BRYA

After beginning hi
Forbes became a s
and lists among his many
Silence (winner of the British Academy Award)
Whistle Down the Wind, *The L-Shaped Room*,
King Rat, *The Raging Moon* and *The Stepford
Wives*. Subsequently he became Head of Pro-
duction at EMI's Elstree studios where he was
responsible for eighteen films, among them *The
Go-Between* and *The Railway Children*. He has
written ten novels including *The Distant Laugh-
ter*, *The Rewrite Man* and *The Endless Game*.

He is married to actress and author Nanette
Newman and they live in Surrey.

BRYAN FORBES

The Memory of All That

HarperCollins*Publishers*

HarperCollins*Publishers*
77–85 Fulham Palace Road,
Hammersmith, London W6 8JB

www.**fire**and**water**.com

This paperback edition 2000
1 3 5 7 9 8 6 4 2

First published by
HarperCollins*Publishers* 1999

The Author asserts his moral rights and no reference to any person,
except those actually named who were alive during the period of
this story, is intended or should be inferred.

ISBN 0 00 651278 X

Set in Postscript Linotype Galliard by
Rowland Phototypesetting Ltd,
Bury St Edmunds, Suffolk

Printed and bound in Great Britain by
Clays Ltd, St Ives plc

This book is dedicated
to the memory of
RAOUL WALSH,
who
once saved my life

The way you wear your hat
The way you sip your tea
The memory of all that
No, no, they can't take that away from me.

The way you hold your knife
The way you sing off key
The way you changed my life
No, no, they can't take that away from me.

They Can't Take That Away from Me
Music and lyrics by George Gershwin and Ira Gershwin

1

LOS ANGELES 1952

Now I come to think about it I've always swum against the current. In my early dog days, when many of my contemporaries had already crossed the Rubicon, my sexual fantasies were pathetically naïve. I was convinced that, as in *The Age of Innocence*, unrequited love would somehow provide much-needed inspiration as I struggled to finish a first novel. The only snag was that, living in a tenement in Queens, NY, unlike Wharton's hero I never found a local Ellen Olenska willing to hold me hostage 'across the ruins of time'. The neighbourhood girls lacked the necessary aura of the exotic, their main pursuit being to trap the unwary into marriage.

With my novel finally pushed out into the world of rejection slips, I resisted my father's constant urgings to take a 'proper' occupation and managed to land a summer job as a small part actor at the Westport Playhouse for what proved to be a short-lived stage career. However, within weeks of my arrival in Connecticut, plans for a life of celibate romanticism somehow got put on hold and I willingly surrendered to the charms of a young actress named Janice. I was so happy that summer, I never wanted it to end, for it seemed that brightness fell from the air every day, but Janice left the company for pastures new and although she wasn't a role model for a Countess Olenska, now at least I had a past to mourn.

I also had something to celebrate. In those halcyon days some publishers were willing to take a chance on an unknown, and during that summer my novel – a turgid tale of love and revenge in the Deep South entitled *A Fine and Private Place* – surprisingly found a home after half a dozen attempts. I received a modest advance which I immediately blew on a second-hand Harley-Davidson. I garnered some respectable reviews, one saying that it cried out to be filmed and I began to feel that nothing could go wrong.

Because of its reputation, the Playhouse attracted Broadway and Hollywood talent scouts. I wasn't offered an acting contract, but one such character, a Lou Camboli, who passed himself off as having a lot of muscle at 20th Century-Fox, urged me to become a screenwriter and promised to give me some introductions if I ever got to that place known, inaccurately, as the City of Angels. That was enough for me. I took him at his word, sold my typewriter and the Harley (not without a lot of soul-searching) and as soon as I could, caught the train.

As it happened I never got past the gate at Fox. By the time the Super Chief deposited me in downtown Los Angeles, Camboli was no longer *persona grata* on the Fox lot. In fact he was no longer around anywhere, having seriously blotted his copybook by humping the girlfriend of a Las Vegas hood and being forced to flee town. With only enough funds left to last a few weeks, I took a job waiting table in an eatery called Jiff's which, if memory doesn't fail me, served hamburgers containing a modicum of actual beef. It was there that I met a girl who knew a man whose sister had read and been impressed by my novel and had once dated an agent named Arnold Kosner. I think Kosner must have owed her one because she persuaded him to see me. On such slender threads our destinies hang.

Arnold Milhous Kosner, to give him his full name, was one of a tribe of independent agents around at that time, the majority of whom were eventually swallowed by the big outfits. Hollywood has always been the spawning ground for countless wannabes, all swimming upstream like salmon, but expiring before the final leap. When I came within Arnold's orbit my guess is he was more interested in social climbing than in advancing embryonic careers such as mine. He hailed from the East Coast where he had once practised law, specialising in divorce, which probably came in handy when extricating himself from his own marital disasters. I think he regarded taking his ten per cent from anybody other than a Pulitzer Prize winner as slumming, but like a lot of small-time agents he operated on the hope that there was always an outside chance that maybe the next Harold Robbins would walk through his doors. I suspect it was his current wife's money that payrolled their pretentious lifestyle. When, after the obligatory show of reluctance, he agreed to represent me for a trial period, he was on his fourth wife, who came complete with a face lift, some major dental work and a fancy old house in Pasadena, full of African artefacts she had looted on one of their many excursions.

I ate there on one occasion, but the invitation was never repeated; I suspect every new client was wheeled out once to allow Mrs Kosner Mark IV to pass judgement. She had a permanently turned-down mouth that looked as though it had been applied with a palette knife, and made no secret of the fact that I didn't pass her Wassermann test of acceptability. The house had been done over by the latest faggot designer (gay hadn't yet become part of the politically correct language) and had been featured in *Town and Country*, the particular issue of the magazine ostentatiously left open on their oversized coffee table. There was a lot of marble, I remember, a Hopper over the fireplace, and a Marie Laurencin, no less, above the toilet in the powder room – just so nobody missed it, I suppose. It was an elegant meal – crystal and silver on the table, linen napkins, the wine

3

decanted, all of which was a considerable advance on the catsup-bottle-place-settings at Jiff's. I remember she talked a lot about 'old money'. Hers had come from Chicago – to be specific from hogs' bellies – her grandfather having been a prince of the pork trade. Call me squeamish, but there is something inherently repellent about making a fortune from dead porkers. The evening she allowed me to grace her table, we ate grouse, not pig, the birds being specially flown in from Scotland and, according to my hostess, shot by a member of the British royal family. Since grouse, royal or otherwise, had never before passed my lips, I had already chalked up a black by complimenting her on the quail.

If the truth were known, Arnold bored for America. If anybody had found a way of distilling him into capsule form, he would have knocked Valium off the top spot overnight. Half an hour in his company was like watching Ingmar Bergman's longest epic dubbed into Japanese. Added to which, being a manic ex-smoker long before the current hysteria, he behaved as though sarin gas was being wafted in his direction whenever anybody lit up in his presence. To compensate for his holier-than-thou attitude he endlessly chewed on wooden toothpicks and, for all I know, might die of dry rot instead of lung cancer.

This was 1952, the Korean War was in progress, and I nightly prayed that my draft papers would never catch up with me. Despite meagre sales my novel had proved that the syrup would pour, and it was not part of my scheme of things to end up dead on the 38th Parallel – patriotism, as I believe that heroic English nurse once said, is sometimes not enough. Draft dodging that conflict didn't carry the stigma later attached to Vietnam, but you still had to watch your ass. It was also the time when the House un-American Activities Committee was sitting and a lot of people in Hollywood were keeping a low profile. There was no mistaking where Mrs Kosner's sympathies lay. Although he had long been dead and buried, she still referred to Roosevelt as a communist and openly expressed admiration for what McCarthy and Cohn were doing 'cleaning the stables' as she put it.

'I told Arnold the other day, make sure you haven't got any of those bleeding-heart pinkos on your books, and if you have, get rid of them fast. What are your politics, Mr Peterson?'

'I'm not really a political animal, Mrs Kosner.'

'But you must have some opinions, surely? How old are you?'

'Twenty-four.'

'Well, you'll soon be drafted then.'

'Sad to say I didn't pass the medical,' I lied. 'I have a congenital heart murmur.'

'Well, that must have been a great disappointment. To fight for one's country, especially in a necessary war such as this, is something I'm sure every full-blooded young American craves.'

'Yes, it was one of the worst days of my life when they rejected me.'

'And such good experience for a writer, I would have thought,' she said, with a grimace to Arnold. 'I haven't read anything of yours, of course.' The 'of course' hung between us as pungent as the ripe Camembert she now offered me. 'What sort of books do you write?'

'Book, singular. I've only written one.'

'I must tell you I make it a rule never to mix family business with pleasure, so I never read anything by my husband's clients, do I, Arnold?'

Arnold snapped a toothpick in half and picked up a replacement. 'Secret of our happy marriage,' he said.

They sat at opposite ends of the table with me in the middle and there were times during the periods of awkward

5

silence when I felt like a tennis umpire waiting for play to commence. I made desultory attempts to think of conversational gambits. Wherever I looked in the room frightening masks stared down at me. Taking these as an opening, I tried, 'Africa must have been fun.'

'You don't describe Africa as fun,' Mrs Kosner said acidly. She picked up a porcelain bell and rang for the black maid to clear the dishes. 'Africa is a profound, spiritual experience. One goes there to sample the primitive culture and to get close to nature.' She was so close to nature she had a mink cover on the toilet seat and a genuine leopard rug in front of the fireplace.

It was the first time I had been exposed to somebody like Eleanor Kosner and I began to understand the origins of the French Revolution. With her Chanel suit, her enamelled talons, diamond-encrusted Rolex and solidified hairdo crowning her empty face, she should have been mounted on the wall alongside the other masks. Before that grisly dinner was over, I would willingly have nailed her there myself.

In fairness, Arnold did get me started. Admittedly it was not an assignment that immediately allowed me to go out and buy a new snazzy convertible but it was enough ($200, less commission, a week for three weeks guaranteed) to enable me to rent a Volkswagen Beetle and enjoy a previously denied freedom of movement. I had the good sense to keep my job at Jiff's, serving the late shift – that was my insurance policy.

The job Arnold pushed my way had to be strictly incognito, but I was in no position to resist that. I was to work for a producer with the somewhat improbable name of Woody Solotaroff. As Arnold sold him to me, Solotaroff was an up-and-coming name with a development deal at Columbia who needed what is known in the vernacular as a 'dialogue polish' in a hurry. I was left in no doubt that the only reasons I got the job were (a) I was dirt cheap, (b) I was willing to work without a credit since I didn't belong to the Guild and (c) Arnold had somehow convinced Mr Solotaroff that I was an authority on the Deep South. The script I was given seemed to be an unhappy co-operation between William Faulkner and Mickey Spillane with a touch of Margaret Mitchell thrown in – the heroine was called Vermilion O'Neil. Lesser minds would have run for cover whatever their needs, but I was full of creative heat. I read the script several times prior to meeting my new employer. Even to my inexperienced eye it seemed to lack certain fundamental ingredients: i.e. construction, drama and anything resembling human dialogue. Nevertheless, with misplaced optimism, I convinced myself that I could come up with the goods.

I met Mr Solotaroff for the first time at his house on Laurel Way, a quiet street perched high above the city where the houses came in a variety of architectural styles. As I set out, nursing my coughing Beetle past the Beverly Hills Hotel's pink façade, I was keyed up to a point few of us ever experience more than once in a lifetime. I had omitted to ask Arnold what Solotaroff looked like but, from his surname, I imagined he would be middle-aged, central European, or Russian maybe, with a guttural accent and would greet me with a frayed cigar between his lips.

So much for mental type-casting: Woody was barely out of high school, dressed like a Wall Street banker, was soft-spoken and had that wonderful built-in, American-Jewish confidence which exudes the aura that they alone and not the gentile meek shall inherit whatever spoils are going in the film industry. In some ways he reminded me of photos I had seen of Thalberg, except he didn't have Thalberg's deceptive, baby-face look. With my cheap, off-the-rack jacket and slacks I could be instantly identified as somebody not on the A or even the B list.

I was immediately awed by the casual sophistication of his lifestyle; the piles of books I couldn't afford on his coffee table, the Buffet prints on his walls, the fact that when he offered me a cup of coffee, it was served in bone china by a silent oriental manservant. Most of all, I was disarmed by his charm: he seemed genuinely grateful that I had accepted the job and straight away got down to business.

'What did you think of the script, Robert?'

'Interesting,' I replied guardedly.

'Yeah. About as interesting as last year's Sears-Roebuck catalogue. One thing you should know – you don't have to be polite with me.'

He picked up a copy of the script and flicked through the pages. 'This is probably one of the worst pieces of garbage to hit my desk. You should also know, if you don't already, that fifty per cent of the scripts up for grabs in this town are garbage. So, before we get down to the nitty-gritty, let me give you the bottom line. Like you I'm hungry. OK, not as hungry as you, but we're both looking for a meal ticket, right? About three months ago I parlayed myself a development deal at Columbia. How? My father used to be Harry Cohn's dentist, and Harry had a very bad mouth. Don't look surprised. As things go in this town, that's nothing out of the ordinary. Whole careers have been established on less. I know a producer over at Fox who's never made a picture in six years, but he draws a paycheque every week just for letting Zanuck take back most of it in the gin game. So, my deal was a pay-off for past paternal services rendered. Cost them nothing. I had to take one of three projects they threw at me. The three that came my way were turkeys they'd been carrying on the books for years. I chose this one as the best of a bad bunch.'

He looked at me and gave the ghost of a smile. 'Now we both know how you landed such an unlucky break. Forget Arnold's bullshit. He has to go through the motions.

I knew I wasn't getting Nunnally Johnson. You're new in town, you don't belong to the Guild, and you'll take whatever's offered. That's OK by me, just so long as we don't kibitz each other. I won't chisel you, my cheques are good, you'll get what I agreed, but you'll have to work for it. What you and I are going to do is change all the names, steal a little here, a little there, have it retyped, give it a new title and, presto, they'll believe they're getting their money's worth. Then with any luck they'll pass and pay me off.'

'Pass? Don't you want to make it?' I asked, stunned by his monologue.

'It's a career-ender if I make it, and I have no plans to retire this early. The object of this exercise, Robert, is to get paid and move on. I'm using them to bankroll me to the next project. Stay around and I'll educate you.'

I was more than happy to stay around and let Woody teach me the ropes, which he did. At that time I had little or no idea how a script should look on the page, let alone how to rewrite one, but Woody knew all the angles. Under his tutorship, and goaded by his manic energy, we pasted together a new version, a hodgepodge of every film about the Deep South that, between us, we could recall. I poured my heart and soul into it until Woody put me back on the right track. 'Don't try and write well. I want cliches, not golden words. Shit, don't risk turning this into something that actually makes sense.'

We had fun with the character of Vermilion (which after long deliberation we changed to Maybelle). She now became the illegitimate daughter of the tyrannical master of the big house. He was having an affair with a neighbouring woman who had slave blood in her background. We put in a bodice-ripping scene when the plantation was overrun by the Unionist forces and had Maybelle commit suicide rather than cling to the belief that tomorrow was ever another day. I'll say this much for our version, it never strayed far from

9

parody, and after the third draft Woody pronounced himself happy.

'Are you sure they'll pass?' I asked.

He shook his head. 'Never underestimate their lack of taste, Robert. We must hope to catch them on an off day.'

While it was being typed up he took me to the Beverly Hills Hotel for lunch to celebrate, but not until he had furthered my education.

'Mind if I get personal?' he asked.

'No, go ahead.'

'I wouldn't be doing you a favour if I took you to lunch looking like that. You need some different clothes. Right now you look as though you're on Welfare.' He led me into his bedroom and opened a walk-in closet almost as big as my motel room.

'We're roughly the same size, I guess. Try these.' He lifted a selection from a rackful of jackets and slacks. 'And you'll need some swimming trunks. Don't panic, you won't catch crabs from them.' He gave me a brand-new pair, which still had the price tag on them. 'The only time you can get away with looking as though you haven't got any money is when you've got money and don't give a shit. This town has a rigid caste system, as you'll find out. Like, I can afford to join the Hillcrest Country Club, but I can't get in. Why not? I'm a Jew. Funny thing, the Jews invented Hollywood and for the most part still run it, but some doors are still closed. Yet this whole town revolves on chutzpah. Know what I mean by that?'

'Not really.'

'Give you an example. A Jewish boy is found guilty of murdering his mother and father. Before the judge pronounces sentence, he asks the boy whether he wants to say anything in mitigation. The boy says, "Yes, I would like to throw myself on the mercy of the court on account I'm an orphan." That's chutzpah.'

10

For some reason he seemed to feel protective towards me. We drove down to the Beverly Hills Hotel in his car, a souped-up Buick, which was valet parked. Although the temperature was into the eighties outside, a log fire burned in the hotel lobby, presumably to give the air conditioning a workout. I noticed a number of blue-rinsed ladies ogling the mink coats in the fur shop; some of the coats were floor-length and the size of small tents. As we passed the desk a man was saying, 'Unless you want to lose my business, move those fucking tourists out of my regular bungalow.'

'Tell you something about this place,' Woody said. 'It was designed by a black architect, but when it was finished, he was never allowed inside. They didn't welcome niggers as guests.'

He led me down to the lower level, exchanging familiar greetings with members of the staff as he went. The lobby taking us out to the pool had other shops, including a barber's. 'Good place to get your hair cut,' he remarked in passing. 'No telling who you could be sitting next to. And that place there –' indicating a small coffee shop – 'is a must for breakfast.' I was flattered he thought I could afford them.

The walk to the pool took us through gardens that assailed my senses with the beauty and scent of unrecognised plants. At the entrance Woody was welcomed by a blond young man he addressed as Sven, who was dressed from head to toe in white, like an operating theatre attendant. Sven selected some pristine towels and led the way down to the pool where he neatly draped the towels on our sun-loungers. 'Have a great day,' he said before leaving.

'Let's go change,' Woody said.

'You seem to know everybody.'

'I know everybody who can be useful to me. Take Sven. Be nice to Sven and you get front-row seats. Get to know head waiters, palm them a big tip the first time you dine and thereafter there's always a table. I never stand in line. That's a big giveaway, means you know you're not on the A list, comprendo?'

'Yes, I think so.'

'Robert, I fear what would have happened to you if you hadn't met me.'

We changed into swimming trunks and picked up some more towels before going back to our places by the pool. Woody handed me a menu from the side table. 'Ever had the McCarthy salad?' he asked.

'No.'

'Specialty of the house. Try it. What d'you want to drink? Beer, wine?'

'Beer's fine.'

He picked up a phone, asked for room service and passed the order, selecting cold lobster for himself. 'What dressing you want on your salad?'

'I'll leave it to you.'

'Thousand Island,' he said into the phone. 'How about dessert? They've got strawberry cheesecake.'

'Sounds great.'

'Make that two cheesecakes, and give us a side order of French fries.'

The meal order accomplished, he lay back and surveyed the scene. On the opposite side of the pool a group of men, uniformly tanned as though sprayed with an airbrush, were watching two of their companions playing a noisy game of backgammon. From time to time one of the spectators would leave the group, climb to the high diving board and execute a perfect swallow, surfacing again at the far end, then strut around the pool, stomach pulled in as though auditioning for Tarzan.

'He's good,' I said, as one of the jocks emerged from the water.

Woody shrugged. 'Only tourists and midnight cowboys looking to pick up a trick use the pool. The serious players come here for business and to be seen.'

At frequent intervals the voice of a switchboard phone operator would issue a metallic command from the concealed loudspeakers: '*Randy Agovino pick up a white phone, please*', or '*Troy Friedman for long distance*.' Noting my interest, Woody said, 'Want to hear your own name called?' Without waiting for my reply, he picked up a phone and spoke to the switchboard. 'Try Robert Peterson for me, willya? I think he's by the pool. Thank you.'

'You're crazy,' I said. 'What do I do?'

'When she pages you, get up, walk casually to another phone and pick up. Then talk to me.'

'What about?'

'Wing it.'

Sure enough, a few seconds later my name boomed out across the stretch of chlorine. Feeling foolish, I got up and did as he had told me. On the other end of the line Woody said, 'See, you're no longer Mr Anonymous. Now everybody around the pool knows your name.'

Shortly afterwards our lunch order arrived. The waiter brought it on a tray completely covered in plastic, which reminded me of the times my mother came home from the hairdresser's after a perm. I was staggered by the quantity of food.

'Enjoy,' the waiter said as he withdrew.

'Tell me something,' Woody said, 'what brought you here?'

I gave him a brief history as a million calories slipped down my throat.

'Is Westport your home town?'

'If only. No, I was born and brought up in Queens. My stint at the Playhouse was just an escape route. All I really want to do is make a career as a writer.'

'So then this friend said he could pull rank at Fox and you came West. Who was he?'

'Lou Camboli. D'you know him?'

'I've bumped into him a couple of times. He's bad news. Never take it for granted that anybody is going to do you a favour unless there's something in it for them. That includes me.' Woody cracked a lobster claw. 'This place looks big when you fly over it, but the bit that matters is Smallsville with a capital S. It's not what you really are that counts, what counts is the last thing people read about you. You might be the greatest thing since Sonny Tufts, if you'll pardon the expression – and that's a local joke, by the way – but that's not enough. I know plenty of people with talent who can't get themselves arrested. Why? Because they don't know how to work the system.'

He abandoned the lobster and forked some cheesecake. 'The ones who call the shots here are a tight little group on the double A list, and you don't get invited to join unless and until you're somebody they really want. Outside, circling like Indians around the covered waggons, are a whole tribe of second-raters who'll step on your face to get where they want to be. Even so, a lot of these deadbeats still pull down a steady hundred grand a year. Why? Because they've perfected the art of kissing ass.'

I listened intently as Woody shared his ground rules for survival, trying not to be diverted by a bizarre couple having a spat in a nearby cabana.

'Take me and this present deal,' he continued, 'I'm not looking to build a career on schlock, but I've learned how to play their game. See, somewhere along the line some jerk at Columbia probably paid top dollar for the piece of crap we've been working on and he doesn't want Cohn to think he fucked up. He wants me to be the fall guy and prove that I couldn't lick it. Then he can go back and tell the front office that I didn't come through, which allows him to save his face.'

14

'Where does that leave you, though?'

'I'll have done him a good turn, he'll owe me one, that's the way it works.'

'I see . . . sort of.'

'You'll find most people you meet are crap shooters hoping to throw sevens every time. It's like the army, it operates on a daisy chain of fear. The officers give the sergeants a hard time, the sergeants give the corporals hell, the corporals kick the enlisted men in the gonads. Right now I'm on shit-house fatigue, but that's fine by me because I'm working on a master plan. My day will come. Watch this space.'

Now Woody was momentarily diverted by the couple in the cabana as the woman suddenly whipped off the man's toupee and dunked it in a bowl of spaghetti, then gathered up her things and minced off. The man dived for cover.

'Recognise her?'

I shook my head.

'Dolores McDowell. Couldn't act her way out of a paper sack, but reputed to give the best head since Gloria Swanson.'

'How d'you know all these things?'

'I make it my business to collect personal details. You never know when they'll come in handy. And I'll give you another piece of advice. Don't waste your time sweet-talking Arnold, get into Lucy's good books; she's the powerhouse in that office. Arnold can just about sell gold bricks if somebody points him in the right direction, the rest of the time he's out to lunch. Cultivate Lucy, take her flowers, pay her compliments, she'll blossom. And if she likes you, you'll work. If she takes against you, forget it, leave town.'

Lucy was Arnold's girl Friday who sat in the outer office and, according to Woody, decided which phone calls were put through. Perhaps 'girl' was stretching it a bit: she was one of those mousy creatures of indeterminate age who on

15

first acquaintance looked like your old high school teacher, but was actually made of solid teak.

'One last thing, don't let your hair down the first time you meet anybody. For all you know, they could badmouth you around town. Play it close to the chest, reinvent yourself.'

I drank it all in – the Gospel according to Saint Woody, and mine for free. Sitting there, wearing his borrowed swimming trunks, I wanted to become like him, I wanted his savvy, a transfusion of his self-confidence. I couldn't believe how lucky I was to have chanced upon somebody of his sophistication. That day, in my innocence, it didn't occur to me that Woody was another hopeful like me, a few rungs further up the ladder, better dressed, with more money, brimming with chutzpah but, underneath, just another player.

As we sat there a small plane circled overhead in the solid blue sky, trailing an ad for a preview that night.

'Want to go?' Woody asked.

'What film is it?'

'Who cares? It's important to be seen at these things. I'll ring around and fix us up with some talent. You never know where chance may lead,' he said with a smile. 'By the way, you're burning, better put some clothes back on.'

While I was dressing in the changing room, a middle-aged man came out of the shower and stood, stark naked, in front of the mirror combing his sparse locks into place. Seeing me glance in his direction, he turned and smiled.

'Hi! Didn't we meet at Jerry's the other night?'

'Jerry's? I don't think so.'

'You're Mike, right?'

'No, sorry.'

'My mistake. How funny, I could have sworn we shook faces at each other. Apologies.'

He made no attempt to cover up and I kept my eyes

firmly at chest level. Where I came from middle-aged men did not flash their family jewels at total strangers.

'Can I buy you a drink to make up?'

'That's kind of you, but I'm with somebody.'

'So I saw.' He smiled again. I left.

Rejoining Woody, I told him about the encounter. We watched until the man appeared and took a stool at the bar. There, he turned and looked in our direction.

'Oh, that tired old queen,' Woody said. 'One of the fixtures. Always looking for new trade. Probably thought we're a twosome. He's been busted a couple of times down at Malibu, but got away with it.'

'How come?'

'How come? The agency squared it.'

'Agency?'

'William Morris. He's an agent, handles a couple of their top leading ladies. A lot of women feel more secure with a queen. They don't come on to them and they can share girl-talk. You're his type.'

My education continued in other directions that night. I called in and told the manager at Jiff's I'd come down with a virus, an excuse I'd found was readily accepted in Los Angeles where, even before the smog took a stranglehold, every second person seemed to suffer from some allergy. 'A sinus of the times' as one wag punned.

I met up with Woody again in the crowd outside the Bruin Theatre in Westwood, which in those days still retained a village feeling. He arrived with two girls he introduced as Ilana and Rachel. I had never been exposed to their type before: these two openly displayed their sexuality in a way that denoted they knew exactly what they wanted and how to get it. There was little to choose between them except one was blonde and the other a redhead.

Maybe Woody had already started inventing my new personality because the first thing Ilana (who turned out to be

17

my date) said to me as we went through the crowded lobby to our seats was: 'The film you've written sounds really sharp.'

'Oh, yeah,' I mumbled, 'we've got high hopes for it.'

'Are there any women's roles in it?'

'Quite a few.'

'Well, I'm available,' she said, and took my arm. When we were seated she immediately gave me some thigh contact. I thought, it's turning out to be quite a day – first propositioned by a queen at lunchtime and now this.

Before the lights had dimmed Woody surprised us with, 'Listen, guys, we may not sit this out to the end.'

'Why, something wrong?'

'I checked. It's a Universal epic starring Jeff Chandler.'

'Is that bad?'

'Cary Grant he isn't.'

'I like Jeff Chandler,' Rachel said.

'We all like Jeff Chandler,' Woody replied, 'but maybe not for ninety minutes.'

As it happened we stayed the course. The film was no great shakes but entertaining enough, nicely shot and with some good action sequences. I watched intently, anxious to learn whatever I could now that Woody had showed me the rudiments of the medium. At one point in the drama, just as Ann Blyth was poised to lose her virginity, Ilana glided a hand into my crotch, but mindful of Woody's advice to reprogram myself as a cool operator, I lifted her hand back on to the armrest.

As we left the auditorium we were handed pencils and preview cards to be filled out. To this day the studios still place a misguided faith in soliciting evidence at sneak previews. Woody had cogent views on the subject, which he expounded over dinner at the Brown Derby, the first fashionable restaurant I had ever eaten in.

'They're a wrist job. I mean, come on, give the public

cards and they immediately become expert critics. I bet if you had a chance of reading them you'd find a high percentage panned the editing or photography, and what the fuck do they know? They've seen a film for free and probably loved it, but they feel compelled to find something wrong because they've been made to feel important. Suddenly they're all Bosley Crowthers. So what happens? The studio studies them like they're tablets handed down from the mountain. Bet your bottom dollar the entire front office are in a huddle right now analysing the crap and tomorrow they'll be back in the cutting rooms re-editing, simply because a lot of freeloaders have sounded off. It's a joke.'

'Woody's right,' Rachel said, anxious to show that she was hip. 'I mean when it asked "What scene did you like least?" I wrote "The love scenes" because I felt I had to write something.'

'There you have it. How about you, Ilana?'

Ilana pulled a face. 'You're a mind-reader. I put the photography was too dark.'

'That's because the projection was lousy and it was the first, ungraded print.' He turned to me.

'I marked everything "Terrific".'

'They'll probably use that as a quote on the billboards.'

'So how did you rate it?'

'I put "Not since *King Kong* have I been so gripped" and signed it "Fay Wray".'

'Funny,' Rachel said. 'You're so funny, Woody.'

I saw several famous faces among the other diners and I felt that I had really arrived, that the future was rosy. The only thing that bothered me was trying to anticipate what the fadeout was going to be that evening. Ilana, although no hardship to behold, was coming on very strong. I lacked the technique to deal with aggressive women. Fortunately, Woody took me off the hook. As soon as dinner was over and the two girls had that what-happens-next expression on their faces, he called for the check and announced that we'd drop them off at their apartments because he and I had to work. 'The finished scripts are waiting for us.'

'Sure you don't want any help reading them?' Rachel asked. 'Know the old saying, all work and no play makes Woody a dull boy?'

'Well, sweetie, I guess tonight Woody and Robert are going to be dull boys.'

They didn't bother to conceal their annoyance. Both flounced off to the powder room.

'OK by you?' Woody asked. 'I mean, if you were hoping to score tonight, just say. We've got time for a quickie, but those types always want to make a night of it.'

'No, like you, I want to see how the script came out.'

The two girls returned to say that they wouldn't put Woody to the trouble of seeing them home but would get a cab. If they expected Woody to relent they were mistaken. 'Dealer's choice,' he said. 'Another time, guys.' Again, I admired his technique.

When we arrived back to his house I have to admit that even though my name wasn't on the newly typed and bound scripts, I still felt pride of part authorship. We took a copy each and read through them.

'What d'you think?' Woody asked as I turned the last page. He didn't wait for my reply. 'Borderline.'

'Borderline?'

'I can't make up my mind whether it's so fucking bad they'll bin it, or whether it's in there with a chance.'

It was the first time he had betrayed doubts in front of me. He paced the room, then stopped by the large picture window and stared at the myriad twinkling lights stretching to the horizon. 'You have to squeeze everything out of this city before it squeezes the life out of you,' he said after a long pause. 'I sometimes sit here for hours at night. During the day it all looks so serene, ordinary, but at night you can sense it's seething like an ant hill, and I ask myself, how many poor saps are down there, dying for a piece of the action they're never going to get?' He turned back to me, as if ashamed that he had revealed too much of himself. 'You going to write a novel about this place?'

'I hadn't thought.'

'You will. Every writer who ever comes here tries it once. But I can only think of one who got it right.'

'Fitzgerald?'

'No, not Fitzgerald. Schulberg. Mind you, he had an inside track, his old man ran a studio. Fitzgerald was always the poor little boy with his face pressed up against the candy store window hoping somebody would invite him inside to sample the goods, and few did. His fictional Thalberg was a fake romantic. The real Thalberg was cold as ice, just a smart little Jew like me.'

'I wouldn't say you're cold. Smart, yes.'

He waved the script at me. 'That's because I was romancing you to get my money's worth. Go home, Robert, I'm going to stay up and think some more about this.'

'You don't want me to help?'

'No.' He was suddenly strangely abrupt, as though whatever current had flowed between us previously had been switched off.

'Well, it's been a great experience, Woody,' I said. 'I'm really grateful for everything. You've taught me a lot, it was a big break for me.'

'Don't depend on it.'

'And thanks for dinner too.' I hesitated, unwilling to believe that it was all over. 'I hope it works out the way you want, and if anything else comes along, let me know. Maybe we could work on something else together?'

'Yeah. Good night, Robert.'

At the door, I clutched at a last straw. 'How should I get

these clothes back to you? You want me to drop them off in the morning?'

'Keep them. I've got others.'

'You sure?'

'Good night, Robert,' he repeated. He had opened the script again and didn't look up at me.

It was nearly a year before I saw Woody again.

2

After the excitement of those three weeks with Woody, my life slid back into a routine minus any adrenalin. I showered twice a day to get the smell of Jiff's hamburgers and fries out of my hair. The clothes that Woody had given me I kept protected in my closet against the day when I might need to make an impression. I rang him a couple of times but only got his answering service telling me he was out of town. I left messages but they were never returned. Remembering his advice, I spent some of my money buying Lucy a pot plant for her desk and a box of See's candies. Although she became increasingly motherly towards me she didn't find me another job. For the most part, when not at Jiff's, I stayed in my cramped little room with the shutters drawn against the fierce light, trying to write, but nothing took flight. Sometimes the customers at Jiff's left behind copies of *Daily Variety* and the *Reporter* and I would eagerly scan the small ads for jobs going. Not having a Writers' Guild card, there was seldom anything for me until, one day, I spotted a box headed 'Rosebud International Pictures'. The ad said Rosebud was looking for new writers to work on feature films. The address was way downtown, on a street called Bonnie Brae, close to MacArthur Park, not yet made famous by the pop song.

Anxious to try anything, I called Lucy to see if she'd heard of them, which she hadn't.

'I wouldn't touch them,' she said. 'They sound very

dubious to me. Those sort of ads are only put in by dead beats.'

'You've got nothing else, I suppose?'

'Not at the moment, Robert. Everything's very quiet, but I'm working on it.'

'How's Arnold?'

'Mr and Mrs Kosner are in Sedona looking for Indian rugs. They'll be back next week. But I'll be sure and tell him you called.'

Ignoring her advice, I followed up on Rosebud International. If I had expected to find them operating from a smart professional block I was quickly disillusioned. I located them in a one-storey house built of faded clapboard that had seen better days. That went for most of the houses on Bonnie Brae. There was a pick-up truck with a flat tyre parked outside the house and the only visible sign of anything remotely connected with show business was a bent television aerial on the shingle roof. A sign on the front lawn said, optimistically, 'THESE PREMISES PROTECTED BY ARMED RESPONSE'. I went to the screenless front door, over which a bare bulb still burned even though it was midday, and rang the bell. After an interval the door was opened by a girl glowing with perspiration and wearing a loose cotton dress and no bra. She had an air of desperation about her and was immediately aggressive.

'Yeah?'

'I came about the job.'

'Who sent you?'

'Nobody sent me. I read your ad in the *Reporter*. About wanting writers. This is Rosebud Films, isn't it?'

'Yeah.'

'Well, I thought I'd apply.'

She stared at me for a few seconds, then turned and called back into the house, 'Gordy, you wanna deal with this?'

24

'Deal with what?' a male voice shouted back.

'Some guy answering your ad.'

She left me standing at the door. Eventually the owner of the voice appeared. Middle-aged and with a beer-drinker's gut, he greeted me wearing a sweat-stained T-shirt, khaki shorts and a baseball cap. He was the type who gave 'designer stubble' a bad name long before it became fashionable.

'Which ad? I've got several running,' he said, also with a hint of aggression.

'In the *Reporter*,' I said again, already regretting the trip. 'The one about writing for feature films. Can I ask you what's involved?'

'Sure you can ask me. I'm Gordon, the President of the company. The buck stops with me.' He looked me up and down. 'You got an agent?'

'Yes.'

'Who?'

Some instinct made me invent a name. 'Solly Kretzer.'

'Never heard of him. All agents are finks. I should tell you I don't deal with ten-percenters. To me they're the scum of the earth, ruining this business. You work for me, you don't need no agent. What's your name?'

'Robert. Robert Peterson.'

'Well, Bobbie, you read the ad. I ain't looking for any fancy writer with big ideas of his own importance. Rosebud is an outfit that's beginning to go places, so if you want to do yourself a favour by getting in on the ground floor, that's another story. That what you want?'

I wanted to escape, but having got that far I thought I might as well hear the rest.

'Yes, I'd like you to consider me.'

'OK. Long as you know the score. Come inside.'

The front door opened directly into the main room. First impressions were not good. It was furnished in a style that

25

art directors would term 'Tobacco Road Casual': a broken-down leather couch with a mangy Irish wolfhound spread across it, half a dozen unframed film posters on the walls, a coffee table piled high with trade magazines, scripts and the remains of a Chinese dinner, two director chairs, cans of film stacked in a corner by an old Moviola, a tailor's dummy with a racoon coat draped around it and, most disturbing of all, a life-size cardboard cutout of Betty Grable.

'Excuse all this junk, we were working late last night,' Gordon said. 'Can you use a cold beer?'

'Sure.'

'Jody,' Gordon called to the girl, 'bring us a couple of beers.' Then to me, 'Take a seat.'

'Get it yourself, I'm busy,' the girl shouted back.

'You heard me, move ass.'

I sat in one of the sagging director chairs. The dog slowly eased itself off the couch and loped over to me. The effort made it cough and it wheezed some terminal halitosis in my direction.

'Shows he likes you,' Gordon said, whacking the dog's rump. 'He doesn't go for most people. Sit, Bonzo; sit, boy.'

Jody brought in two cans of beer, a brand called Brew One O Two, which was heavily plugged on the local tele-vised wrestling matches from Long Beach, which starred such muscle-bound attractions as Gorgeous George and a joke character calling himself Lord Blairs of England, who was usually the fall guy in the ludicrous, rigged bouts. Jody slammed the beers down on the coffee table and left.

'What's with you?' Gordon shouted after her. 'So listen, Bobbie, I've got a good thing going here. See that?' He pointed to one of the posters on the wall. The crude artwork depicted a half-naked girl in the clutches of a werewolf that bore more than a passing resemblance to Bonzo. Under the title *NIGHT CRIES*, was a credit that said: *Produced, Written and Directed by Jay T. Gordon*.

'That was my breakthrough movie,' Gordon said without a glimmer of humour. 'Got back its negative cost in three months. Should have won prizes. Now I want to capitalise on it, but I need some new blood. I can't do it all myself. It's tough being a triple-threat man.' He went to the coffee table and riffled through the pile of scripts, then handed me a thin folder. 'Take a look at this synopsis I just ran off. It'll give you the idea of our product. Next time out I'm aiming to go further up-market.'

I opened the folder and stared at the title: *Little Pussy Red Riding Hood*.

'That's just the working title,' Gordon said. 'You can probably come up with something better.'

'Difficult to improve on this one,' I murmured. There was no air conditioning and the heat plus Bonzo's foetid breath and doggy smell was making me feel faint. I wondered how I was going to extricate myself. Gordon never took his eyes off me as I read the three pages.

'Snappy, huh?' he prompted. 'It needs work, but the basics are there.'

The basics were built around a small-town beauty queen named Pussy, who got involved with a Mafia hood and, with him, embarked on a Bonnie-and-Clyde-style rampage, robbing banks until they both died in a hail of bullets.

'Definitely snappy,' I said.

'Yeah, I can feel this one in my balls.' He rubbed his crotch to give added emphasis.

I felt the time had come to plunge. 'You do realise, Mr Gordon, that I don't have many credits, nor do I belong to the Guild. That might make it difficult for you.'

'Credits! I'm not looking for some flogged-out Guild hack. You strike me as a hip kid who understands a character like Pussy. All her brains are between her legs, right? I've got a hunch about you and I'm usually right about these things. I think you could do a great job and I'm willing to give you the chance. Not many people would do that, understand me? The deal is: no money up front, but the day I start principal photography you take home two big ones. In addition your agent needn't know, because I'm not about to tell him, so you save ten per cent.'

'It's a very tempting offer,' I said, 'and I'd certainly like to think about it.'

'What's there to think about? I'm giving you the plot, all you gotta come up with is some sexy dialogue.'

'I just wonder whether I do know enough about a character like Pussy.'

'What's to know? The girl is a tramp, the guy is a two-time loser, they meet up, they get the hots for each other, maybe she cock-teases him for a couple of scenes, finally he gets her in the sack, they hump, rob some banks, the Feds chase them and gun them down. I'm not looking to remake *Song of Bernadette*, this is a caper movie. I'll cast a good-looking chick with a Jane Russell chest, of which there are plenty, and we make ourselves rich.'

'Yes,' I said, 'sounds a winner. Don't you think . . . you know the plot so well . . . don't you think you should write it yourself?'

'I've got too many deals running at the moment. I have to use my time putting the finance together.'

There didn't seem to be any way out. The dog was still wheezing over me, and I felt a sense of doom descending like ash from a distant volcano. If only I'd listened to Lucy. 'Fine,' I said. 'Right. Well, let me take this away and work on it. I'll give you some trial pages by Monday.'

'Monday at the latest,' Gordon said. 'I want to get this thing rolling. And don't let that synopsis outta your sight. Never know who's gonna steal a good idea.'

'It's safe with me.'

28

I made good my escape. Even though I was desperate for a job, everything told me that *Little Pussy* was not a major career move. I was beginning to realise that one of the Hollywood blood sports was treating writers like dirt. Jay T. Gordon was just another schlock merchant, living hand-to-mouth on the outer edge, somebody who, like his dog, gave off the smell of failure like BO. I showered again the moment I got back to my room, then tore the synopsis into small pieces and put them in the trash can. If Gordon ever tried to locate me through the non-existent agent I had invented, he would draw a blank. I felt reasonably safe, but the encounter had shaken me. All the bright hopes I had packed at the start of my journey on the Super Chief were rapidly tarnishing.

That night, as I served the burgers and eggs-over-easy with side orders of hash browns, I took stock of my situation. My meagre funds would soon run out. Jiff's paid me scale, and none of the clientele were big tippers. The help turned over frequently; few of the waiters stayed long. Like me, most of them believed the job was just a stepping stone to something better, the big break – that one day a casting director would wander in and discover them. We had all read the Lana Turner–Alan Ladd biogs: somebody spotted you in a drugstore or at a gas station and whisked you away to instant stardom. But as I automatically refilled the coffee cups that evening and pocketed the odd quarters, it was difficult to believe that my luck would miraculously change.

The longest-serving member of the staff was the chef, a Pole, who spoke broken English. He worked with manic intensity, brushing oil on the griddle for the bacon, flipping the burgers on to the charcoal grill, his fat-splattered apron like a Turin shroud imprinted with the image of his life. I tried hard to get into conversation with him in those rare intervals when business was slack and he was able to rehydrate with a beer, but he didn't welcome intimacy. The

29

manager was a ferret-faced individual whose main aim in life was to score with the buxom cashier. He lived in a constant state of agitation and suffered from the delusion that he was running a three-star joint.

That particular evening we had a new trainee, a young girl who bore a passing resemblance to Veronica Lake. I later discovered that she had once had a few days' work doubling for Miss Lake in long shot, which seemed to be the pinnacle of her career thus far. She spent all her wages on a voice coach and during her rest periods read Stanislavsky's bible on acting. I helped her out when she got her orders mixed up, and Tony, another one of the waiters, made a play for her but she was a professional virgin, saving herself for her art. My own sex life, like my career, was non-existent. I did cruise the Strip a couple of times on Saturday nights when the Mustang convertibles full of rich Beverly Hills kids looking for some action made the circuit, but all the available girls operated in safety groups, and I lacked Woody's chutzpah to make the initial approach. There were hookers around, of course, but that wasn't my scene. I still carried the tattered flag of romantic love but my emotional barometer remained below zero. I wanted to prove myself as a novelist but, like every writer looking for any excuse to delay actually getting down to work, I convinced myself that I couldn't do my talent justice in longhand. I had to have a typewriter to be taken seriously as a professional. I scanned the small ads and finally located a portable Smith Corona in a store handling repossessed goods. It had seen better days, but once I'd fitted a new ribbon and remembered to hit the 'a' key extra hard every time, it did the job.

Commencing a novel is like setting out without a reliable map on a journey stretching to infinity. After half a dozen aborted attempts I thought, break yourself in, don't try and run the mile, go for the hundred-yard sprint at first. This produced a couple of short stories, mood pieces really, heavily Saroyan-esque, but a daring young man on the flying trapeze I was not. As Woody had accurately prophesied, the stories were Hollywood-based, a big mistake. After only a couple of months I felt I had a lock on the place, which of course I didn't. I came across one of those early efforts in the back of a drawer the other day and was astounded by how third-rate it was, though when first it came hot off my typewriter I know I believed I had licked it.

The thing I remember most was the loneliness of those early months. I served table, saved my money, ate alone, rang Lucy every day and at least twice a week took in a movie, usually a matinee at the theatre that used to stand on the corner of Wilshire and Beverly and is now an Arab bank. It was all a far cry from the chaotic rough and tumble of the Westport Playhouse, where at least I had an identity and life had been witlessly gregarious.

Then, late one evening, something happened which changed my life and my luck in more ways than one.

It had been a quiet shift, never more than half a dozen customers at any one time. We were just about ready to refill the catsup and sugar bottles for the next morning when a threesome came in – a middle-aged man with a younger male companion whose face was vaguely familiar, and a stunning-looking girl. They sat at one of the tables on my station. Both men wore suits and ties – expensive, beautifully tailored suits – and their accents were unmistakably British. I took them for tourists.

'What's the specialty tonight?' the younger man asked me, looking down his nose at our menu.

I felt tired, but loose, and the manager was out of sight having a row with the black kitchen help.

'The specialty here is there's no specialty,' I said. 'Just what you see, sir.'

'Oh well, we feel like slumming, don't we, Billy?'

31

'I like these places,' the older man replied. 'And I know exactly what I'm going to have. Some home-made apple pie and ice cream.'

'What flavour would you like, sir? We've got strawberry or vanilla.'

'Oh, give me both. With hot chocolate sauce. Now how about you two?'

The girl hadn't yet spoken. Now she said, 'You'll be sick, Billy.' At close quarters I found her beauty very disturbing. Luxurious auburn hair crowned a face glowing with health; a full, sensual mouth devoid of lipstick and a smile that displayed perfect teeth. A stunner. 'I'll have the cheese-burger, please,' she said.

'Lettuce and onions, miss?'

'Yes.'

'Raw or fried?'

'Raw.'

'Nobody's going to be sleeping with you tonight,' the younger man said.

'Nobody's going to be asked.'

'You want the fries with that, miss?'

'Oh yes, the lot, all the trimmings. When in Rome.'

The young man said: 'How can you be so fucking conventional? I might join Billy . . . No, I won't. I'll take a chance with the lemon chiffon pie topped with whipped cream, which probably tastes like shaving foam.'

'Absolutely,' I said, 'but it leaves your skin soft, sir,' thinking, *fuck you*.

'You asked for that, Oliver,' the girl said.

Surprisingly, he didn't take offence. 'And a very black coffee. Is it fresh?'

His manner of speaking was the languid British, bored variety, and I tried not to react to the way he had spoken to the girl.

'I'll make fresh,' I said. 'Is that coffee for everybody?'

'Yes, Billy?' the girl asked when he didn't answer.

Billy looked at the nametag on my uniform jacket. 'No, I shall ask Robert to bring me a malt shake.'

'Then you'll definitely be sick.'

Either they had just arrived in town or else the girl was somebody who guarded her English complexion, because she hadn't got a trace of a tan. Her classic features reminded me of Vivien Leigh. While I was tidying up I watched them eat and laugh together during their meal. Over coffee the older man lit a cigar while the younger one smoked a cigarette in one of those Dunhill holders that filtered the smoke through a crystal filter. They all intrigued me. From time to time the older man looked in my direction and gave a smile. When they left he dropped me a twenty-dollar bill for a meal costing thirteen fifty.

Back in my room it was the girl more than the tip that occupied my night thoughts. It's always the unexpected in life that holds a special attraction. I doubted whether I would ever see her again but she came closer to my Ellen Olenska ideal than any other. Her beauty and the scent she wore were otherworldly, and I fantasised about her before I fell asleep, wondering about her setup. Was she the property of the older guy or the younger one, or just tagging along as an escort? I had often seen girls like her among the audiences at the Westport Playhouse during a Broadway tryout – rich, unattainable girls who wintered in Aspen and spent the summer in Martha's Vineyard on their fathers' money; girls with unreal, shiny hair like the models in the shampoo ads; girls with fancy Rolexes on their wrists, who looked right through you if you stared too long and seemed as though they inhaled a purer air than the rest of us.

3

It must have been at least a month later when, by chance, I again saw the man called Billy who had given me the big tip at Jiff's. We were both in the now-vanished Hunter's bookstore on Little Santa Monica Boulevard. Still struggling to make headway with a new novel and being a chronically bad speller, I had decided it was time I acquired a decent dictionary and a cheap thesaurus.

What first drew my attention to him was the heady aroma of a good Havana. I looked around the shop to see who was smoking it and found him lingering in the corner where they kept a small section devoted to pornography – mostly anonymous Victorian reprints like *The Pearl*, *The Oyster* and *My Secret Life*, together with some pathetic twentieth-century imitations, which only the sexually desperate would dream of reading. Despite the weather being in the high seventies he was wearing an incongruous heavy tweed suit. Having made his selection he came up to the counter as I was paying for my own purchases and I saw (for he made no attempt to conceal his choice) that he had chosen three or four of the tawdry modern paperbacks. In a good light and closer to me I noticed that he had a harelip, which had the effect, full face, of giving him a half-smile.

He glanced at me and said: 'It's you, isn't it? The waiter from that place?'

'Yes, sir.' I was flattered that he remembered me from such a brief meeting.

'I thought so. I'm rather good at remembering faces. Can never remember names, probably because they never seem to fit faces. Remind me of yours.'

'Robert.'

'Ah, yes, Robert. For some reason you look more like a Jimmy. I see what you've purchased. Are you working your way through college? Such an admirable American trait, I think, unlike England where most of the undergraduates are layabouts.'

'No. I left college a long time ago, sir. I'm a writer, but not very good at spelling.'

'A writer?' He handed his collection to the assistant without the embarrassment I would have felt in his place. 'That's even more admirable. Do they have any of your books here? Because, if so, I'll buy them. One should always support budding authors.'

'I doubt if they stock it,' I replied. 'I've only written one and it didn't exactly set the world on fire.'

'Well, let's ask. What is the title?'

'*A Fine and Private Place.*'

He turned to the assistant. 'Do you happen to have a copy of this young man's book? What name do you write under, Robert?'

'Peterson.'

The assistant at least had the grace to lie for my sake. 'We've sold out of Mr Peterson's book, sir, I'm afraid, but I'm sure we could order you a copy if it's still in print.'

'Yes, do that. Order three.' He turned back to me. 'I'll give the others to friends. Let me pay for them now. How much will they be?'

'Around five ninety-five, at a guess, sir.'

'Well, take twenty dollars. That should cover it.'

'Could I have your name, sir?'

'William Fisher. Send them up to the Beverly Hills Hotel when they come in.'

To be on the spot when somebody actually bought my novel was a rare and heady experience. I stammered my thanks.

'Not at all, Robert. I am sure I shall read it with even keener interest now that we've renewed acquaintance. Is it heavily autobiographical?' he asked as we went out to the street where a Lincoln limo was waiting. A muscular young chauffeur stood beside it.

'Hardly. It's set in the Deep South and I was brought up in Queens.'

'With queens? How interesting. Did they adopt you?'

'No, sir. Queens, the district in New York.'

'Oh, I see.' He sounded vaguely disappointed. The chauffeur had opened the passenger door for him, but Billy made no attempt to get in. 'Would you care for a drink, or a cup of tea, or both? I always take tea before a cocktail.'

'Well, that's kind of you, sir, but I have to work this evening.'

'When?'

'My shift starts at seven.'

'Oh, you've got plenty of time. Come back to the hotel and tell me more about your writing.' He got into the car as though the matter was now settled and my acceptance taken for granted.

'I've got a car,' I said.

'Fine. Well, make your own way and just ask at the desk for my bungalow.'

When he drove off, I still hesitated on the pavement. There was something about him that made me cautious. I wasn't used to strangers being nice to me, but it seemed ungracious not to accept in view of his kindness in ordering my book. Perhaps he was just a British eccentric, given to such generous acts. I collected my battered Volkswagen and drove up Beverly, crossing Sunset and entering the hotel's curved drive. If the valet felt any surprise at being required to park my heap, he betrayed no sign. I walked inside and went to the desk.

'Mr Fisher,' I said. 'He's expecting me.'

The desk clerk dialled a number. 'Your name, sir?'

'Peterson. Robert Peterson.'

'Mr Fisher? I have a Mr Peterson at the front desk. Shall I have him shown to your bungalow?'

He put the phone down and beckoned a bellhop. 'Take this gentleman to bungalow 7.'

The bellhop, a midget wearing a red uniform and a pillbox hat, aping the famous Philip Morris ad, conducted me through the hotel and outside into the gardens. Tony, at Jiff's, had told me that the hotel bungalows were usually occupied by big spenders like the legendary Howard Hughes, who was reputed to keep one permanently reserved even though he never used it for months on end, and then only arriving in the middle of the night. From the outside they seemed to me very unprepossessing. I followed the bellhop along a series of winding, paved paths, bordered on both sides by shrubbery, until we arrived at Number 7. The bellhop rang the bell for me and said, 'Have a great day,' in a high, piping voice.

I was admitted by the muscular chauffeur. Whereas the façade resembled something put up for a temporary film set, the interior decor was luxurious and tastefully furnished. All the shutters were closed but there were lights blazing everywhere and the contrast from coming out of the strong sunlight was pronounced. Two deep sofas flanked by matching side tables, and between the sofas an oversized coffee table set longways before the fireplace where, as in the hotel lobby, logs were burning. The coffee table was strewn with scripts, newspapers, glossy magazines, a selection of recent bestsellers and half a dozen unopened, gift-wrapped parcels. While I stood taking all this in, Billy appeared. He had taken off his tweed jacket and was wearing a patterned, silk dressing gown, but still had a cigar in his mouth, which he immediately laid in an ashtray, went to a side table and selected a new one from a full box.

'Do you use these? They're Havanas. I can't stand those local green things people chew on out here. You might as well smoke asparagus.' He handed me one shaped like a torpedo.

'D'you mind if I save it for after work?' I put it away carefully in my shirt pocket.

'Nice to have a fire, isn't it?'

'Yes, very.'

'I always feel cold,' he said.

'Even in this climate, sir?'

'Don't call me "sir", makes me feel a hundred. I don't go out much during the day, this afternoon was an exception. It was just that I didn't have anything worth reading. I can't wait to get your book. Is it racy? I love racy books.'

'Well, only slightly. I hope you won't be disappointed.'

'Oh, I have a good feeling about you.' He swept a clear place on the coffee table, knocking a pile of books on to the floor as the chauffeur came in with first champagne in an ice bucket, then returned with a tray of tea and cookies. Billy immediately ate one and offered the plate to me. I couldn't help noticing that there were also several bottles of prescription pills on the tea tray.

'What would you like?' he asked. 'Some of this, or tea?'

'I'll have the champagne, please.'

'Help yourself. I'll join you in a minute, but I must have my cup of tea first. One has to keep up appearances, otherwise you lose all identity in this place.' He poured himself a cup, shook some pills into his palm, swallowed them down with the casualness of somebody eating jellybeans, took a second cookie and slumped down on to one of the sofas. I raised my champagne glass to him. 'Well, thank you again, Mr Fisher. It's the first time I've ever seen anybody buy my book.'

' "Mr Fisher's" even worse. Call me Billy. Everybody else does.'

I searched for a conversational opening. 'Are you and your friends here on holiday, Billy?'

'Good God, no. I never take holidays, they bore me. One only sees people in shorts and sandals, a really disgusting way of dressing I always think.'

He sat with his legs crossed and I noticed that one leg twitched all the time.

'Am I right in saying you didn't recognise our Oliver the other evening?'

I shook my head, my mouth full of a cookie.

'I must tell him that, it'll annoy him. Don't you go to the movies?'

'Yes, usually twice a week.'

'British movies?'

'I've seen a few. Not many.'

'Did you ever see *The Last Victim*?'

'Was that the one set in wartime, where the girl discovered that the soldier she married was really a German spy? Jean Simmons, wasn't it, didn't she play the girl?'

'Not Jean Simmons. Dorothy Prentiss.'

'Oh right, my mistake. Yes, I did see that. I liked it.'

'Well, Oliver played the soldier,' Billy said.

'Really? Yes, of course, now you've told me. He was very good. Just that I didn't connect him that evening. Was that his wife?'

'Was who his wife?'

'The young lady who was with you both?'

Billy choked on his cup of tea. 'Oh, that's rich. Oliver would find that very *outre*. No, she's just a friend of both of us. Have you ever written for films?'

'Not really. Well, that's to say I have worked on one film, but it was just a rewrite job.'

'I produce pictures,' he said casually. '*The Last Victim* was one of mine.'

'Very rude of me not to know.'

'No reason why you should. Nobody reads credits.' He eased himself off the couch and rummaged around on the floor among the debris, then handed me a book that had been on the *New York Times* bestseller list for the last ten weeks. 'Take this home and read it. Let me know what you think. If you like it, you can do the screenplay for me.'

I stared at him. 'The screenplay?'

'Yes. I own the rights, but I haven't done anything with it yet.'

The book was the latest thriller from Larry Westbrook, who had a growing reputation and was being compared to Eric Ambler.

'The thing is ... and don't think I'm being ungrateful ... I don't really have any proper experience.'

'Everybody has to start somewhere. Most of the established writers out here are such prima donnas. Life is too short to be bothered with them.'

'The other thing is, I don't belong to the Guild.'

'Oh, we'll cross that bridge when we come to it. I never worry about that,' he said airily.

I turned the book over and over in my hands. 'What can I say? Thank you very much, but are you sure you want to give me a crack at it?'

'When you get to know me better, Robin, you'll find that's the way I always operate. The best decisions are always those one doesn't think about too much. And you see I have the great advantage of being my own master. I don't have to ask anybody's permission to spend my own money. What I want, I usually get. Don't look so worried. The great thing to remember is it's always more pleasant to receive rather than to give.'

He had called me Robin, but I didn't correct him. When he had first appeared in his dressing gown it had immediately crossed my mind that he thought of me as a pick-up, but nothing in his subsequent manner, gestures or dialogue suggested that he was homosexual. Eccentric, certainly. Mad, even. I couldn't believe that he was really offering me the chance to work on a classy screenplay. People didn't act like that. Or perhaps the British did? I had nobody to compare him with; he seemed to be the inhabitant of another planet. He didn't talk like Woody or the ghastly Jay T. Gordon but, as he rambled on, walking about the room in search of something he didn't find, occasionally waving the cigar at me and ignoring the ash falling on the carpet, his British accent and soft speaking voice meant I sometimes failed to catch everything he said. Conscious of the time, I waited for a polite opportunity to interrupt him.

'Billy, you'll have to excuse me, but I have to go. The manager at that place I work is a tyrant. I'll read this tonight and let you know as soon as I can. Nothing like this has ever happened to me before.'

'No hurry,' he said. 'Take your time. I'm glad we bumped into each other. Give me a ring when you're ready.'

He was taking a different coloured pill as I left.

By the time I drove away from the hotel the combination of two glasses of gulped champagne and the amazing turn of events made me light-headed. On the way to Jiff's I stopped and used a pay phone to call Lucy.

'Lucy,' I shouted. 'Does the name Billy Fisher mean anything to you?'

'Yes. Very respected British producer.'

'Well, I've just met him and he offered me a job. He gave me a novel to read and said, if I liked it, I could do a screenplay for him.'

'Well, well,' Lucy said. 'Let's hope you like it.'

'Tell Arnold.'

'I will when I can reach him. At the moment they're still away.'

'So, what's new?' I said.

4

I stayed up most of that night and read the Westbrook novel at a sitting. As Billy had said, it had a very complicated plot, many of the British expressions were difficult to follow and much of the dialogue was foreign to me, but nevertheless it held me gripped, for the writing was superior to the usual run of thrillers. The hero (whom possibly Billy saw as a role for Oliver?) was a young doctor accused of a brutal murder. There were several other good characters, especially a Scotland Yard detective, and the *Rebecca*-type climax, played out on the Cornish cliffs, had a last-minute sting. The prospect of turning it into a screenplay was daunting but in those days ambition quickly routed self-doubt. I left it until around ten o'clock the next morning (something told me Billy was not an early riser) and then rang him.

'I finished reading the novel,' I began.

'Who is this?'

'Robert.'

'Robert who?'

'Robert Peterson.'

'Do I know you?'

'Yes, Billy, we met yesterday and you gave me the novel.'

'What novel's that?'

'Westbrook's new thriller.' The conversation was not going the way I had imagined. 'I liked it very much and if you still feel the same way I'd like to take a crack at it.'

I heard something fall over and smash and there was a long pause.

'So, is that all right? You want me to go ahead?' I asked.

There was another pause before he answered, 'Go ahead?'

'Write a screenplay for you, like you said.'

'Do what?'

'A screenplay.'

Silence. Then he said: 'I have to go to New York.' His speech was muffled and distant. 'I'll get back to you when it's convenient.'

'Well, any time's convenient for me, Billy.' I tried to keep the rising panic out of my voice. 'I'll give you my number, shall I?'

'Give it to George.'

I assumed George was his secretary, or maybe the chauffeur who doubled as a valet. 'Right. But meantime, shall I start work?'

'When I get back, let me know what you think. I have to go now.'

The line went dead.

I spent the rest of the day trying to think of possible explanations for his sudden change of attitude. He was drunk, he had taken too many sleeping pills, I had caught him at a bad moment with somebody else in the room, he had gone off the idea or, more to the point, he had gone off me. I blamed myself for not acting on Woody's advice; why hadn't I made myself sound more in demand instead of immediately blurting out the threadbare details of my life?

Later that afternoon I phoned the hotel again and asked to be put through to Billy's bungalow. A man answered.

'Can I speak to George, please?'

'George? There's no George here. Who is this?'

'Robert Peterson. I spoke to Mr Fisher earlier and he asked me to leave my telephone number with George.'

'He gets everybody's name wrong. Wait a minute. I'll put you on hold and you can talk to Greg, that's who he meant.' It dawned on me that it was Oliver who had answered.

After a pause another voice came on the line. 'Yeah, can I help you?'

'Yes. My name's Robert Peterson. Mr Fisher wanted me to give you my number so he could contact me on his return from New York.'

'New York?'

'That's what he said. Isn't that where he's gone?'

'Yes, if he said so. OK, give me the number.'

I passed it to him. Then, panicked and bewildered, the moment I hung up I called Lucy and asked her what she made of it.

'They all behave like that,' she said. 'If they sound too keen, they're afraid your price will go up.'

'I don't have a price and I don't care what I get paid as long as I get the job.'

'Well, you'll just have to wait and see.'

'He seemed so nice yesterday.'

Lucy signed off with: 'They all seem nice yesterday.'

By the time I clocked on at Jiff's that evening I had convinced myself that I had blown it. The others noticed my gloom and, distracted, I twice served wrong orders. Our rodent manager gave me a hard time. 'Do that once more and you're out,' he shouted. 'Those were two of our regulars' – blustering as though our regulars were all millionaires who would withdraw their valuable custom. The only time I ever saw him turn on the charm was when any of the Beverly Hills cops came in for a freebie. It had been made crystal clear to me the first day I was employed that the police were never to be given a check.

I was having a smoke in the rest room, sitting on the john, still preoccupied with the day's disappointment, when

45

the door opened and Leyla, the new waitress, walked in.

'Oh, pardon me, sweetie,' she said, with a flirty look I could have done without at that moment.

'Not your fault, Leyla. I should have locked it.'

Leyla was forty or thereabouts, but dressed nineteen with a lot of cleavage and blonde hair that might have come off the Scarecrow in *The Wizard of Oz*. I believe her folks were Turkish, or maybe Armenian – anyway somewhere in that part of the world. She had a pretty thick accent and her dialogue was peppered with 'dahlinks', the word drawn out like she'd been at night school with Zsa Zsa Gabor. There was something sad, almost grotesque, about the way in which she tried to ogle our Polish chef. I guess she was desperate to keep the job because, after she had been with us a week, she confided in me that she had a child to support. The husband was back in Detroit. 'I had to leave him, dahlink, he beat me up something incredible. You should have seen the bruises, all over my body.' She touched her ample bosom. 'Especially here. After I had his baby he said my titties were too large. You think they're too large?'

'No, they seem fine to me.'

'American boys like big titties, don't they, dahlink?'

'Yeah.' I had an awful feeling she might be about to flash hers at me.

'He was a real shitheel, dahlink, and pink all over like a pig, with that hair like pigs have.'

'Sounds a real charmer. What made you marry him?'

'Dahlink, I had to. I had to get my green card and at the beginning he wasn't too bad. He was still a shit, but not too much of a shit, I could live with that if I had to. I mean, all men are shits once they get what they want . . . Not you, dahlink, you're a sweetie pie, I ain't including you. Now when I get money, I divorce him. I never want to see that bastard again.'

After that, my having made the initial mistake of being a

sympathetic listener, she buttonholed me with horror stories of married life in Detroit at every opportunity. Once she asked if I'd like to go dancing with her on our evening off. 'I'm a great dancer, dahlink, you should experience it.' Seeing the reflection of the firing squad come into my eyes, she added: 'No funny business, dahlink, just dancing.'

I pleaded I had to work and after a while she gave up on me and concentrated on the chef. She was popular with the customers and went along with any suggestive dialogue since she knew it usually meant a larger tip.

My excuse to Leyla was not a lie. I spent all my spare time poring over Westbrook's novel, underlining passages I thought were important to the plot, and writing a detailed outline. I wanted to be prepared when Billy got back from wherever he'd gone so as to impress him with my diligence. I stepped up my visits to the movies, anxious to glean whatever help I could from the finished product.

I gave it a week, then rang his hotel again. The front desk told me he hadn't returned.

'Do you know when he'll be back?'

'Mr Fisher didn't give us a date, sir. He's in England at the moment.'

'Oh, I see. Did he leave any message for me?'

'I'll connect you to the message desk, sir.'

When the girl came on the line I repeated the question. 'My name's Peterson. Mr Fisher should have left a message for me.'

After a pause, she said, 'No, nothing, sir. Peterson, you said?'

'Yes. Or it could be under just Robert.'

'No. We have a package from Hunter's bookstore and a slew of messages for him, but not one for you. Sorry.'

This, more than the last conversation I had had with Billy, really deflated me. I had yet to learn that the career I was trying to follow specialised in rejection. However unpalatable, the obvious explanation was that he'd realised he'd made a big mistake and had thought better of it. Rather than face me with it, he had decided to be elusive, leaving a false trail. Before disappearing to wherever, he hadn't even stayed long enough to pick up the three copies of my book. It was more than possible that he had given instructions that, if I called, the hotel staff were to give me a phoney story. I imagined that you could behave any way you liked if you were rich enough to stay in a bungalow at the Bev Hills Hotel.

Back in my room I stared at the Havana cigar he had given me, and which I hadn't smoked, thinking what a dummy I had been. I couldn't bring myself to tell Lucy and when, eventually, she contacted me to ask if there'd been any progress, I lied and said Fisher was still away but had called me to apologise for the delay.

'Well, that's hopeful,' Lucy said without much conviction in her voice.

But hope was no longer uppermost. Once again I remembered something that Woody had said that evening when he stood by the window and looked down on the lights of the city. Billy's odd behaviour had certainly squeezed some of the life out of me. Thus far, starting with the false promise that had lured me to the West Coast, every encounter had led to a dead end. In an effort to stop feeling sorry for myself, I decided to go out. I called Tony at Jiff's to say I wouldn't be clocking in that night and would he alibi for me.

'What d'you want me to tell the creep?'

'Tell him I was in a road accident,' I said, and immediately touched wood. 'Tell him I'm concussed.'

It wasn't too far from the truth; I felt brain dead. I showered, put on Woody's jacket and trousers, took thirty dollars of my hard-earned savings and went out in search of . . . what? A singles bar? No, God forbid. There was plenty of action out there if you knew where to find it, something for every age group of either sex plus the two-way swingers. The trouble with being a writer is that one is always trapped in that no man's land between imagination and reality. Your invented life is always more vivid than the one you are living.

So instead, I drove aimlessly, taking Sunset Boulevard's winding route to the coast, then hanging a right on to the Pacific Coast Highway towards Malibu – the highway that stretches far north to Carmel, sometimes scenic, often dangerous. I had been to Malibu before, but only during the day. Now, at night, it assumed a different character – a seaside resort out of season, near deserted, with a main street that had never been completed. The coast road was in the slide area, bordered by irregular, terracotta cliffs trussed with heavy-gauge steel nets to catch the frequent landslides; notices warned motorists to watch for small rocks that penetrated the net. Hit one of those babies at speed and it would rip through your tyres and send you careering into the oncoming traffic. Although the area wasn't heavily developed, there were scattered houses perched perilously close to the edge of the cliffs, presumably owned by people with a lemming complex. I had seen pictures of the vast palace – nicknamed Versailles by the Sea – which old man Hearst had built for Marion Davies, but since those good old days of the Hollywood deer park, most of the structures fronting the beach looked like chicken huts. I'd been told that they were mostly weekend homes for the well heeled, with swishly furnished interiors hung with expensive art soaking up the salt air to their detriment.

I drove slowly, looking for somewhere to stop, finally pulling across the road into the forecourt of a brightly lit restaurant that advertised fresh fish as its specialty. I took an outside table on the wooden deck and had a drink while studying the menu. When my waitress came back with my beer I asked her to recommend something.

'How about the Dover sole? Should I go for that?'

She shrugged and brushed a strand of damp hair out of her tired eyes. 'You're eating it, not me. Just don't depend on it having been too near Dover recently.'

'Isn't it all fresh like it says?'

'Not as fresh as some of the customers. Take the tuna steak.'

'How's it done?'

'We cook it,' she said with a bored smile. I recognised a fellow sufferer. It was late, she'd been on her feet since six, and she probably never wanted to see another fish for the rest of her life. Why should she bother what some john wanted to eat?

'You get a house salad, baked potato, squash and choice of dessert with it.'

'Sounds a steal,' I said. 'I'll go for it.'

I watched her as she walked away: a neat ass and good strong legs that you needed for her job. The shoes were a giveaway, though, the heels worn down on one side. I sipped my beer and watched the surf break and crash down on the shingle below. It had a hypnotic quality. The spume rose high, like a whale blowing, rainbowed by the restaurant's rooftop floodlighting. I could hear a piano playing, mostly Gershwin and Porter, though every so often the pianist would break the pattern and go for some Joplin. He was good and after I'd finished my meal I began to feel vaguely human again. I went inside.

There were a dozen or so other people in the restaurant, mostly single guys like myself, sitting around nursing their beers and listening to the music. I had expected to see a black guy at the piano, but it was a white boy tinkling the ivories wearing a T-shirt, and a faded denim jacket hung over the back of his chair with the letters UCLA appliqued on it. I took a spare bar stool, ordered another beer and swivelled round to watch him. He played without pause, segueing from one number to the next.

I sat there, enjoying him, until I was the last one in the place. He finished with Ellington's 'Blues in the Shadows', closed the piano lid, and stood up to flex his tired muscles.

'That was great,' I said. 'You're very good. Do you play with a band?'

He put on his jacket before answering me. 'Oh sure, I'm just filling in until Dorsey sends for me. If I played with a band I wouldn't be playing here. There's a limit to how many free fish suppers you can eat.' He shouted a goodbye to my waitress, which she didn't return. I followed him out into the empty parking lot and saw him make for an old Harley-Davidson chained to the fence.

'I had one of those,' I said. 'Back in Connecticut. Had to sell it. Almost broke my heart, but I needed the dough to get out here.'

'Oh, yeah?'

'Now I'm driving that heap.' I gestured towards my Beetle.

'Not the same,' he said, and sat astride the bike.

'You keep yours in good condition.'

'Yeah. Treat it better than I treat myself.' At first he had shown little inclination to be sociable, but people who ride Harleys have an affinity.

'Too bad you had to sell yours,' he said: 'What year was it?'

We swopped technical details for a few minutes and he sympathised, as though we were discussing the loss of a close friend.

'Man, I can't imagine getting rid of this.' He stroked the worn saddle leather. 'Mind you, I had to sell my piano, and that hurt. So what made you come here? My name's Mike, by the way.'

'Robert. It's a nothing story. I had the promise of a job

51

at one of the studios, but it'd blown out by the time I got here.'

'What sort of job? You an actor?'

'No, I write. I'm a writer. Well, that's the game plan, but right now I'm a waiter. How about you?'

'Likewise. I compose when I'm not in the fish factory.'

'I write when I'm not serving hamburgers.' We exchanged a conspiratorial smile during the pause. 'Maybe we should team up.'

Mike said, 'I've heard worse ideas. You write the lyrics, I'll write the tunes.' He gave me a searching look. 'You want to come back to my pad and have a few beers? I'll play you some of my own stuff and you can tell me how lousy it is. Everybody else does.'

'Did you take music at college?'

'What college?'

I pointed to the letters on his jacket.

'This is communal property. We take turns.'

'We?'

'Five of us room in the same pad. All for one and one for all. Why don't you follow me?'

'Will I be able to keep up?'

'If you lose me, it's fifty-two thirty-six West Knoll. Know where that is?'

'No.'

'You know the Strip? Take the slip road down to Holloway and it's on the right. I'll try and keep you in my mirror.'

He kick-started the Harley. It roared into life immediately and he gunned the throttle a couple of times for my benefit before accelerating out into the highway. Despite what he had promised I had lost sight of him within half a mile. I took Wilshire Boulevard this time, hoping to make better speed on the flat, but it wasn't until I cut up Doheny to Sunset that I saw him again. He sped off once more when

I flashed my lights and this time I managed to keep up with him. He stopped in front of an all-night liquor store and I waited until he came out and threw me two packs of beer. Then he led the way to a small, one-storey house with an overgrown front lot that more or less obscured most of the house from the road.

'Don't expect anything fancy,' he said as he opened the front door. 'The landlord doesn't believe in maintenance. Come on in and meet the gang.'

Apart from Woody's place it was the first time I had been inside a real house for months. I guess by Hollywood standards it was old, maybe built in the thirties when lots were cheap. Wooden structure, stucco finish, one main room, a couple of bedrooms, what the realtors call one and a half baths and a kitchen. I later found out there was a semi-basement den because the site sloped down at the rear into an unkempt garden.

The first time I went there the whole place was lit by candles and Mike explained that the utility company had cut off the electricity for non-payment. Mike introduced me to two of his fellow lodgers: Linda, who greeted me wearing only a man's pyjama top, and Paula, who, from the way he greeted her, I took to be his girlfriend. Both girls were in their early twenties. They didn't seem at all fazed by my arrival. Linda was the more obviously attractive of the two, or maybe it was just the way she was dressed, but it was Paula that I looked at most. I've always been drawn to girls who don't need make-up to create an impression, and she had an odd face – a full, slightly crooked, inviting mouth, and amazing hair, so thick you couldn't imagine how she ever ran a comb through it. There was a third girl, Marsha, whom I didn't meet until later – she was sleeping off a hangover apparently – and the final member of the menage was a guy called Charlie, referred to as 'the Lone Ranger', who was out on the prowl.

When we arrived both girls had been attempting to heat a pan of water over three candles.

'You're such a louse,' Paula said. 'You promised you'd pay the bill and get the electricity back on.'

'I forgot. I'll do it tomorrow.'

'We've been trying to boil water for some coffee, but I don't think we'll live long enough.'

'Forget it and have a beer.'

Mike played some of his numbers on a guitar. None of them took me by storm, but they were easy on the ear, if a bit derivative, just as my stories were derivative. Nevertheless, glad of the company, I enthused. We ate crackers and stale cheese and I gleaned that Linda, who hailed from San Francisco, was a beautician at Bonwit's, doing face jobs.

'Can't they make up themselves?' I asked her.

'They come to try out new products and get a freebie. Even with my efforts most of them are a long way from Miss America, but it pays the rent.'

Paula was an aspiring actress and told me she went to class every day, took ballet lessons and had a voice coach.

'They must be expensive,' I said. 'How d'you afford them?'

'She doesn't,' Mike interjected. 'Daddy does. Daddy is a big wheel.' I detected a hint of criticism.

'Well, don't knock him. Daddy also pays my dues here,' Paula replied.

I liked both girls. They had spirit and a good sense of humour. We exchanged horror stories about agents, casting directors and store managers, all of whom had given us a hard time.

'How d'you make out?' Paula asked. 'Where are you rooming?'

'In a motel.'

'Jesus, that's rough, man,' Mike said. 'Listen, the Lone

Ranger is shipping out at the end of the week, why don't you move in with us?'

'You serious?'

'Sure. We need to make up the numbers. We split everything five ways.'

I looked at the two girls. 'Is that OK with you?'

'Mike's the den mother,' Linda said. 'The lease is in his name.'

'That isn't what I asked you.'

'OK by me,' Paula said. 'You can write me some audition pieces.'

'Yeah,' Linda said. 'Just don't hog the bathroom like Mike.'

'The house rules are, we take it in turn with the chores,' Mike said. 'You use the phone, you put the money in the piggy bank. Any cheating carries the death penalty. All messages must be written on the pad. That's another federal offence if you fuck up and somebody loses a job. You'll sleep downstairs in the den when the Ranger departs. Paula and I have one bedroom, Linda and Marsha share the other. Can you cook?'

'Toast, eggs-over-easy and hash browns.'

'OK, you've got the breakfast fatigue. You and me empty the trash bins and once a month blitz the kitchen for cockroaches. The girls handle the dirty dishes unless we have a party when everybody pitches in.'

'Sounds a great setup,' I said.

'It's worked so far. Oh, one other thing, no politics and no total nudity unless the situation demands it. Partial nudity is allowed, especially since we don't have air conditioning.' He turned to the girls. 'Have I forgotten anything?'

'Warn him about Marsha.'

'Ah, yes, our sleeping beauty. Marsha has only one failing. She can't hold her liquor.'

'Don't make her sound like a lush,' Paula said. 'Two

drinks are her limit,' she explained to me, 'then she passes out. Something to do with her metabolism.'

'Otherwise, she is a child of nature. So . . . are you in?'

'I'm in. I can't believe my luck.'

'Know what clinched it?' Mike asked. 'You're a Harley-Davidson freak like me. That's a blood pact in my book.'

5

I have to admit that it sounds really gauche, but in 1952 I had never lived with a girl, let alone three girls. I lost my virginity at the elderly age of eighteen with a distant cousin during a holiday in Vermont, a baptism that for both of us owed more to the necessity of getting it over and done with than any shared pleasure. Maybe the fumbling ineptitude of that episode is what triggered my Edith Wharton period, for years making me an odd man out, the object of derision to the rest of my gang; it wasn't until I got to Westport that the lure of celibacy faded in Janice's bed. Come to think of it, her bed was the only one I had ever shared with a girl – the deflowering of my cousin took place on the back seat of a borrowed Pontiac, the accepted trysting place for anybody who didn't have a place to go to, and in my neighbourhood in Queens nobody I knew had a place to go to. Maybe if a shrink ever got me on the couch he'd wheedle out the fact that, pre-Pill, what also influenced my curious lack of experiment was the fear of knocking a girl up. During my time at Westport a pretty kid in the wardrobe department died from a cheap abortion that went hideously wrong. I kept vigil with her frantic boyfriend when, all-too-late, she was rushed to hospital. That was not a good scene and it scared the life out of me, just as it extinguished hers.

So, moving in with Mike and the three girls meant some major adjustments, but I gradually came to terms with my new situation. The *menage à cinq* seemed to work surprisingly well. For one thing everybody in the house had different schedules. The girls seemed to be out most of the day while Mike and I worked evenings. This suited me because until I had to sign on at Jiff's, he and I had the house to ourselves. I wrote in the den and Mike worked at his music upstairs. He had an ambivalent attitude towards all three girls, especially Paula – where she was concerned, I had to believe that they had worked out a relationship that suited them both, because they seldom touched each other in front of other people or exchanged any of those coded remarks most lovers devise to protect their intimacy.

Marsha, whom I finally met the second day after I moved in, was totally different from the other two. A cheery, uncoordinated girl, with one of those sweet, chocolate-box faces that seem to go with fat bodies, the type that Renoir painted. She taught the first grades in a swanky school on Doheny, where the Beverly Hills rich sent their kids. Her big hang-up was doughnuts – it wasn't the age when diet was an all-American obsession; if you were fat you stayed fat, and Marsha was fat and happy about it. After a while you didn't notice the flab, you only saw her beautiful face. Her ambition was to make enough money to go to Africa and join a mission for homeless children. According to Mike she had enormous success with men. 'She laughs them into bed,' he said. He rolled his eyes. 'And always skinny little guys, isn't that a hoot? Two opposite types, both wanting to explore unknown territory, I guess.'

He could be crude, sometimes referring to Marsha as 'thunder thighs' to her face when he was in a mean mood, which I found embarrassing, because it obviously offended her. I don't think he liked women – to him they were just objects to be used – and nothing pleased him more than to boast about the number of his past conquests, and is there anything more boring than that when your own life is empty?

'Tell me your type,' he said in the middle of yet another autobiographical monologue. 'Or put it this way, if I wasn't around would you try and hump Paula?'

I phrased my answer very carefully. 'It's academic, isn't it? She's your girlfriend.'

'That's no answer. Nobody is off limits. You fancy something, you go for it.'

These exchanges made me nervous. It was as if he was reading my thoughts. I did find Paula attractive and maybe it showed.

'How about Jean Peters?' he continued.

'Jean Peters? I don't know her.'

'Who said you did, dummy? I don't know her either, but I'd sure like to fuck her. I saw her once, getting out of a limo in front of Grauman's. What a knockout. She could sit on my face any day.'

'Yeah, she's very attractive. I love all her films.'

'Know something? I wrote her a song once and sent it to the studio.'

'And?'

'Nothing.'

'Isn't she in the Howard Hughes stable? You'd better be careful.'

'Careful gets you nowhere. Which stars do you fancy?'

'Never thought about it.'

'Oh, come on! You must have smacked the monkey thinking about somebody when you were a kid. Right?'

'Yeah, maybe.'

'Who?'

'Ann Sheridan.'

'The famous picture in *Life* magazine, right? Yeah, that had me going too. She was kneeling on a bed – remember? – wearing a shiny silk top and you could see her nipples pushing through it. Jesus! I must have had her a hundred times. Who else? Turner? How about her? I'd just like to score with one of those really fancy broads the once.'

There was an underlying anger to him, you sensed he felt the world owed him a living but was never going to deliver. He was older than he looked, twenty-seven going on twenty-eight, and had served on a destroyer in the Pacific fleet during the war. That explained why, unlike me, he wasn't anxious about the draft. The threat that sooner or later my papers would catch up with me still occupied my thoughts and I could see the danger of staying in one job too long and having the authorities track me down.

Those evenings when we were all in together we usually watched television on a temperamental, black-and-white set – Jackie Gleason in *The Honeymooners*, Milton Berle or, favourite of all, Groucho Marx. We used to wait for him to include his trick question on his quiz show: 'OK, for fifty dollars, who's buried in Grant's tomb?' – delivered with his trademark leer to the studio audience whenever a seriously dumb contestant had failed to win anything.

Our combined finances were always delicately poised and I sometimes despaired of ever getting ahead of the game. I longed to be able to afford a decent typewriter that didn't miss every third letter when I hit the keys. Being so close to it all, to such unattainable wealth, was like living in a vast toyshop, where everything tempted but you were prevented from ever touching the goods. On fine days the roads would be crowded with fancy convertibles full of Beverly Hills kids partying; they flashed by my old Volkswagen, radios blaring, on their way to pleasures I couldn't afford to sample.

After several lame starts I finally got under way with another novel, this time blatantly influenced by Isherwood's Berlin stories, using Mike and the girls, thinly disguised, as my fictional characters. The trouble was, Hollywood in the fifties lacked the outward decadence of pre-Nazi Berlin to wrap around my borrowed plot – everything was too bland and washed by sunlight and, try as I might, I couldn't produce a believable Sally Bowles. Paula, as a struggling actress, was the role model for my Sally, but on my endlessly rewritten pages she refused to come to life. Likewise, myself as a surrogate Isherwood emerged as a pale imitation of the original. I became convinced that my first novel was doomed to be my last. I pestered Lucy most days, but there was never any further word from Billy Fisher. Then one day, scouring the trades for any mention of him, I spotted an item in the gossip columns which stated that he was back in town prepping his next movie.

I rang the Beverly Hills Hotel and my luck was in: I was put straight through to him. I decided to use a bit of Woody's chutzpah.

'Billy, this is Robert. I'm so glad you're back. Have you been trying to ring me?'

'Have I? I can't remember.' From his tone it was fairly obvious he needed to be reminded who I was.

'Robert Peterson, the waiter at Jiff's, remember? We bumped into each other at the bookshop and you kindly bought some copies of my novel.'

'Of course. I read it.'

'You did?'

'I read everything. Unlike some people.'

'What did you think of it?'

'I liked it. Very good.' I could hear other voices in the background.

'I wondered if you'd come to any decision about the screenplay.'

'Which one?'

'The one you asked me to write.'

'Remind me.'

'You wanted me to script that thriller, by Westbrook.'

'Oh, that, yes. Look, I'm busy right now. But let's have dinner and talk about it.' I heard him shouting to somebody else: 'Where are we eating tonight?' before coming back to me. 'Join us at Romanoff's around eight. Can you make that?'

'Oh sure, yes. At Romanoff's.' I tried to sound as though eating there was an everyday occurrence.

'Good. See you tonight then.' He hung up.

I rushed to find Mike. 'You'll never guess what. You know I told you about that British producer guy who wanted me to write a screenplay, well I just rang him and I think it's on again.'

'The faggot?'

'I didn't say he was a faggot.'

'You said that when you went to his pad he changed into a dressing gown. That's definitely faggot country.'

'Well, you're wrong. Anyway, he just invited me to dinner tonight. At some place called Romanoff's.'

'He's a faggot.'

'Will you stop? Where's Romanoff's? Is that some fancy place?'

'And how!' He whistled to show he was impressed. 'A collar-and-tie job. Nobody gets a table there without some muscle, so this limey must rate. It's run by some dude who called himself Prince Michael Romanoff. Word is he's a fakeroo, but everybody goes along with it. The bigger the phoney you are in this town, the more they suck up to you. Listen, you're going to be amongst the money, kid.'

'Christ! Well, then, I'd better go and buy a decent shirt and a tie. Can you stake me until the end of the week?'

He lent me thirty bucks. My luck was in, there was a sale in the men's department at Magnin's, and I bought a dress shirt and a new tie. Linda was home when I got back and had already been told my news.

'You look as though you've slept under a stone for six months,' she said as I came out of the shower. 'Let me fix you up.'

'How d'you mean, "fix me up"?'

'Don't panic. Just put on a little base, make you look rugged.'

'No thanks.'

'I'll do it real subtle. Trust me.'

'Linda, no way.'

'Well, let me at least fix your hair.'

'I'm not going to sleep with the guy.'

'What's the matter with you?' Mike interjected. 'I thought you were ambitious?'

'You want to look your best, don't you?' Linda asked. 'Stop being so picky. Sit down and let me work my magic.'

When she had finished, she said: 'Have a look in the mirror and tell me if that isn't an improvement.'

I had to admit that she had a point.

'One final touch. You need a Windsor knot.'

'What's that?'

She stood behind me and made a series of complicated manoeuvres.

'You've done this before,' I said.

'Only on house calls. There, that should impress the British.'

I kissed her, just a boy scout kiss with nothing else in mind, but to my surprise she slid her tongue into my mouth in a way that left nothing to the imagination, and if I hadn't had a date with Billy at Romanoff's, the evening might have developed into an interesting situation. 'Remind me to thank you properly when I get back,' I said.

'I'll hold you to that.'

I thought more about kissing Linda on my way to Romanoff's, and I couldn't think why I had been so slow on the uptake. I pondered my stupidity and plotted my next moves while following Mike's directions to Romanoff's, which was located in the street alongside the old Beverly Wilshire Hotel, next to Dunhill's where they sold the best Havanas, hundred-dollar briar pipes and solid gold lighters.

Like Romanoff's it's disappeared now, but at the time both places were where the elite shopped and dined.

I parked some distance away, not wanting anybody to see my shabby Beetle. I had one last look in the rear-view mirror, and then walked slowly to the restaurant. The maitre d' was really elegant – black tie and with a shirt so white it dazzled.

'I'm joining Mr Billy Fisher,' I said, as diffidently as I could, but my voice came out as a croak.

'Mr Fisher's party isn't here yet, sir. Would you care to wait at the table or have a drink at the bar?'

'The bar's fine.'

I ordered a whisky sour, which sounded right, and attempted to pay.

'That's OK,' the barman said. 'I'll put it on your tab. Which table?'

'Mr Fisher's.'

I pocketed my money again, feeling self-conscious. Maybe it was a social gaffe to stick your host with a check before he'd even arrived? Looking around, feigning casualness, I recognised a number of familiar faces – Crawford was there, Lucille Ball, Farley Granger, Shelley Winters and Donna Reed. I could almost inhale the sweet smell of success in the room. The whisky sour hit my empty stomach like a bomb, and I declined the barman's invite to a refill.

It was some fifteen minutes before Billy and his party came in – five of them and the only one I recognised, apart from Billy, was the girl who had been with him that first evening at Jiff's. There was a middle-aged couple and a flamboyantly dressed woman who stopped to talk to several people on her way to the table. I saw the maitre d' greet Billy obsequiously, then he turned and looked to where I was sitting at the bar. I got up and went to the table.

The first thing that happened was that Billy introduced me as Robin to the couple, a Mr and Mrs Zachary Gelb, if

I heard correctly, but it could have been 'Gold' because Billy's British delivery was hard to pick up on. The flamboyant woman was wearing a lavender and lime-green suit which, contrasted with her leathery tan, gave her a reptilian look. She seemed to be wearing Tiffany's entire inventory. In addition, she had also hosed herself down with a cloying perfume. Her name was Dolly Martinez, and she spoke with a high-pitched, Minnie Mouse voice.

'Amanda you've met before, Robin,' Billy said, misnaming me a second time.

'Robert,' Amanda corrected. She smiled at me.

'Who's Robert?'

'This is Robert, you called him Robin.'

'Don't be ridiculous, Amanda, of course I didn't.' He waved his cigar as I sat down between Amanda and Dolly. 'Robert is a brilliant novelist,' he added, recovering his composure.

Mrs Gelb said: 'I envy people who can write. Me, I can hardly fill a postcard on holidays.'

'You don't have any trouble writing cheques, though,' her husband said.

'What's your latest?' Dolly asked as the champagne arrived.

'*A Fine and Private Place.*'

'Give me a copy. I'll try and find time to read it.'

'You could buy one, like I did,' Billy said.

'I never buy books, I get so many to plug.'

'I've read it,' Amanda said, helping me out. 'It's terrific.'

Dolly changed the subject abruptly. 'Billy, before I forget, what you've got to do for me is to get me tickets to see Olivier when I'm in London.'

'When are you going?'

'Next week, after Florida. Then I'm off to Paris to do a piece on Coco Chanel . . . What's today's date?'

'The seventeenth.'

'You sure?'

'No, I'm never sure which day it is,' Billy said. 'I rely on somebody to tell me.'

'Today's the eighteenth,' Mr Gelb interjected, consulting a pocket diary. He raised his glass. 'Here's to the success of your next, Billy.'

'Wait a minute, wait a minute,' Dolly continued. 'So I shall be in Paris on the twenty-seventh for two days and then get into London. Get me a pair of stalls for the thirtieth and have your people leave them at the Connaught. Billy, have you got that? Make a note?'

'I'll remind him,' Amanda said.

'You stay at the Connaught, do you?' Mrs Gelb said. 'We always stay faithful to dear old Claridge's.'

'Can't think why,' Billy interjected. 'One has to rub shoulders with all those decrepit foreign royals.'

For the next ten minutes they swopped hotel stories while studying the menu. They all spoke over each other, talking about places I had little hope of visiting, and trashing reputations. It was loose, fragmented stuff, unfailingly bitchy, knocking films they had seen, dishing marriages, comparing who was sleeping with whom, what producer was on the skids, which stars, male and female, were getting face lifts. I latched on to the fact that Dolly was a gossip columnist for a women's glossy magazine, one of the pack that leeched off the famous. Her voice was at a particular pitch that could not be ignored and she seemed unconcerned that her barbs could be heard by the adjoining table – maybe that was her intention. I had yet to learn that badmouthing was an art form in their circle. When I glanced at Amanda to see how she was taking it, she smiled naughtily and rolled her eyes.

At one point Mike Romanoff himself, working his room, came up to pay his respects. He was a dapper little creature with stiff, close-cropped hair and affected what I took to be a Russian accent. He fussed over the table and pressed us to start with caviar and blinis, which was no hardship, and for the main course persuaded everybody to take the beef done in pastry and smothered in a rich wine sauce. Amanda and I were the only ones who actually seemed to enjoy the meal, the others merely dickered with their food, talking non-stop. Billy in particular seemed to have little or no interest in what was set before him, being more concerned with prompting Dolly to revealing all the latest salacious pieces of news.

'London's so dull,' he said. 'Everybody gets on with each other.'

'Give me Paris any day,' Mrs Gelb said. 'Paris or Bermuda.'

'Good golf in Bermuda,' her husband said, making one of his rare contributions. 'Played recently, Billy?'

'Good God no! Not recently, not ever. I'd have to be certified before I picked up a golf club.'

'What d'you do for exercise then?'

'I walk to the car.'

'Oh, I couldn't do without my golf. Only thing that makes life worth living.' This was aimed, pointedly, at his wife, who affected not to notice.

I sensed that Amanda found most of the conversation as boring as I did and several times we exchanged conspiratorial glances. I was both intrigued and appalled at the indiscretions being exchanged. Being excluded, I drank too much of the vintage wines that were constantly replenished. I couldn't think why I had been invited and at one point when Dolly got up to table hop, I whispered to Amanda, 'D'you know everybody they've been talking about?'

She framed the word 'no'.

'Why isn't your boyfriend here?'

'Who d'you mean?'

'Oliver Hanson.'

'He's not my boyfriend. God forbid.'

'Oh, sorry. I jumped to conclusions.'

'Wrong,' she said, but she was smiling. 'He threw one of his sulks and went to bed.'

Still whispering, I asked: 'Why d'you think I got invited?'

She shrugged. 'Billy likes new people.'

'Have you really read my novel?'

'Yes.'

'I thought you were just being polite.'

'When you get to know me better you'll find out I never say what I don't mean.'

I liked her use of the word 'when'.

Dolly came back to the table at that moment and immediately launched into a lurid account of a recent drama at Universal. It appeared that the studio had bought off the Palm Springs police department when one of their male stars had been discovered *in flagrante delicto* with an underage boy in the Racquets Club. 'They weren't even in the bedroom, they were doing it in the cabana,' she elaborated. 'What makes my job so frustrating is that half the time I can't use the good stuff.'

'You'll find a way, Dolly,' Billy said, lighting another cigar.

'The studio have arranged for him to marry his secretary. I've got an exclusive on that at least.'

'We wouldn't have types like that in my golf club,' Gelb said. 'No way, different world altogether.'

'Your club's got its share, depend on it,' Dolly pronounced.

'It's got its share of bores, that's for sure,' Mrs Gelb said. 'Don't I know it.'

Billy had hardly directed two words to me during the entire meal and the subject of my scripting the Westbrook was obviously not on his agenda that evening. I couldn't think of any way to bring the conversation around to it; they were all so overpowering, so sure of their own importance. They fascinated and revolted me in equal measures and I just wished I had the talent to put them down on to paper. The Gelbs made several pointed references to their wealth and their various homes scattered around the globe. I gathered that Gelb owned a family firm of timber merchants, though quite how his and Billy's interests dovetailed was unclear. Maybe it was just simply that the rich naturally gravitate towards each other. I later discovered that Billy's wealth flowed from a family trust, in his case the fortune had been founded by his grandfather, who had made a killing in rubber during the pre-war period when the sun never set on the British Empire.

'Where should we go now?' Dolly said as the meal ended.

'How about Ciro's?' Mrs Gelb suggested, naming the fashionable nightclub of the time. 'I want to catch the act there, the Will Mastin Trio everybody's talking about.'

'Quite good, I'm told, although it's a coon act,' her husband said.

'D'you mind if I excuse myself?' Amanda asked. 'I have a meeting over at Fox in the morning and need to look my best. Thank you, Billy dear, that was a lovely dinner.' She turned to me. 'You have to cut, too, don't you, Robert?'

'Er, yes,' I said, gratefully picking up the cue. 'I'm afraid so. I'll drop you off.'

'Give me a ring,' Billy said. 'I want to talk to you about something, don't I?'

'I hope so, Billy.'

'Don't forget to send me your book,' Dolly said. 'Or better still just tell me what it's about and I'll give it a mention in my column. I don't have time to read.'

'Thank you,' I said with as much grace as I could muster. I made my goodbyes to Billy and the Gelbs and left with Amanda. The moment we were outside she started to giggle. 'Oh my God, what about those three? I loathe that poison-ous old cow, Dolly. I can't think why Billy's so fond of her, except he collects monsters.'

'You're not a monster. Am I?'

'No. We're part of his East Lynne complex. He likes to play Svengali and take young people under his wing. How d'you think I got here?'

'How did you?'

'Billy spotted me in some half-arsed play at the Garrick – that's a theatre in London. He goes to every first night when he's home. For some reason he thought I was good and gave me a contract.'

'Is Oliver under contract to him too?'

'Yes, he discovered Oliver too and made him into a star. Let's hope he does the same for me.'

'Is he going to put you in one of his films?'

'One of these days, touch wood. He's crazy in many ways, and you have to get on to his wavelength, but I think you can trust him. And he knows everybody. Since I've been here he's got me a couple of screen tests, so fingers crossed.'

'What favours does he demand in return?'

'None, if you mean has he made a pass.'

'Could that mean he swings the other way?'

After a slight hesitation, she shook her head. 'I don't think so. I don't think Billy's anything really. He just gets his kicks second-hand through other people. He loves all the intrigue and infighting in this business. Well, you saw that tonight.'

'What was the dinner in aid of?'

'Nothing. He can't bear to be on his own. Every night's the same. Different faces, but the dialogue as before. I have to tag along.'

She took my arm as we walked to the parking lot. 'So where d'you want to go?'

'I don't mind, where d'you want to go? Don't you have to be up early for your meeting?'

'No, I just pretended – anything not to endure another minute. Why don't we go back to the Polo Lounge and have a drink?'

'Where's that?'

'At the Bev Hills.'

'Fine.' When we arrived beside my car, I apologised for it.

'It's sweet,' she said. 'I love these cars. They're fun. I had one once, named Daisy.'

'You called your car Daisy?'

'Yes, very puke-making, I admit, but I'm like that. I also had a cat called Cat.'

When we got to the hotel she led me through to the Polo Lounge. It was almost pitch-dark. When my eyes adjusted I could make out three or four couples smooching in the booths. Amanda looked around then said: 'No, it's like a morgue. Let's go to my suite.' She marched out to the elevator.

I hesitated. 'Can we do that? Won't we get a visit from the house dick?'

'Don't you know, you can't take guests to your room late at night, but a suite is OK? The hotel morality code says that nothing can possibly take place in a suite. Plus the fact they wouldn't dare upset any friend of Billy's.'

She led me down a corridor where every other door had a room service food trolley outside laden with the debris of half-consumed meals. When we arrived I was stunned by the opulence of her suite. The living room was the size of the entire ground floor of the West Knoll house, with matching sofas and armchairs, a coffee table with an enormous basket of fruit on it, a writing desk, television and a practical fireplace.

'Jesus wept!' I exclaimed. 'Is this all yours?'

'Not bad, eh? And this is just one of the junior suites. You should see the penthouse. Billy had it for a few days when his usual bungalow was being renovated. Make yourself at home.'

'Can I use the bathroom?'

'Take your pick. There's one through there, or one through that door on the right.'

The only time I had ever seen a bathroom like it was in those glossy magazines you read in dentists' waiting rooms. I stared at the array of clean towels, bathwraps, complimentary tablets of unused soap in shell dishes on either side of the double washbasins. It all made me afraid to piss. Because I didn't dare unwrap the soap, I just rinsed my hands under the hot tap.

It's staple fare in those hard-bitten detective novels for the gumshoe to come back into the room and find the lady has slipped into something more comfortable. You know the sort of thing – '*The-broad-was-wearing-a-pair-of-earrings-and-nothing-else*' school of literature, perfected by Chandler. Amanda hadn't gone that far, but she had changed into one of the bathwraps and let her hair down. I felt some return gesture was expected of me, so I managed to unravel Linda's Windsor knot and took off my tie.

Amanda picked up a copy of my novel from the coffee table. 'See! I was telling the truth. I did read it. That fucking Dolly was so bloody condescending to you, I could have killed her.'

It was curious, and maybe something to do with the British accent, but the word 'fucking' didn't sound coarse from her lips.

'What made you choose to write something like this? Do you come from the Deep South?'

'No. New York. I was searching around for a plot and came across an item in *Time* about a brother and sister who were parted at birth, and then met by chance twenty years later, fell in love and married before they found out the truth. I twisted it around quite a lot, of course.'

'Did you find writing the sex scenes difficult?'

'I find everything difficult. I don't believe those writers

72

who give interviews saying their books wrote themselves. That's horseshit.'

'But I'd love to know if when you write about two characters having it off, d'you imagine yourself as the man?'

'In a way, I suppose. Yes. I mean, how else would you get it on to paper?'

'I don't know, that's why I'm asking. Did you fantasise about the girl, your heroine, when you were writing it? Do you mind me asking all these questions? I'm fascinated.'

I began my answer slowly, feeling my way across that minefield we all have to cross at the beginning of a relationship. I recognised the coded message she was passing to me. A mating ritual had begun. 'Yeah, I guess I might have made use of my own experience when I got to those bits. Can I have a drink?'

'Sure. Help yourself.'

'How about you?'

'Yes, please. Open some champagne. Are you still a waiter?'

'I'm waiting on you right now.'

'Do you like that?'

'Which question am I answering? Yes, I like waiting on you; no, I'm sick of waiting at Jiff's.'

'So leave.'

'Easier said than done. I can't afford to right now.'

'I think Billy will rescue you. He likes strays. He's a walking Battersea Dogs' Home. Sorry, you wouldn't know what that means. Local joke.' I handed her a glass of champagne. 'Tell me more,' she said.

'About what?'

'How you write those sorts of scenes.'

'To tell the truth, I don't remember. When I pick up the book now I can't remember how I got any of it down on paper. You don't, you know. It's like some stranger wrote it.'

'Really?'

'Yeah, I met another writer up in Westport and he said the same thing.'

'I think it must be amazing to actually finish a book.'

'It's amazing to even start one. D'you know if Billy even read it? He's never said.'

'Yes, he told me he had.'

'He did? He didn't tell me. Did he say what he thought of it?'

'I think he liked it, but maybe it wasn't raunchy enough for him. He likes sexy books. He's always buying those trashy paperbacks.'

'The second time I met him he was in Hunter's bookstore buying porno.'

'That figures.'

'Why? Doesn't seem to go with the rest of him.'

'Horses for courses,' she said enigmatically.

As she curled up on the sofa, I glimpsed her long, bare legs. 'We're two of a kind, aren't we, you and me?' she said.

'You think so?' I sat opposite her, knowing that very shortly a line would be crossed. For the first time in ages I felt really relaxed and happy. 'What makes you say that?'

'We're both hoping to make it, one way or another. No holds barred. I haven't been here long, but I've already figured what makes this place tick.'

'Let me in on the secret.'

'Spread the bullshit thickly, they lap it up.'

'Is it the same in jolly old England?'

'Oh, no, quite different. There, it's how you speak, what fucking posh school you went to, who you know. It's all class distinction. You should hear the way some West End actresses speak, so la-de-bloody-dah, you wouldn't believe.'

'Do some for me.'

She put on a voice. 'Oh, Deddy, do I really have to marry that beastly Steven? He's arse-paralysingly boring and he

doesn't hunt.' She laughed, enjoying her own impersonation. 'Either that or the other end of the scale – cockney
maids and tarts with hearts of gold all talking Gor Blimey.
Pathetic. The British theatre when I left was in a time warp.'

'Is that why you prefer it here?'

'Who said I did?'

'Don't you?'

'Some of it.'

'Have you had fun?'

'Yes and no. I can live with this,' she said, taking in the
room. 'Not having to pay the rent or make the bed. I think
I was born to room service.'

'What don't you like about here?'

'Most of the people I've met are so fucking phoney.'

'You like using that word, don't you?'

'What, "fucking"? Yes. Does it offend you?'

I shook my head. 'No, I love hearing you say it in that
accent. Have you dated anybody since you got here?'

'Yeah, a couple. Arranged for me by Billy, of course. He
likes to think of himself as a matchmaker. It's the Jewish
thing in him.'

'And?'

She pulled a face. 'None of them were my type.'

'What is your type?' I found myself sounding like Mike.

'Guess.'

That was the moment when, according to the rules of
the game, I should have joined her on the sofa, but I still
hesitated. There was something intriguing but dangerous
about her which held me back. I was also pretty certain that
I couldn't afford her. My reading of the situation was, I
was available, she was bored. Now she allowed her wrap to
gape open just enough to give me a glimpse of a white bra.

'I was always told you British girls were ice maidens.'

'And I was brought up to believe that you American jocks
just jumped on us.'

'Maybe we both got it wrong.'

'Maybe.'

All the time we were carrying on this small talk, an inner voice was urging caution. Was she just playing with me – the technique of a practised PT? As with Billy, I couldn't get a bead on her. Instead of pursuing the topic, I switched subjects.

'Tell me more about Billy. Is he for real?'

'Real? Course he's real.'

'I meant, is he on the level? First of all he said he was going to give me the chance to write a screenplay for him, then he seemed to forget who I was and disappeared. That was until tonight when he invited me to dinner to talk about it and never mentioned it. I don't know where I am with him.'

'Billy's a law unto himself. Just ride with it. I do.'

She gave a sly grin and her face relaxed, half-shadowed in the soft lighting. I couldn't help thinking again how white and translucent her skin was, like the fine bone china dinner had been served on, so different from the tanned Amazons who frequented the Malibu beaches. She had curled herself on the couch, and I thought, why am I holding out? On the face of it, everything was perfect – alone with a beautiful girl in an opulent apartment – how often had such an opportunity presented itself? I went over and sat beside her and put my arm around her, but she evaded my lips when I bent down to her face.

'I should tell you, I don't go for one-night stands,' she said, 'and I'm very choosy whom I go to bed with.'

'That makes two of us.'

'Will you fall in love with me?'

'Is that what you want?'

'It's the only way I can do it.'

'How about me? Do you get to fall in love with me?'

'Depends.'

'Sounds a one-sided deal.'

'That's to keep you guessing.'

Her mouth was responsive the moment mine touched it – open, fleshy and pliant, but cold from the champagne. She kissed with her eyes closed and the kiss became prolonged and more intense as our tongues probed. I was the first to end it.

'That was nice,' she said. 'So, will you fall in love with me?'

'It's certainly going through my mind.'

Her expression changed. 'D'you always talk like that?'

'Like what?'

'So precise and calculated.' She mimicked me. '"It's going through my mind" – as if you're taking out a mortgage on a house. Try saying it like you meant it.'

'OK. Yes, I could easily fall in love with you.'

'Good. I fancied you the first time I saw you,' Amanda said.

'It was the way I waited on table, was it?'

'No. You've got a sexy arse.'

'Butt,' I said. 'Or ass, but not arse.'

'And I felt sorry for you.'

'Why?'

'Oliver put you down.'

'Did he? I didn't notice.'

'Oh, yes. That remark about slumming. Pompous prick. He's such a snob about food. And it's all an act. He's as common as muck underneath it all.'

She looked at me intently, then got up from the couch and went into the bedroom. After the briefest of hesitations, I followed her. The bedroom was in darkness but some light filtered through from the living room. I stood in the doorway as she took off her wrap, then unfastened her white bra. Her ripe young breasts came loose. That was the moment I kissed goodbye to Newland Archer for ever.

'So?' she said.

'Look, I wasn't expecting this, so I don't have a rubber with me.'

She laughed. 'That's such a funny word for them. What d'you call erasers?'

'Erasers.'

'Well, don't worry. I wear a coil.'

I let my own clothes fall in a heap on the floor, thankful that they were new and not my usual work clothes. We kissed again as my hands roved her breasts. When we came up for air her voice changed. 'Don't be in a hurry,' she said. 'Do it slowly, very slowly, we've got all night and I like the trimmings.'

6

Looking back, I don't think I ever truly understood any of them – Amanda, Billy, and most certainly not Oliver, nor was I ever completely on their wavelength. All three of them possessed, in varying degrees, that slightly 'off' attitude towards us ex-colonials. Oliver, in particular, always gave the impression that his friendship was a favour that could be quickly withdrawn, especially to anybody he considered beneath him in the pecking order. He brought the same mannered aloofness to his acting roles, making it his hall-mark and giving out a sense of his own superiority. Amusing, yes, a great teller of bitchy anecdotes that left a queasy aftertaste: you could be pretty sure that the moment you left him his next audience would be treated to an unflatter-ing story about you. I've since met a few expatriate Brits like him in the profession, and they all seem to rely upon a kind of acid humour to make an impression. As far as I can judge they never quite accept the Hollywood scene. They want the glory and the spoils – Catholics who finally get to Rome and kiss the Pope's ring – but at the same time feel they have to withhold their total affection. It's as though unless they find fault – the Californian weather is hot but boring, all producers are philistines, the steaks are too big, the wines don't travel, the women are ball-breakers – they're somehow committing the unforgivable sin of going native. Some I've met have a certain charm, but they turn it on and off like garden sprinklers: sometimes you're deluged, sometimes left high and dry.

Amanda I found easier but, then, of course, I was sleeping with Amanda. She certainly wasn't the ice maiden I had first suspected, more a sleeping tiger easily aroused, different from any girl I had ever known. There was a directness about her, her emotions were always laid bare. I was desperately in love with her and I guess she took advantage of that. She demanded a lot from me once the affair began: frequent protestations of love before, during and after making love, and she was given to odd mood swings that often threw me.

'I expect you'll put me in a novel one day, won't you?' she once said, after a bout of love in the afternoon. 'All writers do.'

'Do they?'

'Yes, you told me yourself.'

'When did I tell you that?'

'The first time we went to bed.'

I traced a circle around one of her nipples reflectively. Her breasts totally fascinated me; they seemed to have an unreal, perfect shape. 'I don't remember that but, OK, if you're right, how would you want me to describe you?'

She put her tongue in my ear and whispered, 'Like somebody no man can resist. Immortalise me.'

'Oh, something modest you mean? Anything else?'

'Yes. Then dedicate it to me.'

Moving her head, she bit me on the collarbone where the neck and shoulder come together. 'And write me lots of love letters that I can tie in ribbons and keep for my children to read.'

'Just your children, not mine?'

'We won't last long enough.'

'You don't think so?'

'No, we'll burn ourselves out.'

'Why? Why can't we go on for ever?'

'No. That's film jargon. A happy ending before the fade-out.'

'What's wrong with happy endings?'

'I want to go out with a bang, not a whimper.'

'You've just had a bang.'

'Oh, not worthy of you. How d'you leave your women?'

'I haven't had that many to leave.'

'Do the harem you room with fancy you?'

'Maybe.' I've noticed that nothing concentrates a woman's mind more than the possibility of a rival.

'Really? Tell me, which one?' she asked.

'The beautician, maybe.'

'Well, does she or doesn't she? You must know.'

'The only quote "intimate" unquote thing that ever happened is when she fixed my hair the night of that dinner at Romanoff's, I gave her a kiss.'

'And? Then what?'

'End of story. Perhaps if you and I hadn't become a number . . .'

'Oh, God! I don't want to be thought of as a "number".'

'Sorry, I meant I fell in love with you and I didn't want anybody else.'

'Has she moved on you since?'

'No.'

'But you all live in such close proximity you told me, there must be times when you see her nude.'

'Yeah, once or twice. We only have one bathroom.'

'How sordid.'

'Yes, well we can't all be kept in luxury by Billy Fisher.'

'I'm not kept, don't insult me.'

'What d'you call it then?'

'I'm a property he's investing in. So, has she got a good figure?'

'Yes.'

'Better than mine?'

'No.'

'When you kissed her, did it do anything to you?'

'At the time, yes. But I didn't follow it up because I met you. This is a pointless conversation.'

'No, it's fascinating. I like hearing about your secret life.'

'If I could afford to, I'd move out and get a place of my own. It all depends on Billy. Has he mentioned anything to you lately?'

'No.'

'Do you ever ask him?'

'No. None of my business.'

'You don't care, in other words?'

'Billy moves in his own way, in his own time. He doesn't like people pressurising him.'

'You don't think he's jealous, do you?'

'What about?'

'You and me. See, I don't believe what you told me, that's he's non-sexual. Everybody gets their rocks off in one way or another.'

'Rocks off! Oh God, for a writer, you do use the most hideous expressions.'

'Sorry, sorry. OK, why are you so sure he does nothing?'

'Because he once said a very revealing thing to me: "I'm Quasimodo."' Seeing my puzzled expression, Amanda explained: 'His harelip, stupid.'

'Funny he should feel like that. You don't notice it after a time.'

'I guess you do if it's on your face. Sometimes he knocks on my door late at night, often very late. Then sits on the end of the bed and talks. Nothing in particular, gossip mostly. He's just lonely. He likes me to read to him. One of those ghastly books he's addicted to.'

'The porno, you mean?'

'Yes. Desperate stuff, most of them.'

'Well, there you are. He has to get his kicks somewhere. Beautiful girl reading porn to him must be a turn-on.'

'Billy's a latter-day Proust, standing on the sidelines, observing all and filing it away.'

'I read a biography that said Proust did a lot of cruising whenever he left his cork-lined room . . . Have you told Billy about us?'

'I didn't have to, he guessed. If you must know, I think he arranged it. That's why you were invited to dinner that night. I told you it amuses him to be a matchmaker.'

'Well, who am I to complain? Lucky me.'

'Lucky me too,' Amanda said, her mood changing abruptly again, as though conjecturing about Billy's sex life had excited her. She sat astride me, bringing her breasts tantalisingly close to my lips.

'I can't,' I said. 'I don't have the strength.'

'Try.'

'Is this your method? First tantalise, then kill your lovers like a queen bee?'

'No, this is my method.' She squirmed on my lap. Sunlight squeezed through the closed shutters, striping her bare body and then happiness took over again.

7

During the next two months I became progressively ragged at the edges. Billy disappeared again for a time and I despaired of him ever taking a positive decision on his screenplay offer to me.

It was events at Jiff's that concentrated my mind. I turned up for my evening shift after a pointless row with Amanda that lovers sometimes have – a slow puncture rather than a blowout, but which still deflates. It had started with a chance remark I made about her new hairdo. Second only to her breasts I had a thing about her hair, but the relationship women have with their hairdressers is a foreign country and men trespass there at their peril. She had been persuaded into trying some new snipper in town who called himself 'Maurice Rene, late of Paris' – Paris, Texas, I suspect rather than France. He had wreaked a Samson-and-Delilah in reverse on her, shearing her beautiful locks in a misguided effort to make her look like Ingrid Bergman in *For Whom the Bell Tolls*.

I tried to keep the shock out of my face when first confronted with the result, but obviously made a bad job of it.

'What happened?' I asked.

'Like it? I've just had it styled by this genius hairdresser Arlene Hathaway told me about. She pulled rank and managed to get me a cancellation. Otherwise I'd have had to wait for weeks, he's so swamped. Do you like it?'

'It's different.'

'Of course it's different, that's the whole point.'

'Takes getting used to,' I said, struggling to regain lost ground, but it was all too late.

'You don't like it.'

'I do like it. Yes, I like it.'

'I can tell you don't. What don't you like about it?'

'Nothing. I like all of it.'

The conversation went round in circles and there was no way out. The fact was, I hated it. She knew I hated it, and she resented I hated it. Maybe she hated it too, but she wasn't about to admit it. And so, what I had fondly imagined would be one of our tumbled afternoons in bed ended in mutual sulks and I departed to Jiff's in a frustrated mood.

I found the place in an uproar. There was a shouting match going on in the kitchen between the rodent manager and the Polish chef. Watched by half a dozen amazed customers, a sobbing Leyla was being comforted by Tony.

'What the hell's going on?'

'He told me I was a whore, dahlink.'

'Who did?'

'Who d'you think?' Tony said. 'That prick we work for.'

A customer at the counter shouted: 'How about some service around here?'

'Give us a break,' Tony replied. 'Can't you see we've got problems? Help yourself if you want to – it's on the house.'

Two of the customers got up and left. The guy at the counter seemed uncertain how to react, then leaned forward and took a Danish.

'Bobbie,' Leyla said between sniffs, 'you know me, I am always a lady, I am doing nuffink to make him say these bad things to me.'

'What started it?'

'He walked in and found her and Stanislav having a little schmooze,' Tony explained, 'so he fired her.'

'Stanislav is making a proposal of marriage to me.

Everythink above board, dahlink, like the perfick gentleman he is.'

At that moment our despised manager appeared from the kitchen. He ignored Tony and me and turned on Leyla. 'Why're you still here? I told you you're through, you Turkish whore, so take your things and get out.' He moved to the customer at the counter. 'I apologise for you having to wait, sir. What can I get you?'

'Hey!' Tony grabbed his arm and pulled him back. 'Asshole, don't talk to her like that. You fire her, I'm walking too. So is Robert. Right, Robert?'

'Sure,' I said without hesitation, catching the general mood of rebellion.

'You can't do that.'

'Watch us.'

Now Stanislav joined us. He was no longer wearing his apron and chef's hat. 'I quit,' he said.

'You can't quit,' the manager screamed. 'The rest of you can't quit either, you're all under contract.'

Stanislav produced a kitchen knife and backed him against a wall. He let rip with a string of Polish expletives interspersed with his garbled English. I roughly made out that he was telling the manager to make his own hamburgers, and when he'd made them to stick them up his ass with the contract. Putting a protective arm around the sobbing Leyla, he shouted: 'We open own place, put you out of fucking business.' The manager edged towards the phone, but Stanislav beat him to it and ripped the instrument out of the wall, which was impressive. The guy at the counter left hurriedly, munching his free Danish.

'Keep away from me, you bloody Polack! You touch me and I'll see you in jail.' The manager was craven now, all his old bombast having evaporated. Denuded of his authority over us, he now appeared just a joke – with his thin moustache and carefully pomaded, sandy hair he was like a fall guy out of a silent movie, the type who always caught the custard pie right in the kisser. Stanislav made a pass with the knife a good yard away from him just for effect, then hurled the knife at the counter, shattering the glass container holding 'freshly squeezed' orange juice which was in fact diluted concentrate bought by the gallon. Having made his gesture, Stanislav shepherded Leyla towards the street, shouting: 'We have the happy hour. We vamoose this bastard.'

He waved and bowed at the remaining customers, two of whom applauded, and swept Leyla out of the door. Tony and I followed.

We ended up in a downtown Polish bar where Stanislav was greeted like the King from across the water, and we started to give some native schnapps a thrashing. The happy hour extended to three, by which time we were all well and truly sloshed. I dimly remember that Leyla burst into song at one point, standing on a table and belting out her national anthem. Although my memory is clouded beyond that, I believe that just before she passed out Stanislav proposed to her again on his knees. I have no idea whether he knew she was still married to the Detroit wife-beater, but I don't suppose the prospect of bigamy would have deterred him. The floating population of Los Angeles, of which he and Leyla were founder members, were just that: drifters who went wherever the tide took them, possessed with a benign conviction that they could beat the system. I hoped Stanislav acted the 'perfick gentleman' on the wedding night and I remain grateful that their drama propelled me into a decision about my own life. I had needed something to spring me from Jiff's – looking back I can't imagine how I lasted all those months, kidding myself that I needed the regular pittance to survive, whereas, in fact, it was a false insurance policy that was never going to pay out. I came to the realisation that the sheer, boring grind had diluted my creative urges as surely as the management adulterated the orange juice.

Surfacing just before noon the next day, I found myself alone in the house, lying on the floor by the side of my bed, fully dressed and horrendously hungover. It took me a while to realise that what had raised me from the dead was the phone ringing. The slightly sibilant voice of Greg, Billy's chauffeur-cum-valet, didn't register for a few seconds.

'Who?' I said.

'Mr Fisher wants to see you.'

The phone cord was twisted and I knocked the instrument to the floor.

'You still there?' Greg asked.

'Yes, sorry. Say again.'

'Mr Fisher wants you to come up to the hotel.'

'Ah, Mr Fisher. Of course. Right. The hotel . . . When?'

'Now.'

'Tell him . . . Certainly . . . I'll be there as soon as . . .' I juggled with the phone and dropped it again . . . 'as soon as I've got rid of some people.'

I staggered to the bathroom, shedding clothes as I went, and was just about to take a cold shower when the phone went again. This time it was Amanda.

'Where were you last night?' she began, sounding as though she had a mouthful of ice cubes.

'I got involved.'

'Well, I guessed that. Who was she?'

'No "she". It wasn't like that. Look, darling, I can't go into it now. Billy wants to see me and I'm late.'

'I don't like being stood up.'

'Yeah, I'm sorry, really. I'll make it up to you.'

'You'd better. Ring me when you're through with Billy. I might be in, and then again I might not.' There was no mistaking the freeze-out.

Billy received me rumpled and in his dressing gown,

brogue shoes and tartan socks, with the inevitable cigar glowing. He seemed to be in an unusually irritable mood; it was the first time I had seen his urbane, British mask slip and I feared I might be the cause. Oliver was slumped in an armchair reading *Daily Variety* with the intensity of a monk studying the Dead Sea Scrolls. He ignored me.

'The reason you haven't heard from me about the script,' Billy said, as his cigar shed a shard of ash, 'is because I've been waiting for those morons at Columbia to give me an answer as to whether or not they want to do it. All they keep telling me is their people in New York are considering it. I couldn't care less what "their people" think and I know why they're stalling. They can't bear the fact that I don't need them and they can't screw me on terms.'

I listened, still feeling as though there was a full orchestra playing discords inside my head, and made an effort to concentrate.

'I'm certainly not going to be pushed around by them, so I want you to start on the script right away. I shall pay you myself, so don't worry about that. Did I give you a contract?'

'Not yet, Billy.'

'Well, I'll talk to your agent. Remind me of his name.'

'Arnold Kosner.'

'Why on earth are you with him? He couldn't negotiate a right turn even if the light's green. Leave him and go with a nice old cow, like Minna Wallace.' He dropped his lighted cigar into an ashtray, but it struck the edge and fell on to the floor. I bent to pick it up, which was a mistake, and nearly passed out.

'Well, I've only just joined him,' I said as I stood up again and waited for the roving liver spots before my eyes to recede.

'Never be loyal to agents, Robert.'

Oliver interrupted at that moment. 'Listen to this balls.

"Latest romantic duo in town is Oliver Hanson and Dawn Williams seen having a close tete-a-tete in Ciro's. Do we hear wedding bells?" No, you fucking well don't. That's your bloody friend, Dolly.'

Billy ignored this. 'Jonathan Clayburn is flying in to work with you on it. I did a deal with him while I was in London. Do you know him?'

I shook my head, which was another mistake, given my condition. 'I've heard of him.'

'Well, he's going to direct it. Perhaps not the easiest person to get on with, so don't be put off the first time you meet him.'

'No "perhaps" about it,' Oliver interjected without looking up. 'He's a walking nightmare. And barking mad to boot.'

'Of course he's not,' Billy snapped.

'Have it your own way. For my money he's a fucking egomaniac and a pain in the arse, so just be warned, Robert. You heard it here first.'

'He happens to be a perfectionist. Don't take any notice of Oliver, he's peeved because Jonathan didn't use him on his last picture.'

'I turned it down. For God's sake let the beast of Pinewood get over his jet lag before you sic Robert on him,' Oliver said, 'otherwise the collaboration will be short-lived. He eats writers.'

'Do shut up, Oliver! Ring me tomorrow,' Billy said to me. 'Leave it until the afternoon, I'll have talked to Arnold by then. If he's in,' he added.

I left the bungalow in desperate need of a hair of the dog. I went to the Polo Lounge where the barman fixed me the elixir for restoring life, which gradually reduced the orchestra in my head to a string quartet. It was only then that Billy's news began to sink in. I began trying to calculate what he might pay me if Arnold didn't screw up. I used the pay phone and rang his office to forewarn him, but naturally he wasn't there.

'They took off for a long weekend,' Lucy said.

I told her of the latest development.

'That's lovely, dear, just the break you deserve. Now don't worry, I'll handle it when Mr Fisher rings. Did he mention a price to you?'

'No.'

'No, they never do. But leave it with me, I'll see you get a proper deal.'

'He said he'd take care of the Guild. Any idea what he'll go to?'

'No, but certainly enough for you to quit your job.'

'I already have.'

'Oh, good. I didn't like to think of you in that place.'

Reassured, I went back to the bar and this time had a black coffee while I mentally began to spend the money I was about to earn. Although filled with a newfound confidence, I took note of Oliver's warning about Clayburn, but filed it away at the back of my mind. I'd read that Clayburn was the latest white hope of the British cinema with the reputation for being an original stylist. He had had a couple of critical and commercial successes, one of which – a dark and moody piece taken from a Henry James short story – had travelled across the Atlantic and been exploited on the art-house circuit. I had seen it in New York and been impressed. The Westbrook novel was obviously going to be a sea change for him as well as a watershed for me.

Something cautioned me not to blurt out the good news to my fellow inhabitants in West Knoll Drive; better to wait until the ink was dry on the contract before crowing, but I couldn't wait to tell Amanda when I saw her later that day. I found she had decided to treat me to an impersonation of Bette Davis in *Jezebel*, determined to rub it in about the previous evening.

91

'Don't ever do that to me again,' she said.

'I promise, darling, but I can explain. I quit my job at Jiff's.'

'So?'

'Well, it was quite dramatic. We all quit, the chef, me, another waiter and the chef's girlfriend. A mass exodus.'

'So?'

'So then we celebrated. Not wisely, but too well.'

'There is such a thing as a phone, you know. That wonderful, efficient American phone system you all go on about.'

'Look, I'm sorry and I apologise, but when it happened I guess we all got involved in the drama of it and I didn't think to phone you. I should have done, it was thoughtless of me, I can't excuse it, what else can I say? Anyway, don't you want to hear my good news?'

'About Billy, you mean? I know already,' she said, puncturing my excitement.

Beautiful women always know when they have us in thrall and can twist the knife an extra notch. Maybe beauty and cruelty go hand in hand; maybe those who are born with it realise everything fades in the end and want to exact the maximum penalties while the bloom is still on them.

'Anyway, since you're about to come into the money you can take me out to dinner,' she said.

'With pleasure, but not if you're going to freeze me out all evening. I've said I'm sorry.' I attempted to kiss her.

'Not now,' she said, still glacial. 'Let's go and eat.'

Thinking it might amuse her and thaw the atmosphere, I took her to the Cock and Bull, a restaurant with mock-Tudor decor where the waitresses were dressed like Anne Boleyn and a Hungarian violinist from Central Casting, done up as Henry VIII, worked the tables playing authentic Elizabethan madrigals from the Blue Danube songbook, if you get the picture. The specialty of the house was Ye

Veritable Roaste Beefe [sic] of Olde England, corn-fed in America – the cuts so large they overlapped the plates – served with a strange, glutinous side order called Yorkshire pudding. If I imagined such ersatz reminders of home would restore the status quo, I was wrong. After ordering, I started to say, 'I can't believe I've finally got my break,' when she lobbed a smoking hand grenade across the table.

'You've told me all that,' she said. 'Don't you want to hear my good news?'

'You've landed the role you auditioned for at Fox?'

'No, but I got landed with something else.'

'What?'

'A positive report from the lab.'

'What lab?'

'The one where they inject rabbits.'

I still didn't get it.

'I'm pregnant,' she said.

'How?' I said, which was about as foolish a question as any man can ask in the circumstances.

'Oh, use your loaf. How d'you think?'

'But we . . . I mean, you said you had one of those things fitted.'

'I do, but presumably it didn't work.'

I stared at her.

'Don't just gawk at me with your mouth open. I'm not having it. What did you think I would say? "Let's go to Vegas and get married"?'

I gave a mumbled, 'No.'

The first course arrived at that moment. 'Be careful how you touch the plates,' the waitress warned, 'they're very hot. Enjoy.'

Enjoyment was no longer on the menu. I stared down at the sizzling hunk of meat and fought off a rising nausea. In a matter of minutes my whole world had turned upside down. 'You couldn't have made a mistake, could you?

Maybe you're just late?' I asked without much conviction.

'No. I've missed two periods. And I never miss. The test came back positive yesterday. That's why I was so upset when you stood me up last night.'

'I see. Yes, I see,' I said as misery engulfed me.

'Haven't you ever had it happen to you before?'

I shook my head.

'So, we have to do something about it.'

'Yes.'

'Quickly. You'll have to arrange an abortion.'

Amanda calmly cut into her meat as though what she had just said was as simple as having her eyes tested, while my thoughts went winging back to the time in Westport when the young girl in Wardrobe had died. I kept my voice low. 'It's illegal, you know that? And dangerous.'

She shrugged. 'Not if you do it soon enough, and it's done properly.'

The violinist arrived at our table and started to play some bloody czardas. I waved him away. He gave me a pained look but moved on.

'How would I go about it?' I whispered. 'I don't know how to start finding that sort of doctor.'

'Then ask around, ask some of your friends, ask that beautician who's so keen on you. Those sort of people listen to girl talk all day. Women always tell everything to their hairdressers.'

'Are you saying they talk about things like this?'

'Oh, believe me.' She was tucking into the Yorkshire pudding.

'How can you eat?'

'Because I'm hungry.'

Her calmness was baffling and not for the first time I realised how little I understood women. There I was, a nightmare vista opening up before me, while Amanda was consuming half a steer. The whole scene was unreal.

94

'I suppose if you can't come up with something, I'll have to ask Billy,' Amanda said.

'Billy? You can't ask Billy!'

'Why not? I bet he'll know a doctor we can go to. Or Greg will.'

'Greg?'

'Yes. He's Billy's fixer. He supplies Billy with all his pills.'

Now the waitress returned. 'Everything OK for you, guys?'

'Great.' I cut into my meat, but the moment blood oozed on to the Yorkshire pudding I knew it was a lost cause. 'Are you crazy?' I resumed when the waitress had left. 'How d'you know you can trust Greg? I don't think we should tell him or Billy. I'm just about to start working for him.'

'What's that got to do with it?'

'It gets me off on the wrong foot, that's what. Jesus, what a mess.'

'Well, what's your suggestion?'

There was a new note in her voice, the one girls use when they are poised to produce the ultimate weapon – tears.

'Don't cry,' I said.

'I'm not.' Her round, green eyes were fixed on me. The thought that she might make a scene in public terrified me.

'I'll find a way, trust me.' I reached for her hand across the table and squeezed it. 'Perhaps you're right. Perhaps Billy is the answer. And maybe he'll advance me the money. I imagine it'll cost a lot to get it done properly, and of course it has to be done properly . . . I suppose there's nothing you can take, is there?'

'Like a bottle of gin and a hot bath, you mean?'

'Does that work?'

'Who knows? It's an old wives' tale.'

'Some of those old-fashioned remedies do work, though.'

'There is one thing that's supposed to work.'

'What?'

'A girl friend back in England said it worked for her.'

'What? Tell me.'

'She said if you go at it like stoats several times.'

The idea of sex was not uppermost in my mind at that moment, but I was desperate enough to clutch at any straw. 'Does that do it?'

'Can do, or at least she swore it did with her.'

'Well, then, maybe we should try it.'

'Say it as if you want to.'

'Of course I want to. And not just for that reason,' I added quickly as her expression changed again. Praying that I would be capable of performing, stoatlike, when the moment came, I made a pact with God that, once I'd managed to extricate myself from this mess, I would swear off sex and concentrate on my career. Newland Archer had been smart enough never to consummate his love for the Countess. Out of the corner of my eye I sensed our concerned waitress hovering.

'Something wrong?' she asked.

'No, everything's fine,' I said.

'Would you like to change your order?'

I wanted to change my whole life. 'Thank you, no. It looks great, but I'm not that hungry. You can take it away.'

'Would you like it in a doggy bag?'

'I don't have a dog.'

'Sure I can't get you anything else?'

'No, thanks, nothing.'

When she had retreated I went straight back to the subject. 'It's safe, is it?'

'Safe?'

'Going at it, I mean? It won't harm the . . . ?' I was incapable of completing the sentence.

'Of course not, stupid.'

'Just wanted to make sure.' I watched her finish her meal, trying to make small talk, but wondering what my performance in bed was going to be when the time came.

'We can cut whenever you like,' I said.

'I'd like a coffee refill, if you can wait that long.' I ignored the sarcasm in her voice.

'Of course, sure, no hurry. How about dessert?'

'Just coffee.'

It was another fifteen minutes before we left and drove back to the hotel. I couldn't rid myself of the feeling that everybody in the lobby knew what we were going to get up to. I felt eyes boring into me. It was as though I was carrying a billboard which said 'THIS MAN IS ABOUT TO KILL HIS UNBORN CHILD' in red letters. By the time we reached Amanda's suite what little confidence I had started out with had all but disappeared. I'd read somewhere that erections were conditioned by a mental attitude. Amanda didn't help. She assumed a somewhat clinical approach.

'D'you want a drink first?' she said, rather in the way that condemned men are offered a last cigarette. I tried to remember whether, in the past, alcohol had improved or ruined my performance.

'Open a split of champagne and bring it into the bedroom,' she said.

I hesitated. 'I suppose . . . No, doesn't matter.'

'What?'

'I was just going to say . . . if you don't want to go through with this thing, I'm willing to . . .'

She waited, but I couldn't finish. 'Marry me, you mean?'

'If that's what you want.'

'You are kidding, of course?'

'No.'

'Well, don't be a hero on my account, because it wouldn't work. I don't know what your game plan is, but mine doesn't include being stuck with a baby at aged twenty. Nice of you to offer, but no thanks. I really like you, Robert, you're a nice guy, and I like the sex we have . . . maybe I like it too much and that's why we're in this mess. But that's the way it goes. So don't look so worried.'

'How can I not be worried?'

'Just get the champagne and we'll test whether this does the trick.'

She was already undressed and under the covers when I took in the two glasses. I sat on the edge of the bed. 'You're quite sure this is safe?'

'Yes, silly.'

'Well, let's drink to success,' I said. I gulped my champagne and the bubbles went up my nose, bringing on a coughing fit. After I had recovered I slowly took off my own clothes, folding them neatly over the back of a chair to delay the moment of truth as long as possible. The instrument of deliverance between my legs resembled a piece of string and I hurriedly got into bed. On all previous occasions the first contact between our naked bodies had always resulted in spontaneous combustion, but this time down in the forest nothing stirred.

'Maybe not the missionary position, huh?' I said with a light-heartedness I did not feel.

'Why not?'

'Well, you know, maybe my weight on . . .'

'Do it any way you want.'

Tentatively, I started to kiss all her usual erogenous zones, hoping this would have a counter-effect on me, but the engine refused to fire. I felt as though I had levitated above the bed and was watching my own performance with a detached, pitying look. At one point I reached down to feel if the bloody thing had dropped off, and found that it had retracted like a plane's undercarriage. Panic set in and panic in such a situation, as we males know, launches us on the downward slope. In normal times whenever I kissed her glorious breasts they never failed to ignite my lust like a rocket, but now there was no liftoff. Amanda, on the other hand, seemed to be having a reasonably good time as I increased my ministrations, but she was travelling alone. I slid further down the bed, trailing kisses over her torso, past her belly which was not yet like a mound of wheat as depicted in the Song of Solomon, though it seemed to me to be larger than usual, until my lips grazed her pubic hair.

'Oh, yes,' she murmured, as I came up for air, 'more of that please. You've no idea how sexy that is.'

I renewed my efforts and after a while Amanda said, 'Let me do the same for you.' We assumed the position that presumably those artful French invented, or at least took the credit for. Amanda performed manfully (though that might not be the ideal expression), and for a few precious oral moments worked the miracle. I extricated myself quickly and attempted the *coup de grace*, but the delusion of pleasure was momentary.

'I'm sorry,' I said. 'Don't know why that happened. Over-anxious, I guess.'

'Doesn't matter.'

'Well, of course it matters. It matters to me.'

'Have a rest and we'll try again.' She snuggled up to me, now using her hand by way of encouragement. I made two further attempts to rise to the occasion, but to no avail. By then I was a wreck, but to give Amanda her due, she didn't seem to bear any grudge, which made it much worse.

'Poor darling,' she said. 'Don't be upset.'

'It's so bloody humiliating to be impotent.'

'Hardly impotent, darling.' She patted her stomach. 'The proof is already in the oven.'

'Well, obviously I'm never going to be able to do it again.'

'Oh, darling, don't exaggerate.'

'This is hardly an exaggeration,' I said, pointing at the offending, withered object. 'If I can't do it with you, I obviously can't do it with anybody. It's the end of the road. *La fin du jour*.' I was behaving absurdly, but I felt absurd.

I swung myself off the bed and went for my clothes. All I wanted now was to get the hell out and nurse my wounded ego in private.

'What're you doing?' Amanda asked. 'You're not going, are you? How can you leave me now?' The quaver in her voice gave an ominous hint of impending precipitation, as they say in the weather bulletins. 'Don't be so horrible.'

'I feel horrible. I probably am horrible.' Reluctantly I went back to the bed and climbed in beside her, careful not to make bodily contact. 'What are we going to do?' I asked.

'I guess you'll have to go through with it.'

'It's bloody unfair. Why did God make our pleasure so complicated?'

'Because He's a spiteful God, full of wrath. Didn't you ever read the Old Testament?'

'Not for a long time.'

'Put your arm around me.'

I did as she asked.

'I don't know why you're so upset and cold,' Amanda said. 'After all, I'm the one who has to face the music.'

'You don't have to remind me.'

'All you have to do is find the way.'

'Yes.'

'Do what I suggested and ask Billy. Promise?'

'All right.'

'Say it.'

'I promise,' I said, lying in my teeth.

8

Even though Amanda's situation was in the forefront of my every waking thought I still couldn't bring myself to solicit Billy's help. Instinct told me it would be a bad career move for me to involve him in my personal problems. In any case it seemed crass to ask that sort of advice from a bachelor who, even if not homosexual, was not exactly fine-tuned to feminine problems of that nature.

He did help, but not in the way that Amanda had suggested. On his own say so he gave me a generous deal on the screenplay: if I stayed the course I was to receive fifteen thousand dollars for three drafts, plus a further five thousand on the first day of principal photography. He also repeated his promise that he would pull strings and get me into the Guild. 'Since you're working for me, I'll also pay your initiation fee, outside the contract, in cash,' he said. 'That way you won't have to pay Arnold commission.'

'That's more than generous, Billy.'

'I like you, otherwise I wouldn't do it.'

I told him about the fracas at Jiff's, which he loved, and then I confided that, having turned in my job there, I was more or less broke and asked if he could advance me a couple of thousand dollars before the contract was signed. He wrote a personal cheque there and then. Armed with this, and having given it much thought, I confessed my situation to Mike.

'Going to cost you,' he said when he had listened to my sorry tale.

'I know that, but can you help?'

'Yeah. No sweat.'

'Really? It has to be done properly, with no risk to Amanda.'

'It's not a no-risk problem.'

'The least possible risk then. D'you know somebody?'

'I got a contact, yeah, but he ain't cheap. You're gonna have to find five or six big ones for the guy who does it and a couple of hundred for the fixer.'

'Fixer? What fixer?'

'Get real. These things ain't easy. Nobody deals direct, you have to have a go-between.'

'And you know of one?'

'I can put out feelers.'

'You said "the guy who does it". He will be a proper doctor, won't he?'

'What d'you mean by "proper"?'

'Qualified.'

'Well, it ain't going to be done at the Mayo Clinic. It'll mean going out of state.'

'Jesus!'

'I had to take my girlfriend down to Mexico the time I was in danger of being a prospective father.'

'Why Mexico?'

'Less risk and cheaper.'

'I'm not looking for cheap, I want it handled right.'

This conversation took place late at night when I invited him out for a meal, ostensibly to celebrate my contract. I didn't want the three girls to know (the other suggestion Amanda had made – that I should ask Linda – had filled me with horror. Linda was still making up to me whenever she got the chance and I had run out of excuses). Mike, on the other hand, took my situation in his stride – no condemnation, not even any sympathy, just matter of fact. He might as well have been discussing a trade-in on his Harley.

'So how do we go about it?' I asked him.

'Well, I'll need a couple of days to contact my fixer. He moves around a lot. And be prepared, he'll want his money up front.'

'He's reliable, is he?'

'He does it for a living.'

'That isn't an answer. Is he straight?'

'Straight guys aren't fixers. You want straight, go to Cedars of Lebanon and ask if they take Blue Cross.'

'OK, don't get uptight, just asking. How does he deal?'

'What's it to you? You pay him, he comes back with the place and the date.'

'It's done by a proper doctor, though?'

'I've told you already, don't expect him to be a Nobel Prize winner in paediatrics on the staff at the Mayo. When the arrangements have been made, you deliver your girl-friend to the address you're given, pay the money, strictly cash, and a few hours later you drive her back here. End of story.'

'God!' I exclaimed. 'It all sounds so sordid. How did it work out after with you? Were there any complications?'

'What d'you call complications?'

'Well, like was she all right?'

'It was rough on her, but she got over it.'

I wished I had a touch of Mike's callousness. No, that's not really true. I didn't want to be like him. I was shit-scared of the whole business, scared of what might go wrong. That night, over dinner, I gave him the cash up front for the fixer, feeling like an amateur punter placing a bet on a horse that might not run. That night when I eventually fell into a disturbed sleep, I had dreams of an unknown country where Amanda and I were searching for a house we could

103

never find, and I woke drenched in sweat. All I could think of was it seemed a long way to go to kill something.

There wasn't an opportunity to tell Amanda the next morning because an early phone call from Greg alerted me that Jonathan Clayburn was ready to start work. Apparently he had moved out of the Beverly Hills Hotel and into the Beverly Wilshire.

'I can't stand all those poncy little hustlers milling about taking breakfast meetings in that pink palace,' he said as soon as the introductions were over. 'I like the oldness of this place and the fact that the rooms are dowdy. Makes me feel at home. Back in London my flat could win a prize for dowdiness. I prefer it like that. It means nothing distracts me. Where has Billy put you?'

'Nowhere. I'm staying with friends at the moment.'

'How can you bear that? I loathe staying with anybody, one always feels so obligated to be tidy.'

He wasn't at all as I had imagined him. Rather shabby in appearance. Shabby and shaggy – his unfashionably long hair needed a wash. I guessed he was around thirty-five, with strong features but pale eyes, the sort you sometimes see on overbred dogs, which at times gave him a sort of mad look. He was having breakfast when I arrived in his suite and ate as he moved around the room rearranging the furniture. I was to learn that he was always restless, as though he constantly needed to burn off surplus energy. His accent was quite different from Billy's or Amanda's – he had none of their clipped vowels, but spoke in a softer brogue that I could not place. He later told me he came from the West of England.

'So that we both know exactly where we stand, let me tell you I'm not crazy about working with beginners, and in any case you seem a strange choice for this material,' he began bluntly. 'But it's Billy's theory that I need somebody uncorrupted by Hollywood I can bounce off, so I suppose I'm stuck with you. Did he get you cheap?'

I ignored the slur. 'Yes, I'm not in the top league. Not yet anyway.'

'And are you uncorrupted?'

'I guess you'll have to find that out for yourself.'

'Personally I like a bit of corruption. You know where you stand. How come you know Billy?'

'He liked a novel I'd written.'

'Oh, so you're one of those, are you, a novelist, not a screenwriter? And now he's sicked you on me. What have you heard about me? I dare say word came down that I'm a difficult bastard.'

'No,' I lied.

'Well, I am. Have you seen any of my films?'

'I saw the Henry James adaptation you did. I liked it.'

He picked up a copy of Westbrook's thriller. 'This isn't exactly Henry James. Nor is it Graham Greene. Just a competent potboiler that needs a lot of work.' He poured himself another cup of coffee but didn't offer me one. From the amount of trays and crockery littered around the room he seemed to have ordered several breakfasts. 'How d'you function?'

'Function?'

'Yes. Don't you understand English? How d'you work? I'll tell you how I operate. I like to talk things through for at least a month before getting anything down on paper. Does that grate on you?'

'No, whatever suits you.'

'That's right. Whatever suits me, and what suits me is living on expenses for as long as it takes.'

'I'm not on expenses,' I said.

To my amazement he suddenly produced a Bowie knife and threw it at the door. It stuck, quivering, in one of the panels. Still talking to me, he prised it loose. 'You should know I'm at a crossroads at the moment, deciding which

105

way to go. The biggest mistake you can make in this business is to make hasty decisions. Don't you agree?'

'I wouldn't know. I've never had the luxury of choosing between two jobs at once.'

He threw the knife again, but this time his aim was erratic and it bounced off the door and shattered a lamp on a nearby table. I made a move to help him pick up the pieces, but he stopped me.

'Leave it, somebody'll pick it up when they do the room. My first thought is we should move the whole thing to France. England's so bloody dreary at the moment.'

It took me a second or two to take that in.

'Ever been to my side of the water?'

'No.'

'You haven't missed anything. Austerity, bombsites and we've still got rationing for certain things, would you believe? Forget "to the victor the spoils". Your bloody government bankrupted us, gave us a few clapped out destroyers and then proceeded to empty our coffers. So this is my way of getting some of it back.' He threw the knife a third time and this time it stuck. 'Setting it in France might jump-start it,' he said, reverting to his other line of thought.

'Will the plot work in France?'

'Why not?'

'Seems very drastic. All the characters are British.'

'So? We change them. If nothing else, moving it to France would mean better unit catering. The French are a pain in the arse. They've never forgiven us for winning the war, but their food's wonderful. You've no idea what food in England's like. We're still eating wartime shit. Ever had horse meat?'

'No.'

'Very sweet. Let's kick the idea of France around for a while, see what we come up with.'

106

He threw unrelated sentences at me with the same casualness that he threw the knife.

'Fine, whatever you say.'

'Don't agree with me every time. I hate yes men. Give me an argument. You watch any French films?'

'I've seen a couple.'

'They know how to handle sex. Hollywood doesn't have a clue. I'll tell you something else, everything sounds better in French. Especially love scenes. If we make the two lovers French, they could speak in their own language and we could use subtitles.'

'Will Billy go for that?'

'Fuck Billy. If he wants me to direct it, he'll go for what I decide, or else he can get somebody else.'

By the end of the first session he had thrown out half a dozen different approaches, none of which bore any relation to the novel that Billy had bought. There was a manic intensity about him, like somebody on a caffeine high. Several times I got the impression he was humouring me, testing the water as it were, to see how I reacted. I played it straight, unsure of my ground. I did venture one small query when I asked him whether he felt Westbrook, the author of the novel, might object if such drastic changes were made to his work.

'Who cares?' Jonathan said. 'He sold his virginity when he took the money for the screenrights. Authors are so bloody two-faced. They run all the way to the bank with the spoils, then cry they've been raped. We can do anything we damn well like with his brainchild. It isn't the first folio of Shakespeare. Think about France.' He paused and stared out of the window at Rodeo Drive. 'D'you like living here?'

'I like the weather.'

'Yeah. The weather in the South of France is good too. Maybe we should both take a trip there, scout some locations. I'll suggest it to Billy. Even if it comes to nothing, at least we'll get a paid holiday.'

Amanda, not France, was uppermost in my anguished reckoning. Before I could give my entire energies to the screenplay, I had to resolve her situation, but there was no way I wanted to reveal that to Jonathan.

'Let me work on Billy. He's not really interested in the nuts and bolts. Haven't you found that?'

'I don't know him well enough.'

'I'll say this for him, he doesn't hang around your neck once the script and cast are set. What we have to watch out for is getting lumbered with his latest leading man. Have you met Oliver?'

'Yes, a couple of times.'

'There's no way I'm ever going to have him in this one. He acts like he's got a broom up his arse. And that's another reason for distancing it from the novel. I'm so tired of all those toffee-nosed English stars giving themselves airs. Their problem is they've all made so many bloody war films they play everything like they're waiting for somebody to pin a DSO on them.'

Because I had hardly slept the night before, I found it increasingly hard to concentrate when he launched into a further diatribe about the industry back in England, which I took to be another way of putting me, the beginner, in my place – Jonathan Clayburn treating the untried student to a lesson from the master. A certain irritation crept over me. I knew I was being patronised.

Then, just before he dismissed me, he went off at another tangent. 'I've just had a different idea for the beginning. The two main characters, the girl and her boyfriend, are on holiday, for the sake of argument in France. On the way down to the South they stop and have some lunch at an outside cafe, in Versailles maybe, and at some point the boyfriend leaves her and goes to the loo.'

'Loo?'

'What d'you call it, the john, the toilet?'

'Oh, right.'

'When he comes back there's no sign of the girl. At first he's not too concerned. Then he asks the waiter. "What girl?" the waiter says. "You were on your own." He produces the check. "See, you ordered one salade niçoise and a beer. There was nobody else with you."' He stopped pacing and stood directly in front of me, twirling the Bowie knife. 'Intriguing?'

'Yeah,' I said, trying to keep amazement out of my voice. 'What happens next?'

'Don't ask me. You take it from there. Play around with it, see what you come up with. I'm just throwing out ideas to get you thinking.'

By now I was convinced I was dealing with a lunatic.

'Sleep on it,' he said, 'and let's meet up again tomorrow. I've got some calls to make and then I have to go out and do some shopping. I never bring anything with me, it's such a drag travelling with luggage, don't you think?'

When I left him I slowly drove up Beverly to Amanda's hotel, bracing myself for the encounter. Bypassing the front desk, I went straight to her room. She was in bed, naked, her breasts slack and pale and looking altogether too attractive for my state of mind. I was suddenly in a funk again.

'You look distracted,' she said. 'How did it go with Clayburn?'

'Oliver was right, he's a madman. He throws knives at the door.'

'Knives?'

'Yes.'

'Stupid prick. I'm so bored with people in this business who think they have to be characters.'

'And he's got some crazy idea of changing the setting from England to France.'

'Is that crazy?'

'Well, wouldn't you think so?'

'I haven't read the novel. Anyway they change everything in films.'

'We've got to talk.'

'O K, come and talk in bed.'

I did nothing. 'I've made some enquiries about you-know-what,' I said, stumbling over my words. Amanda stared at me, but made no attempt to help me out. 'It could mean a trip out of state. To be on the safe side.'

'Where to?'

'I don't know yet. The man I spoke to is going to get back to me.'

'O K,' she said, taking me by surprise by her indifference.

'You don't mind?'

'The place doesn't matter as long as it's going to be done right. But I'm sure you'll see to that.'

'Of course I will, but I've got to trust this guy. I'll pay whatever it costs for it to be done by a legit doctor, not some quack.'

'I know. I trust you. But the sooner the better as far as I'm concerned. I was sick this morning. I hate being sick more than anything else; it's the worst feeling in the world.'

I wanted her to see reassurance in my face instead of fear, but all I could give her was another promise: 'I shall stay with you the whole time.'

'Stay with me now. Come to bed.'

I undressed slowly and slid under the cool sheet she lifted. I wanted everything to be ordinary again, but of course it wasn't and, although this time I was able to make love to her, I was back in the country of uncertainty.

9

'My man has upped the ante,' Mike said the moment I walked into the house. 'He wants more.'

'How much more?' I wasn't too surprised. I had expected it – illegal favours are seldom on offer at sale price, and for all I knew Mike was taking a cut for himself. I wasn't even sure the fixer existed.

'Another hundred for him, non-returnable like the first instalment, and the actual job'll cost you seven not five.'

'But has he fixed it?'

'Providing you come across,' Mike said. 'When he gets the extra dough tonight, he'll give me the details you need. He likes the money in his hand before he gives out information. Says it'll be a different place from last time. I guess the good doctor has to keep on the move to stay ahead of the fuzz. He's no longer in Tijuana.'

'I still think I ought to meet him.'

'You'll blow it if you do.'

When Mike returned late that Tuesday night he gave me the thumbs up sign. 'All squared away. Friday morning, Phoenix, Arizona. Here's the address.'

I stared at the piece of paper. 'This doesn't say Phoenix, it says Mesa.'

'It's part of Phoenix.'

'And the doctor's name isn't on it.'

'He doesn't give names.'

'Jesus, Mike, I'm having to take your word for everything.'

'That's the way it has to be, buddy.'

Faced with an actual date, I felt sick. I was a condemned man finally knowing the date of his execution. Except it wasn't my execution. I spent a long time going over the options. There weren't many. Unless by some miracle Amanda had a miscarriage in the next few days, we would be making the journey – to what? I didn't want to think further than that for the moment. The next day I used some of Billy's advance to rent a decent, air-conditioned car so that she had some comfort, especially on the return journey when it was all over.

There were other problems to solve, not the least of which was how to explain my absence to Clayburn, but as it turned out when I rang him the next morning I didn't need to launch into my prepared, phoney story.

'Glad you called early,' he said before I had got my first words out. 'Something's come up. I have to go to Palm Springs for a few days. No sweat, we can pick it up again after the weekend. Use the time seeing if my idea about shifting it to France works, and play with that opening I gave you. Do me a one-line step-outline so we've got something to kick around.'

'Right, OK.' I tried to sound confident.

'See you Monday.'

'Right. Hope it goes well in Palm Springs.'

'It's not a business trip, I'm hoping to get laid,' he replied, never missing a chance to impress me. I compared my coming weekend with his, hating his bright assurance.

The only reaction I got from Amanda was relief that the uncertainty was over. In contrast to my continuing fears, her composure amazed me. We made a list of things we thought we should take with us, trying to think of possible emergencies, but my scant knowledge of female physiology being what it was, I didn't press Amanda for too many details. I spent the rest of Wednesday attempting the step-outline Clayburn had demanded. His idea for a beginning was intriguing, but once I got that down on paper, invention failed me; the more I tried to substitute France for England the less believable it became. A second wave of panic swept over me. If I failed to come up with the goods for Clayburn and he fired me, in all probability I would have to return Billy's advance, and a good proportion of that had already been spent. It was also in my mind that Mike's contact could be a con man. Maybe the abortionist didn't exist either. This thought began to obsess me.

'What if your man crooks me?' I asked Mike. 'How do I know he can be trusted?'

'You just have to take my word for it.'

'Your word isn't his. Let me meet him before we go.'

Mike shook his head. 'He only deals through third parties.'

'That's suspicious in itself.'

'No, just good protection. If anything goes wrong you're both protected. He doesn't know you, you don't know him.'

'So something could go wrong?'

'Listen, what can I tell you? Your girlfriend's not having a tooth filled, so there has to be some risk. You don't have a choice. The guy's a careful Joe.'

'You sure?'

'Listen,' he repeated, 'if I'm wrong I'll let you off the rent for two months.'

He was right, of course. I didn't have a choice. Like the poor bloody infantry in World War 1, the whistle had blown and I had to put my head above the parapet.

I was grateful for the air conditioning in the rented car. The moment we left behind the sprawl of Los Angeles and

113

pushed on into semi-desert country a fierce and different heat began to build up, shimmering the road ahead so that often I momentarily lost my bearings. I had never driven in the desert and before we had gone a hundred miles I had to force myself to stay alert. We had set off early, hoping to make good time, and for the first hour Amanda surfed through the radio stations trying to find her favourite brand of music. Then she gave up and was silent for a while.

'You feeling all right, darling?' I asked.

'OK.'

'I'm sure it's going to be fine.'

'Are you? Bully for you.'

'My friend Mike says this doctor's very good.'

'Oh well, if your friend Mike says so I've got nothing to worry about, have I?'

'Tell me if you want to take a rest or anything and I'll pull off the road.'

'No, let's get there.'

She leaned back and closed her eyes. I tried to put myself in her place – what did it feel like to know you were going to terminate the life forming within you? A sense of shame swept over me because, despite my fears for her, I had a cowardly need to have the whole thing over and done with. Keeping my eyes rigidly on the straight and dusty road I wondered what method this unknown doctor used. Something Mike had said stuck with me. 'She's not having a tooth filled.' During the incident back in Westport I had gleaned odd pieces of second-hand information, and all of them evoking revulsion. The fact that, from necessity, it had to be done in this hole-and-corner manner – journeying to a strange town and then trusting Amanda's life to an unknown doctor – tempted all the worst fates. It was awful to need the services of a stranger to kill something, like hiring a hit man. Did he ever feel remorse? What single act had committed him to that way of interpreting his

Hippocratic oath? Was he like a priest who turns away from God to perform the Black Mass? Even though the cold air from the ducts played on my face I could feel the sweat trickling down the back of my neck.

Whether Amanda slept or merely kept her eyes closed to avoid conversation I had no means of telling. After driving for four hours I pulled into a roadside cafe and gas station. When I killed the engine she sat up.

'Are we there?'

'No,' I said. 'Roughly halfway, by my reckoning. I thought you might like a break and a drink. I need to top up the gas as well. Better to be safe than sorry in the desert.'

She went inside while I filled the tank and checked the oil and water. The cafe was fairly basic, but clean, with an attempt to look like a cowboy saloon – bare boards, scrubbed tables and sawdust on the floor. We ordered Western-style: eggs, bacon and hash browns, but neither of us cleared our plates. There was a counter display by the side of the cash-till where they sold a few Indian belts, trinkets and fetishes. When I paid the check I bought Amanda a small bear fetish carved out of soapstone.

'To bring us luck,' I said. She took it, but said nothing. 'Why don't you stretch out in the back for the rest of the trip?' I suggested, but again my attempt at cheerfulness failed.

'I hate being in the back. It makes me feel sick, especially the way you drive.'

'I thought I was driving carefully.'

'It's when you brake, you jerk the whole car.'

I left it at that. When we resumed the journey the interior of the car was like a furnace and the steering wheel almost too hot to touch. I set the air conditioning to maximum, but even so, Amanda took off her skirt and blouse (such a curious British word, I've always thought) and sat in her bra and briefs with her feet on the dashboard close

115

to the air-conditioning ducts. At other times I would have found it erotic, now it was just scary. Everything scared me.

'Don't get us arrested,' I said. 'Not on this trip.'

'Stop fussing. If we see any of your wonderful police I'll slide down out of sight.'

But for the rest of the journey we didn't see a single highway patrol and for the most part we had the road to ourselves, just the occasional truck that came into sight in a ball of dust. Our windscreen was constantly spattered with the blood and exploded remains of insects.

'When this is over,' I said, 'I'm going to really spoil you. I'll be able to; Billy's given me a really good contract.' I started to tell her more about the changes Clayburn wanted me to make to the script, expecting her to share my amazement, but she surprised me.

'He's smarter than you think. Those dreary British films don't go down over here.'

'You're a patriotic lot, aren't you, always knocking your own country?'

'Well, hopefully, I'm never going back.'

'Won't you miss seeing your family?'

'No. My parents are divorced. My mother married again, a real prat. And I never see my father. He went to Australia, so there's nothing to go back for. I'm going to make it big here, nothing halfway. I may not have been here long, but I've figured out you're either somebody or you're nobody. And I don't intend to be nobody.'

As she said it, I saw with terrible clarity that, whatever the outcome on Friday, the day would come when I might not share her future. 'I'm sure you will,' I said. 'You don't have to convince me. I'm just sorry I got you into this mess.'

'Stop being nice to me.'

'How should I be?'

116

'Anything else. If you keep being nice to me, I'll burst into tears. Let's play a game.'

'A game?'

'Yeah, a guessing game. I'll start. Who starred in *It Happened One Night*?'

'Male or female?'

'Female.'

'Jean Arthur.'

'No.'

'Bette Davis.'

'You're not even warm. Give you a clue. She also took a bath in asses' milk.'

'In the same film?'

'No, another one.'

'I give up.'

'Claudette Colbert. Now you think of one.'

'OK. I'll make it really difficult. Who played opposite Garbo in *Camille*?'

'Never saw it. Give me another. And make it more recent.'

'That's cheating, you didn't even try ... Let me think. OK. Who played Vivien Leigh's father in *Gone with the Wind*?'

'Easy. I saw it ten times. Thomas Mitchell. That's two to me.'

We passed an hour in such pursuits until she got bored and lapsed into silence again. There was so much I wanted to say to her, but somehow I couldn't form the words. We reached the outskirts of Phoenix around seven that evening, having made another stop at a gas station some fifty miles out, where I had bought a local map in order to work out where Mesa was. It wasn't too difficult to find and I drove around looking for a suitable place to spend the night, finally deciding on a motel that, from the outside, looked reasonable. Amanda let me do all the talking. Recently reminded

117

of *It Happened One Night*, I anticipated we'd get some suspicious looks when we checked in, but the old guy who ran the place couldn't have cared less. I gave our names as Mr and Mrs Wilson from Westport, Connecticut.

'You folks are a long way from home,' he said as he directed us to a cabin.

'Yeah, we're touring around. Thought I'd show my bride the Wild West.'

The cabin was neat and clean with two single beds.

'Sorry we don't have a double left,' the old guy said. He switched on the television. 'Television works real good, though. Anything else I can do for you?'

'Is there anywhere to eat round here?'

'Chinese place two blocks down. Haven't tried it myself but folks say they serve a mighty fine meal.'

When he left us I turned to Amanda. 'Fancy Chinese?'

'I don't fancy anything. Anyway you're not supposed to eat before an operation.'

'You're not having an operation.'

'What would you call it then?'

'Well, I meant not that kind of operation.' Nothing I said that night did anything for her.

'You go and eat if you want to.'

'I wouldn't leave you here on your own.' I tried another approach. 'Do you want to go for the Walls of Jericho routine? Or should we put the two beds together?'

When the penny didn't drop immediately for her I explained: 'Gable and Colbert, remember?'

'Oh, that. Let's just use one bed, I want you close to me tonight. What made you choose the name Wilson?'

'Edmund Wilson, one of my heroes?'

'Who's he?'

'A writer, one of our best. I studied him for my thesis at college.'

We undressed and got into the bed. Cuddling up to her

118

in the cramped space my hand inadvertently rested on her stomach. She brushed it away.

'Don't,' she said. 'Just hold me.'

She fell asleep almost immediately, her head nestled against my neck. But I didn't. I lay awake for hours, and once I heard the distant cry of a coyote, strange to my city ears, that seemed, in the still of the night, like a child in pain.

10

Our Walls of Jericho proved paper thin that night. My fitful sleep was disturbed by shouting from the next room: the unknown couple seemed so close they could have been just behind the headboard of our bed.

'I want that bitch out of our life!' It was a high-pitched, woman's voice.

'How the fuck was I to know she'd be at the party?' the man answered.

'You knew. You knew all right, you lying bastard. That was why you were so anxious to come here.'

'I swear I didn't know.'

'You fuckin' liar. I know you set it up with that bitch. Well, you'll be sorry, I'll make sure of that.'

The man mumbled something I couldn't catch. Then something crashed to the ground and the woman cried out, 'Don't touch me, you two-timing bastard.'

Amanda slept through it as the row flared spasmodically, but I must finally have closed my eyes because the next thing I knew she was shaking me and saying, 'It's gone eight, we overslept.' I came to out of one of those dreams where you are always searching for somebody and constantly miss them.

'For God's sake, don't let's be late,' Amanda said as she went to take a shower. The room was already hotting up despite the air conditioner.

'Let me see if I can rustle up some coffee and breakfast.'

'I don't want anything. Just in case they give me an anaesthetic.'

I stopped dressing. 'What d'you mean, "just in case"? Of course they'll give you an anaesthetic.'

'You don't know.'

She was right, of course. I didn't know. I stared at her nude outline behind the frosted glass of the shower, wishing I had a piece of her calmness, but maybe she was just putting up a front. She seemed to have so much more capacity for courage than me. I couldn't forget what lay ahead in the next few hours, and I couldn't not fear. I went and stood outside the shower and when she emerged, groping for a towel with wet, blind eyes, it was my arms that enfolded her.

'What?' she said. 'What's the matter?'

I kissed her in the hollow of her neck, tasting the scent of the soap she had used. 'I love you,' I said.

She eased herself away from me, but I took the towel from her and dried her body like a nurse with a patient. Everything I did was wrong, I knew that; I should have been strong, not over-solicitous, but I couldn't help myself. It was all I could give her.

While we both dressed, we heard the sound of car doors slamming outside and then the voice of the woman from the night before shouting: 'I'm not gonna forget, don't kid yourself, you two-bit jerk.'

'Those two kept me awake last night,' I said. 'You didn't hear them, did you?'

'No. Do you have the rest of the money?'

'Of course.'

'Show me.'

'I've got it, believe me.'

'Show me.'

I took the bundle of notes out of my back pocket and spread them on the bed. 'OK? Why did you need to see it?'

Amanda stared at them. 'Because,' she said, then turned away and ran a comb through her dank hair.

Outside the heat hit us like a thick, enveloping blanket. The interior of the Pontiac was hot enough to bake bread in. I switched on the engine and air conditioning.

'You quite sure you don't want even a cup of coffee? We've got time.'

'No, I'm fine,' Amanda said.

I left her to return the room key to the desk and pay the bill. When I came back she was still standing outside the car.

'You OK?'

'How do they do it, d'you think?'

'I don't know, honey, I wish I did . . . Listen, even now, you don't have to go through with it, I told you that . . . It's your call, and whatever you decide is OK by me.'

She took a long time before answering. 'No. Let's get it over with.'

I looked at the address I'd been given and consulted the map. 'As far as I can tell it's about three miles from here.' I squeezed her hand, then put the car into reverse.

Before we had gone three blocks heavy drops of rain started to disperse the grime on the windshield. The palms and Mexican pepper trees along the route began to sway as a wind got up and small dust twisters span out of vacant lots like demented dancers. Suddenly, sheet rain came down and within moments the roads were awash. I flicked the wipers to maximum speed, but even so I could hardly see where we were going. Rather than risk anything I pulled in to the side of the road and waited for the storm to abate. Rain drummed on the roof of the car.

'Dramatic, eh?' I said. 'Should cool it a bit, though.' When she said nothing, I tried to think of anything that would take her mind off the abortion. 'Does this remind you of home? It always rains in England, doesn't it?'

'Not always.'

I stayed parked until the downpour eased off before venturing out into the flooded road. Brown water carrying broken palm fronds rushed by on either side of us. Consulting the map several times I threaded our way through suburban streets until we came to the one I was looking for. The houses were mostly one-storey, neat but nothing special.

'Can you spot the number? We want 1504.'

'I imagined something different,' Amanda said.

'Nice quiet neighbourhood, though.'

'That's a plus?'

'Well, you know, it looks respectable.'

I drew up outside 1504. I couldn't bring myself to ask her once more if she wanted out. Part of me longed for it all to be over, and another part was sick with fear for what she had to face. We both sat there staring at the house, then Amanda made the first move and got out of the car. I reached for her hand as we walked to the front door and rang the bell. The door was opened almost immediately as though we had been observed driving up. I don't know what I had expected – somebody dressed like a nurse maybe – but the woman who answered our ring was middle-aged and wearing ordinary clothes.

'Come on in, honey,' she said to Amanda in a flat, matter-of-fact voice.

Amanda stepped inside and I followed. The woman closed the door and turned to me.

'Have you got the money?'

I gave it to her and she counted it. 'Right,' she said, 'you drive off some place, young man, and come back in three hours.'

'Don't I get to stay with her?'

'No.'

'Why not?'

'House rule.'

'I must stay with her.'

'That's not possible.'

'Tell me why.'

'Don't make things difficult. Either do as I say or else you can have your money back and take the young lady away. We make the rules, not you.'

I was holding Amanda's hand tightly. 'Do as she tells you,' Amanda said. 'I'll be all right.'

'You sure?'

She nodded.

I turned back to the woman. 'Three hours then. Make sure you take good care of her.' I kissed Amanda on the cheek. 'You're so brave, darling. It's going to be all right,' I whispered. She looked like a ghost as I left her.

Those next three hours were the longest I had ever spent. I drove around until I found a coffee shop, ordered some breakfast I couldn't swallow, all the time going over the worst scenario – that I had abandoned Amanda to some nameless, incompetent quack and she'd probably die during whatever they did to her. I cursed myself for not being stronger and insisting that I stayed with her. They wouldn't have returned the money and not gone through with it, of that I was sure. I sat there staring at the eggs congealing on my plate wondering how I could have been such a weak shit.

'Something wrong with your eggs?' my waitress asked.

'No, I wasn't that hungry, I guess.'

'Can I get you something else?'

'No, thanks.'

'How about some more coffee?'

'No, just the check.'

The normality of everything around me – the grizzled, weather-beaten faces of three old men at the counter bent over their steak sandwiches, the fat girl with spectacles

124

sitting alone dunking her doughnut, a mother spoon-feeding two infant children – only increased my sense of isolation. I wanted somebody to confess to, to share my guilt and fears with somebody, anybody. Looking at my watch, time seemed to be standing still, like on a long plane trip – only forty minutes of the three hours had elapsed. Standing up to go to the cash desk I was suddenly made dizzy by the thought of losing Amanda. The parting remark I had made to her – 'It's going to be all right' – came back to remind me of my ignorance. I saw it for what it was, the sort of phoney piece of comfort parents trot out when you're young just before you face something horrid.

Outside the heat hit me again. I felt as though I had no bones in my body. I sat on the pavement until the spasms in my legs eased, then, conscious that passers-by were staring at me, I pulled myself up and went into a gift store on the opposite side of the road with the thought of buying Amanda a gift. I didn't want to give her some stupid tourist gimmick that would always take her straight back to this moment and this place. I settled on a small silver heart on a chain which the shop assistant assured me was authentic Navajo. It probably wasn't, but I had it put in a box and wrapped. The episode had only wasted another twenty minutes. They always tell you that desert heat doesn't make you sweat, but when I took to the sidewalks again I was quickly drenched, sweat running down the sides of my face and into my eyes. I walked back to the parking lot and sat in the car with the air conditioner going full blast until the sweat dried on me, all the time making bargains with God like some alcoholic who swears that this drink will be his last. Except, in my case, I was promising I'd never again put a girl in this situation. Then I drove around in circles, anxious not to lose my way, while the minutes ticked by with agonising slowness. At one point the whole situation overwhelmed me and I gave in to a fit of crying, making those choking sounds you surrender to when you are alone.

When, finally, two and a half hours had passed, I found a grocery store and bought a bottle of iced water and some sodas, which I put in the portable cooler. Then, trying to time it so that I arrived back on the dot, I returned to the house. Before ringing the doorbell I opened the trunk and took out the emergency supplies I had packed. I put these on the back seat and kept the engine running while I went to the door because I wanted the car to stay cool for her.

The same middle-aged woman answered my ring.

'How is she?' I blurted.

'A little dozy, but she'll be fine if you take it easy. Stay there and we'll bring her to you.'

She closed the door behind me and disappeared. The room I waited in was furnished like any other suburban house of its kind. I suppose I had imagined that it would look like a clinic, but I found myself looking at a leather three-piece suite, a large ginger cat curled on one of the matching armchairs, a fireplace with an arrangement of dried flowers in it and a nondescript framed print above. It could have been my aunt's living room back in Brooklyn and had no connection with the activities taking place in another part of the house.

I heard the sound of voices and then Amanda came into sight, supported by a man wearing a white coat. He had slicked-back dark hair crowning a face that bore no resemblance to my preconceptions: it was neither sinister nor reassuring, there was nothing written on it at all, just the face of a man who would pass unnoticed in a crowd, a man whose name I would never know. Amanda walked unsteadily, her eyes not focused.

'Have you got far to go?' the man asked.

'Quite a way. We came from Los Angeles. Was it all OK?'

'I believe so,' the man said evenly. 'Have you got anywhere you can stay tonight?'

'What d'you mean, "anywhere"?'

'It'd be advisable if you got her to bed somewhere until it's over.'

I stared at him, stared at his bland face. 'It's over now, isn't it?'

'No,' he said abruptly, as though I had asked a tiresome, unnecessary question. 'This is just the first stage.'

I couldn't take that in.

'You have to appreciate I take a considerable risk to help people like you. I promise you it was done clinically and expertly and will have the desired effect in due course.'

'What do you mean, "in due course"?' I heard my voice getting louder.

'Normally between one and four hours.'

He passed Amanda to me and she sagged against me. 'What sort of answer is that?' I said, a splinter of anger entering my voice.

'I have every confidence that your young lady will make a complete recovery and be none the worse. But . . .' he gave the briefest pause, 'she may experience a certain degree of discomfort. Keep her quiet and get her into bed as soon as possible. Take these.' He handed me an envelope. 'Give her two of these in about an hour's time, then another two if she needs them at two-hour intervals.'

'What are they?'

'Just tablets to ease any pain she might experience.'

'She'll have pain?'

'It's a natural consequence of any operation. Now I suggest you don't ask any more questions, but get on your way.'

He stepped past me and slid the latch on the door. 'And please remember, you have never seen me and you have never been in this house. That would do me a service, just as I have done you a service.'

I held Amanda all the way to the car and gently lowered

her into the front passenger seat. She immediately slumped back, her eyes closed, like a rag doll. I was filled with a new panic.

'It's all over, darling, nothing more to worry about,' I said, Judas-like. 'You just take it easy and I'll get you home as soon as I can.'

'Home' was as false as the note of comfort I tried to put into my voice. Neither of us had a home. We were both adrift in a nowhere city. I eased the car into gear and pulled away slowly. Disoriented by the emotions I was experiencing I made two wrong turns before finding my way on to the route that took us back to Los Angeles. In view of what the man had said I was trying to decide what was the best plan of action.

Amanda stirred. 'D'you have anything to drink? My mouth's so dry.' I stopped the car and reached back for the bottle of water, holding it to her lips. She took several sips then waved the bottle away. I took my handkerchief and soaked it in the cool water and bathed her forehead.

'You poor darling,' I said. 'You were so brave.' I took the gift box out of my pocket and put it in her hand. 'Something I got for you while I was waiting.'

She looked down at it, but made no attempt to open it. Her eyes closed again. The box lay in her lap.

'I don't know if you heard what he said, but it seems it would be better if I got you into bed. Not the same place we stayed at last night. I'll find somewhere better this time, someplace really nice. OK?'

She gave the slightest of nods.

'How d'you feel? D'you have any pain?'

Again she nodded.

I started the car and the gift box rolled off her lap. 'Let's think,' I said aloud. 'Maybe if we went into Phoenix we could find a decent hotel. Only trouble is, I'm running a bit short of cash.'

'My bag,' she said. 'I've got money in my bag. Use that.'

'I'll pay you back.'

She waved her hand weakly, dismissing my offer, then closed her eyes again.

I felt I was in the grip of a new nightmare as I drove towards Phoenix. Ever conscious of the time factor, I chose the first small hotel I came across that advertised vacancies. There was a brassy blonde behind the reception desk when we checked in. She gave Amanda a penetrating look.

'How long you staying?'

'Oh, just the night,' I said. 'We've been driving since early this morning and my wife's a little car sick. Can't blame her.'

'I'm the same. Fix a chain on the back. That's what my boyfriend did. Works wonders. Let it drag behind you, touching the ground. It earths the electric current or something. Does the trick for me.'

'A chain, eh? Really? Thanks, that's a good tip.'

'You can get breakfast from seven. Check-out's noon, else you pay another day.' She handed me the key. 'Down that corridor, last room on the left. Hope your wife feels better.'

'All she needs is a good night's rest.'

Once inside the room, I locked the door and sat Amanda in a chair while I arranged the supplies we had brought with us. Although I knew from nothing, I knew enough to imagine she would probably haemorrhage, so before I undressed her and helped her on to the queen-size bed, I carefully arranged our own towels for her to lie on. Then I gave her two of the pills as instructed, supporting her head while she swallowed them with some water. Her body was cold and I covered her with a blanket, closed the blinds and switched off the air conditioning. I lay beside her on the bed and held her hand. She gripped mine tightly, her nails pressed into my palm. I think I must have dozed off after

129

a while, exhausted by the worry of it all, because the next thing I knew I was alone in the bed and for a second or two I couldn't get my bearings, unable to think where I was.

'Amanda?' I shouted. I staggered to the door, but it was still locked, then I went into the bathroom. She was curled up on the tiled floor, her head pressed against the side of the tub, a mass of toilet tissue all around her, stained a bright red. There was more blood in the toilet bowl. I dropped to my knees beside her and cradled her head in my lap. I put a finger on her neck, feeling for a pulse like I'd seen in the movies. I thought I could detect something, very weak.

'Darling, can you hear me? What happened? Why didn't you call me? What happened? Tell me.'

Her eyes flickered open. 'No time,' she whispered. 'When it started, there was no time.'

'Oh Jesus,' I said. 'You should have shouted or something. I needed to be with you.'

Her eyes closed again. Somehow I managed to lift her up and carry her back to the bed. She was shivering violently and I doubled the blanket and put the cover over her as well. I massaged her wrists and stroked her wet hair back off her forehead, trying to remember what my mother had done to me whenever I had a fever, all the while wondering what was the correct thing to do. 'Have you still got pain?' I asked.

'Different,' she whispered.

'How about if I got you a hot drink? Would that help?'

She nodded.

I rushed outside to the desk, but the blonde was no longer there. Now there was a young guy on duty. He had his name pinned to a card on his lapel.

'Can you help me, Tom?' I said. 'We checked in earlier

and my wife's been taken sick. Is there any way I can get her a cup of tea? I'd really appreciate it.' I held out a five-dollar bill.

'What room you in?'

'Number 28.'

He consulted the register. 'Mr and Mrs Wilson?'

'That's right.'

'Oh, yeah. Jeannie said your wife wasn't feeling too good.'

I wanted to scream at him to get moving, but kept a smile on my face. 'If you could, that would be terrific.'

'Can't promise you it'll be any great shakes. I make a lousy cup of tea.'

'As long as it's hot.'

'Give me a few minutes and I'll bring it along.'

'You're a buddy, Tom. Thanks a million.'

I hurried back to the room, made sure Amanda was as I had left her, then cleaned up the bathroom as best I could, flushing the toilet half a dozen times to get rid of the soiled tissue. When Tom knocked on the door I only opened it halfway, blocking his view of the bedroom, and put a finger to my mouth. He handed me the mug of tea.

'You're a prince,' I said.

Going to the bed I gently nudged Amanda. 'Darling? Here, sip this, and take another of these pills.' I lifted her head up and she sagged against my shoulder. She didn't drink much, just enough to get the pill down before waving the mug away.

'What about the bathroom?' she asked weakly.

'All done, finished.'

She stared at me. 'How ghastly for you.'

'No. Ghastly for you.'

'I'm sorry. Sorry.'

'Nothing to be sorry about. I'm just so furious I wasn't there to help when you needed me. Are you warm enough?

131

Want another drink of tea?' She took a few more sips. 'Are you still bleeding?'

'I think so.'

I went to pull back the covers, but she stopped me. 'Don't look, I don't want you to look. I'll deal with it when I feel better.'

'Doesn't worry me.'

She slept for a while and, watching her, several times I saw her face crease as pain seized some part of her body. I had no idea what a human embryo looked like at two and a half months. As I kept vigil by the bed I found myself wondering what sex the child would have been and whether he or she would have looked like either of us. Studying Amanda's sleeping face was like trying to read through somebody else's glasses and I realised how little I knew about her. How little I knew about myself for that matter. Nothing had turned out the way I had once imagined. Pity and concern for Amanda was mixed with pity for myself. The unattractive truth was, I wanted a different hand from the one I had been dealt, or someone to show me how to play the cards I had. Maybe I, too, slept that long night; I can't remember now. The only thing I hung on to was that, mercifully, people don't remember pain. My mother told me that, talking about giving birth to me. She had a bad time of it apparently, some sixteen hours in labour and in the end I was a forceps delivery. 'I wanted to die,' she told me, 'anything just to have the pain go away, but the funny thing is that, when it was over, I had no memory of it. It was wiped clean, like chalk off a blackboard.'

I sat hunched in that hotel armchair, wishing that for Amanda. There was one big difference, of course. She had the pain, but there was no compensating end product, no baby. Jesus, women have a really lousy time of it any which way. I don't know why anybody calls them the weaker sex.

The next morning I showered without waking her and

went in search of some breakfast for us both. Walking in the sunlight made me feel better and I started to convince myself that the worst was over. I found a deli open and ordered some Danish and coffee to go, together with a carton of orange juice. When I got back I was relieved to see Amanda sitting up in bed.

She greeted me with, 'I thought you'd gone.'

'You nut,' I said, 'as if I'd ditch you. I crept about because I didn't want to wake you.'

'Where did you go?'

I bent and kissed her forehead. 'To get this.' I took a hotel glass out of the bathroom and poured her some orange juice. 'This was cold when I left the deli.' She drank it without comment, then ate the Danish. 'How is it this morning?'

'Like somebody kicked me in the stomach.'

'You want another pill? I've still got a couple left.'

She shook her head. Finishing my own Danish, I lit a cigarette. 'Don't,' she said. 'Makes me nauseous.'

'Sorry.' I stubbed it out.

She got out of bed and took a couple of unsteady steps. I went to support her, but she waved me away and closed the bathroom door. I pulled back the covers and saw that the towels she had lain on were stained with blood. She stayed in the shower a long time and before she came out I again cleaned up as best I could, folding the soiled towels and stuffing them into a hotel laundry bag.

She finally reappeared with a towel wrapped around her, gathered up her day clothes and went back into the bathroom to dress.

'D'you feel OK to travel?' I asked when she emerged again. The lipstick she had used accentuated the pallor of her face.

'What's the alternative? Another night in this place? I never want to see this room, or Phoenix, ever again. Let's go.'

133

It was a strange journey, going back. For the first hour or so we hardly exchanged a word and I had that feeling, like you do, that we'd left something behind. I couldn't think of the right opening with which to start a conversation and yet I knew that we needed to talk and the longer I left it the worse it was going to be. Two or three times I reached for a cigarette, then remembered and thought better of it. The monotonous desert road stretched into infinity and I had to fight to retain concentration. Finally, I said, 'What're you going to tell people?'

Amanda took her time before replying. 'Tell people? What people?'

'Well, Billy and Oliver, for instance.'

'What is there to tell them?'

'Nothing, I suppose.'

'Exactly. You didn't imagine I was going to walk into the hotel with a big grin on my face and say, "Guess what Robert and I did this weekend. We took a trip to Phoenix to get an abortion."'

'No, I didn't imagine that.'

'So why ask the question?'

'I don't know, darling. I guess I'm all mixed up.'

She didn't let me off the hook. 'What about?'

'You and me.'

'Well, we can't go back, we can't undo things. It doesn't work like that.'

I knew what she was saying, but I didn't want to believe it. We were like two fugitives running away from the truth. Because of what had happened she wasn't the same, I wasn't the same, and it was a question of who faced up to it first. I would have welcomed her blaming me; I wanted to take all the blame. I wanted Amanda to show anger, something I could use to reduce my guilt, but she didn't afford me that escape route. I couldn't frame the one question I was desperate to put to her, and, after that initial, non-conclusive

134

exchange, she remained silent and distant until we stopped at the halfway point to have a rest and top up the gas tank.

'You want a cola or a coffee or anything before we go on?' She was on her way to the rest room.

'I'd like a drink,' she said without looking at me. 'A brandy.'

Before going inside I took the laundry bag out of the trunk and dumped it in a trash bin. It wasn't the sort of place that got any call for brandy. All they had was a cheap bourbon. I told her this when she returned.

'That figures in a dump like this.' She raised her voice. 'OK, well get me a bourbon.'

Eyed all the way by the locals, I went back to the bar. When I put the glass in front of her, I said quietly, 'I know what you're going through, what you're feeling, but don't act like this.'

'How am I acting?'

'Like I'm an enemy. I never wanted this to happen.'

'That makes two of us.' She downed the drink. 'Can I have another, please?' with an emphasis on the 'please'.

'Maybe that's not a good idea, darling. Not with the tablets he gave you. We don't know what they are.'

'I'll be the judge of that,' she said.

Reluctantly, I bought her a second shot, which she drank immediately. I sensed we were on a collision course if I didn't play it carefully.

'Might be a good thing if you got the hotel doctor to pay a house call when we get in,' I suggested gently. 'Just to be on the safe side.'

'Proper little Florence Nightingale, aren't you? Stop fussing. It's my body and I'll do what I like with it.'

'OK, darling. I'm only trying to think what is best for you.'

The way she was reacting didn't really surprise me. What the hell did I know about what was going on inside her head? She was right: it was her body that had been violated in a way that no man could ever comprehend. My feelings were of little consequence.

I played it cool on the remainder of the journey back to the Beverly Hills Hotel.

'Do you want me to stay with you tonight?' I asked when we reached her suite.

'Up to you.'

'Well, if it's up to me, I want to be with you.'

'Fine.'

There was no energy in her response and she made no protest when I helped her undress and put her into bed. She fell asleep almost immediately. I sat by the bed for a long time, just looking at her and trying to sort out my own thoughts. Beyond loving her, I wanted to help her, but I didn't know how.

11

Some people keep dream diaries, believing they contain significant portents. I slept alongside Amanda that night, afraid to have any bodily contact, treating her as one would somebody injured, and so much for portents because my dreams were happy, divorced from the trauma we had just lived through. Waking early, I dressed as quietly as I could, left her a scribbled love note saying I would be back as soon as I had finished work, and drove back to West Knoll to pick up the notes I had done on the screenplay, pitifully few though they were.

While I was shaving Mike wandered into the bathroom and closed the door.

'So, how was it on a scale of ten?' he asked.

'God, you're a cold bastard.'

'Takes one to know one. I'm asking, how was it?'

'It's over,' I said.

'Any problems?'

'I don't know yet.'

'What's that mean?'

'I guess the major problem is solved, but who knows what happens now?'

'How has she taken it?'

'Don't ask me. How can I tell? It's too early.'

'But it worked, huh, and you're in the clear?'

'It worked, yes.'

'Well, thank you, Mike, for fixing it.'

137

'Yes, thanks.' My thoughts were splintered – yes, I was grateful to him, but at the same time I knew that, at some future date, I would push some of my guilt on to him. It's easier to forgive people you have wronged than those who know your own secrets. 'Can we leave it?' I said. 'I know it wouldn't have happened without your help, so don't think I don't appreciate it, but I guess I'm slightly screwed up at the moment.'

Clayburn was on the phone when I arrived, giving a hard time to his agent. 'Well, check it out,' he was saying. 'If the money's right I'll consider it. I'm not locked into this thing; all I agreed was I'd give it a whirl, and it was one way of getting here for free.'

'How was your weekend?' I asked when he'd hung up.

'If you're asking did I score, the answer is yes, and if you're also asking did I enjoy it, the answer is no. How about you?'

I had the feeling that recent events had been indelibly stamped on my features and that everybody could guess what had taken place. 'My weekend? Oh, nothing much, I was mostly working on the script.'

'Yeah, well I've had some further ideas. I've gone off France. Anything shot in France is automatically labelled "art house" and gets a lousy release. I need a commercial movie.'

Mentally I crossed my fingers. 'So, it's back to being set in England, is it?'

'No, I still think that sucks. My new thought is the story could work a treat in Chicago. Set in the Roaring Twenties,' he added, picking up his knife from the desk and stabbing a legal pad with it. 'Bring in Prohibition and G-men. D'you know Chicago?'

'No.'

'Me neither. I hear it swings. We should take a trip and check it out.'

I couldn't figure out who he was jerking off – Billy, himself, or me. But it was obvious that he powered his career along on indecision, keeping everybody in the dark as to his ultimate intent and quite happy to pull down a thousand dollars a week expenses while he played everybody at the guessing game. He never even asked to see what I had done with the French variation and it was only a few years later when I caught an old British film on late-night TV, *So Long at the Fair*, that I realised he had stolen the idea. His career was to peter out within the decade, probably because he played hard to get once too often. Nobody in the front offices minds the real difficult bastards, but they have to come up with a hit at regular intervals to stay in the game. Clayburn thought he had it all made for a time, but he failed to realise that outsiders have to be better than the natives if they are to keep their place in the firmament.

That morning I was grateful for him going off at tangents, and I only half concentrated on his wandering small talk; it allowed me to think about Amanda and how I would handle our situation. If he was happy to string things out, I could go along with that. I left him, with nothing resolved, checking with a travel agent about the flights to Chicago and the best hotels.

Amanda was still in bed when I rejoined her. 'How is it now, sweetheart?'

'I'm still bleeding on and off,' she said.

'Shouldn't you really see a doctor?'

'No.'

'What harm can it do?'

'He'd know what I'd done.'

'But is it safe to let it go on like this?'

'I'm tough,' she said. 'I'll get over it.'

I took her hand. It was cold. 'Do you still have pain?'

'Bits and pieces.'

'Bits and pieces, on and off . . .' I mocked, trying to raise a smile. 'Have you got any of those tablets left?'

'A few.'

'Don't they help?'

'Not for long.'

'Have you eaten?'

'I don't feel like eating. Look, I know you mean well, but I just want to be left to sleep it off. You go off and amuse yourself. If I feel like eating later all I have to do is ring down for something.'

'Have you seen Billy since we got back?'

She shook her head. 'I haven't seen anybody. I put a block on the phone.'

'Won't he find that odd?'

'If he does I'll tell him I'm recovering from a hangover. Now stop asking questions and let me get some sleep.'

'Well, promise you'll call me if you need me.'

'Promise.' She closed her eyes.

As I was driving back to the house in West Knoll certain decisions began to crystallise. Ever since Billy had given me money and a contract, I had thought it was time to look for a pad of my own. Although grateful to Mike and the girls for taking me in out of the cold, the arrangement had begun to pall. Communal life has more attractions for failures. Mike's life wasn't going well. He spent most of his time mooching around the house and was drinking more than usual, often slumping asleep on the couch while watching television. At night, I could hear him and Paula having prolonged rows. Now, with the abortion behind me, I felt the need to break the link.

The next morning on the way to another session with Clayburn, I stopped off at a realtor's to see whether they had anything immediately available on their books.

'Nothing too expensive,' I said. 'But something with a bit of character. And quiet. I'm a writer.'

She consulted her list. 'Well, it so happens something's just come on the market which might suit,' she said.

'Furnished?'

'You don't want furnished?'

'Yes, I do – I don't have any stuff of my own. How soon could I see it?'

'Let me ring the landlord. If you're a writer it might be just what you're looking for. It's supposed to have once been rented by Raymond Chandler, so it should have good vibes for you. Reasonable rent too.'

'What d'you call "reasonable"?'

'Three hundred a month, plus utilities.'

'Yes, OK, I can go to that. How big is it?'

'Two rooms, bath and kitchen.'

'Fine, well check it out, please.'

She made an appointment for me to see it later in the day.

By the time I got to Clayburn's hotel I had convinced myself that things were looking up. I would take care of Amanda and in time, with patience, the horror of the abortion would fade from memory. With any luck both our careers would prosper.

My mood of optimism quickly took a knock when I arrived and Clayburn greeted me with: 'Billy really pisses me off.'

'What's happened?'

'I ran my idea past him, about shifting it to Chicago and setting it in the twenties, and he raised all sorts of objections. Said it had to be shot in Europe. As far as I'm concerned that's a deal-breaker.'

I listened with foreboding as he ranted on and indulged in another bout of petulant knife throwing.

'So where does that leave us?' I asked when he drew

breath. I used the collective, but I was really thinking: 'What happens to me?'

'I have to rethink my position.'

'You want to bounce some more ideas around?'

'No. What I want is for people to realise what they're getting when they get me. They buy me, they buy my conception, period. I don't compromise. Take the day off and I'll let you know what I decide.'

I called Amanda from the lobby but her phone still had a block on it. Then I took in a movie until it was time for my appointment with the realtor. She drove me to a furnished apartment in the Hollywood Hills, one of a dozen in an old building, old for Los Angeles that is, with a lot of character. Whether the landlord was conning or not about Chandler, one look and I decided to take it. Returning to the woman's office, I signed the lease there and then, putting down the first month's rent in advance and with what little cash I had left I bought a bottle of Scotch on the way home as a way of softening the blow when I broke the news to Mike and the girls. We all got a little sloshed. Marsha passed out early, as usual, and Linda became very tearful and emotional. 'We could have made it,' she said, 'but you didn't give it a chance.'

Amanda showed no great enthusiasm when I told her the next day but I put that down to the fact that she was still groggy.

'When you feel up to it I'll entertain you in my own pad,' I said. 'Of course it doesn't have his and her bathrooms and I'm the room service waiter.' But if I thought that would raise a smile I was mistaken. Next I told her about the Chandler association.

'Is he somebody important?'

'One of the immortals.'

'Never heard of him.'

'I'll buy you some of his books.'

'What sort does he write?'

'Thrillers, but very special thrillers. Classics. He is the best of them all.'

'I don't like thrillers,' she said, and that was the end of that conversation. I tried various other gambits but couldn't draw her out of her mood.

'Have you seen Billy yet?'

'Yes, he came by last night.'

'What did you tell?'

'Nothing. Tell Billy anything and you might as well put a full-page ad in *Variety*. Anyway, all he wanted to do was beef about your director. Billy thinks he's discussing another picture.'

'Billy's right, and I'm terrified that if Clayburn walks, my deal's kaput. I need that money if I'm going to take care of you.'

'I can take care of myself.'

'But I want to spoil you. I haven't had a chance so far.'

She gave me her Gioconda look, and when I left her I had no idea whether our relationship was back to normal or whether I was faced with a burned-out case. And I still had to reckon with Clayburn.

'You know I've been thinking,' he began the next morning. 'Is a run-of-the-mill murder story the right move for me at this juncture in my career?' He affected that casual tone he used when about to change direction again. 'Do I really want to give nine months of my life to a mundane thriller? What d'you think, Robert?'

'I wouldn't say Westbrook is run-of-the-mill or mundane. I'm not an expert, but he seems to me to be superior to the average.'

He ignored this. 'Put yourself in my shoes. If you were me, with my track record, would you want to wear yourself out trying to upgrade this material?'

'You seemed to like it originally.'

'I liked it, yes, but that's not the same thing as being obsessed. One needs to be passionate about a subject, otherwise it's paid masturbation. I suppose, between us, we've breathed some life into it.'

What life? I thought. We haven't come up with anything yet. All I've done is listen to your crazy ideas.

'I was lying in bed last night with a cute little blonde and found I couldn't perform because this thing was nagging at me. That's always a pointer with me. Do you find that?'

'Can't say I do.'

'Plus, I don't find this town sparks me. The lack of sophistication's so enervating.' He cleaned a thumbnail with the tip of his Bowie knife.

'So, what would you like me to do?' I asked. 'Come up with something completely different?'

'I don't think so. The trouble is, Robert, one has only one life. It's easier for you, you've got nothing to live up to, but I've a reputation to protect.'

'Does Billy know you've had second thoughts?'

'Not yet.'

'How d'you think he'll take it?'

'He's been there before. These things happen. I only agreed to come and explore. It was a very loose arrangement and it hasn't cost him much, just the air fare, a hotel bill and a few weeks' per diems, which I'm sure he'll get back from the studio. That's pocket money to them; I can't lose any sleep about that. In any case I've probably saved them from making a major turkey.' He stopped pacing around the room and smiled. 'You look shocked. Don't worry, I won't land you in the shit-house. I shall take all the blame; my shoulders are broad. Fuck them, chum, fuck them all, they'll fuck us every time if it suits them. You think they'll send a wreath to our funerals? No way.'

'I thought we were getting somewhere at last.'

'We were, we were, in a wanky sort of way, and it's all

experience, mate. I'm sure Billy will shunt it off to some other director and you'll get another eight weeks' money. I've probably done you a favour. You'll come out smelling like a rose and I shall be the villain of the piece. Not that that worries me. Big mistake to be Mr Nice Guy all the time. One must never be in bondage.'

'What will you do? Go home?'

He hesitated. 'Not immediately. Have you ever read any Moravia?'

'Moravia?'

'Italian writer, very hot at the moment.'

'No, can't say I have.'

'You should. By coincidence I met a producer up in Carmel last weekend who's bought the rights to Moravia's latest novel. Gave it to me to read and I must say it's very much my cup of tea. Have you seen any of the recent Italian films?'

'A couple.'

'*Bitter Rice*, did you catch that?'

'Yes.'

'Gave me a hard-on for a week. Those tits! Are you a tit man?' He didn't wait for my reply. 'I'm crazy for tits.'

'I thought you said European films went straight on to the art house circuit.'

'Some of them . . . depends. But my roots, my whole culture's in Europe, I've got to stick by that, not get side-tracked.'

'So is that what you've decided to do?'

'Well . . .' He resumed his pacing. 'Nothing's written in stone, but let's just say that I'm tempted.'

'And, after all,' I said, 'if it doesn't work out it's just another air fare and a hotel bill. With a few tits thrown in this time.'

He grinned. 'How quickly you've got to know me, Robert. Look, don't feel too badly. I've enjoyed the time

145

we've worked together. I like to think I may have taught you a few new tricks. I might send for you to collaborate on the script in Rome, if it comes to pass, who knows?'

'When will you tell Billy?'

'I'm having lunch with him today. I like Billy. I'm very fond of her, actually, but she can be as devious as the next one when she wants to be,'

'She?'

'Don't quote me. Just being wicked. I don't know what Billy does between the sheets and, frankly, I don't care. He's probably neuter, if you ask me, but a bit of an old woman when crossed, so I shall have to be at my brilliant best at lunch.'

I've no idea how he squared it with Billy, because when I rang him the next day to say my goodbyes he had already checked out and doubtless was on his way to the Eternal City to make acquaintance with all those Roman tits. I knew Billy was inwardly seething, but all he said was: 'Jonathan's main problem is he suffers under the delusion that he's indispensable,' striking a match to light his cigar and then finding it was already lit.

Just then Oliver came into the room and picked up on Billy's last remark.

'No,' Oliver chimed in, 'Jonathan's only problem is he's a working-class prick with ideas *au-dessus de sa gare*, if I may quote Mr Rattigan.' Oliver slumped down on to the sofa. 'He's quit, right?'

'Yes.'

'Predictable. What was his excuse this time?'

'He felt it wasn't him,' Billy answered in an edgy voice.

'Well, you're well rid of him. He'd have fucked it up anyway with his fancy camera angles.' He finally conde-scended to notice that I was also in the room. 'Poor Robert, fancy exposing him to that.'

'I was never going to go along with his stupid ideas,'

Billy said, anxious to defend his corner, 'but as you know, I never interfere until I have to.'

'Until it's too late, you mean. I told you he'd act true to form, but you never listen to me.'

'Oliver's in a bad mood,' Billy said. 'He did a test over at Fox, but they thought he was too English. Funny really, because his family's Hungarian Jewish.' He switched back to me abruptly. 'Don't worry, I shall find you something else. In fact, I know what, you can do a screenplay of your novel. It's a much better story, anyway, what're you doing tonight, Roland?' all in the same breath, reverting to getting my name wrong. Sometimes I was Roland, sometimes Rupert or Robin, depending on how many pills he'd taken, and I had given up correcting him. I sensed that behind his mask of casualness he was thrown by Clayburn's defection.

'Tonight? Nothing.'

'Well, I shall take you and Amanda to dinner. Do you want to come, Oliver?'

'No, I'm going to the theatre to see what a cock-up the locals make of *The Tempest*.' He poured himself a drink and sauntered out of the room.

'Shall we have a drink?' Billy asked. 'Or would you rather have tea?'

'I'd rather have a drink.' I gave it a second, then I said: 'Amanda hasn't been feeling too well lately.'

Billy bypassed this. 'Are you sleeping with her?' he asked as he lifted the whisky decanter.

Taken off guard, I answered with a mumbled, 'Yes.'

'When I asked her, she denied it.' He handed me an over-large Scotch. 'But I have a second sight about these things.'

'Do you approve?'

'None of my business,' he replied, but there was something behind his voiced indifference. 'She'll always get where she wants to go. I knew that the first time I spotted her.'

147

'Are you ever wrong?'

'The thing about a screen career, Rupert, is that it doesn't depend on whether you can act or not. Being able to act helps, of course, but good stage actors very often fail on film. What matters is whether the camera loves you.'

'And you think the camera will love Amanda?'

'Yes, she's got the bone structure and marvellous eyes. It has to be in the eyes. If the eyes are dead, the face is dead.'

'Well, I'm glad for her.'

'Have her by all means, but just don't fall for her.'

'What if I already have?'

It was the first time I had ever admitted it to another person, and I knew I was taking a risk with Billy, but in a way it was a relief to share my fears.

'Oh well, I'm the last person you should ask. I don't know anything about love.'

'It's never happened to you?'

'No,' he said abruptly.

'For want of opportunity, or what?'

He gave me a sly smile. 'It takes too much effort and I prefer my own company in bed. Let's eat at the Wilshire this evening for a change,' he continued, stubbing out his half-smoked cigar. 'It'll give me an opportunity to find out what unpaid bills Jonathan has left me to settle.'

'You must resent the way he messed you around.'

'Oh, I'm used to it. I never expect loyalty.'

'At least you know I won't run out on you.'

'Given time,' Billy said, with a smile that, as ever, drew attention to his harelip. 'Given time.'

I had never eaten in the Wilshire's main dining room – a hushed, swanky room with a period atmosphere, subdued lighting and napkins so starched you could cut yourself as you opened them. It was a jacket-and-tie job, unlike the hotel's Pink Turtle coffee shop which always had a welcoming, boisterous atmosphere frequented by diners in a hurry, much more my style. I was handed a huge leather-bound menu like a First Edition of the Ten Commandments and written in French which I always find daunting.

It turned out to be a strange evening. Billy was in restless mode, stabbing at his food, and talking non-stop. Amanda was quiet and seldom spoke. I ordered something I had never eaten before and thought I would like but didn't and the wine that Billy ordered (which, I noted, set him back a monstrous seventy bucks) went straight to my head. Half-way through the meal a man with a vaguely familiar face approached our table. He greeted Billy effusively, then as he straightened up and took in Amanda and me I remembered where I had seen him before: he was the agent who had displayed his all in the locker room at the Beverly Hills pool the time I was there with Woody.

'Join us,' Billy said. 'You've met Amanda. Do you know Robert?'

'Hi, Amanda, you're looking great. But, then, don't you ever? Well, Robert and I did meet once, but we never got introduced. I'm Julian Sugarman.'

There was a discernible squeeze to his handshake before he sat down.

'Julian's a very pushy agent,' Billy said. 'So watch him, he'll try to sign you.'

'Oh, I'm sure you've got them both firmly under your wing, Billy.'

'Only Amanda. Robert's with Arnold Kosner.'

'If you'll pardon the expression,' Julian said, pursing his lips, 'I'm amazed Arnold's in town long enough to sign anybody! I thought he was permanently on holiday with Madame Defarge. Now, stop it, Julian, you mustn't be bitchy. So tell me all, how's your project going? Clayburn behaving himself?'

'No,' Billy answered. 'Drove Robert insane with his changes to the script, then decided it wasn't for him.'

'Oh, he's such a bore. Did exactly the same to Pandro last year. Have you got another director? You should use my new find, Lance Coogan, he's brilliant.'

'I shall probably put it in turnaround,' Billy snapped, biting off the end of a cigar, 'and let Robert script his own novel instead.'

'You've written a novel, have you, Robert? I must read it and give you some casting ideas.'

'Didn't I tell you he was pushy?' Billy said.

'Send me a copy, Robert. I'll read it overnight.'

'Buy it,' Billy said. 'Better still, buy several.'

'All right, I will. Give me the title.' He took out a small notebook and gold Cross pen.

'*A Fine and Private Place.*'

'Sounds intriguing.'

'Do you want to eat with us?' Billy asked.

'I'd love to, but I can't. I've got a little *crise* to sort out with Farley. I sometimes think I missed my vocation; I should have been a maternity nurse the way I'm made to look after my clients. I have to breastfeed most of them. So nice to meet you again, Robert. I shall be in touch the moment I've read your book. Where do I get you?'

'You can always reach me through Arnold.'

'Oh, I don't want to give him the wrong idea that I'm poaching. Though I am, of course,' he added with an arch smile. 'Can't I have your private number?'

There was no escape. He wrote it down and then handed me one of his cards. 'That's my direct line.'

He wandered away and before he was out of earshot Billy said: 'You don't want to go with him. He's dangerous.'

'In what way "dangerous"?' Amanda said, speaking for the first time in ages. 'Seems harmless enough, just another swishy queen making eyes at Robert.'

'Don't be clever.' There was an unaccustomed bite to Billy's voice. 'It isn't clever to say that sort of thing. He has a lot of influence in this town. If word got back to him that you'd said that he could do you a lot of harm.'

'Pardon me for living in the real world.'

The exchange produced a distinctly chilly atmosphere for the rest of the meal. When Billy received the check he signed it without looking at it. 'Look, I have to see somebody. You two can amuse yourselves, can't you?' He got up, dropping an inch of cigar ash on to the table. 'Ring me in the morning, Roland, and we'll discuss the other thing.' He left without another word.

Amanda and I looked at each other.

'What got into Billy?' I said.

'Who cares? He was in a bad mood when he drove me here.'

'You were right about that queen. The first time I met him he was stark naked and waved his prick at me. Give me a break!'

'Where was that?'

'In the locker room at the Bev Hills pool.'

'If he's that influential perhaps you should have given him some encouragement.'

'Thanks a lot. Well, what should we do? I could use some more coffee. But not here, this place is too stuffy. Let's go to the Pink Turtle.'

'OK.'

We had to pass Julian's table on the way out. He was deep in conversation with a young actor I recognised, but glanced up and waved at me. I gave him a thin smile and walked on.

The Pink Turtle was fairly crowded, but we managed to get an empty booth after a short wait. 'Actually, I'm still hungry,' I said. 'I hated what I ordered.'

'So I noticed.'

'What I really fancy is a large piece of cheesecake. Want to join me?'

'No thanks, but I'll have a mint tea.'

At that moment a voice from the past said, 'Dahlink!'

I turned and there was Leyla wearing a pink apron and a bow in her blonde hair, which made her look like an overblown Judy Garland in Oz.

'Leyla!' I exclaimed. 'How long have you been here?'

'I started last week, dahlink. This is the Ritz compared to that other place.'

'How's Stanislav? Are you married yet?'

'Not in the eyes of God, dahlink. But one day, please Mary and Jesus.' She was staring at Amanda.

'Excuse me. Amanda, this is Leyla, an old friend.'

Leyla rolled her eyes. 'Such a beautiful girl, dahlink. You've done well for yourself.'

'Haven't I?'

She bent closer to Amanda and whispered: 'This is a good boy. No funny business with this boy. Trust me.' Then it was back to me. 'You want to order?'

'Yes. A mint tea and a coffee and a piece of cheesecake.'

'Strawberry or blueberry?'

'Blueberry.'

'Right away, dahlink. I'm so happy to see you.'

'Me too.'

She flounced away.

'We were at Jiff's together,' I explained to Amanda. 'Remember I told you we all walked out *en masse*? Stanislav was the chef, a Polack, who fell for her. She has a kid from a previous marriage.' The memory of Phoenix was still raw enough to make me immediately regret mentioning Leyla's child and I covered up quickly. 'How about that accent and figure? Pity Jonathan never met her.'

'Why Jonathan?'

'He's a tit man. That was one of the last pieces of personal information he gave me.'

Leyla returned with our order. 'Here, dahlink. A special

big portion. Are you eating enough? You look thin. Always feed your man, keep his strength up for the bedroom, sweetie.' This was directed at Amanda with a knowing smile and again I felt uneasy. 'She means well,' I said, as she left us, to clear an adjacent table littered with half-eaten food.

Amanda said, 'She reminds me of a crazy aunt I had back home. A family scandal that everybody pretended was nothing to do with us. She dressed like a teenager until she was past sixty and went through three husbands. If you ever see me done up like that, shoot me.'

'You mean when you're sixty?'

'I'll never make sixty.' She stared past me for a moment as though somebody had just stepped on her grave, then she said: 'Are you writing anything for yourself as opposed to Billy?'

'I started a new novel, but it went nowhere. I can't find any juice right now.'

'Use our story if you're lost for an idea. You once promised to put me in a novel.'

'Maybe when we're both sixty,' I said. I forked a piece of cheesecake and offered it to her, but she shook her head.

'I have a test next week for Jean Negulesco, the same film Oliver tested for.'

'And didn't get.'

'Good. He needs a few rejections. Negulesco had me read for him before we went to Phoenix. He says if I get it they'll sign me to a term contract. You did some acting once, didn't you?'

'Not really. A few walk-ons. I was terrible.'

'Shall I fresh your coffee, dahlink?' Leyla interrupted.

'No, thanks, Leyla. What days are you on?'

'I do Monday, Tuesday, Wednesday and weekends.'

'I'll come in again now I know you're here.'

She tore my check off her pink pad. 'The cheesecake's on me, dahlink, for old times' sake.'

'You shouldn't.' I left her a generous tip.

'Poor Leyla,' I said as I waited for my car to be brought round. 'She's a born loser, I'm afraid. She hasn't got much going for her, but what she has she flaunts.'

We arrived at Amanda's hotel the same time as Oliver drove up. 'How did you enjoy the play?' I asked. 'Did the natives do the Bard proud?'

'Hardly.'

I waited for him to say something pleasant to Amanda, but he ignored her.

'I'm going to call it a night,' she said to me. 'Thanks for the coffee, dahlink.'

'Good luck with the test. Call me when you're through, I'll be dying to know how it went.' I kissed her. She walked into the lobby.

'Is that all you gave her – coffee?' Oliver said as we took our parking tickets from the valet. 'You got off cheap. I thought you were both having dinner with Billy.'

'We did, but he left us for another date after the meal. We went to the Pink Turtle.'

'Such a dreary little watering hole, I always think. Full of failures. D'you fancy a nightcap? I've had a fucker of an evening.'

It was the first time he had ever been sociable towards me. 'Yes, OK.'

We went to the Polo Lounge bar, which was near deserted, and slid into one of the semi-circular booths. 'What'll you have?' he asked.

'Scotch, straight up.'

Oliver ordered a brandy, stipulating a brand they didn't have, and with a grimace of annoyance switched to vodka with a twist.

'So, the play was a turkey?'

'Not the play, it was what the cast did to it. An act of total masochism on my part, although I stuck it out to the end. *The Tempest* should be like a swan-song soufflé; this was like over-cooked pasta.'

'Have you done a lot of Shakespeare yourself?'

'Fair amount. It's the only way to get noticed in England. You can act your balls off in modern plays, but unless you go to Stratford and ponce about in wrinkled tights to a lot of worshipping tourists, you're not considered serious. Cheers. Have you heard the story when the Master went to see a performance of *Coriolanus*?'

'The Master?'

'Noel Coward.'

'No, I haven't heard it.'

'Well, he was at the Old Vic, that's a theatre in London originally made famous in the twenties by a monstrous harridan called Lilian Baylis. They all cut their teeth there – Gielgud, Olivier, Edith Evans. Anyway, on the particular night Coward sat in the front row, which at the Vic means you're almost sitting in the footlights, and afterwards somebody asked what he thought about it.' Here Oliver zapped into an impersonation of Coward's clipped delivery: 'There was a juvenile, ablaze with acne, insufficiently bowled and with hammer toes prac-ti-cally up my nostrils.'

Oliver laughed before I could show appreciation of the in-joke. 'Forgive my ignorance, what does "bowled" signify?'

'A form of make-up, a solution of permanganate of potash which stains your body.'

'Ah, I see. You know Coward, do you?'

'I've met the Master, yes.' He switched topics abruptly, perhaps peeved that his anecdote hadn't gone down as he expected. 'Who did Billy leave you for?'

'No idea.'

'I'm sure he's planning revenge. Jonathan's exit really pissed him off. He wouldn't let on to you, but I got the brunt of it.'

'It was shitty thing to do.'

'Shit is Jonathan's middle name. Tough on you pulling the short straw your first time out.'

Although I suspected he was only passing the time with me for want of anything better to do, Oliver intrigued me and I longed to find out what made him tick. He had such confidence, such an urbane disregard for the usual niceties, which only the conceited or the very rich possess. Even so, I was unprepared for his next question that he shot at me as he languidly sipped his vodka.

'How're you making out with Amanda?'

'Making out?'

'I assume you're trying to get into her knickers, if you haven't already. Forgive me for asking, but I've been observing her progress from English wallflower to a would-be *femme fatale*.'

'We seem to have hit it off, yes. I like her.'

'I'm amazed Billy lets her off the leash. He usually plays Svengali to the hilt. He's a jealous old thing, really, one has to watch he doesn't take over one's life. He tried it with me, but I wasn't having any. I'm grateful for his sponsorship, of course, but he has a mean side to him, as you'll find out in due course. It won't have done Jonathan any good to have flown the coop. Billy will make sure that word gets around and Billy has many ears he can bend. He doesn't forget slights in a hurry.'

He leaned forward to extinguish a cigarette and the small light on our table briefly illuminated his even, bisque tan. I noticed that his nails were beautifully manicured and that he was wearing cufflinks with small diamonds in them.

'No, don't mess with our Billy. I dare say you've guessed his setup?'

'Setup?'

'With Amanda.'

'No.'

156

'Their relationship.'

The way he said this made my heart pump. 'She's told me he's masterminding her career.'

'Oh, that, yes. I meant what he gets up to with her. He always tries to give the impression that he's emotionless. Fools most people, but not yours truly. He's got this hang-up that he's physically unattractive to women – the harelip thing – he never kisses anybody, have you noticed? He's had plastic surgery, but it didn't work, just tidied it up. But he titillates himself with those pathetic erotic paperbacks he reads, and afterwards he likes to be serviced.'

'Serviced?'

'Yes. Have girls go down on him. He never touches them, it's all one-way traffic. You get nothing for nothing in this business. Amanda's here on the premises, she depends on him for her livelihood, and it saves him the trouble of going out searching for it.'

I swallowed the remains of my Scotch to conceal my panic. 'Really?' I said, as calmly as I could.

'You didn't suspect?' He paused with the vodka glass halfway to his lips. 'Oh God! I shouldn't have mentioned it. Forget I ever said it.'

'How do you know all these things?'

'I've been around Billy a long time, and when he's taken too many of his happy pills, he lets his hair down.'

It was dawning on me that, far from an uncharacteristic urge to be sociable, Oliver had deliberately chosen this moment to shatter my illusions. I remembered Amanda's quick denial that evening at Romanoff's when I asked if Oliver was her boyfriend. I could believe that he'd tried to come on to her and been rejected. My thoughts went all the way back to the first time I had seen any of them at Jiff's, mistakenly counting Amanda as the beard for two queens. I had been wrong on all counts, the hick colonial who hadn't been able to penetrate their British code.

157

'Same again?' Oliver held up a hand to attract the bar-tender's attention.

'Not for me, thanks. I have to do some writing before I hit the sack.'

'Just another vodka.' The bartender took away the empty glasses. 'We should have dinner one night.'

'Let's do that,' I said, getting up. 'Thanks for the drink.' How conventionally we behave at moments when our world has collapsed. The last thing I remembered as I walked away was his arrogant, actor's face.

12

Billy wasn't a major player – on the Hollywood Richter scale of monsters he would probably have only registered a 4. Others before and after him made him look like a cuddly teddy bear. He was a rich maverick who had an eye for talent and taste for material, plus he knew everybody who mattered, entertained lavishly. He engineered his own ultimate downfall because he was either too lazy or too easily bored to push himself the extra mile. He had successes, primarily in Europe, but I never felt he was wholly at ease within the studio power system, and lacked the final, killer instinct of the genuine Hollywood sharks that separates the men from the boys. It's almost impossible to give a complete and rounded impression of anybody, and the memories I retain of him are scattered, like pieces in a jigsaw puzzle that one never completes. The film industry has always been over-populated with improbable characters who don't seem out of place in that corporate Vietnam, but who elude description to outsiders. Paint them with total accuracy and they emerge as stereotypes, attempt to explain them and their motives and they appear implausible. How can you explain the fat cats who are capable of nothing except the exploitation of what others create and yet command salaries beyond the dreams of avarice and wield power on a par with Genghis Khan?

No, Billy wasn't in that league and when drugs took him off, Hollywood forgot him before the ink was dry on his obituaries. A recluse to those not in his intimate circle, a foreign import to most, possessing few of the more overt local characteristics, when he first arrived his very foreignness probably worked for him, but over and above that the reasons many doors opened for him was the fact that he was seriously rich. A society driven by the almighty dollar respects wealth above all else. Ultimately, of course, he was like everybody else, as disposable as Tampax. Hollywood used him, Hollywood discarded him and Hollywood forgot him. There has always been a supply of Billy Fishers, drawn to the film industry as trout are drawn to the fly.

I couldn't complain. For a period while I was under his wing, some of his mystique rubbed off on me. Since the studios couldn't pigeonhole him into any familiar category those, like Amanda and me, whom he had decided to nurture, started with an advantage: offend us and they offended Billy, and while they wanted what Billy could supply, Billy was not to be offended.

After the debacle with Clayburn he was as good as his word: he put the Westbrook novel into turnaround and swiftly set up a three-picture development deal at MGM, engineered through a friend called Bill Getz, who was married to one of Mayer's daughters – true Hollywood royalty. He included my novel in the deal, together with two other projects he owned.

Mayer had gone by then, bitter and unforgiving, and Dore Schary was running the studio. I had seen photos of Schary when he had gone to Washington to testify at the un-American hearings and he looked more like a college professor than a studio head, with a studied, academic air in contrast to the carpetbagger flamboyance of the Brothers Warner or Harry Cohn, but he had his moment and for a time put MGM on the map again with a string of intelligent movies, reversing the decline of Mayer's last years. Even after Mayer's departure, MGM still had a hundred writers, a hundred stars, forty producers and forty directors under contract, turning out thirty or so films a year.

'I'm amazed they accepted my novel in the deal,' I said to Billy when he broke the news. 'How did you sell me?'

Billy gave me his Cheshire cat look. 'You're such a naïve boy, Robin. So unworldly in matters like these. The front office are not buying you, they're buying me. You don't think Dore took your novel to bed with him, do you? He has to have a stream of product to feed the distributors. If two out of twelve on the roster get the green light, he's happy.'

He procured a contract for me, open-ended, which paid a thousand dollars a week, as part of his overall deal. I was suddenly living on Easy Street. When I expressed my amazement, he shrugged my gratitude aside. 'Just accept it, Roland. I enjoy playing them at their own game.'

Of course I accepted it. As it happened, Amanda was also in luck that week. Her test at Fox had gone well and she had landed the role.

'Darling,' I said, 'that's wonderful. I'm so thrilled for you. You deserved some good news. It is a decent part?'

'Yes. Not very big, but showy, only two scenes, and they're both with Peck.'

'I bet Billy was pleased,' I said.

'Yes and no. He was in one of his strange moods when I told him. He's such a funny old thing; he blows so hot and cold. Then a few hours later he came to my room and threw a packet on my bed. I opened it and it was this.' She shook her wrist revealing a gold bracelet set with three sapphires.

'God!' I said, truly impressed. I thought of the cheap Indian heart I had given her in Phoenix.

'It was his way of apologising for being disagreeable. Billy can't ever actually say he's sorry, he has to buy his friendships. Haven't you found that?' She twirled the bracelet. I caught hold of her wrist and drew her closer to me.

'How are you now?'

'Great.'

'I'm not Billy. I can say I'm sorry.'

'Oh, that,' she said. 'That's behind us now.'

She let me kiss her. It wasn't the same as before, but nor was it a rejection. I put the image that Oliver had planted to the back of my mind. I knew then that I would rather share her than lose her. The first kiss developed into a second, more prolonged, more passionate. I started to undress her and she made no protest. When she was naked I held her against me. 'You're wearing a different scent,' I said.

'No. The same old one. I never change it.'

I wanted to believe that everything was the same as before. We made love between her cool sheets that were changed every day, and in the lazy aftermath we planned a shared future. I was now under contract at MGM and she had a role in a major feature. It seemed too good to be true, but we didn't touch wood, we touched each other and life was blissful.

When Billy and I moved into MGM, he had his own suite of offices in the Thalberg Building, while I was tucked away in a room at the back of the writers' block. God, I can still see it so clearly – more a cell than a room, on the second floor with a single window that looked out on to the plasterers' shop. It came with a desk, chair, typewriter, paper, a decrepit couch, a supply of legal pads, a dozen pencils ready sharpened and the use of the secretaries' pool to type up the finished pages. However sparse, to me it was all unbelievable luxury. To actually have a pass to the MGM lot and to walk to work between the hallowed stages was something that had previously been beyond my imagination.

On my first day there I spent most of the morning doing

little else but contemplate my good fortune. At lunchtime I found my way to the commissary by following the crowd. It was larger than I had imagined, and teeming with people all making a tremendous buzz: actors and actresses heavily made-up and in costume, several of whom I recognised as familiar feature players. Unlike me, everybody seemed relaxed, at home with each other and their surroundings. Many of the items on the menu were attributed to the stars – *Katharine Hepburn Avocado Salad, the Clark Gable Burger, Mickey Rooney Clam Chowder* and so forth. Finally finding an empty table, I ordered the dish of the day, a *Judy Garland Ham on Rye* with a *Margaret O'Brien Strawberry Soda*, which seemed as exotic as you could get.

No sooner had I sat down than two young girls, with hard little faces like porcelain dolls and wearing abbreviated sailor costumes, asked if I minded if they shared.

'Be my guest,' I said with an attempt at worldly non-chalance.

They ignored me the moment they sat down and immediately embarked on a casting session post-mortem.

'What did he say to you then?'

'Well, the first thing he said was, "Why have they sent you in? You look like a Scarsdale princess kidnapped from Bloomingdale's." '

'What a prick! Did you walk out?'

'No.'

'I would have done.'

'I wanted the part, didn't I? So I read for him. I thought I read it pretty good, but all he said was, "You are the avatar of the average." '

'Avatar? What does that mean?'

'I've been trying to figure it out. I asked my agent, but he didn't know.'

'Incarnation,' I interrupted. In the ensuing pause they both stared me down.

'Sorry?' the main speaker said.

'That's what "avatar" means. Incarnation.'

'Oh. Thanks.'

'Well, it was only a lousy one-day part anyway, so screw him,' her companion said. She gave me a dirty look as though it was all my fault. Then they both ignored me again because, I guess, I had intruded on their private grief. I wished I had kept my mouth shut.

When I got back to my office I found the door open and a strange man in a crumpled linen suit lying on my couch smoking a cigarette. He had a ravaged face crowned with salt-and-pepper grey hair that looked as though it had been left out in the sun too long. In his sixties, I guessed, or maybe older, unshaven, and with a high-blood-pressure complexion, I thought at first he was an intruder who had somehow got past security at the gate.

'Hi,' he said, giving me a smile that revealed uneven, stained teeth. 'Heard there was a new boy on the block, so I just dropped in for a friendly chat. Jack Reeves.'

'Robert Peterson.'

'Glad to meet you, Robert. Welcome to the penitentiary.'

There was something too hail-fellow-well-met about him that made me instinctively wary.

He swung his legs off the couch. 'I live across the hall. Well, maybe "live" isn't the right word. Let's just say that I'm just serving out my sentence. Been here too long, Robert. I'm known as the Count of Monte Cristo, though I'm not about to make a break for it. Too cold outside. Seen 'em come, seem 'em go, but I'm still here. Had my moment and then blew it. Now I don't try for the title shot, I'm just content to do whatever they throw at me and keep those old paycheques landing on my desk every week. Like Faulkner kept saying, "They're gonna pay me Saturday." Three ex-wives, Robert, come expensive. You married?'

164

'No.'

'Keep it that way. Writers weren't meant for the domestic scene. Love them on the page, sport, but steer a straight course away from the nuptial bed. We're whores and we should stay with our own kind, don't you agree?' This time he laughed. 'Threw that at you from left field, didn't I? Don't take it to heart, it was meant kindly. So, what brings you to Xanadu?' There was a slurred twang to his voice and I wondered if he was drunk.

'I'm doing a script for Billy Fisher.'

'And who might he be?'

'He's a well-known British producer.'

'Are there such creatures? What's the subject?'

'I'm scripting my own novel.'

'Ah! A double-threat man.' He ground his cigarette out on the floor with his heel. 'God! I've worked for them all, the good, the bad and the downright ugly.'

'Are you engaged on something yourself?'

'In a manner of speaking. Engaged but not married as they say. I'm the resident script doctor, sport. Mr Fixit. King of the Additional Dialogue. Master of the from-here-to-a-fast-comedy-finish. I don't write screenplays any more. I only rewrite other people's screenplays.'

'That must be depressing for you.'

'Depressing?' He put his little finger in one ear and screwed it around as though about to extract some wax. 'No, I wouldn't say that. Just a way of earning a regular buck. This is a cutthroat world, sport. Dog fucks dog. Or put it another way, writers fuck other writers. That's not official Guild policy, of course. According to the Articles we respect each other's work.' He went to my desk and picked up a totally blank legal pad. 'You've made a good start, I see. I'll give you a useful tip. Don't turn in the pages too quickly. String it out, make the good times last. It spoils the market, shows the rest of us in a bad light. Hope you don't mind me mentioning that. I'll give you another tip. These are bad times, sport, the nights of the long knives and dropped options, careers that mysteriously disappear.' He tapped the side of his nose. 'You can be as pink as a baboon's ass for all I care, just don't tell me, and I won't confess to being a lifelong member of the Comintern. It ain't the climate for heroes.'

By now I was convinced I was dealing with somebody who was two sandwiches short of a picnic.

'You're from back East, right?'

'Yes,' I said.

'Me too once upon a time. And like you I suspect, they seduced me out here on the strength of a novel. I could have been – should have been – another John O'Hara, but I kept my appointment in Samarra in this nowhere city and never wrote another book. Joined a distinguished band out here, all hoping to play the same tune. We thought we were coming to Valhalla. Instead, it turned out to be the dying days of the Garden of Allah where we all took to the bottle.' He replaced my legal pad and stared out of the window, suddenly breaking into song with a croaky voice. '*The way you wear your hat . . . the memory of all that*' . . . he stopped as abruptly as he had begun. 'As it happened, the sacrifice of my talent had no epic grandeur. Am I going too fast for you?'

'No.' I didn't know what the hell he was talking about. It was only later, when I got to know him better, that he filled in the blank spaces of his life. His crack about 'epic grandeur' was something he had coined from a saying of Scott Fitzgerald's describing his own broken career. The Garden of Allah Jack referred to was a legendary watering hole on Sunset which a famed collection had once claimed as their own – Dorothy Parker and Benchley among others in the fast lane – during the time when all the studios imported any writer from Europe or the East Coast who had a name. He had worked for everybody in his time – Thalberg, Mayer, Jack Warner, Cohn, Zanuck, starting like Faulkner as a 'junior writer' pulling down $200 a week if he was lucky, and he had stories to tell about all of them, though I suspected some of his anecdotes were apocryphal. He insisted that Harry Cohn had installed a working electric chair in the executive dining room – 'Presumably,' Jack added, 'on the assumption that meeting him in the flesh was not frightening enough for a new guest. Mayer, of course, cried at the drop of an option, and although he imported talent, he paid the price of caviar and then treated talent like stinking fish. I was often assigned to projects that already bore the imprint of three or four other minds. The Guild was in its infancy then, lacking muscle, and writers feasted on each other's work like cannibals.' He ended that first meeting with another homily. 'I always remember a piece of advice Raoul Walsh gave me. Know who I mean? A rough son-of-a-bitch, but a gentleman – you might come across him one day if you're lucky. Know what he told me? Writers only have one pair of hands, so if you get into a fight, don't use your mitts, use a club. On that, I'll leave you in peace. When the going gets too hard, as it will, step across the hall. I make a good cup of coffee.'

He left. Somewhat dazed by the encounter, I sat at my desk and fed a sheet of paper into the machine. I typed the date, the title and FADE IN and stared at the blank page. There I was at MGM, the holy of holies, in my own office, earning a thousand a week and now I had to come up with the goods. I had never felt more alone.

13

The apartments at my new address were grouped around a central, hacienda-style courtyard, which boasted a small pool with cracked Mexican tiles and a faded notice that stated there was no lifeguard on duty. It was fairly obvious that a lifeguard had never been on duty. Most of my fellow tenants were retired senior citizens, wizened, with sunburned features, wearing yesterday's fashions, eking out their life savings. California beckoned the old as well as the young. They usually gathered around the pool when the sun dipped behind the buildings and the courtyard cooled, to share a cocktail or two and talk about their various ailments and the cost of living. There was one old guy in particular, distinguished-looking with a trim goatee and a black eyepatch, who would have been typecast as a French count in the movies. He brought his own director chair and a silver cocktail shaker. I made some discreet enquiries about him and in fact I wasn't too far out: he was a White Russian and had been an actor, once playing the romantic lead opposite Bessie Love, but his career had not survived the advent of the talkies. Now he made a modest living giving English lessons to immigrants. He proved to be the only one of the group with whom I had anything in common and I enjoyed quizzing him about the personalities he had known in the early days of Hollywood, while drinking some of his imported vodka. He had worked for Sennett and told me that Sennett often greeted people while in his bath with a frequently-used spittoon by the side of the tub, and how they would knock off a two-reeler in as many days. He had known Fatty Arbuckle ('sacrificed on the altar of a false morality'), John Gilbert, Mary Pickford and Fairbanks. I pressed him every time we met and he related anecdotes from a past that, to me, was remote but which, to him, was as yesterday. Still retaining a strong accent, he sipped his drink from a silver goblet – his long manicured fingers holding it reverently like a chalice – until his speech grew slurred. 'I had many loves,' he said once. 'So many loves. We worked hard, we played hard, we made love, it was the golden age. You see this?' He extended a hand, displaying a diamond ring. 'I can't get it off my finger now, otherwise I would show you the inscription. Pola Negri gave it to me. I tell you these things because you appreciate what I was. These people here' – he gestured across the sad pool towards a group of the other residents – 'what do they care or know of our profession?' He carried his pride like Cyrano's white plume. Then, abruptly, he would end our session, stand and bow to me, fold his director's chair, and without another word depart unsteadily. I was never invited into his apartment, which was the object of continual speculation among the other tenants, who believed that it was stocked with paintings and treasures he had managed to smuggle out from Imperial Russia.

Then, one day he failed to appear at the happy hour. The following morning the police came to tell us he had been killed jaywalking outside Grauman's Chinese Theatre. Nobody claimed his few possessions – there were no hidden treasures, nothing of any real value, just one icon and the clothes and trinkets of an old man who died a long way from home. The landlord had everything taken away by the Salvation Army, though I claimed a scrapbook in which he had pasted mementoes of his career in the silents, together with a faded, pressed rose alongside an inscribed photograph of a nude girl.

I thought of the poolside scene as God's outside waiting room, and during the time I was there three other residents died. The rest closed ranks, huddling closer together when they met at sundown, as rabbits do in the middle of a cornfield as the reaper encircles them.

Now that Billy had fixed my union card, I was anxious to take advantage of my elevated status, and attended several meetings at the Writers' Guild, fondly imagining I would pick up some useful pointers from established members. Wrong. As Jack had warned, writers *en masse* were a suspicious, disgruntled lot, self-centred and over-anxious to air their personal beefs. The main topic of conversation and debate was the House un-American Activities Committee, then sitting in daily session and carried live on TV. Because of the witch-hunt, many writers were, understandably, running scared since quite a number of them had flirted with left-wing causes in the past, even if they were not actual card carriers. They divided neatly into two camps: those who vehemently denounced anybody known to be or suspected of being a stool pigeon and giving names, and those who felt that the few were bringing down the many and deserved their fate. As a newcomer, my ear was bent by both factions. The fellow-travellers wanted my signature on their petitions and the reactionaries warned me to stay clear for my own good. I was not enamoured of either camp and, with the threat of the draft still hanging over me, I remained chary of signing anything in case, by so doing, I brought myself to the notice of the authorities. I found the quasi-Reds too earnest and dogmatic and the reactionaries inflated with a dubious kind of patriotism.

Despite what has been written since about that shameful period, my impression was that many of those not on the black lists acted out of self-interest, outwardly professing solidarity but, behind the scenes, furthering their own careers, cashing in on the unemployable. The fellow-

170

travellers' special venom was directed at characters like Kazan and Larry Parks, two who had succumbed to the hideous pressure and given names. Kazan eventually rehabilitated himself but, despite his reasoned and affecting defence, Parks's career was finished overnight, poor bastard – he was deemed expendable mainly because no big money was riding on him and the studios were willing to offer up a few sacrifices as evidence of their willingness to co-operate in the cleansing of America. McCarthy, with his permanent five-o'clock-shadowed jawline and demagogue delivery, looked and acted out his part like some third lead in a B picture gangster movie, which is what he was, another instance of the fifth-rate that American politics throws up at regular intervals. The amazing thing is that, until Ed Murrow had the courage to burst his bubble, he lasted so long. The telecast proceedings had a Kafkaesque quality about them and one could only watch with mounting revulsion. My country is never surer of itself than when it allows the rest of the world to witness its shortcomings.

Looking back, I remember those early months at MGM as one of the happiest periods of my life. The despair I had felt working for Clayburn was forgotten, for there is nothing like a little success to change one's whole outlook on the world. I was happy that my relationship with Amanda was back to normal, and she was happy too, now that her career had finally taken off. She often spent the night in my new apartment and seemed to enjoy the change of scenery. 'Hotel rooms close in on you after you've been there for months,' she said.

One night we lay in bed watching an eerie firework display that pierced the skies during a violent electrical storm while thunder rumbled beyond the Hollywood hills. She clung to me, scared, because it brought back childhood memories of air raids during war. 'Sometimes,' she said, 'the searchlights would get lucky and actually lock-in on a plane and we kids used to cheer. You couldn't hear the noise of the planes because of the gunfire. They looked like tiny, harmless fish passing slowly overhead. Not that we ever saw any of them hit with the ack-ack. I think it was mainly a cosmetic barrage.'

'Didn't you take cover?'

'Oh, by then I'd been evacuated from London to Devon with the rest of my school. The raid wasn't for us. The planes passed over us on their way to Plymouth. We didn't even hear the explosions when they dropped their bombs, it was too far away, just quick flashes of light bouncing off the clouds, like now, and afterwards, when Plymouth burned, the clouds turned blood-red.'

There were so many things I wanted to know about her. To be in love compels us to haunt the hidden corners of a loved one's life, to explore those years when he or she was inhabiting the same planet but unknown to us, and a sense of loss pervades us. Listening to her stories about the war years in England I tried to imagine what she must have looked like then: at what point did the chrysalis transform itself into the butterfly? I pressed her to show me photographs of herself when young, but she said she had none with her. 'In any case, I don't want to be reminded of those days.'

As it turned out, the happiness I felt with her was only on loan. The last time we made love was a Friday, I remember, not at my pad but in the luxury of her hotel suite. I had planned something special for the weekend, intending to surprise her and drive out to Palm Springs. I had no premonitions, nothing seemed different, if anything it was how it had been in the beginning and she cried when she came, which before had always been a sign that her pleasure had been complete. When, finally, we slowly came back from that country of astonishment we all visit during the act, and our bodies drew apart, I kissed her damp cheeks, before slipping out of the bed to pour two glasses of wine.

I touched her forehead with the cold glass and she opened her eyes and stared up at me. She had never looked more desirable.

'Want to guess what I've got planned for the weekend?' I said.

'What?' She took the glass of wine from me but did not drink.

'No, on second thoughts, I'm going to keep it a surprise.'

'No, don't. I hate surprises. Tell me.'

I sat on the edge of the bed beside her. 'I thought we'd go somewhere for a romantic weekend. Palm Springs. I've never been, have you?'

'I can't,' she said. 'I've already made other arrangements. Negulesco's giving a party for the cast so we all get to know each other before the film starts. In any case,' she continued slowly, 'I don't think we should see so much of each other. We're both got careers to think about now.'

'What difference does that make?' I slopped my wine on the sheet that partially covered her breasts. 'Why do you suddenly come out with that?'

'Not suddenly. I've been thinking about it for some time. I was waiting for the best time to tell you.'

'You think this is the best time? When we've just made love? I know the film's important to you and you have to concentrate on giving your best, and obviously you have to go to the party – I understand that – but you're talking about something different, aren't you?'

It was only now that she drank her wine as though to give herself Dutch courage for what she said next. 'Yes, I suppose I am.'

'You want to end it?'

'Not end it, just cool it before it's too late.'

'Too late for what?'

'Before it becomes an effort and ordinary and we end up hating each other.'

'What does that mean? A fuck is just a fuck, a sigh is just a sigh, but none of the fundamental things remain?'

'Don't spoil it by being cheap.'

I lost it at that point. I couldn't believe how quickly my world had been turned upside down. It was the more unreal for happening in the immediate aftermath of lovemaking. I knew what she was really trying to say however she dressed it up, and now all I wanted to do was hurt her in return. 'You think that's cheap? I'll tell you what's cheap. Going down on Billy.' I spat it at her. 'But I guess you figured there was no risk of getting pregnant that way.'

She looked at me without a change of expression, threw the rest of the wine in my face and went into the bathroom, locking the door after her.

Desperate, I shouted through the closed door, 'Darling, forget I said that. It doesn't matter, nothing matters except that you and me go on as before.' I rapped on the door. 'Come on, let me in, please. You can't end it like this, not after what we've been through together.'

She made no response. I heard the sound of the bath being run. I stayed there for a long time, pleading with her, debasing myself, but nothing I said brought any response. I thought about writing her a love letter – writers always believe they can persuade by the pen – but in the end I realised that all I would put down on paper would be self-pitying misery. I made one final attempt through the barred door, then walked out of her suite, walked the deserted corridors, past the discarded room-service trolleys denoting that normal life still existed for others.

14

For weeks after we parted my nights brought a personal vision of hell. I would dream I was walking into an unfamiliar bedroom, and there would be Amanda and Billy naked in the bed. She would be kissing him and when she became conscious of me she said: 'I don't care about his harelip.' Sometimes the dream contained Oliver as well, sitting in an armchair. He would look up as I entered and give a knowing grin. The dreams were so vivid that they would stay with me for the whole of the following day. I tried to sublimate myself in work, the writer's panacea for most torments, but my despair surrounded me like a fog-bank that was never going to be burned off by eleven. I felt that my life had no purpose any more. I sent Amanda several letters, desperate efforts to try to win her back, but they went unanswered. I couldn't bring myself to ask Billy to intervene and I was careful never to mention her whenever he and I met. He must have known that we had broken up, for I am sure Amanda had told him during one of their late-night sessions, but for once, given his obsession with sexual gossip, he never asked questions.

Though still hollowed out, I did, slowly, emerge from total despair and forced myself to fold up my old life like a blanket and move on. There were compensations, of course, on the other side of the scale. I was free of debt, with a regular weekly paycheque and, as far as the new screenplay was concerned, left alone. There was no Clayburn insisting on ludicrous changes of plot or location. I worked steadily, pushed along by the urge to prove myself, enjoying the solitariness of writing.

The only breaks I allowed were when Jack Reeves interrupted the flow. Several times I came close to telling him about Amanda, but Jack had a low regard for actresses. 'Most of the guys are fucking bimbos like it's open season for shooting deer,' was one of his mysterious ways of putting it. He liked to talk about the 'museum of fantasy' that Los Angeles had become in his lifetime, speaking with a wounded nostalgia tinged with bitterness and a quota of self-loathing. 'I sold out long ago, kid. There used to be a fragrance about this place when I first arrived, now it's close to decay. I'm decayed, a rusting hulk. Why? Because sooner or later everybody in this town ends up doing paranoia in a serious way, and despite my undoubted intelligence, which you'll have noted with admiration, I'm no exception.'

Curiously, his cynicism did not disillusion me. You can be out of love anywhere in the world, the place doesn't matter, and to me the lure of Hollywood was still fragrant even after the end of the affair with Amanda. I wasn't going to end up like Jack, lacing my first cup of coffee with bourbon, churning out hack rewrites with no pride.

Until I went to work at MGM the only times I had glimpsed any movie stars had been when Billy took me to a fashionable restaurant. Now I trod the same holy ground and came face to face with living legends every day. The first few weeks I tried to keep gaped curiosity off my face, though this proved impossible if I passed Elizabeth Taylor – I had never seen beauty like hers. A few of the resident stars maintained a studied aloofness, but the majority would return a smile. Gradually, I suppose, my own face became vaguely familiar and some passed the time of day with me. Fred Astaire, I remember, once stopped to enquire what I was doing on the lot and lingered long enough to convince me that he was genuinely interested and not just being polite.

One evening as I was driving out of the studio, I passed a parked convertible owned by Kitty Harrison, an actress I'm sure most people have forgotten now, but at that time she was tipped to be a possible successor to Lombard. She had a natural gift for comedy and had made an impression in half a dozen films playing second lead and more often than not stealing the reviews. She wasn't conventionally beautiful but, as Billy once said, the camera loved her. She waved as I went past and I waved back, assuming she might have mistaken me for somebody she had worked with. However, when I looked in my rear-view mirror she was still waving, and I realised she was beckoning me back. I reversed until I was alongside and wound down my window.

'Can you help me?' she asked. 'I can't get this stupid thing to start.'

I got out and she slid over on the bench seat to let me sit behind the wheel.

'I've got gas, haven't I?'

'Yes, nearly a full tank, so it's not that.' At close range I was overpowered by the perfume she was wearing.

'It's really nice of you to help me. I don't know your name, I'm sorry.'

'Robert. Robert Peterson.'

'I'm Kitty.'

'Yes, I know, Miss Harrison. Let me check the battery. Does the hood open from inside?'

'Don't ask me. Haven't a clue.'

I went round to the front of the car, found the catch and sprang the hood. The battery seemed OK and all the distributor leads were properly connected. My own knowledge of the workings of the internal combustion engine was sketchy to say the least, but I acted as though I knew what I was doing. There was a heavy smell of gasoline. 'You could have flooded it,' I said. 'If we give it a minute or two the excess will evaporate and she'll probably fire. We can try that, anyway.'

'If you say so. I don't know what any of that means. I hate machines, especially when they go kaput on me.'

I got back into the front seat beside her.

'Am I holding you up?'

'No, not at all.'

'What d'you do, Robert?'

'I'm a writer.'

'You working on a movie now?'

'Yes.'

'That's great. Anything exciting?'

Not half as exciting as you, I thought. 'Well, I hope it will be.'

The conversation petered out with this exchange. I tried to think of something interesting to say, to congratulate her on her last film, but I couldn't remember the title. Turning the ignition key again, I gently pumped the accelerator pedal. The engine fired once, then died again.

'Nearly,' she said. 'You're a genius.'

I gave it another minute, then tried again with the same result. 'It doesn't want to know.'

'Boring thing, I shall trade it in tomorrow.'

'I don't think it's anything serious. Do you have it serviced regularly?'

'I don't have it serviced ever. My business manager is supposed to take care of those sort of things. I just get in and drive.'

I gave it another shot, this time pumping hard. The engine fired and spluttered for a few seconds before dying again.

'Almost,' she said.

I worked at it, but the bloody thing was obstinate. Much though I wanted to impress her, I had to admit defeat.

'Oh, don't apologise, it was nice of you to stop and try. Look, I hate to ask you another favour, but I don't want to wait around for a cab. Can I bum a lift with you?'

'Of course. Where d'you have to go?'

'Just home. Bel Air. But forget it, that's probably out of your way.'

'No,' I lied. 'No trouble at all.'

'You're not just being polite?'

'No.'

'Well, OK, that's really so kind of you. Let's lock this piece of junk and I'll leave the keys at the gate. They'll get it towed for me.'

We transferred to my car and drove to the main gate where she explained the situation to the studio policeman.

'No problem, Miss Harrison. I'll get it taken care of. You have a good evening.' He gave me a friendly, conspiratorial smile as the barrier was raised.

The Bel Air estate, with its maze of private roads and private police force, had always been an enclave for the well heeled. Most of the opulent houses had been custom-built to their original owners' specifications on large plots, and embraced a variety of styles. It was my first visit and Kitty gave me directions as we wound our way through the densely bordered roads, finally arriving at some impressive, closed, wrought-iron gates. Kitty got out and spoke into a small box fixed to one side of the gates. There was a pause and then they slowly opened automatically. The house itself didn't come into view until we had travelled some hundred yards up the curved drive; exotic plants were in bloom on either side, and I glimpsed a swimming pool and stone cabana through the trees.

'You'll come in for a drink, won't you?' Kitty said. 'It's the least I can do to repay your kindness.'

'Yes, I'd love to. What a fantastic house.'

'Only rented, I'm afraid, but, yes, it is nice. Once owned

by Harlow, so they tell me, but it's probably a lie. Most things are in this town.'

The front was covered in a massive climbing rose planted to one side of the entrance and reaching to the second-floor shuttered windows. I'm not good at describing architectural styles and in any case most Beverly Hills houses in Kitty's price-bracket followed no set rules. This one had a distinct Mexican influence. The carved front door was opened by a middle-aged woman, whom Kitty greeted as Josie. Inside, the tiled entrance hall had a curved staircase with an elaborately carved banister, and I was immediately struck by a large portrait of a nude, the pose reminiscent of Goya's *Naked Maja*, which hung halfway up the stairs.

'Take Mr Peterson into the living room, Josie, and show him where to fix himself a drink. Bring me a glass of orange juice upstairs,' Kitty said. 'I just have to make a couple of calls, but make yourself at home. I won't be long.'

Josie escorted me into a room that opened off the hallway. It was furnished with over-sized armchairs and sofas. Bowls of the same roses adorning the façade of the house were dotted around, filling the room with their scent. There was a well-stocked wet bar in one corner.

'There's white wine in the freezer, sir, if you prefer that,' Josie said. 'Would you like me to open it?'

'Thank you, yes.'

When she left the room I took stock of my surroundings. Three pairs of French windows opened out on to a patio, manicured lawns and groomed flowerbeds. I took my drink outside and stood admiring the view. I couldn't remember whether any of the fan magazine articles I had read about Kitty had mentioned whether she was married, or had a current boyfriend. As I waited for her to reappear, an excited short-haired terrier bounded up and immediately jumped above my waist two or three times, then hooked his two front legs around my leg and started to hump me.

'Oh, do stop that, Jock,' Kitty said as she joined me. 'Get off! Kick him. He's sex mad, that dog. I must get him mated.'

She pulled him away by his collar and gave him a smack. 'Sorry about that.'

'Great garden,' I said. She had changed out of her studio clothes and was now wearing slacks, *a la* Kate Hepburn, and a silk blouse with nothing under it.

'You've got a drink, good. So tell me, what's the script you're working on?' When I'd explained, she said, 'Sounds like a great break. I've met Billy Fisher. I thought he was a refreshing change from some of the characters I've had to work for. Most of them can't wait to jump on you, rather like Jock. Occupational hazard I can do without. This town is full of phoneys. Have you found that? You're from the East Coast, right?'

'Yes.'

'I could tell from your accent.'

I heard myself saying, 'If my script turns out OK, there's a super role you'd be perfect for. I'll suggest it to Billy.'

'Well, that's nice of you. But don't make promises others might not let you keep.'

'How long have you been here?'

'This house, you mean? Oh, about nine months, but I've been in LA three years on and off. I stayed at the Sunset Tower at first, then decided I missed having a garden. I grew up in North Carolina where we had a big garden. Saw this place and fell for it. Let me show you around.'

She walked me to the swimming pool area, then took me to the tennis court, which was equipped with overhead floodlighting. 'Do you play?'

'I used to be able to get the ball over the net when I was at college,' I said.

'You must come up at the weekend and have a game.'

'I expect you're a killer, are you?'

181

'Reasonable.'

'Who does all this belong to?'

'Some merry widow from Florida. This is just one of her five homes. Or maybe she's lost count.'

We went back to the house and she gave me the interior tour this time. There was a panelled library stocked with sets of leather-bound editions – the sort that people who don't read buy by the yard. The dining room had a tented ceiling, with the same silk material covering the walls. 'I call this the Casbah,' Kitty said. 'Not my taste and I usually eat in the kitchen, or outside if it's warm enough. Josie's a great cook. She came with the house.' She then took me off guard by asking, 'Why don't you stay for supper? Or do you already have a date?'

'No. But, are you sure you want me to?'

'I wouldn't have asked you if I didn't. I'm not that polite.'

'Well, then, yes, I'd love to.'

'Let me go and tell Josie we'll be two.'

At that moment the dog made a sliding reappearance on the polished floor and again immediately attempted to get his rocks off on my leg.

'Jock!' Kitty screamed. 'Will you stop that!' Fortunately she grabbed him before the moment of truth and hauled him away. Left alone, I was conscious of a distinct sexual tension in the air, triggered not only by the dog's behaviour but also by Kitty's invitation to dine alone with her. Both in age and sophistication, she was totally different from Amanda, and I had to ask myself, was I attracted to her or just attracted to the thought of being attracted to somebody like her, always assuming, and not taking for granted, that she wished me to be attracted to her?

'They've put me on standby for tomorrow,' she said as she returned and poured us some more wine. 'With any luck they won't get to me, which is a relief. I haven't had a day off for three weeks.'

'Forgive me, I should know,' I said, 'but what film are you in at the moment?'

'In a rut, that's what. Curiously, given that I'm living in this house, the epic I'm doing started out as a remake of an old Harlow movie, but by the time half a dozen writers had jigged around with it, any resemblance to the original has gone out of the window. I turned it down once but they threatened me with suspension.'

'Can they do that?'

'And how. Since I'd just extended the lease on this place, I had to buckle under. We're pampered, but still slaves, you know.'

'Do you have a good role?'

'It's OK. Nothing I haven't played before. Listen, I hope you like Mexican food, if not I can get Josie to rustle up something else.'

'Mexican food's fine,' I said. 'I eat it all the time.' I'd never had any before, but it wasn't the moment to be picky. 'Can I tell you I loved your performance in *Romance for Two Violins*?'

'You can tell me as often as you like. Yes, that was a fun movie. It had a good script and a good director.'

We drifted into small talk about the industry until Josie announced that dinner was served. The table had been laid on the patio, with candles in storm-glasses, fine silver, starched linen napkins and exquisite china and glass. Noting my unconcealed reaction to such splendour, Kitty said, 'None of this is mine. It all came with the house. The lady doesn't do things by half.'

We dined under a clear sky and a full moon. The wine loosened my tongue during the meal and I told my life story to date with some omissions and a few embellishments, seeking to impress her, I suppose. By the time Josie brought us coffee we were exchanging confidences. Kitty confessed she was just getting over an affair, somebody whose name

I would recognise if she revealed it, which she didn't.

Spurred by this and the intimacy of the occasion, I let my guard down and gave her some of my Amanda story, like Kitty, careful to conceal names – I had learned that much – and omitting the abortion episode.

'That's rough,' Kitty said. 'How long did it take you to get over it?'

I looked her straight in the eyes. 'Maybe I just have.'

'You don't know me,' she said after a pause. 'I'm a very complicated person. And it's a big mistake to start a relationship on a rebound.' She got up from the table and went to the edge of the patio. I joined her there, and something spurred me to make a pass. It was a mechanical reaction really, because I had no real thought of taking it to the limit, I just wanted to get close to somebody again. I put an arm around her shoulder. She didn't resist, but her body was rigid.

'Isn't it funny?' she said finally. 'When I left the studio tonight something like this was furthest from my mind.'

'Me, too.' I put the slightest pressure on her shoulders, attempting to turn her towards me. 'Now that it isn't furthest from your mind, what are you thinking?' I kissed her neck.

'Don't,' she said. 'Go home and sleep on it, Robert. We should both sleep on it.'

I relaxed my hold on her shoulders and as my arms slid down they brushed against her breasts and I felt her shiver. 'I doubt if I shall sleep,' I said. Again, I didn't mean it, it was just that I felt I had to say something.

'This is a rotten town for romance.' Then she laughed and turned to face me. 'Oh God, listen to me! That's like some lousy line out of a B movie. We're all such actors, that's the trouble.' She leaned in and kissed me on the cheek. 'I've had a good evening, you're a sweet kid. Don't spoil it now. We'll do it again sometime.'

'Is that a promise?'

'Next time my car breaks down I promise I'll send for you.'

'What if your car never breaks down again?'

'Wait and see how the dailies look to you tomorrow. Sometimes scenes we think we've played well prove an illusion.'

When I drove away from the house I had a strange feeling of relief. Although tempted, I had stayed faithful to Amanda.

15

'Don't be so fucking literary,' Jack Reeves had said when I showed him my first pages of the script. 'It's OK, but forget trying to impress the *New York Times Book Review*. You're writing a film for actors, not the Pulitzer Prize, dummy. Make it real, cut out all that highfalutin descriptive shit. Nobody reads that stuff, least of all actors; they only count their own lines. Learn that and you're halfway home.'

He never minded being interrupted, and that next morning, intrigued by my encounter with Kitty, I had gone straight to his cell. As I entered I narrowly missed being pierced by a dart which stuck in the door surround all too close to my head.

'Jesus!' I said. 'You could have ended a promising career. The last director I worked for threw knives.'

'Just getting rid of my frustrations.'

I saw that he had a photograph of Otto Preminger pinned to the back of the door.

'That Nazi bastard was responsible for giving me ulcers, so every now and then I take it out on him. You want coffee?'

'Let me ask you something,' I said as he poured the coffee. He brewed it cowboy style in a blue enamel jug and it was usually thick enough to float a spoon on. There was always an inch of mud at the bottom of the mug. 'D'you know Kitty Harrison?'

'Sure.'

'Like her?'

'Great little butt.' He fortified his own coffee with a slug of bourbon and waved the bottle at me.

'No, thanks. Too early.'

'Do I detect a hidden agenda in your question?'

'I'm just curious.'

'You thinking of dating her?'

'No, she's out of my league.'

'Bullshit! . . . You're letting the side down. Don't you know that everything in life's rich pageant is grist to a writer's mill? Go for it. As Dr Johnson said, when a man is tired of fucking, he's tired of life.'

'I don't think he actually said that.'

'Well, if he didn't, he should have done. Just don't make it a commitment for life. She's an actress, remember? They're a minefield, tread on them the wrong way and you get your gonads blown off. Don't you listen to anything I tell you? Anyway, I thought you had a steady girlfriend, didn't you tell me that? What happened to her?'

'We came to an understanding not to understand each other.'

'Now that's the sort of dialogue you ought to be writing. Simple, but intriguing. I knew you had it in you somewhere.'

I made my escape before he could pry any further. As I closed his door I heard another dart thud into Otto.

My phone was ringing when I got to my own room. It was, surprise, surprise, the great Arnold Milhous himself, all ten per cent of him, surfacing again after suffering an extended holiday sampling vintage wines in the Loire Valley.

'Robert,' he began without further ado, 'I'm delighted we got you an assignment at MGM. Wonderful news.'

'Yes, isn't it?' I said. 'Except you didn't.'

'What?'

'You didn't get me the job.'

'Who am I taking to?'

'Me.'

He clicked his receiver several times. 'Lucy, I asked for Robert Preston's office.'

'Peterson,' I interjected. 'That's me. Arnold, this is Robert.'

'Oh, good, these bloody studio phones drive me mad. I was saying –'

'That you got me this job, and I was saying that you didn't.'

'You aren't at MGM? Lucy said you were. Wait a minute, let me just check.'

He put me on hold and the line went dead for a few moments.

'Yes, didn't think I'd got it wrong,' he resumed when he came back. 'You're scripting some book or another.'

'My own.'

'On your own? That's good, you'll get a single credit.'

'My own book.'

'Your own book? That's marvellous, you must let me read it.'

'I gave it to you the first time we met.'

'Course you did. I've just come back from a business trip, so I'm just catching up with the backlog. Returned to full desk, but wanted to touch base. Any problems?'

'Quite a few actually.'

'Good, good. Well, let me know if I can help.'

The line went dead. A few seconds later it rang again. This time it was my erstwhile publisher, a man I had never met.

'Mr Peterson?'

'Speaking.'

'Oh, Robert, this is Mike Kennedy at Random House. Glad I've tracked you down. Thought it about time I gave you a bell. I've just read the trades and I see MGM have bought your novel. That's great news. We must get behind it, take out some ads.'

'That might be a waste of money,' I said.

'In what way?'

'You just remaindered it.'

'We did? I can't think how that happened. Must have been a mistake. Let me look into it and get back to you.' He was shouting at somebody as he hung up.

I pondered these two aspects of my newfound fame. In addition to Arnold taking his commission under false pretences I now had a publisher coming out of the woodwork to capitalise on a film sale of a book he had ignominiously dumped. Strip away the chickenshit, as Jack was fond of reminding me, and you get down to the real chickenshit underneath.

And there were more surprises in store for me. I never did get a return call from Kitty and when I enquired at her production office whether she was still on the lot I was told she had completed her role and had flown to North Carolina to visit her sick father. They wouldn't give me her telephone number there so she remained a frustrating, unfinished chapter until Jack filled in the blanks for me.

'Give me a progress report,' he said one morning as we dished the latest studio dirt. 'Did you ever score with Kitty Harrison?'

'Sadly no. She gave me the brush.'

'Well, that figures. I was talking to Russ Saunders who was the First on her last movie. He told me she definitely swings the other way. Said several guys he knew had tried to make it with her, but no dice.'

'You saying she's a dyke?'

'I'm not saying it, I don't know the dame, Russ said it. Did you get a smell of that?'

'No. I thought she was just being cool the first time out.'

'I never understood dykes,' Jack said.

'Nor did Queen Victoria. I read she took the line that they didn't exist.'

This further revelation pointed up the absurdity of my life. I had never had any serious intention of scoring with Kitty; it had been more an attempt at recovering my self-esteem. All it had achieved was to make me even more conscious of the loss of Amanda. I called her late one night when I was drunk, but the hotel switchboard told me she had a block on her line. Before Billy went back to England for a period he said I could have the run of his bungalow suite while he was away, but I didn't take him up on the offer. I wasn't too keen for another session with Oliver, preferring the isolation of my own apartment. I knuckled down to licking the screenplay, exorcising my purple prose as Jack had advised ('Don't get bloody depressed at this stage. It takes years to find your real voice'), leading a monk-like existence, avoiding the commissary and sending the postboy out for sandwiches. I found that the monastic existence had certain compensations and I went for several days at a time without thinking of Amanda. A writer is, after all, most alive when alone. Even so my 'real voice' remained stubbornly silent; in having to adapt my own novel, I was sometimes reluctant to throw the baby out with the bathwater, at other times dissatisfied with the original, seeing it for what it was – a first, immature effort. I took the finished pages home with me at night and worked them over again in pencil, then typed them up again the following morning. The nights alone in the apartment were the worst and I drank heavily, which meant it took an extra hour or more for me to feel human again the next day. Somehow I managed to complete a first draft by the middle of December, handed it in to be Mimeoed and posted a copy to Billy's London office.

I was in my studio cell about a week later writing and tearing up yet another love letter to Amanda when Jack walked in. He waved a copy of my script at me. 'What is it with you? I spell out the ground rules and you walk away from them.'

'What? What have I done?'

'This. You put this into the system without checking with me.'

'How did you get that?'

'How? I found it on my desk with a memo telling me to do a rewrite. Don't you know anything, stupid? The moment you send it to Mimeo they stamp a number on the cover and distribute it like a mail-order catalogue.'

'Oh shit! I didn't know. Billy probably hasn't got it yet. He's going to go ape when he gets back.'

'You did know. I sat you down and told you. Now some front office jerk who fancies himself as Maxwell Perkins has decided it needs a polish, so pushes it out to good old reliable Jack.'

'This is terrible. I need a drink.'

I followed him across the hallway. He closed the door and poured me a neat Jack Daniel's.

'You're lucky it's me,' he said, 'not some other prick out to steal your credit. Good thing I like you, kid, otherwise you'd be looking at a busted flush.'

'But why didn't this guy, whoever he is, come to me to do my own polish?'

'Because in his twisted mind he believes in the divine right of executives to screw artists. Plus he has always conducted his life on the basis that in any given situation two heads have to be better than one.'

'So tell me how I get out of it before Billy knows.'

'Because you're such a pathetic bum, I'll do you a favour. I'll sit on it for a couple of weeks, type up half a dozen of your same scenes on different coloured pages, and our man will be convinced he's reading a new version.'

'Really?'

'Trust me.'

'What if he's right, what if you think it's lousy?'

'He didn't say it was lousy. He didn't say anything. But nothing gets through without a rewrite. Those characters are terrified of giving a first draft the O K. All they're worried about is protecting their asses, in case of any comeback. Kid, we're both on Death Row, you and me, and condemned men have to help each other. I'll fix it for you.'

'What can I do to repay you?'

'You can buy me dinner.'

It was the first time he had suggested that we meet outside the studio and I realised that I really knew little or nothing about his everyday life. 'Any time,' I said. 'What d'you fancy?'

'Let's go the whole hog. Put on a collar and tie and do Chasen's. Live it up for once. Let me make the booking.'

'O K, as long as I pick up the tab.'

'I don't drive any more, by the way, and you'll probably have to scrape me off the sidewalk by the end of the evening, because I intend to hang one on.'

'Maybe neither of us should drive in that case. Let's take taxis.'

The evening started well. Jack arrived spruced up, hair slicked, white shirt, conservative tie and wearing an old, but well-cut suit.

'You suddenly look like a bank manager,' I said.

'I only dress like this for funerals.' He studied the menu while we were having a first cocktail, in his case a highball while I stuck to straight Scotch. 'So, I don't want any arguments tonight. I'm loaded and you're not. I'm picking up the tab.'

'That wasn't the arrangement.'

'Fuck the arrangement.' He produced his wallet and peeled off a few hundred-dollar bills which he slipped across the table. 'Use those.'

'I can't take your money.'

'Take it now because later I probably won't be capable of giving it to you.'

'But the meal's not going to cost that much.'

'This meal is only the beginning, kiddo. I don't celebrate this often. But when I do I like to make a night of it. Just put it out of sight.'

Over dinner, which extended to three hours, he regaled me with stories of a Hollywood that would never come again. Famous names peppered his conversation, for he had worked with so many producers and directors over the years. I questioned him, avid for glimpses into the world of legend.

'You worked for Cukor?'

'Lovely man, even if he was a fag. Literate, civilised, unlike many of them. Great sense of humour, too. Could be blunt, didn't suffer fools or mince his words. Course, nobody ever discussed him being a fag. I got on well with him. We worked on a couple of projects, neither of which ever saw the light of day.'

'Wasn't he taken off *Gone with the Wind*?'

'Yeah.'

'Why?'

'Who knows? Rumour has it that Gable thought he was throwing the picture to Vivien Leigh – Cukor is always better with women than men – and Gable is said to have walked out in the middle of a take saying, "I won't be directed by a fairy." So there was no contest. Cukor went quietly and that was that.'

'Jesus! Tell me more.'

'I wasn't there, for Chrissake!'

'Did you ever work for David Selznick?'

'No, I was lucky. I escaped that. His fucking memos are longer than the scripts. He drives writers mad.'

'Who else? You worked for Preminger.'

'The ulcer producer. I hated the son of a bitch. Yeah, I

worked for him. A total of three weeks. After which I quit. The one I liked was Raoul Walsh. God, he was a character. The man who shot Lincoln.'

Staring across the table at my blank expression, he elaborated although by now his speech was increasingly slurred. 'He played John Wilkes Booth in *Birth of a Nation*. Don't you know anything about the history of the cinema? Griffith took him under his wing when he was still a young buck. Handsome devil, from old photos I've seen. Griffith sent him down to Mexico with a cameraman to film *Pancho Villa*. Came back with footage you wouldn't believe, but a lot of the stuff they couldn't use.'

'Why not?'

'Even in those days it was considered unacceptable.' He poured himself more wine. 'Villa's method of getting rid of his enemies was to bury them up to their necks in the sand and then ride horses over them. Raoul filmed that stuff. Know how they learned their craft in those days? You jumped in at the fucking deep end. The carpetbaggers provided the money and the roughnecks shot the movies. There were no textbooks, they shot off the cuff, making it up as they went along. It was every man for himself. Course, Walsh still cut a dashing figure even after he lost an eye and had to wear a patch.'

'How did he lose an eye?'

'Driving to location in the desert for a movie called *In Old Arizona*. First outdoor talking Western. Walsh was playing the Cisco Kid. Disturbed a jackrabbit and it came through the windscreen. Damnedest thing. Finished his acting career. They recast with an unknown named Warner Baxter.'

I wanted him to go on all night, but spurning coffee when the meal finally came to an end, Jack said: 'Hell, I don't want to sober up and lose all the benefit of this good liquor. The night is young. Let's go on to a cathouse.'

'I don't know any.'

'You're with me. Travelling first class. Get the check.'

I paid and rang for a taxi. While we waited on the sidewalk for it to arrive, Jack came up with, 'How about you and me going someplace else for Christmas? Drive down to the border and hang up our stockings in Tijuana. What d'you say?'

'Sounds good. I wasn't looking forward to Christmas. First time I haven't spent it with the family.'

I've no recollection of the address he gave the taxi driver, but after twenty minutes or so we pulled up outside the closed gates of a mansion. Jack got out, weaving a little, and talked into the speaker grille. Whatever password was needed, he obviously had it, because a second or so later the gates opened to let us in.

Jack was greeted like an old friend by the rugged-looking bouncer and we were led across the marble hall with its curved staircase leading to the upstairs and shown into a room with subdued lighting. It was furnished with sofas and armchairs with lace covers to protect them.

'Homely, eh?' Jack said as he half fell into one of the chairs.

With no experience of whorehouses, I wondered what came next. A younger man came into the room and asked what we'd like to drink and as he was leaving, a woman in her forties entered, neatly dressed, hair coiffured into a bun at the back, not over-made-up and certainly not typecast as a madam. Jack heaved himself out of the armchair and they embraced.

'Jack, dear, why have you stayed away from us so long?' the woman asked.

'Have to ration myself these days, Bee,' he said. 'The sap doesn't rise as fast as it did. Let me introduce a young friend of mine, Robert, who's come to join the club. This is Beatrice, Robert, known to the fraternity as Bee, which stands for "Be on your best behaviour", ain't that right, Bee?'

'I'm sure any friend of yours knows how to conduct himself.' She shook hands with me. It was all very formal. 'I've told the girls you're here; they'll be down in a minute.'

'Busy tonight?' Jack asked.

'No, not very.'

Jack turned to me. 'You can have the pick of the bunch then, kid. How about Pauline, is she free?'

'She could be.'

'Let him see Pauline. You'll like Pauline,' Jack told me. 'She's your type.'

The man returned with our drinks, together with a glass of wine for Beatrice. She exchanged a toast with us, took a polite sip of wine, made some small talk and then excused herself.

'Don't be worried, this is a class joint. Bee runs a tight ship and all her girls are clean.'

At that moment three girls entered the room. Again, I had no idea what to expect. Folklore and general misconceptions on the subject had led me to believe that I would be faced with stereotypes: girls or mature women who looked the part and would appear in scanty negliges. But the trio who now joined us were anything but obvious whores. The youngest of the three, who introduced herself as Pauline and was about my own age, was blonde, wore a silk peignoir and looked like a fashion model. Jack chose the oldest of the three, a dark-haired Hispanic with a wide slash of a mouth.

'Don't feel left out, honey,' Jack said to the third girl. 'I'm saving you for next year when I've matured. Pauline, this is my good young friend Robert. Look after him.'

He stumbled out with his arm around his choice. The unselected girl also left and I was alone with Pauline.

'He's a character,' I said.

'Most of them are.'

'Most of the regulars, you mean?'

'Yes.' She had a pretty smile. 'Would you like to drink some more?'

'No, I'm fine.' I told myself: This is going to be a good experience, it's going to come in useful later.

'You're sure you wouldn't like to see anybody else?'

'Quite sure.'

'Shall we go upstairs then?'

She led the way. I liked the way her body moved underneath the robe. The only sound in the house as we mounted the circular staircase was music being played somewhere, a Nat King Cole standard. I followed Pauline along a carpeted corridor and she opened a door at the far end. The bedroom was not done out like a bordello in some Hollywood Western, but was furnished opulently but simply: a large bed, rattan chairs, a television set on top of an antique chest of drawers and an opened bottle of champagne in an ice bucket. Heavy, drawn curtains and, again, subdued lighting.

'You want to make use of the bathroom?' Pauline asked. From the way she said it I knew I was expected to. There was a man's robe laid across the bathroom stool, bottles of cologne by the washbasin together with packets of condoms. I undressed, sluiced my face and used one of the colognes, then put on the robe and studied my face in the mirror. Back in Queens several of the gang I hung out with had recounted lurid tales of their experiences with whores, who in any case were mostly streetwalkers. Listening to them, I remember I felt a mixture of part envy, part smugness: a touch of envy because the idea of illicit sex had a fearful fascination about it, and smug because I had a regular girlfriend and having to pay for sex seemed a waste of my hard-earned money. Now, as I picked up one of the condoms, it wasn't the novelty of the situation that was uppermost in my mind, but the fact that I had never before done it with a girl without knowing her.

Pauline was in the bed when I returned. I put the condom on the bedside table, dropped my robe and got in beside her. I lay there for a few minutes, trying to think of some way of opening the dialogue. Her naked body when I touched it was strangely cool, and for some reason this brought back the memory of a book I'd read years ago, written by Ralph Bates, a member of the International Brigade who fought during the Spanish Civil War. There was an episode about a torrid encounter he had had with a whore and he described her flesh as burning hot, an image that had always stuck with me.

'Is there anything special you like to do?' Pauline asked.

'No.'

'Would you like me to be on top?'

'Yeah, let's do that.'

It was all so polite.

She leaned over me and took the condom from the bedside table. Stripping the sheet back she began her ministrations while I watched in a detached sort of way. It was her breasts brushing against me that produced the desired effect and the moment that happened she deftly stroked the condom on.

'You can kiss me, if you like,' she said. 'Some of the girls don't care for being kissed, but I don't mind with somebody like you.'

She sat astride me and guided me in, then leaned forward, bringing her face close to mine, and I kissed her. She tasted of peppermint. I put my hands behind her back and pulled her closer as she commenced a slow see-saw motion. Some reflex triggered and when I looked into her face at close quarters it was not the face of a stranger, but Amanda I saw, and when with quiet, clinical skill she brought me to orgasm I made an involuntary cry of 'darling' and for those intense seconds of release I think I believed that it was Amanda who was receiving me. I came back to the reality of the situation slowly. Pauline waited until I slid out of her, then removed the condom and took it into the bathroom. Every act she performed fascinated me. When she came back she went to the ice bucket and poured one glass of champagne.

'Won't you join me?' I asked.

She shook her head. 'House rule.'

'Well, thank you, Pauline. That was good.' I felt foolish as I said it.

'Jack usually stays the whole night,' she said. 'Is that what you'd like?'

'You mean actually sleep with you? There isn't another house rule against that?'

'Bee allows it for favoured customers.'

'How d'you feel about that?'

'You're a friend of Jack's. It's whatever you want. You married?'

It was the first personal question she had put to me.

'No.'

'Then stay if you want to.'

'Yeah. I'll stay.'

She got back into bed with me and I put an arm around her. Her body was warmer now. I have no idea whether she slept, but I was asleep almost immediately.

16

Rather to my surprise, I didn't feel shame, remorse or any of the emotions that, traditionally, are said to be associated with a first visit to a brothel. Apart from a minor hangover, quickly dispersed by the hearty breakfast provided in Bee's establishment, I felt fine. Sex without an aftermath of complications had much to commend it. Using the cash Jack had given me, I settled the bill for both of us, adding extra from my own pocket for Pauline. Jack did not put in an appearance at breakfast and from the amount on his drinks tab I gathered that he was sleeping off a monumental blinder. I arranged to collect his remains later in the day.

'How did I behave last night?' he asked me. He looked terrible.

'Up until the moment we parted company, you were your usual jolly self.'

'I long for the days when I could at least say "the pleasure is momentary, the position ridiculous". Now, it's not even momentary, more a brief memory. Still, I had a good sleep. How about you?'

'I had a good time. Thanks for pointing me in Pauline's direction.'

I drove him home. It was the first time I had ever been inside his place.

'The old curiosity shop,' he said as he ushered me inside. The main room was bookshelved on three sides, the shelves sagging under the weight of books and scripts.

'As you can see I don't entertain here much for obvious reasons.'

He weaved his way to the kitchen and reappeared waving a bottle of Jack Daniel's at me. 'Care for a hair of the dog?'

'I think not.'

He went to his desk, which was strewn with papers, full ashtrays and a variety of unwashed coffee cups. Selecting a cup he poured himself a stiff shot, choking on the first gulp, but managing to keep it down. 'That hit the spot,' he said. 'Sit down if you can find a chair. About twice a year I make the effort to clean up but, what the hell? Who am I doing it for? My last wife had this fetish about a tidy house; this is my revenge on the bitch.' He slumped down against one of the bookshelves, causing a row of books to fall on to the floor. 'I've been working on your screenplay. You're not bad, kid, but you over-write. Keep it sparse. And don't take offence at my revisions. I have reached the happy state of being insensitive to adverse criticism. Years of trying to please potato-brains in those cold storage blocks they call the writers' buildings have immunised me. I urge you to follow my example, because you are looking ahead to a lifetime of working for a collection of tawdry egos who haven't had an original idea in ten years. The only way to survive is to recognise the fact, take the money and, when you've saved enough, get the hell out. Otherwise, you're staring at the end result.'

'But you're good, Jack. Everybody says so.'

'Was good. Was. No longer. Just a hack.'

He poured himself another drink. I thought for a moment he was crying, but maybe his eyes were just watering from fatigue.

'A wiser man than me, Chandler in fact, once wrote, "Any man who can write a page of living prose adds something to our life."'

'You know Chandler?'

'Old pipe-smoking Ray? Sure. He was a big bottle man like me, but the spiky bastard could write like an angel.'

'I'm renting a place he's supposed once to have lived in.'

'Does his spirit walk?'

'Not so far.'

'They have never used him properly out here. What he tried to do was way above their heads most of the time. D'you have a cigarette?'

I produced one and lit it for him.

'Yeah,' he continued after a long drag, 'we need a few more like Ray. He can be a prickly, contentious character when he's had a few jars, but we had good times together. Good times,' he repeated. 'Few and far between these days. But I enjoyed our jaunt last night. We should do it more often. I like you, kid, and I want to protect you.'

'You have already.'

'Keep riding the punches, that's the secret.'

The next time I saw him he was in hospital. After I left he'd gone out to buy another bottle of booze and a carton of cigarettes and was hit by some jerk driving a heap who jumped a red. He suffered multiple fractures and concussion and the accident put paid to our Christmas in Tijuana. I didn't find out for four days, but the moment I was told, I went to see him, smuggling in a bottle of his favourite poison.

'I didn't think flowers and grapes were your bag,' I said. 'How d'you feel?'

'Like I felt working for Preminger. The dumb bastard who hit me didn't have insurance, of course. That hurts more than my goddamn arm.'

'At least you won't have to do any rewrites for a while.' I put two one-hundred-dollar bills on his chest.

'What's that for?'

'I owe you.'

'What d'you owe me?'

'I don't mind you buying me dinner, but I'm not letting you pay for getting me laid.'

He brushed the bills off on to the floor.

'Don't insult a sick man. Pick 'em up and put 'em in your pocket. I've got something important for you to do for me. I want you to go into my office and grab your script. I did some work on it, a few nicks here and there where you went overboard, nothing much and you may even think I've improved it. Type it up, like I said, on coloured pages so you're ready when they come asking for it. You can tell them that you and I discussed the changes and because of this you finished it. Then, when your man gets back, no one's the wiser. Get me a toothbrush mug out of the bathroom and pour a slug of that ambrosia you brought me. They haven't let me near the juice since I got in here and I'm pissing pure water. That's unhealthy.'

Driving back to the studio after the visit, I had further glimpses of the way in which some of the denizens of Beverly Hills celebrated the coming of the Three Wise Men. Apart from plastic Father Christmases on the front lawns, complete with sleighs and reindeer, at least three houses proclaimed *HAPPY BIRTHDAY JESUS* in coloured lights. Hollywood Boulevard had an elaborate, illuminated festive motif strung across the street at intervals and there seemed to be a Santa Claus tolling his hand bell at every second intersection, which must have traumatised those children who still believed.

I did as Jack suggested, retrieved my script and went through the changes he had made. In nearly every instance they were an improvement. Despite the fact that he took pleasure in describing himself as a has-been and a hack, he had a sure touch when it came to fixing the meat of a scene. He had scribbled various comments in the margins: *Don't need this, you dummy, let the actor show the emotion on his face. Think visuals, this ain't a novel.* I went to work on it, slipping in the coloured pages as per Jack's instructions, finishing the day before Christmas Eve.

Whether it's snowing or not (and that year Los Angeles was enjoying a heatwave) Christmas Eve always seems to impart a curious hush over a city. Demented, last-minute male shoppers scurry around, but for the most part the streets are abnormally clear. A sudden feeling of homesickness swept over me. I couldn't face spending the holiday alone in my apartment where the other residents had strung up a few lights around the pool and had announced they were going to hold a Noel barbecue – taking part in some forced, geriatric jollity held few attractions. Wanting more pain, I called Amanda yet again but the operator said she had checked out until after the holiday. Then I rang home, piling on the agony. 'We've got ten inches of snow,' my mother told me as I closed my window shutters to blot out the evening Californian sun. Other members of the family came to the phone to say how they missed me and I was immediately transported back to my childhood and the excitement that had always accompanied the last-minute preparations. At the end of the phone call I was ready to slit my wrists in a warm bath.

I scratched around in my small pile of records and put on some Puccini – Bjorling singing '*Che gelida manina*', a version I had played almost to destruction while writing my first novel and which seldom failed to raise me from the dead. This time the magic didn't work. I left the apartment, got back into my car and headed in the direction of Malibu, thinking I had been lucky meeting up with Mike and maybe lightning would strike twice. The radio didn't help: every station either had 'He's the Little Boy that Santa Claus Forgot' or Crosby singing 'White Christmas' interspersed with the DJs being positively overwhelmed with good cheer. I could understand why the suicide rate jumped at this time of year.

I drove to the marine restaurant where I had first met Mike, but it was shuttered and well on its way to looking derelict. So I drove on, drove for miles with no particular destination in mind and eventually landed up in Santa Barbara – Beverly Hills with more taste. By then I was hungry and cruised around until I spotted a lighted place that looked as though it catered for people under the age of forty.

There were several mixed groups of people my own age all having a noisy good time. I sat at a corner table and wished I'd brought some erudite book to read – philosophy or *Ulysses*, just to emphasise that I was eating alone by choice: single guys eating alone on Christmas Eve signal that they are sexual failures. I ordered steak and fries.

'Don't you want the Christmas special?' the waitress asked.

'No, I'm giving Christmas a miss this year, unless you want to hang up my stocking for me.' I guess she had been listening to that sort of corny come-on all day, and the ghost of a smile she gave me made me disgusted with myself at having made such a puerile remark. It was the sort of line that Jack would have scored through in my script.

I looked at the girls on the table opposite me, taking in their vacant, nymph-like faces, their over-made-up eyes and outlined mouths as they leaned back in their chairs, pouting at their sweating boyfriends and wriggling with God knows what expectations. They were all talking too loudly in an effort to impress. The mating game when you're not part of it has a desperate intensity. Most of my early perceptions about love had been formed from books – Hemingway making it with his nurse in *A Farewell to Arms*; Fitzgerald's Dick Diver and his Rosemary; a collection of stories, whose title I have forgotten, about romance in old Vienna – after I read those I used to fantasise myself as an indolent Hussar officer seducing a series of swooning maidens to the strains of a Strauss waltz, though what affected me most was an account of the tragedy at Mayerling – that haunted me for months. I remember once during the first month with Janice, when we couldn't get enough of each other, asking her if she could ever contemplate a suicide pact if we were forced to separate. The question alarmed her and I never repeated it, although the scene often came to me in dreams. A grand passion that ended in two lovers dying in each other's arms held a strange fascination for me.

Mayerling was a far cry from that restaurant in Santa Barbara, yet with a writer's imagination I couldn't help wondering what the fates had in store for the group seated at the table opposite. I knew, with terrible clarity, how their emotions were reacting, one against the other, and as I cut into my underdone New York strip and washed it down with a glass of beer, I seduced each girl at second-hand, picking out one in particular who caught me looking at her and didn't turn away, but gave that subtle Gioconda smile all women are born knowing how to use, inviting our lusts and, God help us, sometimes murder. Like them, I was looking for love, I felt that keenly, and lack of love drags us down into the pit as surely as any virus. I was as down as I had ever been that night and it wasn't run-of-the-mill self-pity, it was just that I had the feeling I would never find love again. To add to my angst, at that moment one of the boys suddenly leaned across the table, knocking over a glass of water as he grabbed the girl who had smiled at me, pulling her to him by the neck of her lacy blouse so that for a second the nipple of one immature breast was revealed as he kissed her. Whooped on by his companions, he held her trapped until she managed to pull away from him, dishevelled, her lipstick-smeared mouth like a wound. She adjusted her blouse then got up, passing close to me on her way to the rest room to repair the damage, while the boy received the plaudits of his less-venturesome companions. The incident stayed with me on my return journey and I wondered how the night before Christmas would end for her – a fumbled initiation, with no frankincense or myrrh, on the back seat of a Chevvy?

The roads were deserted by now and I made good time home. As I activated the gates of the underground garage and parked, the moment my engine was silent I became conscious of an unusual noise – the sound of somebody sobbing. Getting out of the car, I stood very still and listened, thinking I was mistaken. But, no, at intervals, it was quite distinct. The lighting in the garage was dim, since the landlord seldom bothered to replace any spent bulbs, but I traced the sound to a far corner and went, cautiously, to investigate. Slumped on the concrete floor between two cars I found a girl wearing nothing but a thin cotton dressing gown. I couldn't see her face clearly.

'Hey!' I said, in a voice that I hoped wouldn't alarm her. 'What's happened to you?'

She turned towards me and a pale shaft of light slanted across her tear-stained features. Dark-haired, in her early twenties maybe. I'd never seen her around before.

'Why're you sitting down there, crying?'

'What's it to you?' she said.

'Just asking. D'you live here?'

She mumbled something.

'Come again.'

'I said, yes, I did, but he left town.'

'Who did?'

'What does it matter?'

'It matters, tell me, perhaps I can help.'

'Brodky.'

'Don't know him, but then I don't know half the people who live here.'

'You didn't miss anything,' she said and wiped her eyes on the sleeve of the dressing gown.

'Well, you can't sit there all night, you'll catch pneumonia. Is this guy, this Brodky, your husband?'

'No, thank you. Look, don't bother, mister, it's none of your business, I'll be OK.'

'How can you be OK? If everything was OK, you wouldn't be sitting here crying. You want to tell me anything else? Can you get back into the apartment?'

She shook her head.

'Well, then, you going to stay here all night?'

This time she didn't answer.

'Listen, you'd better come up to my place. I'll lend you a sweater and a coat and drive you where you want to go.'

Again, she said nothing, nor did she look at me.

'Come on, it's Christmas Eve.' I put out a hand to help her up, but she didn't take it.

'You don't want trouble,' she said.

I kept my hand extended towards her. 'Who's talking about trouble? You scared of me or something?'

'No.'

'If you're shut out of your apartment, all I'm going to do is find you some warm clothes. Then you're free to go. No strings, no funny business, promise.'

This time she looked up at me and searched my face. I don't know if she found reassurance there but, still ignoring my hand, she slowly got to her feet. I studiously avoided touching her as we went to the garage exit and walked up to my apartment.

'I guess the reason I never bumped into you before is that I don't mix much with the others.'

'Well, we only moved in two weeks ago.' It was the first time she had responded without caution in her voice.

'That would explain it then.'

I unlocked the apartment door, put the lights on, and then stood aside to let her enter first. She hesitated.

'How do I know you're on the level?'

'That's a good question; you don't.' In the stronger light she had a waif-like appearance, a sad pretty little face, big eyes, wide lips. She was looking past me into the apartment. 'You just have to believe I am.'

'Is there anybody else here?'

'No. Just me. Look, if you're really unsure, stay there and I'll bring the clothes to you. It might help if we told each other our names. I'm Robert. What's yours?'

'D'you have a dog?'

'Dog? No.'

'I'm scared of dogs. I got bitten once.'

'No dogs.'

She finally stepped inside.

'Want me to leave the door open?'

She shook her head, still looking around, taking in the muddle of papers on my desk, the typewriter, the full ashtray.

'So what's your name?'

'Tracey.'

'OK, Tracey, sit yourself down there and I'll look out some clothes. You want something hot to drink? Coffee?'

'Tea. I'll take some tea.'

'Fine. What you should take is a hot tub. You're shivering.' Her scared expression came back. 'Take the clothes into the bathroom, it's got a lock on the door, get yourself thawed out, and when you're dressed I'll have the tea waiting. How's that? Good idea?'

'Why're you doing all this?'

'There was no room at the inn, remember? Stop thinking I'm a rapist and relax. You look perished, so do as I suggest. Whatever you want to do next, you can't go out into the streets looking like you do. That way you might well end up raped. That's the bathroom, I'll pass the clothes round the door, no peeking.' To tell the truth I was beginning to regret playing the Good Samaritan but, having started it, I couldn't back off. She hesitated, then went slowly into the bathroom. I fetched a shirt, sweater and some pants from my wardrobe and pushed them round the door as I had promised. She immediately closed the door and I heard the lock turned. I put the kettle on and poured myself a drink, then sat down to wait for her to re-emerge. She took her time.

There was some colour in her cheeks when she came out and her thick, dark hair was dank. She had combed it away from her face so that it appeared much shorter and with my sweater and baggy pants she looked beguilingly pretty.

'Feel better?'

She nodded. 'D'you have a belt? These are about to fall down.'

'I'll get one. How d'you like your tea? D'you take sugar and cream?'

'Just cream.'

'You should have some sugar. Sugar's good for you after a shock.'

'Sugar's fattening.'

'You should worry.'

'OK, if you say so.'

When I came back with the belt and tea she was standing at my desk, one hand holding up the pants. 'This what you do?' she asked. 'You a writer?'

'Yes.'

'What sort of things d'you write?'

'Well, I've written a novel and at the moment I'm writing a screenplay.'

'You in the movies?'

'Yeah.'

'Show me something you've written.'

I went to the shelf and took down a copy of my novel. She studied my photograph on the back of the dust jacket.

'When was this taken?'

'Couple of years back.'

'I've never met a real writer before. How d'you start writing a book like this?'

'Well, as somebody once said, it's easy. You stare at the blank sheet of paper and wait for the drops of blood to form on your forehead.'

She took this seriously. 'I've often thought about that,' she said. 'I used to write poems. Crazy stuff. I'd wake up in the middle of the night with one in my head and write it down. Then, in the morning, it didn't make any sense.'

'Join the club. So, Tracey, what's next? You got any friends you can spend the night with? You want to call them?'

'I don't know anybody here,' she said. 'We came from Kansas.'

'"We" being you and this Brodky? What sort of guy is he?'

'A total prick. Said he'd marry me.'

'Is that what you wanted?'

'I wanted to get out of Kansas.' She fastened the belt and sipped the hot tea.

'You hungry?'

'No.'

I suddenly looked at my watch. 'Hey, guess what? It's Christmas. Happy Christmas.'

'Yeah, big deal.'

'Don't tell me if you don't want to, but how come you ended up in the garage?'

'We had a fight.'

'What about?'

'Look, mister, don't concern yourself. Soon as I've had this tea I'll get outta your hair.'

'You've got money, of course? You keep a wad in your dressing gown, do you?' That stopped her in her tracks. 'Tracey,' I said, 'it's the middle of the night. The only

211

people out there are drunks and derelicts. Now, why don't you stop thinking I'm gonna jump on you and spend the night here – you have the bed, I'll sleep in the armchair? The bedroom door locks too. And in the morning I'll stake you for a ticket on the Greyhound to wherever you want to go.'

'Why would you do that?'

'Off the top of my head, I don't know. Put it down to the season of good will.'

'Nobody does anything for nothing.'

'Jesus!' I exclaimed. 'You sure as hell are one suspicious character.'

'Maybe I got cause.'

'OK, so do you have a better idea? You tell me.'

'And that's all there is to it?' she answered.

'That's all.'

She took her time. 'OK,' she said finally.

'Fine. We've got that sorted out. You sure you're not hungry?'

'What're you offering?'

'Nothing fancy. I can fix you some eggs.'

'Eggs is fine.'

She settled down in the armchair and opened my book. I went into my tiny kitchen, thinking I'd invited a real cuckoo into my nest.

'What's your second name?' I shouted.

'McCauley.'

'Did you always live in Kansas?'

'Yeah.'

'Are your folks back there?'

'Maybe. They move around a lot. They've always lived in trailer parks. Tell me, what do they pay you for writing a book?'

'Not much.'

She was quiet after that. I put some bread in the toaster

and scrambled three eggs, the limit of my culinary skills. When they cooked I took them into her, but she was no longer in the armchair. She came out of the bedroom.

'Who's that picture in there?'

'My sister.' It wasn't, it was a photograph of Amanda.

'Some good-looking sister. You got a girlfriend?'

'Not at the moment. Here, eat these while they're hot. Want something to drink with them?'

'What've you got?'

'Beer. A Scotch.'

'I'll take a beer.'

I watched her eat. 'Tell me something,' she said between mouthfuls, 'why do men's shirts button on the different side from women's?'

'No idea. Who first thought of brewing beer? Another great unsolved mystery. The world is full of them.'

'Yeah, suppose so. How long have you been here?'

'Two or three months. Are you expecting your boyfriend to come back?'

'He's not my boyfriend. No, he's gone. Took everything and blew.'

'What was your fight about?'

She finished the last piece of toast, wiping her plate with it, before answering.

'The usual. I was working in a department store, in Perfume, and he breezed in one day and shot me a line. Said he'd fallen for me. I believed him, the jerk. I'll take you to LA, he said, you're what the movies are looking for. Oh, he was real convincing. Told me he had connections. Then the moment we got here, he changed. Said his money had run out and I'd have to take a job. Guess what he had in mind? Wanted me to pull some tricks. He was just a pimp. I ran away once, but he found me and brought me back, slapped me around a bit. Then, last night, he turned up with a real hooker and said he was giving me one last chance

213

before dumping me. That's when the fight started. The rest you know.'

I took her empty plate from her. 'If you ask me you got lucky.'

'With you, you mean?'

'No, lucky you got shot of him. And you haven't got a key to get back in?'

'No, he took it.'

'Well, we'll ask the landlord for the passkey.'

'Don't do that, he might stick me for the rent. Sure as hell that cheap bastard left owing.'

'But haven't you got your stuff up there?'

'Nah, nothing I'll miss. That was another thing. When we get to LA, he says, I'll buy you a whole new wardrobe. Tell me about it.'

'OK, well the day after tomorrow, all the stores will be having sales. I'll stake you for some clothes.'

'Why would you do that, mister?'

'Robert.'

'OK, Robert, what's in it for you?'

'Listen, and don't be so bloody touchy. I'm on Easy Street at the moment. I've got a contract at MGM and a weekly paycheque. I can afford a few bucks.'

'I still want to know why you'd do that?'

'Jesus! I'll tell you why. When I first got here I was like you, some guy conned me in the same way.'

'You mean he wanted you to hustle?' A sort of comprehension crossed her face. 'Are you a fag?'

'No.'

'I don't mind if you are.'

'That would make you feel safer, would it? Well, sorry to disappoint you, but I'm not a fag. I was trying to tell you that, like you, I was left high and dry. Had to take a job waiting tables. Then one day somebody did me a favour and my luck changed.'

My story seemed to have bored her. 'How come you don't have a girlfriend?'

I ignored that. 'Look, I don't know about you, but I'm bushed. Take the bed, lock the door, have a good night's sleep. We'll work it out in the morning.'

'Do you have a teddy bear?'

'A teddy bear, no.'

'I always sleep with a teddy bear.'

'Well, you can't win them all. Just let me get a spare blanket and pillow out of the closet and then it's all yours.'

'I've never met anybody like you, mister.'

'Robert,' I said. 'Can't you call me Robert?'

'You don't look like a Robert. You look more like a Gary.'

'Too bad. I'll tell my mother to have me christened again.'

I went into the bedroom and came out with a pillow and blanket.

'Good night, Tracey. Hope you sleep well without teddy.'

'Yeah.' She paused in the doorway. 'Thanks, by the way.'

She closed the door. I listened, but she didn't lock it.

17

I could smell freshly roasted coffee beans, yet I knew I was dreaming. In the dream Amanda (it was still always Amanda) and I were crossing a ravine on a swaying rope bridge. As we took another tentative step forward I felt something tickling my bare feet and struggled to wake from the dream, coming to with rough tongue, parched roof of mouth, a dull ache in my neck. I sat upright in the armchair. As my eyes focused I could make out a blurred shape in front of me.

'How d'you take it?' a voice said.

'Take it?'

'Coffee. I've just made some.'

Gradually the blur resolved itself into Tracey. She was wearing nothing but an old T-shirt of mine which presumably she had helped herself to during the night. She smoothed it down over her flat belly, the action bringing her breasts into prominence. The realisation of who she was and the returning memory of the previous night's events vanquished the last remnants of the dream. I rubbed the back of my neck.

'What time is it?'

'I don't know, haven't got a watch. Around three maybe.'

'God! Have I been asleep that long? When did you wake up?'

'About an hour ago.'

I got to my feet, one leg buckling under me from cramp

and, suddenly conscious that all I had on was a pair of Jockeys, wrapped the blanket around me and went to the bathroom.

'Did I hear you ask me if I wanted coffee?'

'Yeah, I helped myself.'

'Good. I've love some. Black, please.'

I stared in the mirror as I pissed, and mouthed, 'What have you let yourself in for, Peterson?' Then I sluiced my face in cold water and slicked my spiky hair flat. Tracey had a mug of coffee waiting for me when I came out.

'So,' I said, 'did you sleep?'

'On and off. You don't keep much in the ice box, do you?'

'I guess not. But when I get my act together, I'll take you out to eat.'

'Won't be anywhere open. It's Christmas Day.'

'That's right, so it is. I've lost track. Except for hotels. Bound to be a hotel coffee shop open.' I was just about to suggest the Pink Turtle, but stopped myself in time. I didn't want to have to explain Tracey to Leyla. 'Let me have this coffee injection, then I'll get organised. What sort of day is it?'

'Usual. Doesn't it ever rain here? This weather's so boring.'

'Don't let the natives hear you say that.'

I was beginning to find her semi-nudity disturbing. As she moved to look out of the window I saw she had an ugly bruise, like an unfinished tattoo, on one thigh, presumably Brodky's work.

'All those old dudes are having a picnic down by the pool,' she said. 'They've got paper hats on.'

'That's about as jolly as they get.'

'One trailer park we lived in – I was a kid at the time – all the residents threw a party and a guy dressed up as Santa Claus. I actually believed he was the real McCoy. He was the one who gave me my teddy bear. Only thing I had that year.' She turned back to me. 'Was I mean last night?'

'No. And if you had been, you had good cause.'

'What did I say to you?'

'You asked if I was a fag.'

'I did? Well, that was mean, considering.' She smiled at me. 'I read some of your novel this morning. You're deep. Did all that happen to you?'

'No, I made it up.'

'Come on, some of it must have happened to you.'

'Bullshit! If I wrote a murder story would you believe I was the murderer?' I wasn't ready for a literary argument.

'Probably.'

'Yeah, well you've got a suspicious mind. I found that out last night.'

'Did I ever say thank you?'

'Yes.'

She was restless, roaming the room, as though measuring it. 'I've got it now. Everything's the same but in a different place. Like where we were the bathroom was over there. I'm glad I worked that out finally, been bothering me ever since I got up. I remade the bed, by the way. Did you mind me borrowing this to sleep in?' She smoothed the T-shirt again and this time her nipples showed through the cotton. It occurred to me that she meant that to happen.

'Looks better on you than me. Let's go eat,' I said.

We found a place not too far from the apartment and both had the pot roast. She chattered away throughout the meal and I was content to let her talk, mostly about life back in Kansas. Trailer park life didn't sound too hot. She didn't mention Brodky for a while, then suddenly said, 'What if he does come back?'

'I thought you said he'd left town?'

'I don't trust him.'

She looked around the coffee shop as though expecting

him to materialise there and then. I put a hand across the table and touched hers. 'You're safe with me.'

'That's what he said. Sorry, I didn't mean that. I do feel safe with you. I mean, I'll tell you now. I didn't sleep that well. Most of the night I expected you to come through the door and get into bed with me. Most guys would have. Did you think about it?'

'Truthfully, no.'

'Why not?'

'Because I promised I wouldn't.'

She stared at me. 'Yeah, that's right, you did. So, what do we do now?'

'Right now? We could drive to the beach.'

'O K, that sounds good to me.'

On Wilshire I suddenly spotted a cheap pharmacy open and swung over into the parking lot.

'What're you stopping for?'

'Wait and see.' I went inside. There was a lot of unsold Christmas stuff on the shelves and I hunted around until I found a sad-looking teddy bear with a ribbon round its neck. Returning to the car I handed it to her.

'Here. I'm sure it's a poor substitute, but maybe you'll sleep better tonight. Or maybe you don't take gifts from strangers?'

She hugged it to her face. 'You're not a stranger. You're Father Christmas in a way, aren't you?' she said. Then, a moment later, 'Am I sleeping at your place again tonight?'

'Unless you want to book into the Beverly Wilshire. The only snag is they have a habit of asking you to pay.'

'Yeah,' she said, taking me seriously. 'That's true. Tell me, Roberto, if I hadn't been good-looking, would you still have taken me in?'

Streetwise, no doubt about that.

* * *

Her first sight of the Pacific Ocean excited her. For all I knew she had never seen the sea before, but I didn't embarrass her by asking. The surf was big that day and Tracey ran back and forwards in the spume, squealing when the waves caught her.

'Careful!' I shouted. 'Don't get swept away, there's a big undertow.'

A girl riding bareback on a white horse went by, kicking up the sand and followed by two loping mastiffs the size of small ponies. Tracey stood transfixed, watching horse and rider until they were out of sight.

'Wow!' she exclaimed. 'D'you think she's somebody famous?'

'Maybe.'

'People live down here, don't they?'

'The well heeled do.'

'Imagine.'

'Ever go fishing?' I asked.

'Fishing? You ever tried fishing in a trailer park?'

'We could take a boat out one Sunday at Paradise Cove and you could try your hand.' As I said it, I realised I was including her in my future. I couldn't make up my mind whether she'd heard me above the noise of the sea and I didn't repeat the invitation.

On the way back I stopped at a market and bought a few essentials, letting Tracey make her own selection. She chose salted peanuts, Orio cookies, jelly babies and root beer. Diets, like fingerprints, identify lives.

When we'd parked in the apartment garage I made her wait in the car. 'Give me the number of your apartment and I'll check whether lover boy has come back.'

'He's not my lover boy, do me a favour.'

'Sorry. Just an expression. What number?'

'Fourteen B.'

I stopped on my way to the exit. 'That was the old Count's place.'

'Who?'

'Doesn't matter. Some old guy, a Russian, who died.'

'I always thought it was creepy,' she said.

'He didn't die in the apartment.'

I thought of the Count and his silver cocktail goblet as I went up to his apartment and listened outside the door. Everywhere was quiet.

'All clear,' I said when I returned. 'I rang the bell several times, but there was no answer, and no sound either.'

That evening she watched television while I did some more revisions on the screenplay. Quite a domestic scene – Christmas Day with the Petersons, all it needed was some mistletoe. I fixed a couple of things in the script that I didn't like, but I didn't really make much progress. My mind was elsewhere. Stealing looks at her, I thought about what I had said down at the beach, about going fishing. Had I meant it? Now that she was more relaxed, she looked like one of my high school dates. A lot of crazy thoughts started going through my head and the word Fate kept cropping up. Pauline one night and now Tracey – suddenly my empty life seemed filled with chance encounters. When the news came on I sat beside her to watch it, but was careful not to make body contact. Christmas in America always seems to be celebrated with some multiple pile-up on the freeway, and that year was no exception – some fourteen cars had been trashed in Nebraska during a snowstorm. The item was followed by the shots of the President and family attending church, the sacred and the profane sandwiched between ads.

'Fancy a burger instead of that junk you've been eating?' I asked.

'Yeah, any time.'

'Come and watch the fast-order chef at work.'

'Thought you said scrambled eggs was all you could do?'

'I was holding this in reserve.'

'I never want to learn to cook.'

She came into the small kitchen while I prepared the meal. 'I didn't have a choice,' she said, 'but why did you choose to live here? I mean, don't get me wrong, it's real neat, but somehow it doesn't go with somebody famous.'

'I'm not famous.'

'Well, you're working at MGM.'

'Touch wood when you say that. The only reason I chose this place was because the landlord told me that Chandler once lived here.'

'Who's Chandler?'

'A great writer. You should read him.' Mention of Chandler brought back memories of the same conversation with Amanda. 'Anyway, I fell for his sales pitch, then about a month later a buddy at the studio told me Chandler never stayed here. He had a place on Drexel Avenue.'

'What difference does it make if this Chandler guy lived here or not?'

I could see the story had little point for her. 'Just hero-worship, I guess.'

'Would you ever move someplace else?'

I shot a quick glance at her, but there was no guile in her face. 'Don't suppose I'll stay here for ever.'

'We never stayed in one place very long. My father was always in debt, keeping one step ahead of the people chasing him ... Some nights I'd go to bed and when I woke up our trailer would be parked in some other dump a hundred miles away ... I bet it must be great living near the beach. Getting up every morning and finding the sea on your doorstep. You ever wanted that?'

'Who wouldn't? Here.' I flicked her hamburger on to a plate. 'How about that, cooked with style, huh?'

We ate squatting on the floor.

'Tomorrow's the big day,' I said, 'when we buy you some clothes.'

222

She stopped eating. 'I'm gonna ask you again – why're you doing this for me?'

I didn't have a ready answer. I wanted to say, 'Because you're disturbingly attractive and I'm vulnerable,' but I had to get my head together first. I could have said, 'You make me feel protective', or, more honestly, 'When I saw you in my T-shirt this morning I wanted to fuck you.' None of those explanations came out of my mouth; instead I said: 'Because if I hadn't found you in the garage I'd have had to spend Christmas alone.'

'Well, Christmas is nearly over, and that's no answer.'

'Tracey, I don't have an answer, to tell the truth. I wish I did. Something like this has never happened to me before.'

'You sorry?'

I looked at her long and hard. 'No.'

'You took your time. Do I grow on you?'

That made me laugh. 'I guess you do in a way.'

'In what way?'

'Why all the questions?'

'Because I want to repay you.' She suddenly kissed me and then, as if reading my thoughts, 'You want to fuck me? You can, you know.'

Without waiting for an answer she got up and went into the bedroom. I sat where I was, disturbed by the directness of her, thinking how accidental life was. You got yourself killed on the freeway on Christmas Day, or you found a girl crying in the garage and took her in like a stray cat. I had the feeling, however crazy, that if I didn't follow her I was going to miss something that might change my life. The big problem was, did I want my life to change yet again? The whole mixture of love and sex, the importance we attach to it, the way it twists us into knots, the amount of time and energy we expend trying to find it and the pain we have trying to get over it when it fails is always so complicated.

I got up and walked to the bedroom door. Tracey was already in the bed with just a sheet over her.

'Like you said to me, no strings. You won't have me round your neck for ever.'

'There are always strings,' I said. I went closer to the bed and my eyes flicked past her to the photo of Amanda on the bedside table. 'I'll sleep with you, but let's talk it through first.' Even as I said it, I felt foolish; it seemed such a dumb thing to say to a girl who was willing to give herself. She watched me, half her face covered by the sheet, as I undressed and folded my clothes neatly for once, delaying the moment when I joined her. I lifted my side of the sheet and slipped in beside her naked body.

'OK, let's talk about it.'

'What is there to talk about?' she said. 'You either want me or you don't.' She edged closer until our bodies were touching, then leaned over me and I felt her breasts gently flatten on my chest. 'If you don't want to go the whole way I can repay you like this.' She started to slide down my body, but I pulled her back.

'Of course I want you, but it isn't as simple as that. What happens after tomorrow?'

'I don't know. I'll move on, I'm used to that. Don't worry so much.'

I took her head between my hands. 'One of us has to worry. You don't seem to realise where you're at. So, I buy you clothes tomorrow. What then? I give you a ticket on the Greyhound? To where? Back to the trailer park? What's journey's end? Look, and I don't want you to feel grateful to me, I'm responsible for you now. Maybe I should have left you in the garage, but I didn't, I took you in of my own free will, you didn't force me to, so now you think I'm going to kiss you goodbye after we've gone shopping? That's it, nice meeting you, it's been a slice, *bon voyage* and all that?'

224

I didn't really know what I was saying, the words were just tumbling out. The whole scene took on a bizarre aspect. I seemed to float away from her, looking down on us both from above the bed the way they shot it in the movies just before the dissolve. There I was holding a naked girl in my arms, a girl utterly unlike anyone I'd ever known, trying to convince myself that I was going to do the honourable thing and not fuck her. Then, suddenly, everything fell into place and I heard myself saying: 'What if I didn't put you on a Greyhound, what if I asked you to stay here, move in with me?'

'I'd say you're crazy,' she said.

'Maybe, maybe not, but I'm asking you.'

'Why would you do that?'

'Don't answer a question with another question. I'm asking. Do you think we could make that work?'

'If that's what you want.'

'There you go again.' I kissed her awkwardly, then got out of bed, went into the bathroom and took a condom out of the cabinet. When I went back to her she was crying.

'Now what?'

'Nothing,' Tracey said. 'Everything's perfect.'

18

I remember reading that some fancy old British sage pronounced that 'in the dark all cats are grey' when advising his nephew on the pleasures of the bed, meaning, I take it, that there's nothing to choose between women when you get down to basics. I always thought that was a lead nickel. Sex with Tracey was definitely not the same as sex with Janice or Amanda. Once we had got over our initial explorations that first night, she was happy to make love at any time. There was something endearingly tender and fragile about her.

The next morning I set her loose in the shops to get some clothes while I checked in at the studio, arranging to pick her up later. I'd given her three hundred dollars to spend as she pleased, telling her to go to places like Bergdorf Goodman rather than some cheap joint. I stopped off at the hospital to visit Jack since I hadn't seen him for a couple of days and was immediately shocked at his changed appearance. Although he made an attempt to greet me with his usual ebullience, it was obvious he'd taken a turn for the worse. He was hooked up to a drip and his face was the colour of ashes. I had intended to tell him about Tracey, but it didn't seem appropriate.

'Glad you looked in, kid,' he said. 'I want you to do me a couple of favours. Open that drawer and give me my wallet.'

I went to the bedside table. His hands fumbled with the wallet but eventually he took out a key.

'This opens my desk drawer. When you get to the studio, look inside and you'll find two things – a sealed envelope addressed to my old man up in Maine. Contains an insurance policy in my name but made over to him. I don't want any of my exes to get their hands on it, so post it to him for me.' He paused to get his breath back. 'The other thing is a script I've been saving for my old age. An original. I wrote it on their time, but fuck them, I don't owe them anything, they've had their pound of flesh out of me. I want you to have it.'

'What d'you mean "have it"?'

'Just that. Put your name on it and sell it as your own. It's not bad, though I say it myself.'

'I couldn't do that. You can sell it yourself when you get out of here.'

His head fell back on the pillow. 'I'm not getting out of here.'

'Don't give me that crap. Course you will.'

'It ain't the movies, kid. Can't write happy endings to order. Just do what I say.'

'Well, I'll go this far. I'll post the letter for you and I'll keep the script safely until you're better, but there's no way I'll put my name on it.'

'Just do as I say, kid. Don't be a hero. I'd like to think you beat the system for me after I've gone. Poetic fucking justice.'

The effort of talking seemed to have exhausted him. He closed his eyes and lay back on the pillows. The whole conversation alarmed me and on the way out I buttonholed the nurse on duty. 'How's Mr Reeves coming along?' I asked as casually as I could. 'Seems a bit down this morning.'

She gave me a look. 'You are a relative?'

'No, just his best friend. He hasn't got any family to speak of.'

'Well, don't quote me, but he isn't in good shape. He's

got a blood clot on his brain. They're going to operate this afternoon.'

'What're his chances?'

'Difficult to say. He's not in good shape generally.'

She was disinclined to tell me anything more. I went back into Jack's room, but he was asleep. As soon as I got to the studio I went into his office and it looked like the room of someone who was already dead. There was a half-drunk cup of coffee, some cleaning tickets, a full ashtray and a sheet of paper still in his typewriter. On it he had typed: *Words are the only things that last forever.*

I unlocked the desk drawer and took out the envelope and script, then locked it again. I made sure there was nobody about before going back to my own office where I settled down to read the script. It had a title: *The Beginning of the End.* It proved to be a thriller mostly set in Chinatown, Los Angeles, and it grabbed me from the opening sequence. Good characters, tough, sparse dialogue, the work of a man who knew his stuff, far superior to anything I could come up with. I felt cold and guilty reading it, remembering his offer. When the phone rang I jumped as though somebody had discovered me in the act of committing a crime. It was Billy, who had just got back into town and wanted to see me. I put Jack's script into an envelope and buried it under a pile of old magazines before walking over to the Thalberg Building, taking a copy of my own, revised script with me. The excitement I had previously felt about my own work just wasn't there any more.

Of course Billy greeted me by the wrong name.

'Good flight?' I asked.

'No. I came back on Air France. Big mistake, but I couldn't be bothered to go through London. Those snotty French have a stupid rule about not allowing cigars. We had engine trouble or something and put down in a ghastly place called Gander, which is like Siberia. Everybody had to get off the plane and spend five hours in a Nissen hut, which they call a terminal, and of course I'd taken sleeping pills, so it was a total nightmare. Anyway, Roland, I don't want to talk about it. Tell me all your news. Is that the script you've brought me?'

'Yes.'

'I'll read it when I feel better. Are you pleased with it?' He didn't wait for my reply. 'I see from the trades that Jonathan is doing that Italian film. That won't do him any good. I spread the word while I was in Cannes.'

'Did you have a good Christmas?'

'I don't celebrate Christmas. I suppose you spent the holiday with Amanda?'

'No, I didn't as a matter of fact. I think she went to friends. She's busy filming.'

'I thought we three would have dinner tomorrow, so I can catch up on all the latest gossip.'

I hesitated. 'I might not be able to make it tomorrow.'

'Never mind, I'll take Amanda out anyway. If you change your mind about dinner let me know.' He started to dial a number.

'I'm anxious to know what you think of the script. I've done quite a lot of revisions,' I said, but Billy wasn't listening. He swept a pile of letters to one side as he looked for his cigar cutter on the desk. Billy seldom answered letters, preferring the telephone. 'It's a big mistake to put anything in writing unless you're forced to,' was one of his edicts. As I left he was saying, 'Dolly, it's me, I'm back. What's the truth about Orson, is he really going to marry that awful girl?' He was back in the land of trashed reputations.

I returned to my office and collected Jack's script. The envelope addressed to his father I posted on the way to meet Tracey as arranged. The moment she got into the car with her armful of shopping bags she kissed me and presented me with the receipts and thirty dollars change. 'Keep it,' I said, but touched. 'You were meant to spend it all.'

'I had the greatest time, you've no idea! I usually steal clothes, so paying cash was a real bust.'

That night she put on what she had bought, treating me to a fashion parade.

'I still can't get over it,' she said. 'I've never had clothes like these before.' She behaved as though I had treated her to mink and designer exclusives, whereas in fact I saw from the labels that she had bought most of the stuff off the sale racks. While she was changing from one outfit to another I phoned the hospital to enquire about Jack. This time I lied and said I was his brother calling long distance. They said he had come through the op and was stabilised. The next twenty hours would be the critical ones.

It was difficult to switch from thoughts of Jack to Tracey, flushed with life's pleasures, but seeing her in a blouse and skirt for the first time changed her completely.

That night, after we had made love, I told her my fears about Jack.

'Poor man,' she said. 'I'll go with you next time if you think he wouldn't mind.'

'I'm sure he'd rather see you than me.'

He wasn't to see either of us. The moment I woke up the next morning I called the hospital again. This time I was shunted from one extension to another until I finally got somebody who seemed to have some authority.

'I'm trying to find out the condition of a Mr Jack Reeves who had a serious operation yesterday.'

'I'm afraid we're not allowed to give out information over the phone, sir.'

'OK, I'll come in.'

'Are you a relative?'

'No, I've been through all that three times, he doesn't have any family except his old father who lives up in Maine. I'm a colleague of his at MGM, his closest friend. All I want to know is if he's OK. You can tell me that, surely?'

'Let me put you on hold for a moment while I check.'

I waited. The voice came back on the line after fully two minutes. 'Who am I talking to?'

'Robert Peterson.'

'Well, Mr Peterson, although we normally don't give out information of this sort unless to next of kin, in view of what you've told us we're making an exception on this occasion. I'm sorry to tell you that your friend died during the night. Perhaps you'd be kind enough to come in and make the necessary arrangements for the removal of the body in the absence of any close relatives? There's a question of the hospital charges.'

'Of course,' I said. 'Dead men can't pay, can they?'

I hung up and rang Personnel at the studio and explained the position. They were much more sympathetic and helpful. 'Thanks for letting us know, Bob. That's too bad. Jack was a studio fixture, one of the old-timers. Don't worry, we'll take care of it.'

'I'll call his old man,' I said, 'and try and break the news gently.' Then I slung on some clothes and drove to the studio, anxious to clear Jack's office of anything else he would have wanted to keep from prying eyes. There wasn't much – a couple of bottles of bourbon, a telephone book in which I found a number for his father, a few paperbacks, mostly Westerns, his notes about my screenplay and a month-old court order for non-payment of alimony to one of his ex-wives. It didn't seem enough to show for a life. After taking down the dart-scored photo of Preminger from his door, I tore up his script notes and the court order and took the rest with me, including the last sheet of paper in his typewriter. After helping myself to a shot of his bourbon I phoned his father in Maine. The ring at the other end of the line had a strange, old-fashioned sound and rang a dozen times before a voice answered.

'That you, Melvin?'

'No, sir, Mr Reeves, sir,' I said. 'My name's Peterson, I'm a friend of your son.'

'Who?'

'Peterson.'

'Do I know you?'

'No, sir. But I'm a friend of Jack's.'

'Oh, yeah. How's he doing?'

I tried to choose my words carefully. 'Well, I'm sorry to say he met with an accident over Christmas. Somebody hit him. He had to go to hospital.'

'Jack was always a lousy driver.'

'This wasn't his fault. The guy who hit him was a drunk.'

'That sounds like Jack.'

'Mr Reeves, Jack wasn't drunk. It was the other guy.'

'Hold on a minute, got something on the stove.' The line went dead for a while, then he returned.

'Put Jack on the line to me. 'Bout time he called his old man. Never heard from him over the holidays.'

'Sir, your son isn't around at the moment,' I said, floundering for words. I'd never had to deal with death before.

'Never even wrote. Mind you, post ain't reliable these days –'

'Sir. Mr Reeves,' I cut in. 'Jack met with a serious accident and he won't be writing to you . . .' I plunged. 'They did everything they could, but he died, he died from his injuries. I'm very sorry to have to tell you that.'

There was a long silence.

'Mr Reeves, you there? The studio where he worked are taking care of all the arrangements.' Again he did not answer. 'I'm really sorry to have to bring you that news, sir.'

'Jack's dead?' he said finally in a faraway voice.

'I'm afraid so, sir.'

'Appreciate you calling.'

'If there's anything else I can do . . .'

'Appreciate you calling,' he repeated. 'He was a good old boy, always sent me money.'

'Yes, I'm sure, sir.'

'Won't be seeing them cheques any more.' The line went dead abruptly.

I found I was shaking when I put down the phone. The act of telling his father had brought it home to me as well; it seemed fantastic that I'd never be called across the hall again to hear Jack's latest piece of philosophy or get a charge from his thick coffee. In a sense he was the first genuine friend I had made since arriving in Los Angeles; somebody who wanted nothing from me. The news trickled down through the studio grapevine and that lunchtime half a dozen of the other writers and me adjourned to a bar across the street and toasted Jack's memory. They all had stories to tell about him, most of them unprintable in polite society. The one I enjoyed most was his Preminger encounter. Apparently it had been heroic – he had delivered the final draft of his screenplay dressed in Gestapo uniform, then taken an ad in the *Reporter* stating that when he died he wanted his ashes flung in Otto's face. 'Who wants to volunteer for that?' one of the gang asked. 'Any takers?' I discovered something I should have known: that he'd twice been nominated for an Oscar, but had never won. It was typical of Jack that he never mentioned those to me. We raised our glasses to him, then trooped to the cellblock.

His name had already been taken off the door.

19

Tracey never went out unless I was with her, still terrified that Brodky would suddenly reappear. She kept the place spotless, which was a change, and made unwise attempts to cook dinner on a couple of occasions. I gamely ate what she put in front of me, but for the most part we ate out. I took her to unfashionable restaurants where we were unlikely to bump into anybody I knew. It wasn't that I was ashamed of her, but I didn't want to put her at a disadvantage. One Sunday, as promised, I took her fishing at Paradise Cove and she actually caught something, which freaked her out. 'Put it back,' she squealed, 'it's alive.'

'Course it's alive, you just caught it. That's the object.'

'Well, I didn't know they'd be flapping about like that. You do it, you do it, I can't touch it.'

Billy had read my script by now and said he was pleased with it, picking out a couple of scenes in particular, which happened to be the ones that poor old Jack had fixed for me.

'What's the next move?' I asked.

'Well, I suppose we have to find out what they think. Irritating, but they're entitled since they've paid for it.'

I didn't mention that somebody in the front office had already seen the previous draft. There was a chance that, with the submission now coming direct from Billy, it wouldn't find its way to the same man. Billy's approach to films worried them: he didn't fit the usual pattern, and he wasn't craven. One thing I had learned at Jack's knee was that those who inhabited the middle echelons were constantly terrified that their fairy gold would be taken from them. 'They'd have to go back to being the nothing they've never ceased to be,' he would say when their posturing opinions went counter to his own convictions. 'We're not in a civilised society, we're in a Roman circus. That's why they've got a lion on the logo.'

Billy again insisted that I had dinner with him. I'd run out of excuses, but I knew it would be a mistake to take Tracey along. She wasn't ready for exposure to Billy's smart crowd. I told her it was an important business meeting I couldn't duck.

Amanda and Oliver were in Billy's bungalow when I arrived. I caught Oliver giving me a knowing look as I went through the motions of kissing Amanda on the cheek, but thankfully he didn't treat me to one of his oblique remarks. In fact, for him, he was quite gracious and said he had enjoyed my script. As for Amanda, she was friendly but distant, more anxious to relate how well her film was going than to get into small talk with me.

'Have we had any good news?' I asked Billy when I could get a word in.

'Yes, we're celebrating, Robert.'

'Celebrating getting his name right for once,' Oliver observed.

'They liked it.'

'They did?'

'Well, not without reservations, of course. They have to put in their two cents. I agreed with them all and now I shall ignore them. They want to put it in the spring schedule. They even talked about cast.'

'Who?'

'Van Heflin.'

'I like him,' I said. 'What about the girl?'

235

'Janet Leigh. Not that I've agreed to either. I want Amanda to test for it when they assign a director.'

I turned to Amanda. 'Be wonderful if you got it. Have you read it?'

'Not yet, but I remember the character from the novel. Yes, be great.' She had subtly changed since I had last seen her. For one thing she was now wearing heavier eye make-up and a brighter lipstick, neither of which she really needed, and they gave her a hard look that hadn't been there before. Being with her again, even in company, still turned me over. Had it not been for Tracey I dare say I would have carried the torch until it burned my fingers. We ate in the hotel for once and she excused herself early, pleading she was on first call.

'How's her film going?' I asked when she'd left.

'It's a crock of shit, of course,' Oliver said. 'They offered me the second lead in it, but I wouldn't touch it with a barge pole.'

'That's just your opinion, Oliver.' Billy blew cigar smoke across the table. 'Perhaps you should have taken it. Nobody else is standing in line to offer you anything.'

'Well, you're meant to be my *eminence grise*, why don't you get off your arse and find me something? You're so busy masterminding Amanda's career, you should concentrate on people with talent.'

I kept out of it. To my amazement Billy smiled at this venom. He really did enjoy trading insults when he was in the mood and that night he seemed to deliberately bait Oliver. 'You mean somebody like Richard Burton?' he said. 'Trouble is they're difficult to find.'

'God, you can be bitchy sometimes.'

'Whenever I give you good advice, you go against it. Stop wanting to be the next Valentino, dear, and try for Bette Davis's roles, much more within your range.'

'Don't press your luck, Billy.'

'If you're unhappy here living in luxury at my expense, go back to your beloved West End and work for Binkie. He pays two hundred pounds top, I believe.'

They were like two dogs circling each other in an alley, looking for the chance to move in for the kill. It was a revelation to me how the Brits could trade insults in such quiet, measured tones.

'I'm warning you, don't go on.'

'Is that meant to scare me?' Billy said. 'People have been warning me all my life. Fortunately I'm in a position not to care.'

'Yes, well we can't all buy friendships, can we?'

'You should know. I bought you. And Robert here, and he hasn't complained.'

'Well, he hasn't been around you as long as I have, but I'm sure he'll discover your true character sooner or later, if he hasn't already.'

Billy waved his cigar in the direction of the waiter and signalled for the check.

'Go to bed, Oliver, you're being even more boring than usual. Robert and I have business to discuss. Try and wake up in a better frame of mind, otherwise you'll spoil your looks.'

'What's on the agenda tonight – sharing Amanda?' Oliver said, ignoring the fact that the waiter was standing by the table. Billy scrawled his signature across the check in his usual never-look-at-the-amount fashion, but I watched his face and it changed. He dropped a fifty-dollar bill on top of the check.

'Thank you, Mr Fisher. I hope you enjoyed your meal. Come and see us again soon.'

'I'd like a cognac,' Oliver said. 'Delamain. In a brandy glass, not in one of your toothbrush mugs.'

'Certainly, sir. Right away.'

'What has Amanda got to do with it?' Billy said, as the

waiter left. Although it was an attempt to sound unconcerned, his voice was less assured.

'Everything, I imagine. Personally I've never been keen on a *menage a trois.*'

Billy got up. 'Come on, Robert, let's go, leave him to it.'

'It won't come as a surprise to Robert,' was Oliver's parting shot as we left. 'I've told him the scene that goes on between you and your little starlet.'

The only thing Billy said as we walked to his bungalow was, 'I'm thinking of buying a house. Hotels have begun to bore me.'

The moment we were inside he went straight to the pill table, palmed some capsules out of two bottles and swallowed them without water. His hand shook as he lighted a fresh cigar.

'What you and I should do,' he began, 'is sit down and make our own cast list. Janet Leigh and Heflin are very good, but they wouldn't be my first choices. The only reason the studio suggested them is because they're under contract and therefore cheaper.'

'Really? Is that the reason?'

'Of course. If they use somebody not on the lot they'll have to deal with agents. I think we should aim much higher – I'd like Burton, just to annoy Oliver if nothing else, and Jennifer Jones – that would be good chemistry, except that her husband is impossible. All those interminable memos. No, forget her. Life is too short.'

He went to the table he used as a desk and opened the drawer. 'While I think of it, Robert, I owe you some money.'

'Do you?'

'Yes, you're due another payment on the first day of photography, but you may as well have it now.'

There and then he wrote out a cheque and handed it to me with, 'I suppose you'll have to tell your agent? Who are you with, I forget?'

'Arnold.'

'Oh, yes. Dolly tells me that Mrs Arnold, whatever her name is, is totally bald and wears wigs, but that the rest of her body has started to grow hair.'

'God!' I said. 'Perhaps he'll leave her behind in Africa on their next safari.' I was staring at the amount of the cheque. 'Billy, this is too much. The contract was for five thousand.'

'Really? Oh well, I can't be bothered to write another one. Treat it as a bonus for working so hard.'

Maybe the pills he had taken went to work straight away, but for the rest of the time I was there he chattered non-stop about encounters on his recent trip, and how much he disliked the French. 'Still they're no match for a pushy Jewish boy,' he observed as he roamed the room, occasionally picking up some of his mail, glancing at it, then dropping it in the waste bin. It didn't take a trained psychologist to realise he was talking about anything other than the subject we both wanted to avoid. I listened, but my mind was elsewhere. I was still stunned by the amount on the cheque. I'd been bought off, I knew that – quickly, neatly, by a master of the game we were all playing – and an echo of Oliver's gibe hummed in my ears. It was Billy's method of dealing with anything that disturbed his status quo.

'Well, this is just the start, Roland,' he said. 'We're going to do lots of things together.'

'I hope so.'

He suddenly wandered away into his bedroom, returning shortly afterwards with two shirts still in their Cellophane wrappers. 'Here, have these. They're silk, I bought them in Paris.'

'But don't you want them?'

'No, I don't like the colours.' He thrust them at me. 'They'll look much better on you. I have to make some phone calls,' he added by way of dismissal and I took the hint. As far as Billy was concerned everything was back to normal.

239

20

The apartment was in darkness when I got back. As I switched on a light I saw Tracey curled up in the arm-chair.

'Why're you sitting in the dark?' I said.

'He came back.'

'Brodky?'

She nodded. 'Yeah, I heard the loudmouth sounding off to somebody by the pool.'

'But he didn't come up here, did he? Where is he now?'

'I don't know. I hid in case he saw me.'

I cuddled her to me. 'Well, stop worrying, there's no way he can get to you while you're with me. Look, this'll take your mind off him.' I dangled Billy's cheque in front of her. 'Read the numbers.'

She stared at it for a long time. 'Is it real?'

'As real as they get.'

'Where did you get it?'

'The producer I'm working for.'

She took it from me and studied it closely. 'You got eight thousand dollars just for writing?'

'Oh, thanks a lot. It's not just writing. You're living with a hot number.'

'Holy shit!'

When she finally accepted that it was real she began to laugh, not the laugh you use when somebody tells a joke, but the laugh that small children make when amazed. Despite

240

her scare over Brodky's return, she perked up immediately.

'I've thought of a plan,' I said. 'Been going round in my mind for some time and this clinches it. Know what I'm going to do with all this money? We're going house-hunting in the morning. Get away from here, so you don't have to worry about Brodky tracking you down. We'll find the place you always dreamed about, by the sea.'

'You kidding me?'

'On the level. First thing tomorrow we're out of here.'

'But you told me you'd paid for six months here.'

'So I lose some, but I'm rich, who cares?'

She flung herself into my arms and kissed me. 'You're so good to me.' The one kiss led to several and we ended up having sex.

As soon as we woke up we packed all my stuff. I wrote a note to the landlord explaining that I'd had to go back East because of a death in the family, but gave no forwarding address. I made sure the coast was clear before we went down to the garage. As we entered, Tracey suddenly backed off. 'That's his car. He's still here,' she whispered. 'Oh God!'

'Don't panic. He's not in it. Tell you what, shall we let his tyres down, teach the bastard a lesson?'

The idea appealed to her. 'OK, do it.'

We worked quickly and threw the caps away before speeding off. We drove to Santa Monica and went into the first realtor's office we found. I explained to the woman what we were looking for if she had any on her books – a small house, reasonable rent, with a view of the sea. 'That's a must,' I said. She showed us several and we both plumped for the last one, a clapboard with salt-faded blue paint, tucked away in a cul-de-sac. There were three rooms and a shower downstairs, two bedrooms and bath above. It was furnished after a style, not my style, but I didn't worry about that – what decided us was the fact that we had a clear view of the sea from the small redwood deck. The rent was well within my newfound means.

'We'll take it,' I said. 'Just give me time to go to the bank and collect my stuff and I'll be back to sign the papers and give you the deposit.'

'We'd want cash, I'm afraid, if you're moving in straight away.'

'No problem.'

I told Tracey to stay put in a cafe until I returned, then sped back into Beverly Hills, going to Arnold's office first. I put the cheque in front of Lucy.

'How does that grab you?'

'Good gracious. Have you been gambling?'

'Billy Fisher puts his money where his mouth is. He was pleased with the script, gave me the next payment in advance and added a bonus.'

'Well, well. That's unheard of.'

'Now, Lucy, sweetheart, I want a favour. Deduct Arnold's commission and give me a banker's draft, or whatever they call it, for the balance, so I can cash it right away.'

She hesitated. 'All right, seeing as it's you, I'll ring our bank and say it's OK. I hope you're not going to do anything stupid with it. You should save your money.'

'Easy come, easy go.'

'That's not a good rule to live by.'

'Just joshing you. I've just taken a place down at the beach. I'll let you have the address and new telephone number so you know where to find me.'

'Well, I hope you know what you're doing. There are always rainy days.'

She started to write the cheque; I leaned over the desk and kissed her.

'Lucy, you're a definite star. Is Arnold in today?'

She blushed bright red. 'He'll be in later. He had a breakfast meeting with Terry Williams.'

It was now nearly lunchtime. Williams was the current golden boy, nominated for that year's Oscars, who drove a Bentley and was on everybody's A list.

'Well, tell your leader my good news, will you? And ask him what he thinks of the script. Be great if he ever phoned me himself. Maybe he'll stand me breakfast one day.'

I went straight to Arnold's bank and presented his company cheque. After it was scrutinised by the teller, one of the managers came out to see me. 'It's rather a large sum to be carrying around in cash, Mr Peterson. Are you sure you want the entire amount?'

What I find about these bank types is that they always give the impression that handing over your money is somehow an affront, as though you're raiding their personal piggy bank.

'If you don't mind,' I said. 'I have a business deal that has to be concluded today. I'll take it all in large bills.'

He didn't look happy about it, but gave the OK. The seven thousand two hundred was counted out twice in front of me. I put it away carefully. En route to the old apartment I stopped off at a flower shop and sent Lucy two dozen roses, then posted the note to my ex-landlord. When I drove into the apartment garage I saw a man I took to be Brodky circling his car and kicking the deflated tyres in anger. He was about five foot six tall with sleaze written all over him, from his white and tan shoes to his slicked, black hair, that suggested it had been sprayed on – George Raft on a bad day. There was a scraggy-looking blonde with him wearing a halter-top and shorts. He shot me a look as I got out of my car.

'See this?' he said. 'Look what some motherfucker did to me.'

I walked over and clicked my teeth in sympathy. 'Gee, that's too bad, nowhere's safe these days.' Close to, he smelled of cheap cologne. The girl had a doomed, lop-sided face that looked as though her plastic surgeon had left for a date halfway through making her over.

'Can you give me a ride to a repair shop?'

'I'd love to,' I said, 'but I'm running late today.'

As I walked away he shouted, 'Thanks for nuffin, pal,' and I heard him thump the side panels. When I'd gathered up my gear, I went down to the garage again. He and the girl had gone.

I collected Tracey and told her of the encounter with Brodky. Even though I explained I'd left no trace behind us, she was still edgy. 'He's not looking for you, right now he's looking to get his car back on the road,' I said, 'so quit worrying. He's a nothing, just a small-time pimp and he's out of your life for ever.'

I signed all the paperwork with the realtor and put down a year's rent because it worked out cheaper, then we went on a shopping spree, buying a new king-sized bed on condition it was delivered that day, a couple of patio chairs, some satin sheets (Tracey's idea), new towels, a crate of wine, two bottles of champagne, firewood and a carload of provisions. All in all I had blown some five thousand dollars, but I didn't think about that, the adrenalin just kept pumping. Arriving back at the house I carried Tracey over the threshold. The moment I put her down she ran through the house and out on to the deck.

'Look at it,' she said. 'The sea!' And as we looked a school of dolphins soared and dipped half a mile out.

We spent the afternoon rearranging the furniture and finding places for my gear. True to their word, the store delivered the bed. We moved the old one into the garage and bounced on the new.

'Let's christen it,' I said.

'OK, but let me put the sheets on first. I've always wanted to do it on satin sheets.'

Everything she did had an uncomplicated happiness.

Afterwards we sorted out how the heater system worked and took a shower together. I dried her with the new towels, then we opened the champagne and sat on the deck, and watched the changing patterns of the sea until the bugs started to bite. Retreating inside, we lit the fire and made love for the second time in front of it. In the torpid aftermath I tried to catch up on all that had happened to me in the space of twenty-four hours. The only blot on my changed landscape was Jack's death. The funeral had been arranged for later that week. His attorney had produced a will, which contained Jack's sense of humour to the end. He had stipulated that he wished to be buried at Forest Lawn in the Wee Kirk of the Heather Chapel there, claiming that he had distant Scottish ancestry. He requested that bagpipes be played. Much later, I gathered he left very little money and, in fact, the Writers' Guild Benevolent Fund paid for the funeral. Sadly, the long-standing Preminger joke proved to be apocryphal – there was no mention of it in his last testament – and in any case nobody had the nerve.

There was a good turnout for the funeral, mostly writers, together with a dozen producers and directors he had worked with and a few actors whose faces I recognised – Mitchum was there, I remember, with Jack Palance and Gloria Grahame. He got his bagpiper in full regalia who pumped out some skirling tunes. I'd never been to Forest Lawn before, though I couldn't miss the billboards along Sunset extolling the unique advantages of being put to rest there. It's difficult to parody a parody, although Waugh took a crack at it. Death be not proud didn't exactly jump to mind as I looked around at the pristine lawns dotted here and there with churches for all denominations – Disneyland for the Departed. The message from the ads was that if you wanted to do your nearest and dearest proud when they shuffled off their mortal coils, then Forest Lawn was the only place to consider. After the funeral service was over I wandered around and took a look at the main attraction, the largest painting of the crucifixion in the world, the size of a basketball court, and housed in its own amphitheatre where a recorded narration described its virtues, half a dozen showings a day. You could only file out one way when the performance was over – straight into the gift shop. I bought Tracey a Forest Lawn bracelet as a souvenir and, while I was waiting for it to be gift-wrapped, I noticed that the assistant had been cleaning the glass counter top with a bottle labelled 'Cavity Embalming Fluid'.

When she handed me my change I asked her: 'Is that for real?'

She looked around guiltily and whipped the bottle out of sight. 'Listen, don't say I said so, and get me into trouble, but it's the greatest thing for cleaning glass.'

Jack would have enjoyed that.

21

Around this time, articles featuring Amanda began to appear in the fan magazines. She was referred to as 'the latest up-and-coming British import' and romantically linked with a number of young studs. The studio publicity department had lost no time in making her over and the glamour shots that accompanied the articles showed a harder Amanda, indistinguishable from a dozen other starlets.

Since I was no longer required to be at the studio every day, I spent the mornings working on a new novel and the afternoons painting the weathered clapboard exterior. At least once a week I pestered Arnold, and when I managed to get him on the phone, he invariably gave me the standard agent reply: 'I'm working on it, but things are quiet at the moment.' What he really meant was he didn't have a clue – if you read the trades, things were anything but quiet, every studio was humming with activity. I suppose, in my heart, I had fondly imagined that, having turned in a screenplay for MGM, producers would be beating a path to my door. Random House wrote to say my novel was being reissued and, after some prodding from me, Arnold (or more likely Lucy) renegotiated my old contract with them on the strength of the forthcoming film and got me a modest, additional advance. I was happy and relaxed with Tracey, but there was something missing from my life that I couldn't put my finger on. I seemed to be in limbo.

Every so often, and always when Tracey was out of the

house, I would take Jack's screenplay out of hiding and reread it. The more I studied it the more I realised what a long way I had to go before I was in his league. It was so sparse, and yet so rich, each scene ending with a cliffhanger. I remembered what he had said to me the last time I saw him in hospital, about saving it as a nest egg for his old age. That choked me. It's funny how some people, even on short acquaintance, burn themselves into your consciousness. I often dreamed about him and we were always laughing together in the dreams. Once I typed a new title page and put my own name on it to see how it would look, but I gave myself immediate guilt, and destroyed it.

After a few weeks of pure domesticity Tracey and I both decided we deserved an outing. The spectre of Brodky had receded and she seemed to have got over her fear that, even in a place as vast as LA, she would somehow come face to face with him on the street. We drove into Westwood to have a meal and take in a movie, choosing *High Noon*.

I've always liked good Westerns and Tracey had a crush on Cooper. On leaving the theatre at the end, whom should we bump into, but the great Woody.

'How come I didn't get a Christmas card from you?' was his opening line. 'Boy, how soon they forget.' He switched on his smile to Tracey. 'Hi, I'm Woody, the one who made your boyfriend into a star, as I'm sure he's told you.'

Tracey looked to me for help.

'This is Tracey.'

He gave Tracey a searching, up-and-down look that practically undressed her. Since our last meeting he had changed his entire appearance. Gone were the Brooks Bros button-down Oxfords and neatly pressed slacks; now he sported the crumpled, campus-casual look, with a crew cut to go with it.

'Hey, Robert, I hear great things about you.'

'You do? That's more than I do.'

'Yeah, it's all over town that you're the next Charlie Brackett. Just kidding. I haven't heard a thing about you, thought you'd jacked it in and gone back East. Want to go eat?'

'We've eaten,' I said.

'So come and have a coffee with me. Or don't you mix with success any more?'

Without further ado he linked arms with Tracey and propelled her along the pavement. I caught up with them, feeling I had lost control of the situation. He led the way to a noisy, late-night eatery, most of the tables occupied by groups of kids from UCLA.

'So what d'you do, Tracey?'

'She lives with me,' I said.

'How come she got so unlucky?'

I could see that Tracey was bewildered by his wisecracks.

'Woody gave me my first break,' I explained. 'I worked on a script for him. What happened to it, Woody? Did it ever get anywhere?'

Woody removed the top half of his bun and smothered the burger with ketchup. 'Yeah, it got somewhere. The toilet. Boy, was that a near thing! It was touch and go for a while that they might actually ask me to make it. See Tracey, what I tried to teach this innocent was that you have to massage the studios if you're ever going to stay ahead of the game. It's like blackjack, you haven't got a prayer unless you learned to count the deck before they start dealing.'

I could see that it was all double talk to her and I quickly turned the conversation to his own career. 'So what're you up to now?'

'I've got a real sweetheart of a thing going out at Universal,' he answered. 'Big things are on the way.' The casual way he said it made me think he was lying – a splash of his old chutzpah.

'That's great.'

'Yeah. Can't say more now, but wait until you read about it. And what's with you?'

'Well, I got my Guild card finally and wrote a screenplay for MGM. From my own novel.'

'And?'

'I'm waiting to hear.'

'Who'd you write it for?'

'Billy Fisher.'

Woody nodded. 'I've heard of him.' He wiped the ketchup off his lips with a paper napkin. 'Now where have I heard of him? Oh, I know. He was escorting that new British chick at a party the other night.'

The last thing I wanted was for Amanda to come into the conversation and I headed him off. 'Listen, Woody, you know everybody. Can you suggest an agent who might take me on? I'm getting nowhere with Kosner.'

'You and fifty others. He's the kiss of death. Look, now we've met up again, let's keep in touch. Give me your number.'

He scribbled it down in his pocket diary, using a gold pen. 'That's Malibu?'

'Not Malibu itself, not actually on the beach, but close enough.'

'You mean, you can see the sea if you stand on a ladder. I'll come visit.' He called for the check. On the way out he whispered to me, 'Does your girlfriend ever talk?'

'She's shy,' I said, 'and she's not in our business.'

Driving home Tracey said: 'Are they all like that?'

'Who?'

'The people you work with.'

'Woody's OK, he's just full of himself. He was showing off for you.'

'You changed while you were with him.'

'Changed? What way?'

'You talked differently. I hated how he put you down all the time.'

'He wasn't being serious. He likes me.'

'Funny way of showing it. What does he do?'

'He's a producer, he makes movies.'

'What has he made?'

'I can't think offhand, but he's a major player.'

'Now you're talking like that again. Different.'

'Don't be stupid.'

'Well, you want my take on him? He's a phoney and I wouldn't trust him.'

'When I want your opinion of my friends, I'll ask for it. How can you judge somebody after meeting them for the first time?'

'I can.'

'Like you judged Brodky I suppose?'

'You don't know the circumstances.'

'Oh, that's right, yeah. You were desperate to get out of Kansas. That warped your infallible judgement.'

'I don't know what "infallible" means.'

'Put it this way, you could be wrong about Woody.'

We were skirting the perimeter of a row, and I couldn't think why I was defending Woody so vehemently to her. He had put me down in front of her and she was right about the way in which I had quickly slipped back into the flip way of talking that most people affected around the studios.

'Listen,' I said, 'don't let's fall out over Woody. You don't have to like him, but I owe him. He gave me a break when I needed one.'

We drove the rest of the way home in silence and that night was one of the few times since we had moved in when we didn't make love. I slept badly, drifting in and out of a weird dream in which Woody kept taking off a mask, revealing Billy's face underneath. I woke early with the ominous feeling something was about to happen. Tracey was still asleep. I made coffee and sat out on the deck, listening to the plaintive repetition of doves calling and answering each other, while I took stock of my life. Both the dream and the minor disagreement Tracey and I had had over Woody stayed with me. Were her instincts, coming as they did out of loyalty to me, better than my own? There were so many thoughts jumbled up in my head like tangled wires connected to nowhere. A few weeks back things had seemed so clear-cut, everything coming right – the script, the fact that I was suddenly rich, moving into the house, having a calm love life. Now doubts had begun to surface.

I suddenly felt Tracey's arms go around me from behind and she kissed the top of my head.

'What time is it?' she said.

'I don't know. I haven't got a watch on.'

'Why you sitting out here?'

'I didn't sleep too well.'

'I'm sorry about last night. That guy just riled me, I guess.'

'Forget it. It's over.'

'Want me to fix some breakfast?'

After a stack of her pancakes I stopped feeling sorry for myself, took a long shower and went to work on the new novel. It was set in New York, a comedy thriller, totally different from my first, and going reasonably well. On an impulse I typed up a four-page synopsis of the plot, with the idea of rousing Arnold to try and place it. Jack had always said that story editors only had a four-page concentration span. I was quite pleased with the result, but on second thoughts I felt I ought to show it to Billy ahead of Arnold. He might feel hurt if it was submitted by an agent. When I judged he would be up and about, I put in a call to him.

'Billy? Robert. Thought I'd give you a call because I'm

quite excited about what I'm writing now and I wanted you to have first look. Not the whole thing, just a four-page plot outline.'

'Yes, fine, Robert. Post it to the office.'

'I could bring it over now, if you like.'

'I'm busy right now.'

'OK, fine. Hope you like it. Any news on the script?'

'Yes and no.' There was a pause and I sensed he had put his hand over the mouthpiece.

'What does "yes and no" mean?'

'They're definitely going ahead, but they feel they ought to put another writer on it for the final draft.'

I thought I'd misheard him at first. 'You haven't agreed, have you?'

'It's the way the studio likes to operate.'

'But you told me you had the last word, that you always ignore their comments.'

'In this case they made a certain amount of sense.'

'Weren't you happy with my version?'

'Yes, as far as it went, but I can't ignore them completely. They're putting up three million, they're entitled to have some say.'

'That isn't what you said before. Why have you changed your mind?'

'I haven't changed my mind.'

'Then why didn't you tell them I'll do the rewrites? After all, it's my novel.'

'They felt you'd gone as far as you could. You have to remember that you're not a name yet.'

'I know that, you don't have to remind me, but this was my big break. This was how I was going to make a name. I just don't understand why you didn't fight for me. You always said you don't give a fuck about their opinions, that you always go your own way with your own money.'

'Robert, you got paid with my money, plus some extra.'

'I know that. I know I got paid and I'm grateful, very grateful, but that's not what I'm talking about. It's my script, for Chrissake. I'm not looking for any more money, I'd do the rewrites for nothing.' I was dealing with it in the wrong way, but I couldn't help myself. 'How could you do this to me?'

'Do what to you? I wasn't aware I'd done anything to you except give you a chance. Well, you've had your chance and now it's somebody else's turn.'

'Billy, please listen, you don't know how important this is to me.'

'We'll talk about it later when we meet.'

'When? I can meet you any time. Can we meet today?'

'No, I'm busy today. I'll call you. Now excuse me, I have to take an overseas call.' He hung up.

I was in shock. Too shattered to explain anything to Tracey, I got straight in the car, determined to beard Arnold even if it meant sitting in Lucy's office all day. Amazingly, he was in and had nobody with him.

'Such things happen, Robert,' he said, in a matter-of-fact way, chewing on his toothpick. 'But I thought this Fisher character was a close friend of yours.'

'So did I. That's what I can't understand. Didn't you like what I've done so far?'

'I haven't got around to it yet. I'm sure it's very good,' he continued blandly. 'Did they assign a director yet?'

'I don't know.'

'Could be that whoever's directing it sees it differently. Or maybe he's a conglomerate. There are more and more of those.'

'Conglomerate?'

'Writer director. There are lots of reasons why. Could be that the star has asked for changes. It's a hard pill to swallow, I agree, and I sympathise, but they always have the last word.'

254

'Can't you go in there and fight for me?' I fired my bitterness across his desk like shotgun pellets. 'That's your job, isn't it? Can't you go over Fisher's head and protest to Schary?'

'Robert, part of my job is to stop you making enemies. You're just beginning. It won't further your career to get known as a troublemaker. You signed the contract and if you read the fine print you'll see they can ride roughshod over you any way they wish. It's the way of the world, Robert. The world we have to live in.'

'So, you're saying there's nothing I can do? What if they cheat me out of a credit?'

'You'll always get a credit for your novel.'

'That isn't the point.'

'But it's better than nothing. Wait and see. Early days yet.'

I paced his office, chain-smoking, and he reached for a room spray and gave it a prolonged burst, but nothing I said persuaded him to fight my corner. It wasn't until a week later that I discovered that another of his writers, who got treble my weekly rate, had been assigned to the rewrite and that he had done the deal the very morning he and I met.

When I poured out the story to Tracey, she tried to understand but the situation was beyond her comprehension. That night I got swirling drunk and Tracey had to put me to bed. The last thing I remember saying was 'he probably is a faggot at that. Only a faggot would do that to a guy', before I blacked out. I slept until gone noon the next day and staggered up to find the house empty. There was a note stuck to the fridge door: *Gone to get my hair done. Hope you feel better. Love T.*

I was glad she wasn't there to witness my returning rage. Disappointment had been transmuted into hate during the night and I wandered around the house, knocking into furniture, talking and cursing to myself. It took a cold shower and two cups of black coffee before the tightness in my chest eased off. The more I thought about it the more I realised the truth of what Jack had tried to drum into me. You had to screw them before they screwed you.

It was thoughts of Jack that gave me the answer. Dying, he had provided me with the means to get even with the lot of them. Why continue to be Mr Nice Guy?

I took Jack's script from its hiding place and tore off the title page. Then I sat down at my typewriter and fed in a sheet of blank paper. On it I typed: *THE END OF THE BEGINNING. An Original Screenplay by Robert Peterson. Copyright.*

And this time, I didn't feel any guilt.

22

I spent that afternoon mapping out what I intended to do and in what order. Before Tracey returned, I had half a dozen copies of Jack's screenplay Mimeographed with my new title page inserted. Back in the house I searched for and found the business card of the agent who was fond of flashing his cock at strangers, the one Billy had warned me to steer clear of. I rang his direct line.

'Mr Sugarman?' I said.

'Ye-ees. Who is this?' His voice was guarded.

'Well, you probably don't remember me, but we met with Billy Fisher once and you were kind enough to give me your private number.'

'Stroke my memory.'

'Robert Peterson. I'd written a novel which you kindly said you'd take time to read.'

'Robert! Of course. The good-looking one. How could I not remember you? And I kept my word and read your novel. I thought it was just wonderful. I can't believe you're old enough to have all that talent, and to know all about the dark side of life. I've been ringing your number to tell you so, but it's disconnected.'

'I moved,' I said.

'Naughty of you not to tell me. But I'm so thrilled you've called me now. So, what's with you?'

'I wondered if you'd have time to see me.'

'Just name the day.'

'Can you make tomorrow? Is that convenient?'

'Let me just look in the little black book . . . or the large black book, shall we say? . . . Well, tomorrow I was meant to have a breakfast with Anna May Wong, but I can move her to later.'

'Please. Don't cancel her for me.'

'Just teasing. He's just a Chinese waiter I met the other night. You'll probably be saving me from a fate worse than death. So, shall we say breakfast tomorrow? Eight o'clock in the Polo Lounge?'

'Eight o'clock. Right. Well, thanks a lot, Mr Sugarman.'

'We're not going to be that formal, are we? I give you full permission to call me Julian. I'm s-oo pleased you got in touch. I thought you'd gone out of my life for ever.'

It only occurred to me afterwards that had he really wanted to find me again all he had needed to do was ring Billy. Breakfast seemed safe. I'd been worried that he'd ask me to dinner. I was doing the seducing this time and I wanted it to be on neutral ground.

I resolutely didn't have a drink that night and made sure I set the alarm clock when I went to bed. Not being sure how one had to dress for breakfast at the Beverly Hills Hotel, I didn't risk anything, but put on a collar and tie. Taking a copy of Jack's screenplay with me, I arrived promptly. The room was crowded, but Julian was already waiting for me at a corner table with my novel in front of him.

'You look great,' he said with a little too much enthusiasm for that time of the morning. 'And, listen, don't you dare leave without signing this for me.'

He nudged my novel across the table. It was so clean it didn't look as though it had ever been opened.

'Now, what're you going to eat, a growing boy like you?'

Coffee and iced water had already been placed in front of me. 'I'll take some eggs and juice if I may.'

'You certainly may.'

He ordered berries and Sanka for himself. 'Have to watch the figure. That doesn't bother you, of course. Well, I'm all ears to hear your news, tell me everything.'

'I've written an original screenplay,' I said, going for the kill right away, 'which if you think it's any good, I'd like you to handle for me.'

I detected a hint of disappointment flicker across his face.

'Do you have representation at the moment?'

'Well, I'm not signed, but as I think I told you, Arnold Kosner has been fronting for me ... when he's in the country, that is.'

'Yes, I've always thought he ought to come to work with a backpack. Have you met the latest Mrs Kosner?'

'Once.'

'Once is too often, I'm told. Poor Arnold, he was very good in his day, but somebody like you should be with a major office like ours. Well, I'd be happy to read your screenplay, Robert. I'm flattered.' He took a mouthful of berries and stared me straight in the eyes. 'Is that the only reason you called me?'

'The main reason, yes,' I said, hoping I wasn't pushing my luck.

'Does Arnold know you're thinking of moving?'

'No, not yet.'

'Well, that's fine then. How about our friend, Billy? Are you still seeing him?'

'Not as often as before.'

'And how is he?'

'He's busy over at M G M.' I didn't mention the fate of my screenplay and much to my relief he didn't enquire.

'I've got great respect for Billy but the trouble is, and don't repeat me, he's rather a one-man band and has never really fitted in here. Gives a lot of people the impression that he thinks he's too good for us. Rather flaunts his money. To get anywhere in this town you have to stay put, not come and go as he does, and play the game according to the rules. The Brits do make some lovely films from time to time, but of course they're not mainstream.'

I listened while he chipped away at Billy until little was left and I realised the truth of Billy's warning. Julian Sugarman was definitely not somebody to get on the wrong side of. He sprinkled lethal fairy dust over half a dozen reputations during the course of that breakfast, always with the throwaway technique that malicious queens have made their own. I got more and more apprehensive, wondering what the hell I had let myself in for, but the die had been cast and I knew I needed him if my plan was to work. Prior to parting company with Arnold, I had to be sure I had another home to go to.

I signed his copy of my novel before we got up, and gave him my new telephone number.

'You can expect to hear from me very soon,' he said. 'I'm really excited about what we can do together. You've made a wise choice. Oh, Julian, that sounds very conceited. What I meant was, I've got a feeling about you. I can always discern talent and you've got talent written all over you. Plus you're very humpable.'

I pretended I hadn't heard that. Outside, while we waited for our cars to be brought up from the parking lot, he gave my arm a parting squeeze. 'This is the beginning of something beautiful, Robert. We're going to make wonderful music together.'

Those daunting words stayed with me for the next twenty-four hours. I hadn't really expected him to get back so quickly, even given his ulterior motives, because whatever else he was, he was smart, but he rang me the following evening.

'It's brilliant,' he said the moment I picked up the phone. 'And I'm levelling with you because I want our relationship to be squeaky clean from the beginning. We're going to have no secrets between us. I'll always tell it straight, and I have to admit my heart sank a little when you gave me your script. I was afraid I might not like it and have to be polite. But forget that! Your script is something else. I'll go so far as to say I haven't read anything as good in the last five years. Where have you been hiding? You asked, will I handle you? Robert, I'm down on my knees. If you don't come with me I may kill myself and think what a loss that would be to mankind.'

'You really think it's OK, do you?'

'Robert, sweetheart, don't give me modesty. You know it's terrific. I can't tell you how excited I am. Has it been anywhere?'

'No, you're the first to see it.'

'Perfect! Because I know exactly where I'm going to take it. You're going to be a very happy boy by the time I'm through. To say nothing of a very rich boy. Now then, sweetheart, we just have to do things in the right order. Can you come into the office first thing tomorrow and sign the papers? See, I can't represent you until you've done that. Tell me again, you haven't shown this to Arnold and you're not signed with him?'

'No, it was just a gentleman's agreement. I didn't have a Guild card when he took me on. I do now.'

'Has this been registered with the Guild?'

'No.'

'Well, we'll take care of that too. And after you've signed you can let Arnold know.'

'Right.'

'Are you happy? I'm happy. I'm delirious.'

'Yes, I'm very happy.'

'See you in the morning then. And keep lunch free. We'll celebrate.'

'What's happened?' Tracey asked as I hung up.

261

'I just got myself a new agent at William Morris.'

'Is that good?'

'Not just good. Sensational.'

I danced her out on to the patio. 'You ever done it out in the open under the moon?'

'No, but you could persuade me.'

'Let's pull the mattress out here.' We fetched the mattress and a blanket. 'I like it when you get a new agent,' Tracey said, straddling me, which was her favourite position.

All the time we made love leaves fell on us from the white-barked eucalyptus tree that stood in the adjacent lot and overhung our deck. In the lazy aftermath I caught one as it drifted down, crushed it and held it under her nose. 'Know what that reminds me of? Whenever I got a cold as a kid my mother would put a few drops of eucalyptus oil in a basin of boiling water, put a towel over my head and make me inhale. Were you ever made to do that?'

'No.'

We lay on our backs, the blanket over us, sharing a cigarette, watching the winking lights of planes as they climbed out to sea.

'You ever been in a plane?' Tracey said.

'Nope. When I first came to LA I scraped together just enough cash for the train fare. You?'

'Once. Brodky brought me out here on one.'

'You're not still worried about him, are you?'

She took the cigarette out of my mouth. 'Not really. Sometimes maybe, when you're not here. Then, yesterday, when I came out of the hair salon I thought I saw him. I ducked back inside and stayed in their john until somebody banged on the door.'

I put an arm around her and stroked her neck. 'Why didn't you tell me?'

'Well, I thought you'd say I was being stupid. I just get freaked out every now and again.'

'Chances are it wasn't him anyway.'

'Yeah.' She was quiet for a while, then she said, 'You think you and me will make it?'

'Haven't we just made it?'

'I didn't mean that. I meant, you know, get it all together, really together?'

'I thought we had already. You can't get more together than this. What else did you mean?'

'Nothing.'

I knew what she was getting at, but I couldn't bring myself to say what she wanted to hear. I was just beginning to understand the vast reservoirs of doubt and insecurity that lurk beneath the surface of young girls like Tracey, small-town girls who think of the gold ring on their finger as the ultimate prize. They read the sort of magazines that push the Camelot of marriage down their throats in every issue. They study the bridal gowns in mail-order catalogues, and horoscopes that only tell good news. Marriage isn't just a status symbol, it was the big escape from boredom, from trailer parks, crowded tenement blocks and blow jobs on the back seat of borrowed cars while watching Deanna Durbin in a drive-in.

'Getting chilly,' I said. 'Let's go in.'

We hauled the mattress back to the bedroom. It felt damp from the night air. My mother always told me that damp beds gave you rheumatism. That, and that playing with yourself grew hair on your palms. Perhaps she connected them both in her own mind.

Tracey fell asleep before I did. I kept myself awake thinking of my next moves.

23

Having signed the agency papers at William Morris the next morning, I asked Julian how I should go about ditching Arnold.

'Just pick up that phone and tell him.' He pushed the instrument across his desk.

'Wouldn't that be out of line, a little callous?'

'From what you told me, he's probably forgotten he still represents you.'

'I was thinking of Lucy as much as Arnold; she's always been very supportive.'

'Well, you sweet, sentimental creature, that's up to you, but don't think you have to send flowers. People change agents all the time, it's no big deal. But do it quickly, otherwise he'll read it first in the trades. Personally, I'd call him. It's so much easier to be insincere on the phone.'

I filed that remark.

'Now, we're still on for lunch, I hope? I want to show you off.' He made it sound as though I was a new rent boy. 'Before you leave here you've got to be introduced to some of the gang. You're not just acquiring little me, but a whole family.'

He went out to his outer office where his assistant, a willowy youth with a bouffant hairstyle and probably older than he looked, sat behind a piled desk.

'Brent,' he said. 'You've met Robert, our new star writer.'

'Of course. I've already welcomed him to our fun farm,' Brent replied peevishly.

'Robert will be on our A list, natch,' Julian told him. 'That means, Robert dear, that your calls are always put through. Brent can be very picky when he chooses. He has his favourites, of which you'll now be one.'

Brent gave a thin smile as though he had heard the spiel once too often. He excused himself and picked up his phone that was constantly blinking. Julian took me along the corridor where I met four or five of the other senior agents. Names were thrown at me that I promptly forgot. The contrast between the activity at William Morris and the peace that passed understanding in Arnold's office was a revelation. Finally, I was ushered into the Oval Office, as it were, to meet Abe Lastfogel, the head honcho. He was an amiable old man, very gracious, who gave me a warm welcome and he said he was greatly looking forward to reading my screenplay. 'If it's half as good as Julian says, we're off to the races,' he said.

When I left I stood outside the Morris building on El Camino in a daze. Everywhere looked different suddenly. Collecting my car I decided that the advice Julian had given me about Arnold was sensible: I would get it over quickly. I headed for his office.

Arnold wasn't in, of course. He was having a fitting for a new suit.

'Want to leave a message?' Lucy asked.

'What's his diary like for tonight?'

'Tonight?'

'Yes, is he free for dinner? I have something I have to discuss urgently and I thought it would be a nice gesture if I took him out for once, seeing as I'm in the money.'

'Well, that's a nice thought, Robert. I'm sure he'd appreciate it.' She consulted the diary. 'Yes, he is free, as it happens, because Mrs Kosner is in their Lake Tahoe house, remodelling.'

'Herself or the house?'

'Now, don't be naughty, we mustn't speak ill of the boss's wife,' but she smiled as she said it. 'Let me ask him when he comes in. Give me a ring after lunch. You sure you don't want to tell me what it's about?'

'It's personal,' I said, too abruptly as I immediately realised. I saw from the way her mouth tightened that she was offended that I wouldn't confide in her.

Julian had lunch served in a cabana at the Beverly Hills pool and his first words to me as we sat down had been: 'Have you done the deed?'

'I tried, but he wasn't in the office. I'll try again later.'

Julian raised his glass to me. He had ordered the latest fad, a Bullshot – a mixture of beef consomme and vodka – which I had tried once and found nauseating. I stuck to Scotch. 'So, here's to the start of the beginning. Everybody loves your title. It's got box office written all over it. You are a clever boots.'

'Who're you going to send it to?'

'Already sent. Yours truly doesn't let the turf grow under his tiny trotters. I had it biked over to Fox this morning. It's gone to Zanuck.'

'Zanuck? You mean Zanuck himself?'

'Darling boy, you don't shop at Macy's when you've got credit at Cartier's. I know, I just know that Darryl will flip over it. It's so much his cup of tea and Fox are desperate to find another vehicle for Peck. Unlike some, Darryl actually reads. I'll tell you who was livid he didn't get first look at it.'

'Who?'

'Our mutual friend Billy. I rang him after you left this morning and told him the good news, thinking he'd be pleased for you. But no, very put out. Said that he was surprised you'd come up with a good script because the one you'd done for him was third rate. I thought I'd tell you, because it's always useful to know who's badmouthing you, and as I said there's going to be no secrets between you and me. Not that he matters in the least. You've kissed Billy Fisher's ass for the last time, so don't let it depress you.'

'I'm glad you told me.'

'*En passant*, did he ever make a play for you?'

'No, and I never kissed his ass, either.'

'I was speaking metaphorically – wouldn't wish that on you. Just wondered. I expect Oliver keeps him on a tight rein.'

'I don't think they're a twosome.'

'Really? Such a handsome creature, Oliver. But cold. Judith Anderson in *Rebecca*,' he added. 'What's your type, Robert? Who turns you on?'

'Depends.'

'Are you spoken for at the moment?'

'I live with somebody, yes.'

'Are we to be given a name?'

'You wouldn't know her. She's not in the business.' I knew I was being sounded out and already I'd cottoned on that, in Julian's circle, 'her' could be ambiguous. I just hoped that his enthusiasm for Jack's screenplay would be enough to keep him at arm's length.

'Do you look after yourself?'

'Look after myself? In what way?'

'Go to a gym?'

'Not since I got here. I used to play a lot of football at college.'

'Well, you've got a gorgeous figure, you should take care of it. I'll take you along to my health club one night.'

He was a cautious queen, probing me slowly. For the rest of the meal he talked about the plans he had for me, which made more pleasant listening.

I rang Lucy from the hotel lobby when Julian and I parted. She was somewhat frosty still, but said that Arnold was happy to have an early dinner and that she would make a booking in my name for six thirty at Roland's Bistro on Little Santa Monica since Mr Kosner preferred to eat early and Italian. I then rang Tracey to say I wouldn't be home until late and passed the rest of the afternoon looking around bookshops.

Although I had prepared my resignation speech, I didn't launch into it immediately. In any case, Arnold was keen to monopolise the conversation in his usual pedantic way, relating the entire itinerary of their next trip abroad. 'You know all about the Galapagos Islands, of course?'

'Vaguely, yes. I mean, I've heard of them.'

'We thought it would be a complete change from our usual excursions. We've done Europe and Africa to death and this was Eleanor's idea. She's got such a keen spirit of adventure. Normally they don't encourage visitors, but she has friends in Washington who pulled strings with the Ecuador Ambassador and obtained the necessary permissions. Which reminds me,' he added inconsequentially, taking out his pocket diary and making an entry, 'I must arrange to get our shots, we always like to be on the safe side. We don't even trust the water at Claridge's, and apparently the islands are infested with mosquitoes. We shall take protective clothing, of course. What was I saying?'

'Your wife's spirit of adventure.'

'Yes, she's like an inquisitive child when it comes to travelling. Never lost her innocence. I've been reading up about the islands. You know where they get their name, don't you? It's the Spanish word for tortoise. According to the early explorers some of the tortoises weighed as much as six hundred pounds and were strong enough to carry a man.'

'Really?'

'He first thought of the idea there, I believe.'

'Who was that?'

'Darwin. *Origin of Species*.'

'Ah? I didn't know that.'

He elaborated on Darwin throughout the main course and I found myself speculating by what process of natural selection Eleanor Kosner had evolved. It wasn't until we had coffee that I was able to broach the reason for my invite.

'Well, I certainly hope your trip proves a great success. How long will you be away?'

'A month to five weeks. But, of course Lucy will be minding the store as usual.'

'Yes. Lucy's a real treasure . . . Arnold, nothing to do with you going on your trip, don't think that, but for some time now I've been thinking that perhaps I ought to move on.'

'I thought you'd only just moved.'

'Not move house again . . . It's just that I'm very conscious that I haven't really earned you a great deal of commission.'

I fumbled to light a cigarette and Arnold took out a toothpick and chewed reflectively. 'Early days, early days,' he said.

'As you know I was very disappointed at the way the MGM assignment ended, and what with that and the fact there doesn't seem to be anything else on the horizon, perhaps I ought to, you know, look around and try my luck elsewhere.'

He stopped chewing. 'Elsewhere?'

'Yes.'

'Another studio?'

'No, another agent.' I finally got it out on the table. He snapped the toothpick and his eyes looked past me as though wishing to signal for the check, until he remembered he wasn't paying for the meal. 'Well, Robert, it's your life and your career. You must do what you think is best.'

'Don't think I'm not grateful to you for getting me started. I shall always be grateful for that.'

He shot his cuffs back to expose his wristwatch. 'Will you, Robert, will you? Perhaps Eleanor was right about you. She usually is. She couldn't understand why I took you on. Thought you sadly lacking in style. Now you've proved her right. Goodness, look at the time. I have to get back for her call.'

'Of course. I'll get the check. At least I've got the style for that,' I said, getting in one for myself. I paid hurriedly because he was already standing up and ready to depart. There was a Charlie Chaplin impersonator doing his act outside the restaurant. Arnold studiously ignored him until his Cadillac was brought. He tipped the valet, then said: 'Well, *bon voyage* to both of us, Robert.' And that was that.

It hadn't been easy, but on the other hand it hadn't been as bad as I expected. I gave Charlie Chaplin a ten-dollar bill before driving off, rather as a thanks offering for prayers being answered than appreciation of his talents.

24

The moment I arrived home Tracey thrust a Western Union envelope at me. 'This came for you. I never saw one of those before, so I opened it in case it was bad news.'

'And was it?'

She shrugged and pulled a face. 'You tell me. Seems like somebody's pissed off with you.'

The telegram was from Billy. ONE NEVER EXPECTS LOYALTY ESPECIALLY FROM THE UNTALENTED BUT YOU HAVE ESTABLISHED A NEW LOW STOP REST ASSURED YOUR BEHAVIOR WILL NOT GO UNNOTICED AMONGST PEOPLE WHO MATTER IN THIS TOWN STOP I WILL SEE TO THAT. WILLIAM FISHER.

'What the hell did you do to him?'

'Pissed him off, like you said.'

'But why?'

'Too complicated to explain. Don't worry about it.'

'I don't understand the business you're in. That guy sounds dangerous, like another Brodky.'

'No way.'

I wasn't going to admit it to Tracey, but the venom in Billy's telegram had shaken me. It was a reaction I hadn't expected because, still smarting from the way in which he had allowed my screenplay to be turned over to another writer, I had thought of myself as the aggrieved party.

In the weeks to come he made good his promise to bad-mouth me: unflattering snippets started to appear in the gossip columns which I was sure he had placed through his friend, the poisonous Dolly. It was the usual stuff – *Respected British producer, Billy Fisher, has parted company with would-be screenwriter, Bob Peterson. Apparently Bob couldn't cut the mustard.* And *A little bird tells me that the fire has gone out between the beautiful and talented Amanda Boyd and fledgling scriptwriter Bob Peterson. On a winning streak herself, Amanda has wisely called it a day.*

I went to Julian for advice on how to handle it, but he shrugged it off. Julian's philosophy was that nothing mattered as long as they spelled your name correctly. He did get me an interview with Army Archard in the *Reporter*, which evened the score a little, and I accepted that his approach was probably best.

Woody picked up on it, of course; gossip items were his staple diet.

'Who's your press agent?' he asked when he rang. 'I want to make sure I never hire him.'

'Oh, very funny.'

'Listen, buddy, who gives a shit what any of those leeches write? But, between you and me, did you really get blown out of that fancy M G M deal?'

'Yes. I crossed that British producer.' Some inner voice cautioned me not to mention the screenplay Julian had sent to Fox. I was learning.

'Too bad. You and your girl want to have a meal? Make up a foursome?'

I hesitated, remembering how Tracey had taken against him the first time. On the other hand we couldn't live like hermits for ever, nor could I exclude her from everything I wanted to do.

'Yeah, sure, when?'

'Let's make a day of it, Sunday. Have a late brunch, take in a movie maybe, then come back to my pad and I'll have my guy cook Chinese.'

'Sounds good. You still at the same address?'

'No, let me give you the new one. After the last fire I decided to quit the canyons. It jumped my house, but we got scorched, too close for comfort. I've taken a place on the flats, on Roxbury, the right side of the tracks, very elegant, used to be owned by Rosemary Clooney.'

Tracey took some persuading, but I finally convinced her that first impressions of Woody weren't the whole story. 'OK, he's smart and he knows it,' I said. 'You have to be smart in this town to stay ahead, I'm slowly finding that out. But he grows on you, promise.'

'You said that about the other guy, the one who sent you that goodbye telegram.'

'Yeah, OK, I admit, sometimes I'm too trusting. We don't choose our enemies, they creep up on us.'

'So who's to say this Woody guy won't do you down?'

'He's different. He's not employing me.'

'Is he Jewish?'

'Yes, but so what?'

'My father never had a good word to say for them.'

'From what you've told me, your father didn't have a good word to say for anybody. I'm amazed he wasn't in the Klan. Maybe he was. Was he?'

'No.'

'Just an old-fashioned American patriot, eh? The sort that made our country great.'

'You don't have to be so sarcastic.'

'Oh, sorry. I got the impression that you hated your family.'

'No, just the place where they live.'

'My mistake.' Storm clouds were gathering and I decided to cool it. 'You'll probably enjoy it when you get there. We'll have some drinks and food, see his new house.'

'Well, OK, if it's that important to you,' she said with a pout. 'But being around smart people makes me feel what I am, stupid.'

'You're not stupid.'

'I don't have anything to say. I'm not educated like you.'

'You don't have to be educated to talk to people like Woody.'

'Yes, you do. You have to know what they're saying if you want to join in.' Then she surprised me by adding: 'Will you test me?'

'Test you?'

'Yes. I've been reading that *Time* magazine you buy. To find out things.'

I was about to laugh, but then saw she was serious. There was something infinitely touching about her need to make something of herself, but at the same time it scared me. I didn't want the responsibility of her life. The truth was I knew in my heart that she was right, she didn't belong, she would never fit into Woody's crowd, and part of me knew I was forcing her towards another kind of corruption, a world that was always going to be alien. Meeting me, she had exchanged the trailer park for the Beverly Hills Deer Park. She wasn't driven by my ambitions and I should have taken that into account. But the progression of small incidents that erode a love affair – the worms that lurk inside the meat of a seemingly perfect apple – are never totally apparent at the time, it is only later, all too late, that we realise when we said the wrong things, took the wrong turnings. That night in bed she made me question her on the articles she had read in *Time*, a pathetic exercise that I humoured. I didn't have the heart to tell her that I doubted whether Woody and company would use their quality leisure time analysing the Korean War or the latest outbreak of cholera in India.

Halfway through the week I had a call from Julian. 'Tell me I'm a genius,' he began.

'You're a genius.'

'Are you sitting down? I knew I was right about Zanuck. Fox have made an offer.'

'A good one?'

'Not good enough, sweetie, but Julian's working on it. You don't know me when I'm squeezing somebody's balls. I'm taking a meeting with Schneider tomorrow.'

'Schneider?'

'I forget you don't know anybody. VP in charge of business affairs. Walks with a tight ass, and has zip fasteners on his wallet, but I can handle him. I shall ask for twice what they've put on the table and when he's done screaming, he'll settle somewhere in the middle.'

'How much will that be?'

'Enough to make us both very happy, baby. Listen, while I've got you in a good mood, how about our date? What're you doing today? I thought perhaps we could take a steam in the health club, then sit around the pool in my cabana this weekend.'

'Why didn't you ask sooner? I'd have loved to, but I've already fixed to hang out with an old friend.'

'Put him off, I'd be much more fun.'

'I would, but he's only in town over the weekend,' I lied.

'I'm devastated. I was saving myself for you.'

I was doing my best to keep him sweet until the Fox deal was struck and set, but Julian took no prisoners. 'OK, I'll dry my tears, but you have to save next weekend for me. It's going to be party time.'

'You're on.' I sensed he was going to extract a price beyond his ten per cent.

Sunday brunch at a trendy restaurant with Woody and his latest girlfriend, who went under the improbable name of Haze Lamont, passed off without incident. Woody was on his best behaviour, no cracks at my expense and nothing that got up Tracey's nose. In fact, after the ice was broken, I could see that she actually began to enjoy herself and at one point she plucked up enough courage – airing her *Time* magazine studies – to ask Woody whether he thought the economy was showing signs of recovery, a conversation stopper that had Woody floundering for a moment. As for Haze, the immediate comparison that sprang to mind was a Varga illustration: platinum blonde, with a cupid-bow mouth and a pert little nose, an unreal plateau of a bosom that threatened to burst out of her halter-top, she sank three mimosas in quick succession, spoke in a hushed, little-girl voice and giggled a lot. Woody seemed to find her amusing, so I guessed their relationship was at the exploratory stage. After brunch we took in the first showing at a movie house – *The Cruel Sea*, a British import that had been garnering good reviews. Woody and I enjoyed it, but the two girls complained they couldn't understand the accents.

'Do they all talk like that over there?' Haze asked.

'Yeah, they speak a foreign language. English,' Woody said.

Then we drove to his new residence on Roxbury where all the houses represented serious money. They were custom-built in styles varying from Mexican to New Englandish and looked as though they had been painted that day. Woody's was all pale pink brick and leaded windows, with a white picket fence and bougainvillaea climbing up the front – a picture-book illustration of the good life. The moment we stepped inside I realised he hadn't been exaggerating. It was chic in spades: a sunken den with a pool table and wet bar, a full-sized tennis court and a sculptured swimming pool that began inside the house and flowed out into the back lot under a vast picture window that slid upwards at the touch of a switch. The rest of the house, which Woody couldn't wait to show us, was on the same lavish scale – a master bedroom and en suite tub large enough for de Mille to shoot a Roman orgy in. Haze bounced on the bed.

'Once tested, never forgotten,' Woody said with a look to me.

Other guests started to arrive, a motley collection, half a dozen young girls – foxy, tanned girls with great legs, the sort that are bred to be cheer leaders. Their escorts were older, some of them middle-aged, but all aggressively sure of themselves. They seemed immediately at home and, unlike Tracey and me, took the opulence for granted. I'd been brought up that you were asked before you helped yourself to a drink, but the new arrivals went straight to the bar and filled their glasses from the varied array of bottles. Anxious not to be taken for a rube, I followed suit and mixed a couple of highballs for Tracey and me.

'So where's the action gonna be, in the pool I hope,' was the opening gambit of the first man who spoke to me. He was wearing an open-necked silk shirt under a double-breasted blazer with gold buttons and a fake crest on the pocket, completing the picture with monogrammed loafers. 'I'm Don,' he said sticking out a mammoth paw. He reeked of cologne and had a gold chain around his neck dangling in a forest of chest hair.

'Bob,' I said.

'Hey, good to meet you, Bob.' He was looking past me to Tracey, giving her a leer. He walked over to her. 'Where have you been hiding, babe?'

'Nowhere,' she said. 'I'm with him.'

'Don't depend on it.'

There were other names and faces like Don, self-assured jocks who weren't impressed by anything, names and faces that time has since mercifully erased, and that afternoon I was overwhelmed by their easy sophistication, which I lacked. They intimidated me by their self-assurance. The girls, too, had an air of sexual arrogance about them. Several of them immediately disappeared into the house to re-emerge topless and cavort in the pool.

'You two going in?' Woody asked me.

'We didn't bring anything.'

'I seem to remember you never have any trunks. How about you, Tracey, you want a costume?'

She looked to me for guidance. 'OK?'

'Sure, why not?'

'Robert knows me of old. I'm a branch of Saks. Come on.'

He led us into the master bedroom and produced a selection. 'Choose what fits you,' he said. 'Not since Randolph Hearst have you enjoyed such hospitality.'

'Wow!' Tracey exclaimed the moment we were alone. 'Look at all this gear.' She picked up a leopard-print costume and held it in front of her. 'How about this?'

'Don't get carried away.'

'What's wrong?'

'Nothing, just don't get too excited by your first taste of Beverly Hills high society.'

'Well, don't spoil it for me.'

'A few days ago you were telling me you didn't want to be around smart people.'

'Yeah, well I can change my mind, can't I?'

'And they aren't all that smart, just rich.'

She stripped off quickly. 'What's wrong with rich? Hell of a sight better than poor. Aren't you gonna get changed?'

'No rush, is there?'

'I don't want to miss any of the fun.'

'Just watch yourself.'

'What's that mean?'

'They're not your sort.'

'Oh, thanks. I'll see you out there.'

'Take the price tag off before you go. Creates a better impression.'

She stopped and tore it off. 'Don't put me down,' she said. 'I'm enjoying myself for once.' Her face had become petulant.

'I like the "for once".'

The moment she went out I began to regret ever coming there. I changed slowly, unhappy about what I saw in the mirror: I looked as though I had lived in a cave all my life, in contrast to the even tans sported by most of Woody's guests. These were the days, remember, when the good old ozone layer was intact and nobody gave a thought to skin cancers. Some of the men had frazzled themselves to the colour of mahogany. I felt like Charles Atlas before somebody kicked sand in his face.

I helped myself to another stiff drink on my way out to the pool. The first thing I saw was Tracey being held by the waist in the water by the smooth type who had introduced himself as Don. Her breasts were level with his face and before he dunked her down again he nuzzled one of them. Depression covered me like a heavy duvet. I had a sudden premonition that the bottom was about to drop out of my life again. All the aquatic revellers looked so sure and indestructible, as though Woody had rung Central Casting and asked them to supply a selection of identical types for the afternoon. While these morbid thoughts circulated I watched Tracey and Don surface at the far end of the pool. This time she wrapped her legs around his hairy midriff and he bobbed her around while kissing her neck.

Woody appeared at my side. 'Your date seems to have entered into the spirit of the occasion,' he said. 'Where did you find her?'

'In a garage.'

'OK, don't tell me if you don't want to, but watch out for our Don. She's acting like she might be ready for a trade.'

'What does our Don do?'

'Apart from helping himself to another guy's girl? He's an attorney who moves exclusively in the fast track. He also bankrolls the odd movie under the table, using some of the cash he doesn't declare.'

'Close friend of yours?'

'No. I've used him a couple of times to get me out of a hole. Listen, if you don't mind me saying so, the girlfriend seems a strange choice for you. A little on the dim side, maybe? Cute, I grant you. None of my business, but level with me, where did you really find her?'

'I told you. In a garage, crying her eyes out. Some pimp brought her to LA from Kansas to go on the game for him and when she didn't buy it, he roughed her up.'

'So, then what? Enter Robert, the Good Samaritan. Big mistake, buddy. Alley cats never make good house pets.'

'You're an authority, are you?'

'I've taken in my share of strays. You're going places, why blow it on some discard?'

'I happen to like her.'

'Why not? She's no hardship on the eyes, but maybe a touch common?'

'I never thought of you as a snob, Woody.'

'Aren't I full of surprises? Still I never gave you bad advice, did I?' He grinned. 'On the other hand, did I ever give you good advice? Just watch your back.'

When Tracey finally came out of the pool, Don dried her with a towel. Once or twice she glanced around, trying to spot me, but I had carefully put myself in a shaded area and the late sun, low in the sky, obscured me from her view. I sat there nursing my drink and my angst. Later, she disappeared back into the house to change and a short while afterwards I saw Don casually drift in the same direction.

Without wanting to be involved, I was forced into a conversation with a middle-aged man called Walter Berkovitch, who immediately confided that he had made a fortune in bowling alleys. Now he wanted to get into films as a producer.

'Woody tells me you write films.'

'Yes.'

'What have you written, anything I might have seen?'

'I doubt it.'

He had produced his visiting card, but now he put it away again and wandered off.

Tracey didn't find me until the party began to break up.

'Have fun?' I said.

'Where were you? I looked for you, but you didn't come in the pool.'

'Too much competition.' I wasn't drunk, just teetering on the edge.

She didn't say any more until we were on our way back to the beach, then she couldn't hold out any longer. 'Don's promised to help my career.'

'I didn't know you had one.'

'Well, I could have if he puts me in one of the films he finances. You should be pleased.'

'Pleased he screwed you?'

'He didn't screw me.'

'Let me rephrase that. Pleased that he's *going* to screw you. You forget, I saw your Busby Berkeley routine together in the pool.'

'I don't know what you mean.'

'Oh, sorry. My apologies. I forgot you didn't read that in *Time*. I must have got the wrong impression from my ringside seat. I got the idea you were breastfeeding him. When are you starting your new career?'

'Why're you being so mean to me?'

I swung the wheel violently and pulled into a vacant lot. 'I'm being mean? How about you? You spend the afternoon measuring his prick under water and I'm supposed to ignore it?'

'You could have joined in,' she sniffed, the tears ready to roll.

'He wasn't my type.'

'I don't understand why you're getting at me.'

'You understand what being a tramp means, though.'

'I thought if he got me a job like he said, I could help pay you back.'

'The only job he's likely to get you is another blow job.'

'I didn't give him a blow job.'

'No? You could have fooled me. God! You're so stupid.' She started to cry.

'Woody's my friend and you made me look a fucking idiot in front of him. Didn't you think of that?'

'I was just having a good time.'

'Don't I give you a good time?'

'It was a different good time. I couldn't stop him making a play for me.'

'Yeah, I noticed you put up a fight.' I started the car again and hung a right back on to the road. If I had been slightly drunk before, anger had burned most of the alcohol, but I still drove recklessly, wanting to scare her. I hadn't gone more than half a mile when I spotted blue lights flashing in my rear mirror. 'Shit!' I said, 'that's the perfect end to a shitty afternoon.' I pulled over, wound down my window, lit a cigarette and waited for the motorcycle cop to approach me. He was young and good-looking, dressed like he was auditioning for the Hitler Youth Corps.

'What's the problem, officer?'

'Step outside the car, please, sir,' he said evenly. He peered across me to Tracey and gave her a searching look.

'Can I see your licence?'

I reached for it slowly like I'd seen on the movies.

'You know why I pulled you over?'

'I've got a brake light out?'

'You were doing 55 in a 30-mile limit.'

'I was? Gee, I'm sorry. My girlfriend and I were having an argument and I must have missed the sign.'

'That was two miles back. The whole stretch is a 30 limit.

This is a Connecticut licence. How long have you been here?'

'Oh, not long, couple of months,' I lied. 'We came in to see if we wanted to settle here.'

He looked me up and down.

'This your car?'

'Yes.'

'How long have you had it?'

''Bout the same time.'

He nodded in a way that didn't suggest any belief. Then he took out his book to write the ticket. 'You outta-towners have to learn to drive by our rules. You're lucky you've got a clean licence.'

'What's the tab for speeding?'

'Well, I clocked you at 25 over the limit, that's an A1 violation. Going to set you back a hundred bucks and go down on your licence.'

I didn't want to have anything on record the Draft Board could use to track me down. Everybody had told me you don't mess with the LAPD, but I took a chance. 'Can I pay cash?'

'Can do, save you a stamp,' he said laconically.

I took out my billfold and peeled off two big ones, fanning them slightly as I held them out. He took both notes and looked straight at me without a change of expression.

'Maybe this time I'll let you off with a caution, seeing as how you're a tourist. Go easy in future. Some cops would throw the book at you.' He handed back my licence.

'Yes, I will. Thank you, officer.'

He watched us drive off before remounting his bike.

'That was all I needed,' I said. 'Even though I handled it, it still cost me two hundred bucks.' We neither of us spoke or looked at each other for the rest of the journey. I drove with ultra care. When I walked into our little house the contrast between Woody's opulence and mine struck me like toothache. I had such a smouldering urge to change everything in my life.

'Want me to fix something to eat?' Tracey asked.

'Like what?'

'Anything you say.'

'OK, I'll have lobster thermidor with garlic and country-style fries.'

'We don't have any lobster.'

'And if we did, you couldn't cook it.'

She turned away and went into the bedroom. I opened some wine and took it out on to the deck, intending to finish the whole bottle. After a while she came to the patio doorway. She had let her hair down and changed into one of the dresses I had bought her. It was made of imitation silk and clung to her body, doing wonders for her breasts. She knew it was a turn-on for me. That might have been the moment when we kissed and made up, but just then the phone rang.

'Answer that,' I said, then shouted after her: 'If it's Julian I want to speak to him.'

She went back into the house and picked up but didn't call back to me.

'Is it Julian?'

Getting no response I went inside. She was just putting down the receiver.

'Who was it?'

'Just my folks.'

'Just your folks, so you hung up on them?'

She didn't look at me.

'You gave him this number, didn't you? You gave him my fucking number. You gave that jerk at the pool my number!' I threw my glass in the direction of the fireplace. It missed and struck a lamp, smashing both. 'Didn't you?'

'No.'

'Don't fucking lie. It was him. I'm not that dumb. Brodky had you figured right. You're just a little whore.' I made a move towards her and she backed off, expecting me to slap her around.

'I didn't mean anything by it, but he came on so strong. I've never met anybody like him before.'

'Well, depend on it, you're going to meet plenty more bullshitters like him. This town's full of them.'

'Why would he promise to help me then?'

'Why? Because he wants to get between your legs. Can't you get that into your stupid head?'

Maybe it had been bred into her since childhood, the trailer-park mentality glued to her for life. Nothing was ever permanent. We are what we eat, as the saying goes, and we're also stuck with what we inherit, the genes or whatever decides these things. Cancer runs through some families, wanderlust in others. She was fair game for the likes of Don the legal crapshooter, and when he was finished with her, then some other sweet-talking guy would read the Hollywood fairy story to her, and maybe one of them would get her a walk-on in a movie. She had to be a pushover for that kind of come-on to have shacked up with Brodky in the first place. Then I'd done my number, not as corny as the others maybe, but nevertheless a number – why kid myself? Morality was all a question of degree, one man's meat, another man's poison. Her crumpled pretty little face would drive a variety of Pygmalions to try their hand at remaking her because she had that built-in waif's look that challenged the old male ego. I remembered how easily, how immediately, I had fallen victim to her appeal.

'I won't see him again, Bobbie, I promise.'

'Yeah,' I said, suddenly tired of it all.

'Don't you believe me?'

'Look,' I said. 'You don't owe me life-long allegiance.'

'What's that mean? You use such big words sometimes.'

'It means if you think that character can give you what you want, go for it. It's your life.'

I left her and went back on to the deck and continued drinking alone. Far out to sea the sun glinted on the dolphins as they leaped. I felt mixed emotions. Part of me wanted to patch up the quarrel and resume the easy life, but the echo of Woody's remark about alley cats lingered. She had found her way to my door by chance, and I had taken her in and given her a bowl of milk. Now somebody else had promised her fake caviar. I fell asleep on the deck and when I woke up, prepared to bury the hatchet, she had gone. The only thing she left behind was her teddy bear.

25

The house took on a different character without Tracey; it was suddenly just a shell to inhabit, like a rented holiday home. There were times when I cursed my own self-destructive stupidity. I missed the sex, but there were other factors that helped paste over the void; the decks had been cleared: Billy had written me off, I had given Arnold his marching orders, and according to Julian, I was on the brink of a breakthrough in my career. He phoned a few days after Tracey disappeared, opening the conversation with: 'Are you sitting down, sweetie?'

'Actually, I'm lying down.'

'Better still. I had my session with Schneider and, as I predicted, the moment I mentioned a price he went straight into an impersonation of Olivia de Havilland in *The Snake Pit*. I let him get the histrionics off his chest because I knew, and he knew I knew, that what Zanuck wants, Zanuck gets. And does Zanuck ever want your screenplay.'

'So? Don't keep me in suspense.'

'What would you say to forty-five thousand dollars?'

'Are you kidding?'

'Yes. Actually I closed at fifty.'

'You are kidding?'

'No. Plus, Associate Producer if you want it, at another five. Which is just a sweetener, means precious little, but it's an extra credit on the screen.'

'I want it. You're a genius.'

'Wait, not over yet. I was really enjoying myself by then, because I had him on the ropes. I nailed him for another ten after two times negative. But don't spend that in advance because, dream on, with their bookkeeping, you ain't going to see it, but again it's something to quote the next time around. Am I your favourite agent, or what?'

'Julian, how can I ever thank you?'

'Well, you could act like a gentleman and offer to go down on me.'

I glossed over that. 'You're brilliant. When do I sign?'

'As soon as Business Affairs send over the papers, and they'll take a week or so. Then our people will go through it with a fine tooth comb.'

'But it is definite?'

'It had better be. However, on with the good news. We'll be taking an ad in the trades to put your name on the map.'

'Really?'

'Of course, sweetie. When we've got it, we flaunt it, I make sure of that for my people. So how about our date?'

This time there was no escape.

'Can you make next Friday?'

'Sure,' I said.

'We'll spend some quality time together.'

I pushed what that might mean to the back of my mind and savoured the moment. Remembering from whence my good fortune had come, I made a deal with my conscience that, when the Fox cheque was safely lodged in my bank, I would send Jack's father a donation. There had to be some honour among thieves. The prospect of fifty thousand dollars belonged to previous realms of fantasy; it was like sticking a pin into a form card and seeing an unknown horse come in at a hundred to one. I spent the rest of the day doing endless sums, trying to calculate what I would be left with after commission and tax. The only sad part of it was I now had nobody with whom to share the good news. I found myself wishing that Amanda was still around. It even crossed my mind to give her a ring and see if the flame could be reignited. I had always had a sneaking suspicion that the reason for our break-up was not just the abortion but my lack of material success. Amanda had set her sights high, she had admitted as much in an unguarded moment.

In the week after the announcement of the deal appeared in the trades, my previously dead phone started ringing. Apart from Woody, who, despite a show of enthusiasm, could hardly suppress his envy, the rest were people I had never heard of who had somehow obtained my unlisted number. I had calls from three publicity agents offering to further my career, another from a character who ran an escort service ('Listen, you'll be going to premieres and I can supply some sensational chicks guaranteed to get your picture in the fan magazines'), a woman called Stella Firmament (I kid you not) claiming to be a psychic and wanting to give me a free seance, a car salesman, a firm of accountants, three actors offering to audition for me and a man claiming to be a distant relative and looking to share my good fortune.

Before the ink was dry on the contract I was given a pass to the Fox lot and shown to my new office. In contrast to the cell I had occupied at MGM, this was the producers' block, with wall-to-wall carpeting and, luxury, its own toilet. Before parts of it were sold off for real estate, the enormous Fox lot straddled from Pico Boulevard to Santa Monica. It was less gaunt, more informal, than MGM. Most of the top stars, directors and producers had their own permanent bungalows, sumptuously furnished according to individual tastes. Albert Nagy, a popular director of the period and also an accomplished artist, was the first of the residents to seek me out. Word of my script had already gone the rounds on the studio grapevine and Nagy had put down his marker with Zanuck to be considered to helm it, so I figured his immediate overtures of friendship were not devoid of an ulterior motive. He did a portrait of me I remember, quite a passable, romantic likeness. I looked for it the other day, but it must have disappeared in one of my many subsequent moves. Monroe was on the lot at that time as well as Mike's great passion, the delectable Jean Peters, and the studio was buzzing with talent, young and old.

I finally met Zanuck outside the commissary one day, dressed in jodhpurs and carrying a riding whip. One of the few studio heads with hands-on knowledge of film-making, he talked about my script and the plans he had for it in a way that confirmed he had actually read it, for he discussed individual scenes in detail.

'I want to give it a lot of thought before I decide who's going to direct it,' he said. 'Good to have you with us, kid. Keep writing.'

'That's really something,' my new secretary said when I told her of the encounter. 'I've been here four years and he's never said hello to me. It means you're on his A list.' She gave the impression that I had just kissed the Pope's ring and been granted absolution from all my sins.

I got into the habit of having a coffee in the make-up department every morning before going to my office; not only was it the village pump where one heard all the latest gossip, but there were always new faces around – hopefuls of both sexes. Most of them had gravitated to the West Coast, lured, then as now, by the dream of instant stardom. Those who succeeded in making first base were groomed and remodelled, given a glamour stills session, then passed to one of two resident dramatic coaches, handed a scene to learn and put in front of the cameras for a screen test. As a writer it intrigued me to see how, invariably, they eventually emerged from the same mould – the real character painted out of their faces as country girls became lacquered dolls indistinguishable from the stylised bathing beauties that graced a dozen calendars. The males were also given the treatment: new hairstyles and in many cases new names. Nobody was looking to put the average girl or boy next door in films; the studios preferred stereotypes. The men had to be clean-cut and handsome for the camera, the girls dazzlingly perfect. It helped if they had some talent, of course, but talent wasn't the prerequisite. First they needed to have sex appeal. Only a small percentage made it past the initial stage but, if they were considered to be worth keeping, they landed a minimum-term contract with a pocket-money weekly salary. Most of them failed to realise they had signed themselves into bondage, their day-to-day lives circumscribed by the contractual fine print, their futures limited by the yearly option. I felt sorry for them, even those who got a second chance, since they were now part of a male-dominated system that guaranteed a loss of innocence, for every newcomer was closely scrutinised and rated by the resident predators. The girls were considered fair game and unless they got lucky early in the game and found a mentor, they were often passed around from office to office. Sometimes I would find a memo on my desk from one of the other producers on the lot, giving me a new girl's name and a telephone number and inviting me to sample for myself, usually with details of her attributes and sexual performance. I had yet to be in line for my own bungalow, but those who had them regularly used them for something other than script conferences, and don't let anybody tell you different. America isn't called the land of the free for nothing.

I played it cool, friendly but cool, anxious not to appear aloof from the sexual musical chairs but at the same time keeping my distance. I knew I had to be careful in those early days. There was always the fear that somebody might come out of the woodwork and expose the true authorship of Jack's script. He had always been garrulous, often in his cups – who was to say that in a drunken moment he hadn't mentioned its existence? Already several of the directors and writers I socialised with in the commissary wanted to know what else I'd written and whether I had any other originals tucked away. It helped that the reprint of my novel was back in the bookshops, but I was forced to invent a phoney background. Woody's advice came in useful, but it was the writers who worried me most. Writers have a sixth sense where their rivals are concerned, and as I had found when going to Guild meetings, very little charity was extended to their colleagues. I was constantly on my guard, especially since I now began to be mentioned in the gossip columns. Louella and Hedda were still powerful voices in the land, while the third member of the elite pack, Scott Fitzgerald's Sheilah Graham, might be the better journalist, but she was ready to plunge her dagger in the back if the mood took her. In addition, scores of minor truffle hounds, mostly affiliated to foreign newspapers, dispatched weekly copy to keep the rest of the world informed about the mores of tinsel town.

The studio publicity department arranged for me to be interviewed by Isabel Wimbourne, a British member of the Foreign Press Association and a regular columnist for a London daily. She turned out to be a matronly, middle-aged woman, who lived in a modest bungalow on North Doheny with a Union Jack flying outside. First impressions of the press corps often proved to be deceptive, since basically they were all seeking to further their own egos, but Isabel Wimbourne appeared to be more like a maiden aunt writing for the church magazine than a character assassin. She grilled me in an offhand way, taking occasional notes, and when the piece appeared it described a stranger, written in a style that suggested Nancy Drew, girl detective, had forsaken crime and turned her hand to film journalese, but got all the facts wrong. I discovered that I was the hottest young bachelor around, dating a new girl every night and on everybody's party list. In fact the only party I went to during that first heady period was Julian's. That is, if you could call a gruesome twosome a party.

With a quota of premonitions I drove to his apartment after the close of business on the Friday night. He lived in a two-storey block on the South side of Wilshire, conveniently close to the William Morris office. It was furnished expensively and had fag written all over it, little chintzy chairs and matching sofa, wall-to-wall tufted white carpet that was all the rage at the time, and lots of dinky china ornaments and photos of past and current clients suitably inscribed. I was given a guided tour on arrival, Julian acting like a realtor anxious to make a quick sale. 'It's showing its age at the moment, like me, dear, but I'm about to trick it up. A friend of mine thinks I should give it a face lift and go the whole way with Art Deco, but I can't make up my mind. Would I like it? I don't know that I want to live in one of Joan Crawford's old movies. D'you have any brilliant suggestions?'

I wanted to say, 'Yes, burn it and start again,' because it screamed of fairyland, but I acted the polite guest. 'Perhaps it could do with being lightened, but I'm not really the person to ask.'

The bedroom walls were covered in patterned silk fabric, with matching drapes, closed to exclude all light. Joss sticks burned on the bedside tables, and the headboard behind his king-size bed with its black sheets was an elaborate affair carved in wood and depicted Cupids entwined. On the wall facing the bed there were two kitsch oils in gilt frames showing nude youths besporting themselves in sylvan glades. As I glanced at them Julian said: 'I bought those in West Berlin when I went there for the Festival. Paid a fortune, but they just took my eye. The man who sold them to me swore they were Roehm's.'

'Who was he, a famous German painter?'

293

'What lazy boy didn't do his history lessons? If he painted anything it was only to paint himself into a corner. Captain Roehm was a member of Hitler's original gang and leader of the SA until he came to a very nasty end. The Fuhrer had him murdered.'

'Excuse my ignorance.'

'Oh, don't be silly, why should you know? The dealer probably took me for a ride, but I often lie in bed wondering whether those pretty boys became stormtroopers and if they survived the war. What d'you think of them?'

'As paintings?'

'The Aryan Adonises.'

'Interesting,' I said.

'Are they to your taste?'

'I don't really know much about Art.'

'Well, we're not exactly talking about Art, dear. We're talking about their pretty little asses. I wish I'd lived in Berlin during the thirties. All that decadence. Then the Nazis came along and spoiled the fun. On the other hand, if I had been there, I'd be dead by now, so think yourself lucky, Julian. Anyway, this is the holy of holies where I do all my homework, and this is the bathroom where I wash away all my sins.' As we moved towards the bathroom his hand lingered briefly on my waist. I looked in. An enema bag hung on a hook beside a purple kimono and there was an impressive array of bath oils and scent bottles arranged on glass shelves.

'Do you ever think about famous people going to the toilet?'

'No,' I said.

'I do, constantly. Everybody has to shit; it's the one thing that makes us all equal, did that never occur to you?'

'I haven't given it much thought.'

'Royalty, politicians, Zanuck, Rita Hayworth, the Pope, they all have to visit the john and wipe their botties. It's the great leveller.' His hand brushed against me a second time as we went back into the main room.

'Shall we have a little drink before we go?'

'Sure. Where are we eating?'

'Well, I'm going to introduce you to my health club first,' he said, starting to mix a couple of lethal Manhattans. 'I don't know about you, but I need to unwind after a week in the office. All my actors are so demanding, I practically have to breastfeed them.' He handed me my glass and clinked his against it. 'Let's drink to your screenplay. I can't tell you how excited everybody is. I know what I've been wanting to ask you. That time we first met at the Beverly Hills pool, who were you with that day?'

'A producer called Woody Solotaroff I was working with.'

'Oh, him, yes. I knew it struck a bell, but I couldn't think of the name. Ghastly creature. Such a smart little Jew, gives us all a bad name. I hope he isn't a great friend of yours?'

I felt I ought to defend Woody. 'Not a close friend, but he did help me to get started.'

'I bet he didn't overpay you, though. The word around town is that he's a cheapskate. Pity I wasn't looking after you then, though I always sensed we would end up together. I loved your naughty novel, as I told you. I couldn't get over the fact that you knew so much about life at your age.'

'It was fiction,' I said.

'Oh, yes?' He gave me an arch look and I felt the pull of his sexual tension between us. His voice had undergone a change, pitched lower as he skirted around the only topic he wanted to explore further. For a moment I thought he might be about to pounce and I moved to examine a photograph in a silver frame on a side table. It showed a handsome woman standing in the porch of a house with her arm around a small boy.

'This you and your mother?' I asked.

'Yes.'

'Your mother's very good-looking.'

'Was,' Julian said. 'She died two years after that was taken.'

'I'm sorry. Do you have any brothers or sisters?'

'No, there was only little me.'

'Is your father still alive?'

'Yes, the odious bastard is around somewhere. But don't let's get on to the subject of my father and ruin the evening. Drink up and let's get going.'

Directed by Julian, I drove in my car to a district in downtown Los Angeles, finally arriving outside an anonymous-looking brick building that gave no clue to its identity except for a small plaque on the side of the entrance which said: BUDDIES HEALTH CLUB, *Members Only.*

'You're going to enjoy this,' Julian said as he signed me in. But I didn't. It did not take me long to realise that 'Buddies' paid only lip service to health faddists and existed as a covert meeting place for the faithful. Now, thirty years on, when the moral climate has undergone such major changes, the goings-on at Julian's old health club wouldn't raise an eyebrow, but in the fifties things were different. It's boring and pointless to make judgements in retrospect – God knows I'm hardly entitled to – and, after all, there's nothing we heterosexuals won't stoop to, given the chance, but that first glimpse of a hidden world whose existence I had previously only partly imagined, shook me. Borrowing Julian's vernacular, the atmosphere of the place was immediately Dorothy-friendly homoerotic, peopled with the moneyed gay set and their pick-ups openly camping it up. Reluctantly I let Julian persuade me to take a steam, then suffered a massage and a quick dip in the pool where a bevy of corpulent old bods and their pretty acolytes were frolicking.

'There's such a friendly atmosphere here,' Julian said. 'That's why I like it.'

When I was allowed to make my escape, his choice of

restaurant proved to be a somewhat old-fashioned establishment with a predominantly German menu. We sat side by side in a plush banquette. At one moment, taking me through the unfamiliar menu, Julian squeezed my hand, the sort of casual intimacy lovers employ at the beginning of a date. Whether by design to deliberately impress he ordered a rich, imported red wine to accompany the main dish. From nervousness I drank it recklessly, all the time seeking to turn the conversation away from myself.

'I'm fascinated,' I said. 'How does anybody become an agent?'

'How? Well, in my case, when my mother died I was shipped off to live with grandparents out in Pasadena. Grandpa owned a cinema, although that wasn't his main business. The family money came from the rag trade. I was allowed into the projection room and to help rewind the films, so I got to see all the latest releases whatever the category. Occasionally some of the stars turned up for sneak previews. I thought they were creatures from another world, unreal. So film was in my blood from an early age, and when I graduated my grandfather got me an interview at William Morris and they took me on in the post room. After I'd been there two years I happened to catch somebody's eye, nobody you'd know because he's since died. But he prised me loose from bondage and made me his assistant and initiated me into the deal-making process . . . amongst other things –' he paused for that innuendo to sink in – 'taught me everything I know.'

Oh, sod it, I thought, I'll smoke him out, get it over with. 'You ever been married?'

'No, dear. Why d'you ask that?'

'No particular reason. I got close to it myself once. Since I've been here as a matter of fact.'

'Well, a tiny word of advice. Writers should be free. Domesticity doesn't sit easily with creativity. You want to be pushing a pen, not a pram. People here get married for three reasons: they want a meal ticket, the studios make them to avoid a scandal or else it's the only way they can get a piece of pussy. Now you don't need a meal ticket, you're not about to be on the front page of the *Enquirer* and you must have them standing in line for you. Fuck all you like, but steer clear of Mrs Matrimony. She'll hold you back and I want to see you go places. Who did you nearly tie the knot with?'

'Oh, just a girl I roomed with.'

'You're not going to tell me?'

'It's over now.'

We were given the menus again and ordered dessert, which Billy insisted had to be accompanied by a glass of Chateau d'Yquem.

'I'll convert you,' he said. 'Nectar of the Gods. I can see I've got to teach you some sophistication. After that we'll have a sambuca with our coffee.'

The room was beginning to swim by the time the meal was finished and when we stood outside waiting for the valet to bring my car, the streetlights had a fuzzy halo around them.

'Are you all right to drive?' Julian asked.

'Maybe not.'

He got into my car behind the wheel. I fell into a drunken sleep during the journey and only came to when the engine was turned off.

'Sorry about that,' I said. 'I'm not much of a guest. How will you get home?'

'I am home. This is my place. But you're not fit to drive yourself. You'd better spend the night here.'

'No, I'll be fine.'

'Don't be silly. I won't hear of it. You'd be arrested before you'd gone two blocks. The police are very hot on drunk driving. The last thing we want at the start of your career

298

is seeing your mug shot plastered all over the tabloids. Just be sensible.'

Part of my fuddled brain was sending alarm signals, but I was incapable of acting on them. He parked and locked the car and then shepherded me into his apartment.

'Just give me some black coffee,' I said. 'I'll be OK in a little while.'

'Stop pretending.'

I only have a hazy idea of what happened next. I dimly remember that Julian helped me into the bedroom and dumped me, fully clothed, on the bed. Then I think he removed my shoes and trousers and put a cold face cloth on my forehead. After that I assume I passed out. I knew nothing else until some time in the middle of the night when something woke me from a disturbed dream. Only dimly aware of my surroundings, I gradually became conscious that somebody was handling my cock. I struggled awake to find Julian stark naked with his face in my groin and my cock in his mouth.

'Jesus!' I shouted. 'What the fuck d'you think you're doing?' which, given the circumstances, was a pathetic question to ask. I kicked him violently and he fell sideways off the bed.

'Don't hit me, don't hit me,' he moaned. 'I couldn't help myself. The temptation was too much. I'm in love with you,' his voice increasingly distorted with a whine of panic.

'Don't give me that.'

'It's true.' Now he grabbed me around my legs. I saw that he had an erection.

'Just back off. Julian, back off.' I tried to loosen his grip.

'You don't know what you've done to me.'

'Get off me and get a life!' I finally prised his arms from my legs and he fell backwards on to the carpet.

'I won't ever try that again, I promise. Please don't say anything to the agency, please.' His sparse hair, normally so carefully arranged, straggled down across his tear-stained face. I got out of the bed and stepped over him, making for the bathroom.

'It was a mistake, I made a mistake, don't let it change anything between us. Please, Bobbie dear, I beg of you.'

'OK, OK, stop being hysterical.'

'Tell me you won't let it go any further. I'll make it up to you, you'll see.'

In the bathroom I sluiced my face in cold water. Julian followed me.

'Please say you won't.'

'All right, I won't. I just want out of here. Where are my car keys?'

'I'll find them, I'll get them, but first say you forgive me.'

He put his hand on my bare shoulder, but I pushed him away and started to put my clothes on. 'Julian, let's both forget it.'

He followed me around while I dressed but made no further attempt to touch me until, when he gave me the car keys, he tried to keep hold of my hand.

'I'm going to work that much harder for you, you'll see. I'll make it up to you.'

He stood there, naked, as I went to the door. 'You don't know what it's like to be me,' he said.

'You've given me a pretty good idea,' I said, and left.

26

Arriving at the studio on the Monday morning I found a memo on my desk asking me to drop by Arthur Gaynor's bungalow. Gaynor was an established producer on the lot who had a string of formula movies to his credit, none of them particularly distinguished but invariably money-spinners, hence his longevity. He had no discernible intellect, but was held in good odour by the front office for his ability to pare down budgets to the bone and bring his films in on schedule. (What shall it profit a film producer if he wins an award but does not recoup the negative cost?) Physically, he tipped the scales at 220 pounds, and his main claim to fame rested on the fact that he had been an All American, which to many has always been held superior to winning the Congressional Medal of Honor. His detractors liked to suggest that most of his brains had been kicked out on the football field, which was quite possibly true, since most of his observations about scripts made little or no sense. A fervent admirer of Douglas MacArthur, having served on the great man's staff in the Southwest Pacific theatre during the war, he sometimes sported a corncob pipe for effect.

When I arrived at his bungalow he was seated behind his enormous desk, which was bare except for one of his football trophies and a large tobacco jar. The wall behind him was hung with framed citations, not for the films he had produced but tributes to his prowess on the field, the centre-piece being an inscribed photograph of him shaking hands with Ike. An American flag stood in a corner. He was about as unlike the perceived idea of a Hollywood producer as you can get.

'Ah, Robert,' he said. 'Good to have you on my squad.'

This was the first indication I had that my screenplay had been given a production number and that I was now to join forces with him.

'Sit down. Let's kick a few balls around and get to know each other until Luke Curtis joins us.'

'Luke Curtis?'

'Yeah. Darryl wants to push out the boat with this one.'

I received this news with mixed feelings. I was excited that the film had been given the green light, but the choice of Curtis gave me cause for alarm. Although I had not been around very long, I knew of his reputation, for Jack had often regaled me with lurid stories of Curtis's behaviour towards anybody who didn't fall in with his way of thinking. I don't remember how we got on to the subject, but Jack loved nothing better than to badmouth directors against whom he bore a grudge.

'Curtis? A critics' darling and a copper-bottomed phoney. He started out as an actor, worked in some early silents, but he was too ham even for the silents, which is saying something. Maybe because of that he's uneasy around good actors. Plus he's a professional Irishman,' Jack had said. 'That's the worst kind in my book. You know the type, or you will, believe me. They've never been closer to the Blarney Stone than the inside of an Irish bar, but they imitate that fucking Barry Fitzgerald accent to impress because, for some reason I've never been able to fathom, over here the Irish are always given the benefit of the doubt. I'll level with you. Most of the American Irish I've met in the course of business make me want to throw up. All that talk of the Emerald Isle, peat fires and the Liffey water is a crock of shit. In Curtis's case it's more than pathetic because his grandfather was a first-generation Polack out of Chicago who married a colleen straight off the boat, but to hear him talk you'd think he was a direct descendant from the line of Irish kings. I worked for him once. Never again. The dislike was mutual. Caught him out the first day when I asked him if he was going to Finnegan's Wake. "A lot of your fellow countrymen'll be there," I told him, "including Finnegan's widow, Molly Bloom. It's going to be a big event." I knew he didn't have a clue what I was talking about, but wouldn't admit it. "Yeah, sure," he said. "I'll definitely go. Where's it being held?" I guess somebody must have put him wise, because when he found out he never forgave me.'

'He's made some successful films, though.'

'Yeah, I'll give you he knows where to put his camera and he can stage a good fight. That's part of the fake Irish bit too. But you must have noticed his women are always the weak vessels. He likes them to cry a lot and they're always portrayed as holy virgins. Nobody gets fucked out of wedlock in his movies. No, he's not my cup of tea.'

When I first met him, Curtis had some forty movies under his belt. After failing as an actor, he had drifted into directing around the same time as Walsh, Borzage and Clarence Brown, churning out a number of indifferent two-reelers for poverty-row producers until he got a break working as an assistant on a Western. The director got bitten by a rattler and Curtis took over and finished it. His list of films demonstrated that he was an able technician who could handle straightforward action vehicles and Westerns better than most. Those I had seen were entertaining enough in a juvenile way, but subtlety was not his middle name. He painted the screen in broad strokes and favoured using the same leading men time and time again, casting rugged types who could be relied upon not to make waves on the set. He seldom used thinking actors who might give him an argument, for, an autocrat behind the camera, he had little time or patience for discussion about how a role should be interpreted. Actors were there to turn up word perfect, hit their marks and move on to the next shot. Any challenge to his authority was abhorrent to him and treated with a string of abuse. The stories he favoured were about loners who rode into town, did stirring deeds, then rode out again leaving a tear-stained heroine behind them.

Stories of his own florid lifestyle abounded. He was said to keep himself under control while shooting a movie, and then he would take off on a monumental binge that could last a couple of weeks. Jack had told me tales of how he would hole himself up with a whore in some out-of-town hotel with a couple of crates of whisky and drink himself insensible. When his long-suffering wife finally managed to locate him he would be a stretcher case, more often than not fused to the mattress of the bed where he had fucked, drunk and defecated during the self-destructive orgy. The whore and the hotel damages would be paid off and Curtis removed to a nursing home to dry out. The cycle never varied, apparently, and his life contained little else in between. He made a movie, went on a blinder, recuperated, then started another movie. To many in the industry, this lifestyle evoked a grudging admiration, for Hollywood always respected hell-raisers of his kind, especially those who, in their sober interludes, delivered the goods.

'Well, that's amazing,' I said to Gaynor, mustering the required amount of enthusiasm. 'Luke Curtis! He's a sort of legend.'

'Not even a sort of legend. He's the genuine article.'

'Is he happy about my script?'

'Well, I'll let him tell you when he gets here.'

'Do you like it?'

He smiled slowly and started to fill his pipe. Although his hands were the size of dinner plates I noticed that his nails were manicured and buffed so that they shone. 'You wouldn't be sitting here, kid, if I didn't.' The phone rang. He picked it up and listened briefly. 'The answer's no. I don't take calls from that fink.' Then the smile again as he hung up. 'Agents,' he said, as though I was part of his thinking. 'All they do is blow shit in your face. Remind me who you're with.'

'Julian Sugarman at William Morris.'

'Oh, him, yeah. Well, he cut you a pretty fancy deal on this one. Darryl paid top dollar.' He sucked on his unlit pipe, drawing in the air. There was something about all his movements that didn't sit with his bulk.

'Give you some good advice, kid, before you meet the big man, remember this: all great movies are the product of one man's vision. That's something to take home with you and sleep on.' He delivered this as though he had lifted it straight from out of La Rochefoucauld. 'You have any problems, come to me. Curtis is uneasy around writers. I'm going to look after your end, kid. Nobody's going to fuck with this project.'

He was so smooth that everything he said that morning came across like a lie, and I kept wondering how Jack would have dealt with the situation had he been sitting in my chair. 'I'll remember that,' I said.

'Everybody on the lot has been asking where you sprang from. You're a man of mystery.'

'Am I?'

'Scripts like this don't turn up every day.'

'I guess I got lucky.'

'In spades, kid. You got me and you got Curtis.'

When Curtis finally appeared his immediate attitude did nothing to reassure me I was in for an easy ride. He was taller than the photographs I had seen had suggested, with the mottled, bronzed face of a heavy drinker. He came in wearing a battered old hat which he never removed, and kept an unlit cigar in his mouth. I stood up as he entered, which was probably a tactical mistake, but I was nervous.

'You two haven't met before, have you?' Gaynor asked.

'No, we haven't. How d'you do, Mr Curtis?'

Curtis gave me a long look, then directed his question to Gaynor.

'I thought you said I was going to meet the writer?'

'This is the writer, Luke. Robert Peterson.'

'You bullshitting me? This young buck wrote our script?'

'His name's on it.'

Curtis turned back to me. 'OK, I'll go with the flow. And sit down, I'm not a woman. How fast are you?'

'How fast?'

'Yeah, we start shooting in four weeks and we've got things to put right. How soon can you make the changes?'

I shot a glance at Gaynor for his promised support, but he just winked at me.

'Depends on how many changes you want.'

'Plenty.' Curtis slumped into a spare chair. 'Long speeches. Too many words. I hate long speeches. You familiar with my work?'

'Yes, sir.'

'Then you know I tell a story in pictures, not words. I'm casting Hank Boyle in this one and he doesn't need words, his face tells it all.'

Boyle was one of his regulars, a taciturn actor in the Cooper mould, but without Cooper's romanticism. I had never found that his face told anything, in fact it was a strong contender for inclusion on Mount Rushmore, but I wasn't going to risk anything by being negative. 'He can be very effective in the right part,' I said.

'He sells tickets,' Curtis growled, as if that settled all arguments.

'I agree.'

'Don't agree with everything I say. Give me a fight. Stand up for what you believe in.'

'Well, I believe in my script as it is.'

'You do, huh?'

'Yes, sir.'

'You don't think it needs changes?'

'Well, not big changes, no,' I said bravely, though I didn't feel brave.

Curtis turned to Gaynor. 'Where do they find them these days?' Then back to me with: 'How many scripts have you written, kid?'

'Four or five,' I lied.

'And how many films have I directed?'

'I don't know the exact number, but it must be well over twenty.'

'Twenty? I've had my name on forty-two, and I never did pick up a perfect script.'

'Well, if you tell me what you don't like, I'll try and put it right.' I took a risk and it was a mistake. 'Though I thought when Mr Zanuck bought my script he was happy with it as it was.'

'Zanuck isn't directing this movie, I am.'

'What Luke is saying,' Gaynor interjected, 'is that he has a concept. That right, Luke? Listen to his concept, Robert.'

They began to talk concept across me as though I wasn't there. 'Concept' was then Hollywood-speak for changing everything and starting again. Since those days it's been upgraded to 'High Concept' by the latest batch of powerbrokers. Roughly translated, 'High Concept' has come to mean mind-numbing, infantile films, pitched to an adolescent sensibility, that pound audiences into submission. They usually star a small band of actors who command obscene salaries and call the shots. Of course, Curtis and Gaynor weren't operating on that plateau, they were part of the now vanished old guard, shielded by the paternalism

307

of the studio system providing they played by the rules, dinosaurs unaware that within the next decade their days in the sun would be over. The Hollywood they were to leave behind was provincial, isolated from the outside world and ordinary human reality. Not that anything has changed.

As I faced them both that morning Gaynor's early assurance that nobody was going to fuck with Jack's script proved worthless. Fuck with it they did. During that first, disturbing meeting they chipped away at the edges, changing the emphasis of certain key scenes, and leaving me in no doubt that I was a hired hand, only there under sufferance.

'The girl is too ballsy and too young,' Curtis said at one point. 'I hate women who talk like they're wearing a jockstrap. I don't want a dick love story. That's a turn-off for Hank. He won't play that stuff, nor will his public buy it. The way you have it, the guy's a cradle-snatcher.'

'But she has to be young, that's the whole point,' I said. 'That's why he's torn.'

'I'll let you know when I want to remake *Daddy Longlegs*,' Curtis said. Then he spoke past me to Gaynor. 'Jesus Christ! Arthur, you know the girl needs a makeover, right?'

'Right.'

'Stay with the money.'

Although loud warning bells were sounding in my head, I tried to stay calm. 'Hank Boyle's signed, is he?'

'Not signed, but he's going to do it,' Gaynor said.

'What's the point of your question?' Curtis barked.

'Just asking. Who did you have in mind for the girl?'

'Julie Broderick.'

'I don't know her.'

'Nobody knows her yet, but Darryl wants her. Stay around and you'll learn, kid. It's known as sucking the tit that feeds you. Right, Arthur?'

'On the nail.'

(Later I discovered she was Zanuck's latest flame. Her

real name was Isabella von Voorst and she spoke English with a thick, guttural accent. Eva Braun would have been better casting for Jack's heroine.)

'How old is she?'

'Well, put it this way, she ain't just out of diapers. Don't worry about casting, that's not your concern.'

The meeting broke up shortly after that, Curtis announcing he was leaving to go to the races. 'So, we all set?' he asked me as he stood up. 'Make the girl older, and give me a happy ending. Eighty-six all those words,' being his parting shot.

'Great guy,' Gaynor said when the door closed. 'They don't come any classier. You don't know how lucky you are to be working with him, but one thing you should know, he hates talking story. He has a concept and sticks with it. Think you can handle his concept?'

'I'll give it some thought.'

'Yeah, push it out into the water and see if it floats.'

On that depressing note I went home to an empty house and started to wrestle with my conscience. I felt as though Curtis had asked me to redesign the wheel. In a couple of sentences his so-called 'concept' had stood the existing screenplay on its head. Jack had written the story around a man who falls hopelessly in love with somebody twenty years his junior and finally loses the battle against youth and spring. In places it sailed dangerously near to the Hays Office reef of acceptability, but that was what gave it its strength and originality. I knew if I attempted to water it down it would become banal. The girl's existing characterisation, which Curtis had denigrated as 'ballsy', provided some vital humour to the piece. In the first flush of selling it to Fox, I had never given any thought to the possibility that they would want it changed so drastically and despair set in. Except for Julian I had nobody to turn to for help. He now owed me one but I wondered if he would go in and do battle for me. We hadn't spoken since the fateful encounter at his place but, with nothing to lose, I called him.

Brent picked up. 'He's on the other line, natch, but he left word I was to interrupt if you rang, so let me put you on hold and get him.'

There was a short pause and then Julian came on the line, not the bushy-tailed Julian of old, but somebody hesitant, still scared perhaps that his attempted seduction of me had put him in jeopardy.

'Robert? I've been waiting for your call. I don't know how to apologise –'

I cut him short. 'That's forgotten. I want your help on something.'

'Yes, anything.'

'I had a tricky meeting at Fox this morning with Arthur Gaynor and Luke Curtis.'

'Why tricky?'

'Curtis wants to turn the whole thing on its head.'

'Really?'

'Yes, really. And the other thing is he wants to cast Boyle in the lead.'

'Well, you could do worse. At least he's the right age.'

'That's the point. Curtis says he can't be seen to fall in love with a girl half his age. He's told me to make her older. Plus he wants major dialogue cuts. According to him Boyle won't handle long speeches.'

'No, well he's always been Mrs Monosyllabic. Come over to the office. I'll cancel all calls and we'll talk it through.'

'I can't. Just tell me how far do I have to go along with his ideas?'

'Well, dear, he is the director.'

'I know that. I'm asking, can I dig my toes in?'

'Did Gaynor support you?'

'No, he just sat there sucking his pipe and let Curtis do

all the talking. Boyle's wrong to begin with. He can't act.'

'Well, we know he's not Tracy, but he is box office, dear.'

'Do William Morris handle him?'

'No, he's with Paul Kohner.'

'And the agency doesn't handle Curtis either?'

'No, he isn't with anybody. Work comes to him and he's too mean to pay ten per cent.'

'Well, go over their heads to Zanuck. Wouldn't he support me, since he liked it so much?' Julian didn't answer immediately. 'You still there?'

'Yes, of course. Just thinking. Listen, sweetie, everybody goes through this. Usually they get in another writer, but I protected you on that as far as a second draft.'

'And what happens after a second draft?'

'Then they can do what they like.'

'Are you telling me there's nothing I can do about it?'

'It's not personal. They treat all writers the same. And it'd be a shame if you got off on the wrong foot. These are powerful men you're dealing with; they don't like being crossed.'

'Well, fuck them, I'm not going to let them ruin my script, and you and everybody else had better know that.'

There was a note of panic in Julian's voice when he answered. I could almost hear his brain ticking over. He wanted to placate me for a variety of reasons, but at the same time he was anxious to protect his own ass, thinking of the fallout if I made waves. Even though he had sold my script, I was still small fry in the general scheme of things and he wasn't about to risk his daily bread and butter.

'I think you should sleep on it, dear. Don't do anything rash. Maybe, you never know, you're so brilliant, you'll find a way of making Curtis's suggestions work for you. He's a tough old bastard but he knows his stuff. Let me give it some thought and I'll call you back. Other than that you're OK, are you?'

'What d'you mean, "other than that"? What is there other than that?'

I was scared. It seemed that the whole fake edifice I had constructed was about to collapse. The con man had been conned in turn by the fine print. I looked at my contract and there it was staring at me: Paragraph 9(b), honed and perfected over the years, binding the writer like Gulliver. I was entitled to turn in a second draft, but beyond that they could give it to the janitor to rewrite and there was nothing I could do about it. Jack had constructed a Cadillac but they were free to turn it into an Edsel. Curtis's dialogue at the meeting had been peppered with expressions like 'Give me a hook, I need a hook there,' or 'I want a grabber' – shorthand for 'I don't know what I want or how to write it myself, but work it out if you want to keep your name on the credits.'

I seldom moved from my typewriter for the next two days, beginning a score of ideas, but nothing came together or made any sense. The more I tinkered with it, the more Jack's originality faded. I panicked. It had seemed so easy to steal Jack's work and pass it off as my own. Julian's immediate enthusiasm and the fact that he had quickly sold it to Zanuck had lulled me into a false sense of security. There was no way I could come clean now; I had to brazen it out. But how? I didn't have the talent to change it in a way that gave Curtis what he wanted and at the same time kept Jack's conception intact. It was in this mood of desperation that I suddenly remembered the advice Jack had given me when my MGM script required rewrites: *'Sit on it for a week, then retype bits of it on coloured pages and they'll believe they're reading a new version.'* Would that work in this instance? I couldn't believe that Curtis was that stupid. Gaynor, maybe, but not Curtis. But what else was left to me?

I started again, cutting the girl's dialogue but retaining

enough of the original so that she stayed as Jack had intended and trying my best to ape his style. I was at my desk, wrestling with every fresh problem, when Julian rang.

'How about if I gave you some good news?' he began.

'Like Curtis was trampled by a horse?'

'No. But Boyle's out. He's not available. I checked and he's signed to do some African epic for Paramount.'

'Well, yeah, that's something. It doesn't help me with the script, though.'

'It might. The next actor they cast might side with you. I'm going to push Gaynor to use Widmark instead. D'you like Widmark? He's hot at the moment.'

'Yes,' I said. 'He's good.'

'Intelligent, too. Got some grey matter between his ears. Don't despair yet. Call me any time you like, day or night, if you want to bounce some ideas.'

I went back to the typewriter and worked until the small hours. Like Scott Fitzgerald once said, with writers it's always three o'clock in the morning when you're facing the blank page. I finally crashed into bed, without having made any real progress. That night I dreamed that I was exposed as a phoney, stripped of my rank in front of the entire membership of the Guild, like Victor McLaglen on the army parade ground in that old film. I woke up in a cold sweat and the dream stayed with me the whole of the next day. The only original idea I came up with was to devise a new opening sequence, elaborating on an incident Jack had touched upon when describing the hero's background. I felt he would have forgiven me that and it gave Curtis his 'grabber' on the first two pages. I ended up with some forty partly revised pages, duly typed on coloured paper, and at the end of the week I had my secretary type up another two copies and took them to Gaynor.

'Feel good about them, kid?' he asked, having flicked through them as though testing them by weight.

'Well I've tried to come up with what Mr Curtis wanted. One copy's for him. Will you get it to him?'

'He's off the lot at the moment. Gone to Tucson to scout locations.'

'Tucson? Why Tucson? The story's set in LA.'

'He likes Tucson. And, by the way, I've had some of my people go over the old script and they came up with a few gizmos.'

The way old farts like Gaynor talked about 'my people' suggested there was an entirely separate race out there. He slid a piece of notepaper across his desk. It was headed *From the Desk of Arthur Gaynor* under a small logo of a couple copulating.

'Cute, huh?' he said. 'They print them at the Farmers' Market. I'll get some done for you. Makes an impression, people remember it.'

'Yes.' I stared at the ideas his people had given him and felt my stomach go into spasm.

Suggest make the hero a cop instead of a newspaper reporter. Make the girl a nightclub hostess he meets on the rebound from another affair. She was previously involved with a mobster and knows too much. When she and the cop get it on, they kidnap her. Then have the Mob frame him so that he's dismissed from the police force. Now he's on his own. He has to get to the girl before they kill her. Develop this for a big action finale.

'One or two interesting possibilities there you can maybe play around with,' Gaynor said. 'But you're the creative guy, I'll leave it to you.'

'Has Mr Curtis seen these?'

'Yeah, I talked them over with him.'

'And? What was his reaction?'

'Well, when you get to know Luke better you'll see he never comes down hard on either side of the line. That's what makes him the man he is.'

'But these make it a totally different film.'

'They're not written in stone, kid. Just to get you thinking. And by the way, forget Boyle.'

I played dumb. 'Forget him? Why?'

'He's out. The ungrateful bastard took another film, but don't lose any sleep over it, we can do better. Too many of these overpaid hams think they can call the shots. They're killing the business. So, you got any other problems?'

'No, only getting the script right.'

'That isn't gonna be a problem. Like I said, I'm gonna protect you from interference. I believe in letting my creative people have a free hand.'

When I left his office I felt like somebody who had just been told he had a terminal illness. I drove back to Santa Monica, thinking I might as well hang myself in the shower. Then, halfway home, a better idea came to me. I turned around and made for Woody's house. My luck was in for once and I found him at home. I told him what I was going through with Curtis.

Woody listened carefully. 'Give me a copy of your original. Let me read it tonight.'

He rang me early the next morning.

'You clever bastard!' he said. 'You've been holding out on me. I didn't know you could write like this.'

'You like it?'

'I'd kill to get a script like this. There's no way you should go along with what those two pricks are suggesting.'

'But what else can I do?'

'I'll tell you your problem. You trust people. Don't trust anybody.'

'Not even you?'

'Well, maybe me now and again but not too often. But

315

listen to my advice. Haven't I been right, so far? I said what would happen with your alley cat, didn't I? I'm a psychic where sex is concerned. She left you, as I said she would. I saw her on Don's arm the other night at Ciro's, purring. You've got to learn to recognise the shits and start being a shit yourself. How d'you think I've survived this far? I use people. Pick their brains, steal their ideas, use their money, their contacts and anything else they've got on offer. D'you read me?'

'But how does one start?'

'You start here and now. We're going to play Curtis and Gaynor at their own game. What are they? Two fucking old has-beens who've been handed a sensational script on a plate. You owe them nothing, so screw them.'

'But how?'

Woody proceeded to tell me.

27

Woody's scheme cost me a thousand dollars, but it was money well spent. I acted just in time because Curtis went straight for my jugular when I took my next meeting with him and Gaynor.

'You trying to fuck with me?' he said for openers. 'Big fucking mistake, kiddo.'

'I'm sorry, Mr Curtis? I don't understand.'

'This. I'm talking about this.' He waved the coloured pages version at me. 'This your idea of a rewrite?'

'You didn't like it?'

'We think it's kinda dull,' Gaynor got his own two cents in.

'I wasn't born yesterday,' Curtis continued. 'This is a jerk-off.'

'I thought the opening grabber would work for you.'

'It sucks. You were supposed to fix the girl and cut most of the crap dialogue.' He opened a copy of the script and flicked through it. I saw that nearly every page had passages scored out with a red marker pen. 'This is what I mean by cuts. When you cut, cut deep, like a surgeon. Get on with the plot. Take this fucking scene, three pages of dialogue and nothing happens. Who needs it?'

'It's their first scene together and sets their relationship. It's there because that's when he begins to realise he's attracted to her.'

'Luke prefers the idea my people came up with,' Gaynor said. 'The kidnapping.'

'But that makes it into a totally different story,' I said. 'And it's cornball.'

'I'll tell you what's cornball,' Curtis said. 'Having some journalist fall for the poor little rich girl. You want to write about journalists, steal from *The Front Page*. The guy is old enough to be her father, for Chrissake! I told you I can't buy that. Their scenes together will get us all arrested. The kidnapping gives me a hook. This has to have a hook.'

'Originally it had a good one – the difference in their ages.'

'Listen, get it into your head, that's out. You had your chance and if this is the best you can come up with, you blew it. I don't have time to fuck around.'

'Luke and I think we should bring in a new mind. You've done a good job so far, but it never hurts to get a fresh slant.'

'Does Mr Zanuck agree?' I asked, in an attempt to look braver than I felt.

'You trying to be smart? Don't be smart, kid.'

'I wasn't. Just asking a question.'

'Zanuck didn't hire me to be double-guessed by a beginner,' Curtis said. He closed his copy of the script, slammed it down on Gaynor's desk and turned away from me. 'We'll let you know what we decide.'

I was dismissed. I went back to my office and phoned Woody to tell him what had happened. 'Have you fixed it?' I asked. 'Tell me you've fixed it, please.'

'Don't panic, everything's arranged.'

'Will it work?'

'My money's on it.'

'No, my money's on it.'

'Trust me. It begins this evening.'

'God, I hope it works.'

'You know why you're in this mess? You should have brought the script to me. Instead you let your faggot agent

318

talk you into a deal that guaranteed you'd get screwed. Gaynor would tread on his mother's face if he had a mother. And as for that prick Curtis, I can't wait to get even with him. He blew me out of a project once. You're doing me a favour.'

'I'll remember next time. Woody, if you pull this off, I'll be for ever in your debt.'

'I'll make sure of that.'

There was nothing I could do but wait.

28

I spent the next two days anxiously waiting to hear whether Woody's elaborate ploy had worked. When he had told me what he intended to do it had seemed a bizarre idea and I didn't share his conviction that it was failure-proof. If he was wrong then I was on the scrap heap, back to square one. I had not only bitched my own chances, I had betrayed Jack, squandered the legacy he had left me.

Woody had assured me, 'He'll go for it. I know how to cast these things. The broad I chose is a real star.'

'But she's a hooker, right?'

'Of course she's a hooker, but she doesn't pick up tricks on the corner of Hollywood and Vine. She's a class act out of Chicago I've used before at stag parties. I've set it up beautifully. First, she's from out of town so there's no chance Curtis has ever set eyes on her before. Then I prepared the ground, rang his office pretending to be an East Coast agent offering him first look at a hot new actress who would fly in especially to see him. Next I had a chum in New York express some ten-by-eight glossies just to make it look kosher. I knew they'd whet his appetite because she's a very sexy number.'

'And he rose to it?'

'And how. The reason you're paying top dollar is that I've booked her into a suite at the Wilshire, but don't worry, I got a special rate because one of the managers there owes me. He's making sure the room bar is stashed with Curtis's favourite poison.'

'And you think she'll pull it off?'

'If she can't, nobody can.'

So, I waited, fingers crossed, prayers frequently said.

It was the afternoon of the third day when I got a call from Gaynor to go and see him. There was a marked change of attitude from our last meeting.

He greeted me with, 'Oh, Robert, some bad news, I'm afraid, which I thought you should know. Luke's been taken ill.'

I played it straight. 'Nothing serious, I hope?'

'Well, he had a sort of heart attack, and of course at his age, that isn't too good. He carries too much weight, as I've been telling him.'

'No. Gee, I'm sorry. Is he in hospital?'

'Yeah, he's in a private clinic.'

'Where did it happen?'

'He was at a friend's house, I believe,' Gaynor said without a flicker.

'Does he have a history of heart trouble?'

'He's had a couple of run-ins before. None of this is public knowledge, you understand.'

I nodded. 'It won't go any further.'

'The studio will be putting out some sort of story, playing it down. I'm only telling you because it's blown our schedule off course. We need to think again.'

I was enjoying it all by now. 'We? Oh, I must have misunderstood. I thought from our last meeting that I was off the team.'

Gaynor pushed some tobacco into the bowl of his pipe. 'That was Luke not me. You got off on the wrong foot with him. Happens.'

'Are you telling me they're likely to replace him?'

'Could be, could be. Right now it looks doubtful.'

'That's too bad.'

'Darryl hasn't made a final decision yet, but he's talking about giving Howard Jackson the script.'

'Which script are they giving him, the original or the rewrite?'

'I'll have my people check on that.'

'So,' I said, 'Kismet.'

'Say again?'

'Fate.'

'Name of the game, kid. So keep all this under your hat and I'll call you soon as I have any more news.'

'Can I ring Mr Curtis, or go see him?'

'He's not allowed visitors, but I'll pass on your message. It's a shame. He had a lock on this one, a real concept.'

'Yes,' I said. 'Didn't he?'

I couldn't wait to ring Woody. 'You were right,' I shouted. 'He's out of it. Tell me what happened. Did he really have a heart attack?'

'As near as damn it. Our girl gave him the business, but the moment he started on the juice, she didn't have to work hard for her money. Guys like Curtis only need to be topped up and they're away. She got the hell out before he started breaking up the room. I checked with my pal on the front desk. The guests on either side of Curtis's suite started to complain at the racket and the smell. Security were forced to break into the room and take him out in a straitjacket down the service elevator. He isn't going to surface for weeks. What version did Gaynor pitch you?'

'Just that he's recovering in a private clinic.'

'A funny farm more likely. Have they said who's replacing him?'

'Maybe Howard Jackson.'

'Well, that's a plus. Know what you should do now? Have your swishy agent fix for you to meet Jackson pronto, and make sure he reads your original.'

'I already thought of that.'

'Jackson's a different animal to Curtis. He respects writers and he's never put his name on potboilers. But don't hang around, every minute counts in a situation like this. For all you know your name isn't even on the script.'

'Woody, you're a prince. I really owe you.'

'Give it to me in writing.'

Using Julian, a meeting was set up with Jackson for the following day. Woody was right, Jackson was another breed, with none of Curtis's loud-mouthed aggression. He received me in his book-lined study, which I took to be a good omen.

'They sent me two versions,' he said. 'Which is the one you wish to be judged by?'

I pointed to Jack's script. 'That's my original, the other is after I made the changes Curtis and Gaynor wanted.'

'It bears all the hallmarks of inferior minds,' Jackson said gently. 'There's no comparison between the two. Your original is far superior and the only one I would consider directing. And I should tell you my deal is that I produce as well as direct, so you won't be working with Gaynor any longer. I shall want some changes too, but I work with the writer, not against him. I don't think you'll find me difficult. I'd like to read it several more times before we get down to working on a final shooting script. Scripts like this don't come my way too often.' He smiled. 'Flattery first, then noses to the grindstone. I thought we'd work here, away from interference. So what gave you the idea for this one?' Before I could answer, he went on: 'What struck me was its maturity and it touched a chord, perhaps because I once fell for a very young girl and skated perilously near to the abyss. What do they call it now? A mid-life crisis. This town is not for the unwary, as doubtless you will discover, if you haven't already.' Again the smile before he returned to his original question. 'So what spurred you to tackle a theme such as this? You're too young to have suffered the same pangs.'

I invented quickly. 'I knew somebody back East, an uncle of mine, who went through the mangle. The family didn't find out until he died when this young girl turned up out of the blue. He seduced her when she was sixteen, apparently, and they'd had an affair for ten years. I guess his story stuck in my mind.' I surprised myself by how glibly I could lie.

'I thought it must have some personal background. It's too real not to. Very close to home in my case. We're going to have some problems with it, you know that, but nothing we can't overcome. This is a very hypocritical place, selling sex for all it's worth but at the same time forced to purify it. We invented the eleventh commandment: Thou shalt not tamper with the Code. It'll be swept away one day, but for the moment we have to be cunning and find ways around it. Well, I've enjoyed meeting you, Robert. Give me a couple of days to square my deal with Zanuck and I'll get back to you with a game plan. I feel good about this.'

He saw me to the door with old-fashioned courtesy. For the first time I felt I had met somebody who could be trusted. On the way back I made a detour to Forest Lawn, bought some flowers and laid them on Jack's grave.

29

Over the next month I worked closely with Jackson on the final version of the script. There was no pressure. He told me that part of his deal had been to insist that the previous start date be delayed. 'We'll go when I'm ready,' he said. The revisions he asked me to make proved to be nuances, changes of emphasis, here and there suggesting that certain scenes would play better if placed in a different order. If he made dialogue cuts he always explained why, saying, 'I shall cover that with a close-up. It doesn't need any words, it'll be self-explanatory.' Perhaps because of his experience of surviving the same kind of love affair, he knew how to handle the emotional scenes. 'Take *Gone with the Wind*,' he told me. 'A very erotic film as well as being an epic. But did you ever see Rhett hump Scarlett? Never. He carried her up those stairs, dissolve and the rest was left to the imagination. All you got was Vivien Leigh in bed the next morning with a satisfied smile on her face. That's my kind of film-making. Not always achieved, of course,' he added with a smile, 'but something worth aiming at.'

I knew that he had gone to the mat with the studio to keep the script intact and maintain the relationship between the man and the young girl.

'I made sure they knew it was a deal-breaker as far as I was concerned. The marketing boys were scared, and tried to talk Darryl round to their way of thinking, but Darryl backed me. Say what you like about Zanuck, but he's a film-maker first and last, and he likes to fight New York and the distribution arm.'

The more I got to know and like Jackson, the more it became obvious that he was not a compromiser and concealed the proverbial iron fist in a velvet glove. This was proved when he also talked Zanuck out of using Julie Broderick.

'Was that difficult? I was told she was the latest girlfriend.'

'It wasn't as difficult as I thought. I got lucky. Some photographs have just appeared in a German magazine showing her in somebody else's arms and they concentrated Darryl's mind in other directions.'

I was flattered that he also involved me in the casting. I was on the floor when he tested half a dozen unknown actresses, though I stayed out of the way when I saw Amanda's name on the call sheet. Afterwards, when we viewed the dailies one of the hopefuls stood out from the rest, a young girl from Denver, newly arrived in LA, Lauren Taylor, who had an extraordinary quality. She wasn't a great beauty – and in any case Jackson was not looking for an obvious sex-bomb – but she had a quality that the camera loved – great eyes and a mass of luxuriant hair. When the time came to make a decision, before Jackson asked my opinion he wrote a name on a piece of paper and put it in his pocket. 'Let's see if we agree,' he said. 'Tell me your choice.'

'They all had something,' I said guardedly, wondering whether he had chosen Amanda. She had done a good test, which disturbed me when they ran it. I knew the dialogue by heart, and since Jackson had chosen one of the love scenes for the tests, Amanda seemed to be speaking the words directly to me rather than the actor she was playing with. It was a good thing I was in a darkened viewing theatre, otherwise I might have betrayed myself. Part of me wanted her to get the role, because I was still in love with her, but another voice told me I would never survive seeing her every day.

'Difficult,' I said. 'I thought three of them were excellent.'

'And? Don't sit on the fence.'

'I guess my vote would go to Lauren Taylor.'

He took out the piece of paper and handed it to me. 'Great minds think alike.' He had written Lauren's name.

For the male lead he cast Jason Lyons, primarily a New York stage actor, in his fifties, with few screen credits to his name. 'I want somebody with a legit background who knows how to get his tongue around some decent dialogue,' he said. 'I'm bored with having to teach some of our current leading men how to act. Jason will have added impact because film audiences aren't over-familiar with him. Don't get me wrong, he's star material, just very choosy as to what he does.'

'And the studio were happy to go along?'

'Again, Zanuck's a compulsive gambler, never happier than when he's beating the shoe at the chemmy table. He knows this is a gamble, but he gets a charge pitting his cards against the rest of the players. Plus, he's not paying over the odds for the two leads which means I can bring this in at a reasonable budget without cutting any corners.'

Once the shooting script had been put to bed and the main casting set, I wasn't involved again until principal photography. Entirely due to Howard, my contract had been extended. 'I want you around,' he said. 'Be good for you and good for me, because what's written on the page doesn't always play. There's a certain strange alchemy that takes place between the performance on the set and the one that gets trapped on the emulsion. That constantly surprises me, even after all these years at it. Likewise actors, good actors, and I think we've got good actors for this one, bring something extra. One has to be on the lookout for those extras and use them. It's stupid not to. So, although we've

327

got a great script we both have to be elastic. There's always room for improvement. You'll see.'

During the weeks leading up to the first day of shooting there was little for me to do except hang around the art department and production offices. I watched the set designs taking shape on the drawing board, impressed by the detailed work that went into everything. The studio system had many critics, but in its heyday there was an oiled perfection about the various craft departments, peopled by old guys who had spent their lives being the best at their particular jobs. The work turned out by the plasterers and carpenters never failed to impress me, all the more so because their efforts were destined to end up being burned on the back lot when the sets were struck. It was as though armies of artisans had been put to work creating whole cities for others to sack. It wasn't until the next decade that entire films were made on location, the interiors being shot in actual buildings. Occasionally, some structures were preserved – because of its fame, Tara stood for a long time after *Gone with the Wind* was finished, but in general everything was judged expendable: it was cheaper to burn the old and begin again than strike and store. Maybe that's always been part of the American ethos, not just characteristic of the film industry – change your automobile, move house, have the decor made over, take a different job when the old one begins to bore you, keep looking for a crock of gold at the end of somebody else's rainbow and when you've found it, steal it. Don't ever stand still, push onwards and upwards.

While waiting for the first day of principal photography I attempted some work on my new novel, but I was too fragmented to concentrate, caught up in the general excitement that gathers pace during those last weeks when a film is poised for that expensive leap into the unknown. Even Howard privately confessed to nerves.

'Tell you something in confidence,' he said, 'and if you give me away I'll fire you. Doesn't matter how well prepared I am – and believe me I've mapped out this movie in my head sequence by sequence, shot by shot – I still don't have any real idea how it'll come out the other end. Every day I get up convinced that I'm going to make a masterpiece, but usually I have to be content with realising seventy per cent of my dream. The thing you have to be on your guard against is getting too euphoric over the dailies. I've sometimes come out of the viewing theatre and heard people saying, "That's Academy Award material." More often than not those are the shots that end up on the cutting-room floor. It's like a comedian laughing at his own jokes before he's got to the tag line. Nobody knows how a film will play until it gets in front of an audience. Anybody who tells you different is full of crap. Boy, if it was that simple to make a winner every time, we could phone it in. One thing you will find when you watch me work: I don't overshoot. There is the Willie Wyler school that go for take after take until they figure out what they want to do. That's not my method. Nor do I fuck my leading ladies. I might think about it, I might want to, but I don't allow myself to fall into that trap. I've seen good directors pussy-whipped by their stars and forced to slant the movie in the wrong direction. I keep my zip buttoned.'

He had taken me under his wing, treating me like a son. On a couple of occasions he invited me back to his house for dinner with Lee, the Art Director, and Budd Masters, the First Assistant he had used for years, who could thought-read his needs. Lee was an unobvious Southern queen from Baton Rouge who, among his other talents, was a great cook. On these occasions Howard gave his own staff the night off and allowed Lee the run of his kitchen. 'Only reason I hire him to design the sets,' he joked. They were fascinating dinners, which Howard used as vehicles for us to bounce ideas. He was a good listener, always receptive to suggestions how to improve the movie even if, finally, he never acted upon them. Although years later the New Wave French managed to pull the wool over a lot of people's eyes with that *auteur* gizmo, I had an early demonstration that film-making was a collaborative effort. Howard was in control, a benevolent dictator who gave credit where credit was due. I saw how he ensured all the pieces came together at the right time, never relinquishing his overall authority, but willing to experiment.

As the crew assembled I was surprised how many of them were approaching senior citizenship; the average age of the camera crew – Bernie, the cinematographer, his operator and focus-puller – was sixty-one; only the clapper-loader was a comparative juvenile of forty-six. They were all quietly efficient, their only concern to be the best in their chosen field. It was all a revelation to me.

Julian called on a daily basis to see how everything was going. Still anxious to make amends, he was all sweetness and light, constantly telling me he was working flat out to get me another assignment the moment *The End of the Beginning* wrapped. 'This is going to be your year, sweetheart. Tomorrow the world.' But I was learning not to take anybody or anything for granted.

I had a scare when somebody from the Writers' Guild called me to say that the title *The End of the Beginning* had been registered some years previously by another writer.

'Really? Does that mean I can't use it for my film?'

'Well, there's no copyright in titles, but we try and avoid duplication as far as possible. Anyway, this is just to let you know we've checked it out and there was never a script attached that we can locate. So, there's no problem with you using it.'

'Good of you to let me know. Who registered it previously?'

'An old-timer called Jack Reeves. Did you ever meet him?'

'I think I came across him when I was doing a stint at MGM.'

'He died not so long ago. We're running an obit in the next issue of the newsletter. I didn't know him, but quite a character from all accounts.'

I breathed again, but not for long. The next time I had a meal with Woody he went on the attack with, 'You know I've been thinking what a man of mystery you are.'

'I am?'

'Yeah. When you and I first met you weren't exactly the sharpest writer on the block. Me, I'm not a writer, but I knew more than you did about how to put a screenplay down on paper. Remember?'

'Sure, you taught me a lot; I've always acknowledged that.'

'So how come a year later you blossom into a genius?'

'Don't know about genius. I just worked at it. The idea had been in my head for a long time and I suddenly found a way of making it work.'

He gave me a look and I knew he wasn't convinced. I also guessed what was really bugging him: the fact that I hadn't given him first look at it. Although he always liked to give the impression that he had everybody's ear, he wasn't 20th Century-Fox or even Republic, he was still in the minor league, for this was long before the independents like him started to rule the roost. He knew how to work the system, but the system would have to change before he came into his own. His instincts had homed in on my Achilles' heel (he cheated, why wouldn't anybody else?) and I took care to be on my guard. Woody was such a perfect representation of what made Hollywood tick, he knew that those on the inside didn't have to conform to anything other than Rule One: generate product that makes a profit. It didn't matter how you achieved this. You could be as eccentric, as crooked, ruthless and paranoid as you liked providing you came up with the goods.

I don't know why I'm citing Woody as a prime example. Woody clones were thick on the ground and I was already going down the same route as everybody else. My current days in the sun had only come about because of a dead man's generosity, and I wanted them to last. I was so close to the success I craved above all else, but I knew that just one careless remark could tumble my pack of cards. I lived on the edge.

30

Everything went remarkably smoothly when shooting commenced. There was a cathedral-like hush on the large set because Jackson liked calm, insisting that everything be subservient to the actors. He gave little direction to Jason once the moves had been blocked, concentrating on the inexperienced Lauren. She fluffed her lines on the first few takes, but Howard was patient with her and she gained confidence as the days went on.

The shooting schedule was planned in such a way that sequences were shot out of continuity, which in my ignorance I found strange until Don, the Production Manager, explained why. 'It's all to do with cost, kid. Saves money and time. All the scenes that take place in this set are lumped together, regardless of where they come in the script. Which means as soon as Howard gives the all-clear on the dailies, we can strike this set. I know it seems back to front, but it makes budget sense. *Comprendo?*'

'I think so.'

Jason, a detached character, was pointedly aloof from the Hollywood scene, but pleasant, and got on well with Lauren. If the fact that she needed more help from Howard grated on him, he concealed it and their scenes together had a sexual intensity. With me he was approachable but couldn't help revealing a stage actor's condescension towards filming. The fact that Howard was shooting out of continuity jarred on him. 'I know why they do it, but it's hard on one's performance. You don't get a chance to develop the character slowly, especially when there's no proper rehearsals. Still, mustn't complain. One must just use the money to subsidise the things one really wants to do and run all the way to the bank. Don't take me wrong, I think your screenplay is worth doing, otherwise I wouldn't be here.'

He did lose his cool once when, at the end of the third week, the publicity department placed a story that his on-screen relationship with Lauren was continuing after hours. He insisted that the unit publicist be replaced before he would come back to work. Apart from that short-lived hiccup, the shooting ran smoothly.

I was allowed to attend the dailies and had the heady revelation of hearing the screenplay come to life on the screen. The experience should have aroused fresh guilt, I suppose, knowing that the dialogue was not mine, but I basked in the compliments Howard paid to me with only the vaguest pang of conscience. I had sent Jack's father a cheque with a note explaining that it was the proceeds from the sale of Jack's typewriter and books. I never heard back from him, but the cheque was cashed.

At around the middle of the schedule the production moved out of the studio to begin three weeks on location. Howard had dropped back two days, mainly because they had a faulty batch of film stock which had necessitated retakes, but the film was still on budget and he was confident of picking up the lost time. He had rejected Curtis's choice of Tucson and instead had opted for Santa Fe. The entire cast and leading members of the crew flew on a chartered aircraft to Albuquerque, then the majority transferred to coaches, just Jackson and the two stars travelling by car. The construction crew had arrived a week earlier to prepare and dress the locations we were using. There was a rest day before shooting recommenced.

The production had taken over an entire hotel and I found myself allocated a room on the same floor as Lauren. Until Santa Fe I hadn't really got to know her. She took her work very seriously, went to bed early every night and although ready enough to exchange pleasantries over coffee between setups, her mind was always concentrated on what came next. That first night she and a group of the other actors invited me to have dinner with them in the hotel dining room. Howard and Jason and the cinematographer went elsewhere.

All the actors were infected with location fever and in holiday mood, rather like students suddenly released from school after exams had finished. I've since noticed that, while they are working, actors often take on some of the characteristics of the roles they are playing, though in Lauren's case, when she relaxed, she reverted to the exuberance of the college girl she had only recently cast off, then caught herself out and remembered she was now the star and changed personality again. She had yet to emerge from the chrysalis of her life before the film; now she floated between the girl she had been and the girl that she was in the process of becoming. There was no real envy of her new status from the others because actors always believe that their turn must come: it is a resilience that sustains them throughout their careers, sometimes without justification and against all the heavily loaded odds. The more I get to know actors the more I am amazed by their ability to live with the occasional success, the inevitability of failure.

Nikki, Lauren's stand-in, had been included in the party at Lauren's insistence. There is a caste system that operates in the acting profession as surely as it exists on the Indian subcontinent. I came to learn that few stand-ins ever make the grade: they lived in their star's shadow, accepted by the other actors but never fully part of their world. Stunt doubles were higher up in the pecking order and they were required to be a passable likeness so that, in a quick cut, audiences would be fooled. Nikki wasn't a replica of Lauren, but she was the same height and had the same facial bone structure that enabled the cinematographer to fix the basic lighting. Then, when Lauren was called to take her place on the mark, he could finesse the key light and ensure that she looked her best.

Actors being an insulated tribe, never happier than when they are swopping shoptalk, I often felt left out of the conversation around the dinner table. Some of it stemmed from the fact that I wasn't one of them but part of the management in their eyes. Their indiscretions, of which there were many, centred around the poverty of their salaries and per diems. They didn't feel they were getting what their talents deserved.

I was sitting next to Lauren and tried to draw her out. 'Are you enjoying the film, or is it very different from what you imagined?'

'No, I love every minute. Everybody's so nice. There's less bitchiness than in the theatre.'

'Is the theatre bitchy?'

'And how,' one of the actors chipped in.

'So what's the big difference?' I asked.

'On a film everybody wants you to be good.'

'Plus you don't have to do matinees,' somebody else said.

'Know what I like best?' Lauren said. 'Not having to put on my own make-up.'

'And you get your hair done every day,' the girl playing a maid said.

'What do you all think of Howard?'

'Yeah, he's cool. I did a couple of days on a Hitchcock movie once. I might as well not have been there.'

They all had stories to tell as to why they had yet to make the big time. But they were hanging in. If Lauren could make it, why not them?

Lauren excused herself before coffee because she needed to get to bed early and be ready for make-up and hair at some ungodly hour. I lingered on with the others until one by one they all went to their rooms. The only person who stayed the course with me was Nikki.

'Don't you have to be up early, too?' I said.

She shrugged. 'Providing I can stand on the marks, nobody cares what I look like.'

'So shall we go in the bar and have a nightcap?'

'Sure.'

We had a few drinks and ended up in bed together. Perhaps not a night to paste in the scrapbook, but not one to be regretted either, although I am sure that Woody would have classified her as another of my stray alley cats. Nikki was probably one of the industry's ultimate losers, but she had a perennially cheerful disposition and took whatever was on offer. That night I was on offer. She hoped that Lauren would go places, because that meant she would have a career by proxy. But if not, something else would turn up. I liked her uncomplicated slant on life and it was nice to be in bed with a woman once again and to enjoy sex with no strings.

It wasn't until near the end of our stay in Santa Fe that I got any closer to Lauren. At the end of a long day's shoot, she usually had room service and learned her lines for the next day. Then freak weather shut in. We had dust storms, flash floods and no sun. For two days everybody sat huddled in the trucks and Winnebagos, waiting for the clouds to lift. The forward weather forecasts were bad, the storm was expected to last for another two days. The only ones not depressed by the hiatus were some of the feature players on a daily rate – the longer we were unable to shoot the more they made. Howard took me, Lee, Budd, and Bernie, the cinematographer, to look for a cover set. It was the first time I had seen him gloomy, and he took it out on Lee.

'We should have been prepared for something like this,' he said, staring out of the rain-streaked windows of the unit car. 'I blame myself as much as you. Never go on location without adequate weather cover. Look at this shit coming down. Would happen right in the middle of a sequence. It's not supposed to rain at this time of year. Just our fucking bad luck.' It was unusual for him to swear.

'Well, all the forecasts we had were great, but you can never be absolutely sure in the desert,' Lee answered.

We travelled for two or three hours, stopping every so often while Howard considered possibilities. 'If we find something you'll have to do some quick rewrites,' he said to me. 'I can't go back and retake the beginning of the sequence, not only because of time, but because Lauren played it perfectly as far as it went. I don't want to redo it in case she can't repeat it. What a bummer. I had the feeling everything was going too well.'

Eventually we came across an old schoolhouse that was half derelict. We stood out in the rain getting sodden for a long time looking at it while Howard considered all the angles. Nobody else spoke.

'Can we make this work?' he asked finally.

'It'll need a transition shot to get from the other location. Nothing matches around here,' Bernie said.

'Yeah, you're right.'

'Otherwise, I like this. I can rig it, no problem, if that's what you decide.'

'Well, it's the best we've found.' He turned to me. 'Give you any ideas?' Before I had time to answer, he turned to Bernie, thinking aloud. 'I could do it this way. I'll shoot an extra tight shot on Jason and Lauren under a tarpaulin, which you can light to match. They look up into the sky. Cut to a shot of the storm. I'll put some thunder on the track. Then cut back to them without the tarpaulin. They start to get drenched, Jason grabs her and they run for it.

Quick mix, and we pick them up coming inside this to take cover. In a way it might work better if the love scene is played interior. I can make it more moody and avoid all that lust in the dust stuff. I was never too happy about that.' He started to look cheerful again. 'In many ways this'll be much better. Right, that's it, then. Let's go back and get everybody cracking.' He turned to Budd. 'Make sure Wardrobe double up on the clothes and warn the artists to expect some new pages tonight. How long will you need to dress the set, Lee?'

'I'll get my team started tonight. In fact, better leave me here now and have Props and the Set Dresser join me.'

'Give the artists a later call tomorrow, ready for ten, but everybody else as per usual,' Howard instructed Budd.

We left Lee in the schoolhouse working out what he would need. On the drive back to the hotel Howard outlined how he saw the new scene could play for him. 'You'll have to revamp the dialogue, Bob. It can be more intimate now that they're inside. I want it moody, Bernie. Don't give me your Prince of Darkness, I want your best atmospheric. It's a schoolhouse – old school desks, chalked words still left on the blackboard, kids' drawings pinned to the walls, that sort of stuff.' Then back to me: 'Get the picture? The school scene brings home to Jason the difference in their ages and it throws him. When they get inside he takes off her jacket. They're drenched, remember? It's the first time he's touched her. Girls with wet hair always look good. I want you to make her look vulnerable, Bernie. Break our hearts. Maybe he does kiss her. Yes, he kisses her. Nothing heavy, but held long enough to make us believe he won't be able to pull back from the brink. He backs off. We sense she would have let him go further. Tease the audience. Oh, I like it. I think we got lucky having to make the changes. Get to work as soon as we're back, Bob. I want it soonest. Make it poignant, give me a scene they can play the hell out of. Not too much dialogue, keep it sparse, but give it undertones. Don't come out of your room until you've finished, we'll send food and coffee in for you. I can't wait to shoot it.'

His mood infected everybody and the moment we got back I went to my typewriter. I knew this was the proving ground for me. Fortified with cigarettes and coffee I took a long hard look at the scene, made two or three false starts, and then it clicked; I saw the way through. Howard's approach was right. I kept the dialogue sparse, Jason's lines capable of double meanings. Having seen the location, I could visualise how it would play. Once I had got the key to unlock the scene, the rest flowed and I felt happy with it. Howard was happy, too, when I showed him the new pages.

'I think you've licked it, kid. Get Production to run these off and distributed. I really like it. Out of chaos came light.'

I didn't sleep well that night; my brain was still racing. The next morning I went out early with the rest of the crew. The art department had been at work all night, transforming the interior. Prop men and set dressers are a race apart. Where the hell they find the stuff is beyond me. There they were out on their own in a strange town, eight hundred miles from the studio, and yet somehow in a matter of hours they had come up with everything Howard wanted. Now, when I arrived, the painters were at work, ageing various sections to Lee's instructions, using the cobweb gun to Miss Havisham corners of the classroom. The big arc lamps were in place outside the windows on the south side of the building, scrims in front of them, so that, together with dimmers, Bernie could produce a soft light that simulated the storm skies. The generators had been baffled some distance away in deference to the sound crew; honeywaggons, Winnebagos and caterers' trucks were in position on the blind side of the building. It was all stations go, and once Howard had

340

given him the first setup, Bernie started blocking in his basic lighting, using the stand-ins. It was still raining, but rain rigs had been fixed over all the windows in case the storm abated.

By the time Lauren and Jason arrived everything was more or less ready. Jason surveyed the scene and nodded approval. 'I like the new stuff,' he said to me.

'How do you feel about it?' I asked Lauren.

'I like it. Isn't this place amazing?'

'Now it is,' I said. 'You should have seen it last night; there was nothing here.'

They both went off to get made up and changed. I grabbed a couple of cups of coffee and doughnuts and took one to Nikki.

There is something about life on a film location that is difficult to describe to outsiders. I've often thought of it as being like a group of soldiers who suddenly get a furlough in a foreign city and go on the town. You have a team of maybe some sixty or eighty people – cast, technicians, caterers – thrown together, who suddenly cast off their inhibitions. It is as though the escape from the rigidity of the studio routine has released them from their day-to-day strings. The mostly unlikely couples pair off. Perhaps the fact that everything – the hotel charges and meals – is being paid for, means that the period away takes on the character of a holiday, ignites a short-lived abandon. The wardrobe mistress strikes up a relationship with the driver of the generator truck, the soundman has an affair with a local extra, the focus-puller falls for one of the actresses, and for the duration of the location they are inseparable. Then, when the location finishes, in the majority of cases they go back to their normal existence and such is the transient nature of filming, they may never find themselves in the same close proximity again for years, so that the episode remains just a fading memory.

These thoughts went through my mind as I chatted with Nikki. I knew that even if I went to bed with her again, the affair would end with the film. She had a boyfriend back in Los Angeles, a stunt man who took any risk if they paid him enough. 'He's brilliant at falling off buildings,' she said.

'Doesn't that worry you?'

'No, he knows what he's doing.'

'Does he know what you're doing?'

'I won't tell if you don't.'

I hid myself at the back of the room out of everybody's eyeline when shooting began. The new scene played well, just as Howard had predicted. It had a different element to it now, aided by the setting. Bernie had slanted light behind the playing area so that Jason and Lauren were in semi-silhouette. Howard moved in closer for the chaste kiss and printed the first take.

'Perfect,' he said. 'Don't let's try and improve on it. Change Lauren's clothes – don't want you to catch pneumonia, honey. Robert, where are you?'

I came out from my hiding place. 'How was it for you?'

'Like you said, perfect.'

'It's giving me a couple of other ideas too, which I'll spell out this evening. Somebody bring me a cup of coffee.' He turned to the camera crew. 'Put a thirty-two on and let's lay a track. I want to change the angle and then pull back at the end of the kiss.'

The rest of the day went equally well, no snags, and they wrapped an hour early. I went to Lauren's Winnebago to congratulate her on her performance.

'Want to ride back with me?' she asked.

'Yes, I'd like to.'

She had a Teamster driver called Chuck, an excessive bear of a man with a blackhead-pitted neck that became purple whenever he was excited. He was very possessive with Lauren and made sure nobody took liberties with her.

342

Originally from the Bronx, he had one of those non-stop vocabularies that classified everybody and everything according to his right-wing philosophy. Once he was on a roll he was impossible to interrupt and that day he gave Lauren and me his rundown on what was wrong with the world. By the end of the journey we both felt pummelled.

The unit was working a six-day week, Sundays being the only rest days. In the elevator on the way up to our floor I had the sudden impulse to ask Lauren for a date. 'If you're not fixed to do anything better this Sunday, would you like a change of scenery? I thought maybe I'd drive out into the country and have some brunch. Care to join me?'

'Yes, that sounds a great idea.'

'Terrific.' I walked with her to the door of her room. 'And once again, I really thought you played the scene superbly today.'

'Well, you wrote me some good dialogue.'

As I went to my own room I tried to analyse my feelings. Was I attracted to her, or was it the case that, in my mind, she had become, in life, the desirable character that Jack had written? I couldn't decide.

31

That Sunday I waited until a decent hour, then rang Lauren's room. 'How long do you want before you're ready?'

'I'm ready now. I woke up early as usual. I'm programmed.'

'OK, give me half an hour to organise a hire car and I'll meet you in the lobby.'

'We could use my car. Save you money. Chuck likes being on golden hours.'

'I'm not looking to save money,' I said. 'Nor do I want another session with Chuck, engaging Teamster that he is.'

'OK, whatever.'

I had already asked the desk clerk to pick out a restaurant and give me directions, and was just about to leave my room when Howard rang me.

'Sorry to spring this on you, but do you mind working this morning?' he asked. 'The schoolroom rewrite means we have to change the scene in the market, but I've thought of a way of fixing it. Can you come to my suite?'

'Right,' I said, trying to keep the misery out of my voice. 'I'll be along in five minutes.'

I went and knocked on Lauren's door, but there was no answer. Rushing down to the lobby I found her waiting for me, talking to one of the other actors, a young man named Alvarez, who was playing a Mexican.

'I'm sorry but something's come up. Howard wants a script conference. I don't know how long it will take. I'm so sorry.'

'Can't be helped. Work comes first. Don't worry about it.'

'Can we make it later? I'll leave word at the desk. Or shall we say a definite time? How about three o'clock? I should be through by then.'

'Three o'clock's fine.'

Alvarez stood to one side during this exchange, but I got the distinct feeling that he would move in the moment I left.

I went through the session with Howard with mixed feelings and often wandering concentration before going back to my own room to type the revised dialogue. Howard wasn't satisfied by the first attempt and made additional changes, which again I had to type up before he gave his approval. 'Get it to the production office,' he instructed, 'so that the actors can have the new stuff in good time.'

By now it was after three o'clock.

'Can I use your phone first?'

'Go ahead.'

I rang Lauren's room, but there was no answer, so then I rang the front desk. 'Is Miss Taylor in the lobby?'

'I can't see her, sir.'

'Well, if you do, tell her I won't be long. My name's Peterson.'

When I put the phone down Howard gave me a quizzical look.

'Have I screwed up your day?'

'No, it was just a loose arrangement. Getting this right was much more important.'

'You were taking Lauren out, were you?'

'That was the idea.'

'What d'you think of her?'

345

'I think she's going to be terrific, everything I imagined for the role.'

'Apart from the role?'

'Nice.'

Howard nodded. 'A word in your ear, if you need it, which you probably don't. It's always a mistake to read too much into the life we lead. That's to say, be careful you don't confuse filming with real life. We're not real, most of us. How could we be when everything we do is built on wet sand? We manufacture, manipulate emotions for brief periods, and sometimes that fools us into believing they live on after the cameras stop rolling. You're going to write more scripts, work with other actresses.'

It was as though he was reading my mind. He walked to the window of the suite and opened the blinds, flooding the room with blood-red sunlight. 'Take a leaf out of my book, Robert – two failed marriages, both to actresses I directed. Three children I never see and God knows too many one-night stands.' He turned to face me again. 'So who am I to talk? Maybe you'll have better luck. Get out of here. Tell her it was all my fault.'

There was no sign of Lauren in the lobby nor any response from her room. I hung about outside the hotel for a while, kicking my heels. Other members of the crew came and went. Nikki went out on the second assistant's arm, giving me a smile as she passed. I walked around the block a couple of times, but when I returned there was still no sign of Lauren, and finally I went back up to my room. I sat on the edge of the bed. There was a fireplace facing me, empty except for some dusty, fake flowers. Staring at it took me straight back to a time when I was recuperating from a long childhood illness. It had been winter and I remembered that, day after day, I sat beside a log fire in a torpor, mesmerised by the darting blue flames and the hiss of pine sap, pondering the unknown future. That past mood returned and I lay back on the bed and fell into one of those heavy, daytime slumbers that I have always imagined must be akin to drowning. The more you struggle to force yourself awake, the deeper you sink. The next thing I was conscious of was somebody knocking on a door, but I couldn't be sure that the sound was not part of the dream. It took an effort to become aware of my surroundings, for by now the room was in semi-darkness. When eventually I came to and stumbled to the door there was nobody there. I sluiced my face in the tepid water that came out of the cold tap, which helped a little. Then I looked at my watch and found I must have slept two hours. I deliberated and then walked along the corridor to Lauren's room.

She opened the door at my first knock, still dressed as I had last seen her.

'Say it,' she said.

'Say what?'

'Say you're angry with me. I bitched the day, didn't I? I'm so sorry, but there was nothing I could do about it. It just happened.'

'What did?'

'Well, it's the corniest excuse in the world, but it happens to be true this time. When you couldn't make it this morning, Alvarez and a couple of the other actors invited me to drive out to an Indian reservation with them and explore some cliff dwellings. I told them I had to be back to see you at three, but their car broke down – ran out of petrol, can you believe? We were miles from anywhere and one of the boys had to thumb a lift to the nearest garage. He took an age before he returned and I was nowhere near a phone. The moment I got back I knocked on your door, but there was no answer. Do you believe me?'

'Of course I believe you.'

I stepped inside the room and she closed the door.

'Were you furious?'

'Do I look furious?'

'You look ruffled.'

'That's because I fell asleep for the rest of the afternoon.'

'Tired of waiting for me.'

'No, I had a heavy session with Howard. So what d'you want to do now?'

'First of all, am I forgiven?'

'You're forgiven,' I said.

'What I'd like to do right now is have a bath and change. I feel like a cave dweller myself. Then I'll do whatever you want to do. Why don't you stay here and have a drink? I shan't take long. I don't know what I've got over there, the hotel keeps bringing stuff and I don't drink much. Help yourself.'

She went into the bathroom, shedding her sweater as she went. I examined the contents of her bar. There was a hospitality bottle of white wine standing in an ice bucket, but the ice had melted. I opened it. Like the tap water, it was lukewarm. Then I couldn't find a glass.

'Where d'you keep the glasses?' I shouted.

'Do what?' she answered. The bath water was still running.

'Glasses? There don't seem to be any glasses.'

'Have one of these toothbrush glasses.'

'Can I come in?'

'Sure.'

I went into the bathroom. She was half-undressed, standing at the washbasin pinning up her luxuriant hair and I caught a glimpse of her small breasts in the mirror. 'Here,' she said, turning without embarrassment to hand me a glass. Her body had an even tan accentuated by being against the white tiles. I went back into the bedroom and while she splashed about in the bath we conducted a conversation through the open door.

'What were the cliff dwellings like?'

'We never got there. Tell you something funny, though. On the way we stopped at a trading post advertising genuine Indian jewellery and stuff. I picked out a belt, but it wasn't my size and I asked the Indian owner if he had any others. He said he was sold out except for that one, but he was expecting a shipment in from Japan next week. How genuine can you get?'

While she chattered away I looked around her room. She kept everything neat. There was a photograph on her bedside table, a family snapshot, together with a couple of paperbacks. I picked them up to see what she was reading – John O'Hara's *Butterfield 8* and a volume of poems by Robert Frost. She had used an old call sheet to keep her place. When I examined the photograph more closely I saw that it had been taken some years previously when she was a teenager. I took it that the man standing with his arms around her shoulders was her father. In the background I could see the corner of a clapboard house with a covered porch, and the snapshot had the look of a Norman Rockwell cover.

'Where do your folks live?'

'Sorry?' She suddenly appeared in the doorway with a towel loosely wrapped around her.

'I'm being nosy, looking at your things. Where was this taken?'

'At home. In Denver. Ever been there?'

'No.'

'You're from New York, aren't you?'

'Yes.'

I held my glass out to her. 'Want to share this?'

'I'll have a sip.' When she took it from me, the towel slipped from her and for a second or two she stood partially nude before me. I caught the scent of the bath oil she had used. Fixing the towel, she drank a little of the shared wine and handed the glass back to me. Remembering what

Howard had said, I saw the similarities between the scene she had played in the schoolroom with Jason. It was a moment when I might have kissed her and started something. But I didn't. Maybe she felt something, too, because I saw a blush appear on her neck.

'I really am sorry I spoiled our day,' she said.

'Well, we'll have a nice evening instead. What's your call tomorrow?'

'Not too bad. Eight thirty read for ten. And I don't have many lines to learn, unless you've written me a lot of new ones.'

'No, there weren't many changes for you. What d'you fancy in the way of food? American or Mexican?'

She pulled a face. 'Not too crazy about Mexican.'

'Me neither.'

'Let's go American. A steak and fries. I guess I could cut loose for once. Isn't dieting a bore?'

'I wouldn't know, I've never tried it. OK, American it is. Let me go downstairs and organise it.' I finished the drink and put the glass down.

'I'll be waiting in the lobby,' I said. 'Take your time.'

32

Nowadays you can get cured of most vices: go into rehab, join AA, become a born-again religious nut, scrub floors at the Betty Ford Clinic, pay a fortune to subdue your sexual libido. The one thing they can't stomach-pump out of you is the fame virus. Once that's in your bloodstream, forget looking for a cure, it's malaria. Nobody retires in our business. They go on until the coronary, kept afloat by liposuction, nose jobs, a new set of porcelain teeth, hair implants, or a complete makeover. I switched on television the other day and there was a former household name in movies doing a commercial for incontinence panties. Plucky little senior citizen, still in harness, still in show business, still desperate to cling on to the dying embers of fame even when her bladder has given out.

Thinking back, Santa Fe was where the virus entered my bloodstream. It was there, for the first time, that people gave me respect instead of grief, and from then onwards my life took on a different slant. I started to believe I had become a member of the magic circle, that select band who were going to make it in the movies. I became convinced that I cast a golden shadow. I soaked up the compliments like a sponge. People in the movie business always go over-board with praise, though one cynic put it another way: 'This is a business where they wish you well only if they know you're terminally ill.' In a variation of that cynicism, I was equally guilty: the compliments I paid to Lauren owed more to a desire to be part of her growing fame than any sincerity. Privately I didn't think she was that good, but you don't rock the boat until it's reached harbour. Bernie photographed her supremely well because he was a long-time member of the school whose livelihood depended on pleasing female stars. He once told me that he had been one of Dietrich's favourite cameramen. She was away from the Hollywood scene for seven years, and asked for him when she made her return. Viewing the early dailies, she was appalled by what she saw. 'What have you done to me, Bernie?' she asked him. 'I look terrible up there.' He said, 'I'm sorry, Marlene, it must be my fault. You see, I'm seven years older.'

When Bernie had performed his magic, Howard always picked her best takes, sometimes to Jason's disadvantage, and I knew why: Jason could always go back to the theatre in New York; Lauren was the one the studio had its money on; she was the seed corn. A good editor can always improve a performance, fashioning the takes, even using outtakes, in such a way as to fool critics and audiences that they are in at the birth of another Grace Kelly.

The Santa Fe location wound up three days over schedule, nothing disastrous but enough to make Howard edgy. He had another two weeks' interiors in the studio. Lauren stayed at the Chateau Marmont on Sunset while in Hollywood. The Marmont has always been up-market theatrical lodgings for those transients who aren't sure whether their options will be picked up. It stands on the opposite side of Sunset from where Jiff's used to be and has made its contribution to filmdom's legends over the years.

Despite his warning about not dating those you were working with, it was Howard who precipitated my affair with Lauren. I've said he came back from Santa Fe on edge and his mood infected the entire crew and cast. He took me to one side one evening as we came away from viewing the latest dailies.

'I'm worried about Lauren,' he said.

'In what way?'

'Have you noticed the change in her? The last few days her performance has gone downhill. I can't get to her. She seems out of it.'

'Maybe she's having her period.'

'No. I asked Wardrobe, and it's not that. Let me ask you something. You two haven't had a row, have you?'

'I've hardly seen her since we got back from Santa Fe.'

'What happened there?'

'Did I sleep with her, you mean? No, didn't touch her. We had a couple of meals together, but that was it.'

'Do something for me, Robert, because I don't want her to lose it now. She's still got some important scenes to shoot. Let me ask a favour. Romance her a little, try and find out what's bothering her. I've tried but she clams up.'

'OK, if that's what you want,' I said. 'Seems a long shot, but I'll try. Anything for the sake of the picture.'

The following day I made sure I was in early and went into Make-up. I talked to Jason and gave him a couple of small dialogue changes.

'I thought they might play better,' I said. 'Try them, but if they don't work for you, go back to the original.'

He studied the page I had given him. 'You could be right. Has Howard passed these?'

'Yes.'

I helped myself to coffee and a doughnut, then wandered into the next room and stood behind Lauren's chair. Wally was doing her eyes and it wasn't until she looked in the mirror to see the finished effect that she became conscious of me there.

'Hi,' I said. 'How goes it?'

'Fine,' she said in an offhand manner. 'You're around early.'

'Yes, I had to give Jason a couple of new lines.'

'Do they change my cues?'

'No, they don't affect you. It's the scene he has with Alvarez.'

Wally powdered her. 'I'll do the last checks on the set,' he said. Lauren got out of the chair. She still had her hair in curlers. I walked with her to her dressing room. Annie from Wardrobe was waiting for her.

Lauren said, 'I don't need to get dressed yet. They won't be ready for me for at least another hour.'

When Annie left, Lauren sat at her dressing table and fiddled with a nail file. 'So, what's with you?'

'Nothing much. Business as usual.'

'How's it going with Nikki?'

'Nikki? Why Nikki?'

'Rumour has it that you and she have been getting it on.'

'No. I haven't seen her since we got back from location.'

'You haven't seen me either. You were so friendly in Santa Fe. Since then you've hardly said hello.'

'Well, nothing intentional. I kept out of your way because I knew you had some big scenes coming up.'

'Which, as it happens, I've played very badly.'

'I don't think so.'

'Well, Howard does, I can tell. I thought you liked me.'

'I do like you. Even in hair curlers. Look, this is a silly conversation.'

'I know you slept with Nikki in Santa Fe, so don't deny it. She couldn't wait to tell me.'

'OK. But it was nothing, just a short holiday romance that was over as soon as it started. She has a regular boyfriend, as I'm sure she's also told you.' I put my hands on her shoulders and turned her round to face me. 'I didn't know it would have this effect on you. After all, why would I?' It was then that I noticed she had a snapshot stuck in the side of the mirror, a picture of both of us sitting side by side in director chairs on the location.

There was a knock on the dressing-room door and Annie shouted: 'I think they're nearly ready for you, Miss Taylor.'

'Two more minutes,' I shouted back. 'Look, Lauren, you're making something out of nothing. I know you're not working this Friday, so if you still want to have anything to do with me, why don't we make a date for Friday?'

She didn't answer immediately. 'Do you promise me it's over with Nikki?'

'Yes, I've told you.'

'All right,' she said reluctantly.

I leaned in and kissed her on the forehead. 'Until then, just concentrate on being brilliant.' Going on to the set, I took Howard to one side. 'You were right. It was me.'

'Why?'

'The old green eye. I made the mistake of boffing her stand-in.'

'That was a mistake, chum.'

'Not at the time. But I think I squared it. I'm taking her out this Friday. I don't know what you've landed me with, and it runs contrary to all your advice, so be it on your head.'

'Well, thanks. Let's hope her performance improves.'

Feeling a little like somebody from a blind-date agency, I collected her from the Chateau on the Friday morning. Minus her heavy studio make-up, and wearing no lipstick, she looked very young.

'So how would you like to spend the day? You choose.'

'Could we drive to the ocean? I haven't seen a beach since I went on holiday with my parents two years ago. I just want to breathe sea air.'

'OK, how about San Diego as a change from Malibu?'

'Is that far?'

'Take a couple of hours maybe.'

During the drive I casually tried to draw her out. She revealed she had only had one boyfriend who could be considered serious – a high-school heartthrob. 'We were in a production of *Romeo and Juliet* together.'

'And he played Romeo to your Juliet?'

'No such luck. Friar Laurence to my Nurse. We were both miscast. He wore a really ghastly wig that kept falling over his eyes.'

'So it must have been love,' I said.

'And he had braces on his teeth. I think I gave him up because I almost got metal poisoning. How about you?'

'Well, the first girl I fell in love with was a cousin. We used to have long petting sessions when her parents were out of the house.'

'How old were you?'

'Fourteen. I was a late starter.'

'And did you?'

'No, she was a good Catholic girl.'

'I'm Catholic,' Lauren said.

'For real?'

She shook her head. 'I don't go to Mass any more. Haven't for years. But I still believe in a sort of way. Do you believe in anything?'

'No.'

'Nothing at all?'

'Only William Morris.'

'When you say flip things like that you sound as though you've gone Hollywood.' She was silent for a while, shielding her eyes as a fierce reflection of the sun from the car in front blinded both of us. I pulled down the visors. Then she said: 'You're not doing this out of charity, are you?'

'Charity? No. Why would I do that?'

'You were different in Santa Fe. Then, until the other day, you seemed to ignore me. I got the feeling that maybe Howard had asked you to make the effort.'

Her exact reading of the situation surprised me. 'Why would you think that?'

'Because I've learned quite a lot since I got here. Everybody's nice to your face, but they're really only out for themselves.'

'And you think I'm the same?'

'I don't know. I'd like to think you were different from the rest,' she said, looking straight ahead.

She said very little else until we arrived in San Diego. The clean sea air, a welcome change from the city heat of Los Angeles, infected her with a sort of gaiety. I bought us both funny hats, and we walked along the sea front until we selected a restaurant. We had a long lunch in the open air under striped umbrellas, and drank spritzers with our fresh, grilled sea bass. Small sailing boats tacked on the dazzling water, seagulls swooped low over us in search of pickings and a street busker came and juggled for us.

During that lunch I became aware that she made me feel happy in a way that hadn't happened since my early days with Amanda. For too long, when alone, I had wanted to exorcise Amanda for ever, to be rid of jealousy and hate, to make my life a blank sheet again on which somebody else could write. After lunch we walked along the beach for a while where Lauren took her shoes off and paddled. She picked up some pebbles and skated them across the water.

'You know why I was so upset about Nikki, don't you?' she said.

'Not really.'

'Can't you guess?'

'I might make the wrong guess.'

'Didn't it occur to you that you could have gone to bed with me instead of a substitute?'

'No, it didn't if you want an honest answer. I liked you, which I hope was obvious, but I wasn't on the make.'

'You used the past tense.'

'For what?'

'You said "liked".'

'Sorry. I *like* you. Is that better? I like you very much. Come here.' I turned her towards me and kissed her gently. 'You're a very complicated character, you know that, don't you?'

'Why am I?'

'Well, believe it or not, I'm not used to girls offering themselves to me. And, actually, if we want to get everything out of the way, I thought you were attracted to Alvarez.'

'Alvarez? No way.'

'I know he had eyes for you.'

'Well, if he did, I didn't notice. You're thinking of that Sunday, aren't you?'

'Yes.'

'Did you feel jealous?'

'Yes. Jealous I wasn't with you. Maybe if my car had broken down instead of theirs, we wouldn't be having this conversation.'

'So, what now? Shall we begin again?'

'Sure. I'll introduce myself. My name's Robert Peterson. I'm a screenwriter and at the moment I'm lucky enough to be spending the day at the beach with my leading lady, a desirable young actress for whom great things are prophesied. I was wondering whether she'd like to come back to my pad and see my etchings?'

'To which she replied, I'd like that very much.'

I kissed her again and I put my arm around her as we walked to where I had left the car. She was in a happy mood for the return journey.

'So this is where you hide yourself,' she said when we arrived at my place. 'It's great.' She wandered around. 'You keep it so neat.'

'Sometimes. You're seeing it at its best.'

'And is this where you write?' she asked, standing by my desk.

'That's where I try to write.'

There was a sheet of work in progress left in my typewriter. It was a letter I had begun to Amanda. 'Don't read that,' I said, tearing the paper out of the machine and crumpling it up.

Now Lauren found a copy of *A Fine and Private Place*. 'Can I have this?'

'If you want.'

'Will you sign it to me? Or is it your only copy?'

'No, it's just been republished.'

I sat down and wrote an inscription on the flyleaf: *For Lauren, who made my words come alive, With love.*

'Haven't you got nice handwriting. Mine's terrible. Even I can't read it sometimes. I shall treasure this and I can't wait to read it.'

'Come out on the deck, such as it is,' I said. 'We might see some dolphins.'

'Really?'

'Yes, they're usually around. The other day I spotted a whale blowing.'

'Chuck told me Malibu's the place where the grunions run. Have you ever seen that?'

'No. I've been told that too, but I've never met anybody who's actually seen them.'

'What are they supposed to be doing when they run?'

'Mass suicide, I guess.'

'I'm afraid of the sea,' she said. 'My parents took me on a cruise once across the Pacific to Tahiti, and the whole time all I could think of, looking at the water day after day, was that it went on and on down for ever. It's not blue when you're way out, not like they always show you in the ads, it's black. You imagine all the things that are down there. When I swim I never go out of my depth. Other things in life are like that, aren't they?'

'How d'you mean?'

'Haven't you ever started something and then wondered if your feet will touch bottom?'

'Yes, maybe, once or twice.'

'D'you think I'm odd?'

'No.'

'I think I'm odd.'

I left her scanning the flat ocean while I went back into the house and fetched a bottle of wine. When it got to us, we lay side by side on the inflatable mattress. Lauren fell asleep almost immediately, her face very close to mine. The slanting angle of sunlight caught the faint golden down above her upper lip. She had a full, pretty mouth, perfectly shaped. A ladybird suddenly alighted on her hair and I gathered it up and examined it as it rested in my palm. The speckled red shell opened down the middle and the minute black wings fluttered when I prodded it with my little finger. It seemed in no hurry to fly off. I wondered if the lives of insects were complicated like human beings'. *Ladybird, ladybird, fly away home, your house is on fire, your children have gone.* Who the hell had invented that rhyme? And why? I blew on the insect softly and a second later it took off and was lost to sight. Lauren stirred and her lips parted as something in her sleep made her smile.

After a while I eased myself off the mattress without disturbing her and went into the kitchen to prepare something for us to eat. I had some smoked salmon, avocados, potato salad in the fridge, together with some crusty Italian bread. While I was busying myself the phone rang.

'Just touching base,' Julian said. 'How's it going? Have you seen any cut together?'

'I saw an hour's rough assembly when we got back from Santa Fe.'

'Were you pleased with it?'

'Yes. Howard's doing a great job.'

'How's the girl?'

'Good. Very good.'

'I've got two tickets for the ballet tomorrow night, thought you might like to come.'

'Thanks, but ballet's wasted on me,' I said. 'Take somebody who'll appreciate it.'

'Well, didn't want you to think I'd forgotten you. Let's fix to meet next week or whenever. Give me a call when you have a free evening. I've missed seeing you.'

I didn't pick up on that. 'How about any offers coming my way? I'll be out of a job soon.'

'I'm working on it.'

The sound of the phone had wakened Lauren. She came in from the deck, her face still crumpled from sleep.

'Julian, excuse me, I'm in the middle of trying to fix a scene Howard wants for tomorrow. Thanks for calling.'

'Who's Julian?' Lauren said when I hung up.

'My agent.'

'Any good?'

'He got me this job. I haven't been with him long, but long enough for him to make a pass.'

'A pass? My God! How did you deal with that?'

'With difficulty.' I pointed to the food. 'Is this OK? Or we could go out, if you'd rather.'

'No, don't let's go out. This is great. How long was I asleep?'

'An hour maybe.'

'I need to take a shower. My hair feels sticky from the salt air. Can I?'

'Of course. Let me get you some fresh towels.'

'D'you have a hair dryer?' she said when she came out of the bathroom wearing my robe.

'Sorry, no.'

'Men don't, do they? Funny that.'

'We haven't got that much hair to dry. Come and eat.'

She turbaned a towel around her head, sat cross-legged on the floor by the coffee table and began to pile her plate. 'I'm really hungry. Even after our delicious lunch, isn't that shameful? Can we put some music on?'

I showed her my stack of LPs and she selected Clooney singing 'Mr Sandman', which she played twice. 'I love those sorts of numbers. Real mush. I guess I've got no taste in music. No sophistication.'

'What does that matter? I know people who've got sophistication coming out of their ears, and they bore the ass off you.' I told her about the dinner I had had with the Kosners shortly after I'd arrived in Hollywood. 'A mink-covered toilet seat,' I said, 'you can't get more sophisticated than that. Let me play you something else.' I selected a recording of *Tosca* from my somewhat eclectic collection. 'It's a bit scratched because I've nearly worn it out. Puccini, "The stars were shining". Now, some musical snobs think liking anything other than Mozart or Bach shows a lack of sophistication. Puccini's out because he's too popular.' We listened to the rest of *Tosca* as the light faded and a wind blowing in from the ocean chilled the room. I got up and closed the patio doors. 'You want a blanket around you? I'd light a fire except I haven't got any firewood.'

She didn't answer for a moment, then said very quietly: 'We could go to bed – wouldn't that be a better idea?'

'Have you thought of what you'd be letting yourself in for?'

'Yes.'

'I could be bad news.'

'Suppose I don't mind risking that?' she said. She got up and went into the bedroom. I finished my wine before joining her. She was already in bed and as I stood looking at her she pulled the sheet away from her. I let my own clothes drop to the floor and got in beside her. Lauren pulled the sheet back over us and pressed the whole length of her body against me, her breasts soft against my chest, her mouth searching mine, her tongue snaking into my mouth. And so Lauren, the lapsed Catholic who swooned over mushy pop lyrics and didn't like swimming out of her depth, seduced me.

362

33

When the affair with Lauren began the subject furthest from my mind was marriage. I would gladly have married Amanda before Phoenix, with or without our child, but that was different. That was love.

Lauren didn't move in with me. We both abided by conventional Hollywood morality. It was all part of the preservation of the species – it was OK to screw your brains out, but strictly *verboten* to flaunt it by cohabiting openly. All marriages were sacrosanct until the divorce. Some of the biggest whores and adulterers were portrayed as playing Happy Families in the fan magazines. It didn't matter if they hadn't shared the marriage bed for years and were only talking to each other through their lawyers, they still smiled for the cameras until the papers were served. After which the publicity machines would go into overdrive, churning out a new set of fantasies. *Putting her recent divorce behind her, Betty Bloop (seen here needlepointing in her luxurious Brentwood home) is determined not to let it affect her blossoming career. She has thrown herself into work on her latest film and has found consolation in the hundreds of letters of support from her faithful fans. 'I will never forget my public,' she said.*

The film was winding up now and the buzz was around that Howard had come in with a winner. Zanuck decided to hold it back for a Christmas release, opening in time to qualify for that year's Oscars. The rules were that a film had to play a minimum of one week in the Los Angeles area before the end of the year.

Lauren got very emotional at the wrap party. I could understand how she felt; I felt a bit of it myself. End-of-picture parties are strange occasions, part jubilation, part relief, part sadness, difficult to describe to outsiders. The best I can do is to say that, if you're an actor, it must be like the end of schooldays when the familiar is suddenly taken away and you have to face the unknown. Your performance is trapped in the emulsion and, good or bad, there's nothing you can do about it any more. Your career is now in other people's hands – the editor, the composer, the poster artist, whoever decides the campaign of how to sell it, and, ultimately, the fickle public – that great, anonymous, amorphous mass that lies in wait, sometimes well disposed, sometimes unforgiving. It's Russian roulette and you're not even spinning the chambers. You have to wait until the film is exposed. Will it open against stiff competition? Or, by a happy quirk of timing, will it be screened in a week when all its rivals get panned? Will an influential critic come out with an early rave, and the others follow his lead for fear of being considered square? Who knows? Nobody knows anything. All those thoughts go through your mind at the wrap party as you drink the free liquor and eat the provided food, and exchange presents, swop anecdotes about the weeks you are leaving behind, say how you hope you'll work together again, insincerity mixed with genuine feelings, until finally, the lights go out, the stage is bare and you go home to a void, a feeling of let-down. You've forgotten to reprogramme the alarm clock and it goes off at the same hour it has done for the past weeks. You throw yourself over the side of the bed and pad for the bathroom, then suddenly realise there is no need: it's all over.

I think that Lauren was more affected than I was. Now there was nobody attending to her every need, she was just another out-of-work actress. True, she went into the studio several times to pose for publicity shots, but it wasn't the same – everybody had moved on. She had some consolation; Zanuck picked up her option and she was now signed to a term contract, one-sided like they all were, but it held out hope for the future. Even Howard had changed. After taking a short holiday, he spent most of his time in the cutting rooms, and although we had a meal together, like everyone else he was more concerned with what was next going to come his way.

'You got anything you're developing?'

'Only a new novel.'

'Will it make a film?'

'Can't tell yet.'

'Well, let me have first look.'

Before, I had never thought of him as somebody insecure. 'Know the trouble with most of us?' he said. 'We take ourselves too seriously. You'd think from the way some rant on we're remaking the Sistine Chapel every time a camera turns. Sure we make good movies, some great ones, but that's all they are – movies for the masses, this century's most widely available drug. And when television really takes a hold, watch out. You think our business is corrupt? Whoever controls television controls the price of everything, your food on the plate, what news they want to give you, who to vote for – which in turn means who can afford the most dollars for air time. I like this business, it's been good to me, given me everything I have, but I hope I'm never fooled by it.' He switched topics abruptly. 'How is it with you and my young discovery? I hear you're a number.'

'Yes, we've been seeing a lot of each other.'

That was the moment I looked across the restaurant and saw Billy and Amanda being shown to a table. Howard turned his head to see whom I was staring at.

'Somebody you know?'

'Yes, Billy Fisher, a British producer I once worked for.'

'That's one of the girls I tested, isn't it?'

'Yes,' I said, 'he has her under contract.'

Howard stopped looking. 'Going back to Lauren, I think she'll make it if she gets the roles. You should write something especially for her. I think she's good, but having directed her, I think she's limited. Since I threw you together, how serious are you about her?'

'Pretty serious.'

'Well, I wish you luck.' He beckoned for the check. 'We're putting the music on next week. Come along if you have the time.'

'I'll make time,' I said.

On the way out we were forced to pass Billy's table. Amanda gave me a ghost of a smile when our eyes met, but Billy studiously avoided me.

'Hello, Amanda,' I said. 'How's it going?'

'Fine.'

It seemed unjust for her still to be beautiful and calm while I stood there with my heart racing. 'Good,' I said, at a loss. 'Nice to see you again. How are you, Billy?'

'No better for meeting you again,' he replied.

'Likewise,' I said, which was the only rejoinder I could think of before walking away.

The chance encounter rattled me more than I had imagined possible. I thought, will I ever get over her? Hollywood was such a small place; sooner or later you were bound to bump into people you knew. While we were both still in the same place, I would see her again, always rekindling the agony. How many times in the future would I awake with a sense of pain? In the days when we had been together, I had often tried to get her to say that there would be no end to our affair, that eventually we would marry. I would have happily settled for a lie, such was the intensity of my desire never to lose her.

I wasn't clever enough to conceal my mood with Lauren when I returned home.

'Something wrong?' she asked. 'Didn't your dinner with Howard go well?'

'No, it was fine.'

'You seem preoccupied about something.'

'I think I ate something that disagreed with me.'

'Has Howard finished cutting?'

'He's got a fine cut. I'm going to see it next week when they're putting the music to it.'

'Did he say how I've come out? Tell me the truth.'

'He seemed pleased with everybody.'

'But what did he say about me?'

'He thought you'd make a big success. They wouldn't have picked up your option otherwise.'

That night, when we made love, the compulsion grew in me to abandon the past for ever, to do something irrevocable. Lying comes so easily when we are hurt. Curled beside Lauren in the lazy aftermath of the act, I asked her to marry me.

She raised herself in the bed and stared down at me. 'Do you mean it? Don't say it if you don't mean it.'

'I want to marry you,' I repeated.

'Oh, darling, you don't know how I've longed for you to say that. I was so scared you'd just want to go on as we are. I wanted to marry you the first time I saw you.'

'Now you tell me,' I said, with a smile, trying to make light of this strange moment of truth. She had so much more capacity for love than I did; she judged all love by her own. Seen from below, her hair falling over her face, she seemed like a naked child, absurdly young, absurdly happy. I had never felt so alone.

34

'When shall we tell the parents?' Lauren asked over breakfast the following morning.

'Whenever you like.'

'Mummy will want me to be married from home, the full church bit. She's seriously religious when it comes to marriage.'

'Really? She wouldn't prefer somewhere quiet and discreet like Reno or Vegas?'

'You are kidding, aren't you?'

I wasn't, but I pretended otherwise. 'As if I'd start married life by offending your mother. How d'you think your parents will take the news?'

'They'll adore you like I do. How about yours? Why don't you ring them now?'

'Later,' I said. 'Let's buy the ring first, show everybody that we mean business.'

'I like your style, Mr Peterson.'

At the first jeweller we visited we were dealt with by one of those assistants, probably specially bred for the job, who had perfected the art of the put-down: if the customer doesn't immediately zero in on a diamond as big as the Ritz, they swiftly lose interest. We endured the insufferable condescension for a while then, after some mutual body language had passed between us, took pleasure in telling him that nothing he had shown us was up to scratch. It was a different story in Tiffany's. There nobody intimidated us and I further reduced my bank account buying a small blue diamond in a simple, classic mount. Afterwards we celebrated with scrambled eggs and lox, the best in town, at Nate an' Al's.

'Let's ring them from here,' Lauren said. 'I can't wait any longer.'

'OK, you go first.'

She used the restaurant's courtesy phone and I saw her inviting admiration of her ring from the staff while she waited for the connection. When she rejoined me she was crying.

'She hated the whole idea?' I said.

'No, she was over the moon. Started making plans immediately. I always cry when I'm happy. Your turn.'

It took four or five rings before my mother answered. She had never liked phones, treating them as alien objects that seldom brought good news.

'Mother, I'm getting married.'

'Just a minute, dear, I've got something on the stove.' When she picked up the receiver again she said: 'Did you say you were married?'

'No, getting married.'

'Can you afford to?'

'Yes, I wrote and told you things are going well now and I'm earning good money.'

'I hope she's a nice girl. What's her name?'

'Lauren. She's the star of the film I wrote.'

'Have I seen her in anything?'

'Doubt it, this is her first film. We're getting married in Denver.'

'Why Denver, why not here?'

'That's where Lauren's home is, and it's the bride's choice, isn't it? As soon as I can I'll bring her East to meet you. Are you pleased?'

'Yes, if it's what you want, dear,' she said ambiguously.

Too late for that, I thought, going back to our table where Lauren was flourishing her ring to another waiter.

'What did they say?'

'I only spoke to my mother. She just loved the idea.'

'We must let the studio know. They're bound to want to do some publicity. And Howard, of course. If it hadn't been for Howard we'd never have met. I'm so excited, aren't you?'

'Yes,' I said.

Howard was the first person she rang. Never one to let grass grow under his feet if it might help the movie, he took care of publicity and the following day we went to the studio for a joint photo session. The story was given to Louella as an exclusive. When we emerged from the stills studio there was a new Cadillac convertible, tied with ribbons, parked outside. A note on the windscreen read: *Start as you mean to go on, travel through life first class. Enjoy. Love, Howard.*

I hadn't rung Julian, but as soon as he read it in Louella's column he was on the phone.

'Good career move, sweetie, although a loss to the rest of us. I hope we're not going to hear the patter of tiny feet too soon after the blessed event. Dirty diapers tend to blunt creativity. Still, I'm always thrilled when young love blossoms. What d'you want me to give you?'

'How about another job?' I said. 'I pushed the boat out buying the ring, and funds are getting low again.'

We sent a set of photographs to our respective families and gave Hedda Hopper an interview to balance the protocol that existed between her and Louella. Hopper, an ex-actress, had a glacial charm and we were wary about what we said to her. Then, when Lauren had finished all her post-production looping, we decided to christen Howard's Cadillac and drive to Denver. That proved too ambitious. We should have taken the plane because it was a hell of a long way, we stayed in lousy hotels en route and arrived frazzled.

Her parents lived in an affluent neighbourhood, a quiet tree-lined suburb where their pre-war detached house stood on a large plot. Her father was on the board of a pharmaceutical company whose fortunes had prospered as a result of some new wonder drug for arthritis. He proved to be a tall, slightly stooped man with cold, grey eyes and that clipped delivery often affected by those who have spent their lives giving orders to others. He was polite but not over-effusive when he welcomed me into their home. I had arrived dressed in my usual casual clothes and I noted the faintest grimace cross his face as he gave me the once-over. He, on the other hand, wore a formal suit. The house was expensively, but conventionally furnished with nothing out of place. Folklore contends you can always see what a daughter will become when you look at the mother's face. I guessed Mrs Taylor was in her late forties, well preserved, and she had passed on her bone structure and clear skin to Lauren. More talkative than her husband, she fussed over me and was at pains to make me feel welcome. Once she had shown me to my room and made sure I had everything I needed, she and Lauren disappeared to discuss whatever mothers and daughters do discuss on such occasions. I took a quick shower and changed into the suit Woody had given me long ago before joining Mr Taylor downstairs. I found him waiting for me in his study, a panelled room with one wall bookshelved, the shelves holding sets of the classics, the sort of collection bought by the yard. He had mixed some cocktails ready for my reappearance.

'I understand from Lauren you're a writer,' as he handed me a stiff Manhattan.

'Yes, sir.'

'A film writer, yes?'

'Yes.'

'Does that pay well?'

'It can do, sir.'

'I take it you can support Lauren? She's been used to the best, you know.'

'I certainly intend to support her.'

'Strange, having a daughter. You wouldn't know about that, of course. One moment they're sitting on your lap, the next minute they've flown the coop. Where do you intend to live?'

'I have a rented house at the moment, in Santa Monica.'

'Where's that?'

'On the coast, just outside Los Angeles. After we get married we'll be looking for somewhere else, somewhere bigger.'

'Yes. Want to talk to you about that.' He cleared his throat and sat behind his desk as though he was now about to start a formal interview of a new employee. 'As you know, Lauren's our only child, and I've always made certain plans for her. You can see the sort of home she grew up in, and I want to make sure she has the same lifestyle when she gets married. Have you been around?'

'Around, sir?'

He drained the last of his Manhattan. 'Sown your wild oats.'

'I've had other girlfriends, yes, but nothing serious until I met Lauren.' Listening to my responses it was almost as if I was sitting at a typewriter writing a script.

'Bit of a surprise, you see. Came out of the blue. Didn't know of your existence a few weeks ago. You're from New York, I believe?'

'Yes.'

'Don't care for the place myself. Everybody in too much of a hurry. And of course, Hollywood is just a name to me. Can't say that I was over-pleased when Lauren decided to become an actress – chancy profession, one reads some alarming tales.'

372

'I think Lauren's very level-headed, sir.'

'Oh, yes. Not her I was thinking of. Others, the people she has to mix with. What's your religion?' His questions dodged about, coming at me from all angles. 'She was brought up a Catholic,' he continued without waiting for my reply. 'Are you Catholic?'

'No, I'm not, sir.'

'Something you have to think about when you have children.'

Whether he intended to press me further on the subject, or whether he had temporarily lost his prepared way, he suddenly switched topics. 'I saw the car you arrived in. Latest model.'

'Yes, it was our first wedding gift, from the director of Lauren's film.'

'Very generous. People around here don't go much for ostentation. Not the right people, that is. Creates the wrong impression. Do you want a refill?'

'I won't, thank you.'

'One's your limit, is it?'

'On an empty stomach, yes.'

'Well, I'm glad we've had this talk. Course, the rest will be out of my hands. The wedding, I mean. Leave all that to Mrs Taylor.' He got up to straighten a picture on the wall. Relief finally arrived as Lauren and her mother joined us.

'What's Daddy been telling you about me?' Lauren asked, squeezing my hand. 'You haven't been grilling him, have you, Daddy?'

'We thought three bridesmaids,' her mother cut in. 'The first Saturday in September. Put that into your diary, Don. That doesn't give us much time, so we must start thinking about the guest list. You must give me your numbers, Robert. Do you have a large family?'

'Quite a few, mostly on my mother's side, but they're scattered about all over the country.'

'How about brothers and sisters?'

'Two sisters, both married with children.'

'Children get restless at weddings,' Mr Taylor said. 'Run all over the place.'

'I must decide who's going to cater it,' his wife continued. 'We went to the Millers' wedding last month, didn't we, dear? Every course was cold by the time it reached the table.'

For the next half an hour she and Lauren chattered as though planning a full-scale military invasion. Taylor and I were virtually ignored and I sensed he was moving over to my side, on several occasions giving me a conspiratorial look. He insisted on taking us out for a celebratory dinner at his golf club. I offered to drive them in our car, forgetting Taylor's earlier remark about ostentation, and the offer was declined. We went in his Buick. At the club I met a bewildering number of total strangers and had my first experience of being introduced as 'my future son-in-law'. The male members all seemed to have been taken from the same mould. I was careful to drink very little, conscious that I was on trial. Lauren, on the other hand, was completely at ease on her home territory and it became obvious that, for all his reservations about Hollywood and the career she was following, her father was inordinately proud of her. From the way he was treated by the club's staff, he had local clout.

'Do you play?' he asked. 'We could have a round tomorrow.'

'No. Tennis is my game,' I said.

The subject was dropped and most of the conversation over dinner concentrated on the impending wedding, taking in such minutiae as how many layers the cake should have, what flowers should decorate the church, whether they would be able to get the Cardinal to conduct the ceremony and whether the reception should be held outdoors. It was so far removed from the world I had left behind as to be almost incomprehensible. I wondered if Taylor believed that his beloved daughter was going to the altar a virgin and what his reaction would be if he knew the sacred hymen was no longer intact.

That night, lying alone in a strange bed, I convinced myself that Taylor had seen through me, that everybody would eventually see through me. When I finally fell asleep, the portents haunted my dreams.

35

We stayed in Denver for another three days and by then Mrs Taylor had everything buttoned up for the wedding: the date was set, her own guest list drawn up, Lauren's bridal dress was being designed. It wasn't until we set out on the journey back to Los Angeles that Lauren suddenly said: 'Daddy's going to buy us a house as his wedding present. Did he tell you?'

'No, he didn't, as a matter of fact.'

'You sound annoyed. It's just that he wants everything to be perfect for us.'

'Yes,' I said. 'Well, so do I.'

She was silent for a few minutes. 'The other thing is, did Mommy say anything to you about religion?'

'No. But your father mentioned it. He wanted to know if I was Catholic.'

'It's so important to them.' Another silence. 'Would you ever take instruction?'

'You joking? I thought you were lapsed, or whatever the expression is.'

'I am, but that doesn't mean I've left the Church. Once you're in you're in for ever. Would you?'

'No way.'

'Not even for me?'

'That's blackmail,' I said, clamping up.

Once back in Los Angeles Lauren was put to work by Publicity. She did glamour sessions with her sweater padded

376

out and nearly froze to death splashing in the surf at Malibu in a swimming costume. I spent my time in the cutting rooms, keen to learn as much as I could. At weekends Lauren and I went house-hunting armed with the promise of Daddy's money.

'How much did he say we could go to?' I asked.

'He didn't. Daddy's not like that. He just wants me to have something I like.'

'Something we both like,' I corrected.

'Of course.'

We looked at places in Beverly Hills, some on the flats, and others higher in the canyons. The realtor showed us one property on Laurel Way and with a sense of *deja vu* I realised it was the house where I had first met Woody, now done over by a subsequent owner, as all the houses were, given time. Nothing was ever permanent in Beverly Hills and taste with a sell-by date could be bought off the shelf.

I rang Woody that same night and told him.

'Don't buy it,' he said. 'It's riddled with termites and it's in the fire zone. And in any case, how could you afford it?'

'I can't, but Daddy is putting up the bread.'

'Well, good for Daddy. You're a kept man already. Listen, go with it. When the marriage fails you'll get half. Community property law.'

'Jesus, Woody, you're such a cynic.'

'Only way to be. Hey, I keep getting good vibes about your film. Word is you've got your name on a smash. You're such a lucky bastard. When are you going to cut me in? I started you, remember?'

'Of course I remember. One of the reasons I rang you was to ask whether you'd be my best man at the wedding.'

'You want a Jewish best man? What happened to all your gentile friends?'

'Will you?'

'Weddings scare me.'

'This one scares me. Her parents want me to become a Catholic.'

'That *is* scary. You going to do it?'

'God, I don't know.'

'Do you think a good-looking Jewish boy would be a hit at a Catholic wedding?'

'Woody,' I said, 'you're my only hope. Say yes, please.'

'Let me think about it.'

If I imagined the subject would go away, I was wrong. Lauren pursued the idea that same night after we made love, choosing the moment when I was most malleable.

'I had a letter from Mommy today asking if you'd made a decision.'

'Decision about what?'

'You know, whether you'll agree to become a convert. It's so important to her. She's worried we'll be living in mortal sin.'

'Doesn't she know we're already in mortal sin?'

'It wouldn't ever cross her mind. She'd be so happy if you agreed. I know she's talked to the Cardinal and he's promised to push things through.'

I began to perceive a conspiracy. 'What does that mean exactly – "push things through"?'

'Just speed things up. Pass the word to Father Paul.'

'Who's Father Paul?'

'One of the local priests here.'

'How can you go along with this? You told me you don't believe in all that mumbo jumbo any more, yet you want me to join.'

'I didn't say I didn't believe, period. All I said was I don't go to Mass regularly.'

We came dangerously close to our first major row, but I refused to give a definite answer. What with Daddy's money and now this, I was being boxed in and I didn't like it.

'If they feel that strongly, I'm amazed they let you become an actress.'

'Oh, I've always been able to twist Daddy around my little finger.'

The next thing that happened was the studio decided Lauren should go to New York and stockpile a series of interviews for the national magazines, which would then be held to come out just before the release of the movie. I was allowed to go along for the ride; in those days nobody was that much interested in writers unless they had a big name, but they thought somebody might want to do a piece on me about the marriage.

I know it sounds far-fetched today when, despite the endless advertising hypes, air travel is about as glamorous as taking the Staten Island ferry, but at that time people actually dressed smartly when they took a plane trip. No dirty jeans and backpacks. No coach fares – all one class. I'd never flown before so I'd no idea what to expect, but that first trip was a revelation. The plane Lauren and I flew in coast to coast (a Douglas as I remember) had a piano player tinkling the ivories at the rear of the cabin. It was like an airborne, daytime nightclub. The main meal had not been microwaved to the consistency of boiled Nike trainers and was served by air hostesses who didn't look as though they had been seconded from a maximum security women's jail. Those were the good old days before they introduced the pack-them-in-like-cattle era. Roll back the clock.

It was good to be in New York again. I'd forgotten what a shot of adrenalin it always gave me to join the throngs on Fifth Avenue in the sunshine. I loved the blast of noise coming at you non-stop, the books stacked high in Double-day's windows, the demonic taxi drivers, even the sad nags outside the Plaza. After the sterility of Beverly Hills it was like returning to the Promised Land. We had been checked in to separate rooms at the Carlyle, then as now, one of the most stylish hotels going.

While Lauren began to work her way through a punishing schedule, starting at breakfast the first day, I took a taxi to Queens. My father was at work when I arrived home and I was shocked by my mother's changed appearance. She seemed to have aged considerably in the fifteen months since I'd last seen her.

'Why didn't you give me more warning?' she said. 'I'd have cooked something special. Are you on your own?'

'For the moment, yeah. Lauren's working, but you'll see her before we have to leave.'

We sat in the kitchen, which had always been the hub room. I'd forgotten how drab our apartment was. There was a tired scruffiness to it, and overall a musty smell – too many meals had been cooked in that cramped space, the odours trapped in the very plaster on the walls. It reminded me of a set from *The Honeymooners* and I tried not to let my dismay show while I was brought up to date with the inevitable chapter of bad news. Why is it the older generation become so concentrated on ill health, as if only by reciting the misfortunes of others can they hang in? I listened patiently as she ran down the latest list – Uncle Walt had inoperable prostate, her best friend had Parkinson's, the daughter of her hairdresser was married to a wife-beater, a distant cousin had had a breast removed. Looking at my mother, at her lined face beneath the wispy, badly permed hair, I could have been listening to a stranger. It was a long time before she got around to asking about my life and when, eventually, the subject of the wedding was included, I made the mistake of saying I'd buy her a new dress for the occasion.

She immediately bridled. 'Why would you buy me a new dress?'

'Because I want to and because I can afford to now.'

'Your father will buy me what I need.'

'Well, I know that.'

'You trying to make him feel small?'

'Of course not. Forget it.'

'Is it going to be a fancy affair, then?'

'I don't know about fancy. Since she's an only daughter, I guess her parents want to make a bit of a splash. They're inviting over a hundred people.'

'I see. They've got that many friends, have they? I could count ours on two hands.'

'Well you don't have to match them.' I quickly changed the subject. 'What I thought was, tomorrow I could take us all out to dinner somewhere when Lauren has finished her interviews.'

'What's wrong with eating here?'

'Nothing. I'd just like to give you and Dad a treat. Aren't you pleased I'm able to?'

We made more uneasy conversation until my father arrived home. As with my mother, age had crept up on him and his thinning hair was now much greyer. He went straight to the fridge and took out two beers but before he could open them I produced the bottle of Chivas Regal which the film company had left for me in my hotel room. He examined the label. 'Twelve years old,' he said. 'You must be made of money.'

'Open it.'

'No, I'll save this for an occasion.'

'Isn't this an occasion? You can both congratulate me on getting married.'

'I don't touch that stuff,' my mother said.

'When are we going to meet your bride?'

'I explained to Mother, Lauren's busy doing press interviews, but I thought I'd take us all out for dinner tomorrow.'

'OK by me.'

'I'll send a car for you. We'll do it in style.'

'You sleeping here tonight?'

'No, they put us both into the Carlyle hotel. All paid for. You look well, Dad. Been keeping well?'

'Have to pace myself.' He finally opened the Scotch and poured us both a measure.

'He hasn't been well,' my mother said. 'And small wonder, he drinks too much.'

'Now don't start on that. Nothing to do with that.' He raised his glass to me, then took a slug. 'That hits the spot. So, you both sharing a bed at this Carlyle?'

'Course they're not,' my mother said.

'Times have changed, Mother. Young people don't wait like we did.' He winked at me.

'Well, I don't want to hear it.'

'How're things going at work, busy?' My father worked in the dispatch department of a haulage firm.

'Pretty busy.'

We talked of this and that for another half-hour, but it was hard sledding and I made the excuse that I had to leave to meet a producer. 'I'll ring Mother and let you know the arrangements for tomorrow night.'

Lauren had just finished up her last interview of the day when I got back to the hotel. 'Boy, what a day,' she said. 'Am I out of it. That was the eleventh interview on the trot. And they all ask the same questions, have you noticed?'

'No, because I've never done it.'

'What've you been doing?'

'I went back to see my folks, visit the old haunts. You'll finally get to meet them tomorrow. We're all having dinner.'

'At your home?'

'No, I thought we'd eat here. The food's sensational, I'm told, and it'll give them a treat.'

'Oh, that's a pity, darling. I've been dying to see where you lived.'

'It's nowhere special,' I said.

36

Choosing to eat somewhere as elegant as the Carlyle was a mistake. My parents were awed by the whole experience. The formal ambience of the Carlyle dining room freaked them out, the menu baffled them. It took an age for either of them to decide. I felt sorry that I couldn't find a way of putting them at their ease. My father was wearing his one good suit, but the collar of his badly starched shirt stuck out at an angle. I tried to draw out my mother on the subject of the wedding, hoping that she and Lauren would find some feminine ground to talk about, but she remained more or less silent, picking at her food. In her eyes, I guess, Lauren did not fit into the image of the girl next door she had thought I would one day marry and then settle into a facsimile of her own life.

My father, in an effort to make conversation, suddenly asked me: 'What do they pay you for your sort of writing?'

'I got six thousand for the script we've just filmed,' I said, picking an amount that represented six months' salary for him after shooting a warning look to Lauren.

'That's every week, is it?'

'No, for the whole script.'

He looked disappointed. 'I thought you said you were doing well. Mind you, when your mother and I got married we didn't have two hundred bucks between us. How about you, Lauren, do you get paid better than him?'

'Actors always get more than writers,' I said hurriedly.

'Pity you didn't stay an actor then.' He laughed a little too loudly at his own joke and I realised that the wine I had chosen to go with his meal had got to him.

'This wedding,' he said. 'We run trucks to Denver, I'll have to hitch a ride.'

'I'll fly you both there,' I said.

I saw the expression on my mother's face as she dabbed her mouth with the napkin and then folded it neatly as though she expected the next person who sat at the table would be using it. My father then launched on his vague knowledge of Hollywood. 'I expect you see a lot of people like John Wayne and Betty Hutton. Now they're what I call stars,' he said. '*Stagecoach*, that's my idea of a good movie. Is your movie anything like that?'

'Not really, no. It's more a love story.'

'Oh, pity.'

It went downhill from then and my father finally said, ''Bout time I took you home, Mother. She's not used to being up this late.'

I had retained the chauffeur-driven car and we parted company on the pavement. I kissed my mother's powdered cheek, tasting the cheap scent she had used. 'I'll see you at the wedding, if not before,' I said. 'Promise you'll let me know if there's anything you need.'

While Lauren was saying her goodbyes, my father took me to one side.

'I'll never get your mother to Denver,' he whispered. 'She doesn't like to travel far.' He tapped the side of his nose. 'Pity, but there it is. Just make sure you get a regular salary.' He missed his footing as he got into the car and I steadied him. They both sat in the rear seats like statues. Lauren and I watched until the car pulled into the traffic.

In the elevator I said, 'I'm sorry I inflicted that on you.'

She shot a glance at the elevator operator and said nothing else until we were outside her room.

'Why did you lie about what you got for the script?'

'To save his face.'

'Wouldn't he have been pleased for you if you'd told him the real amount?'

'He couldn't have taken it in.'

'I thought they were sweet.'

'They are sweet, but they were out of their depth tonight and that was my fault. It didn't work out the way I'd planned. And another thing, don't depend on them coming to the wedding.'

'What d'you mean? They have to come. It wouldn't be the same without them.'

'Well, let's hope I'm wrong. I just get the feeling they won't.'

'I have to let Mommy know soon because of the catering.'

As I kissed her good night outside the door of her room, she said: 'And you have to give Mommy an answer too. It's unfair to keep her waiting.'

'Is she still on about that?'

'It's just for the wedding, you don't have to be a practising Catholic afterwards.'

'Oh, that's great. That's one cynical attitude.'

She kissed in a perfunctory fashion. 'Do it for me if you love me. I just want the wedding to go off smoothly. And don't forget Daddy is buying us a house.'

'And Mommy's buying us a Cardinal.'

She had one last interview in the morning before we caught the flight back to LA. We rode to La Guardia in the provided limousine in silence and she was withdrawn for most of the flight. I knew she was waiting for me to give the answer that would make everybody happy. *Do it for me if you love me* – the weapon women always used as a last resort. During the night I had pondered whether I did love her enough to make that quantum leap. I had left God behind years ago, never once asking Him to come to my aid, not even during those long hours when I waited for Amanda to emerge from the abortionist. Any prayers I had ever made had never been made from a conscious belief, just a transient panic. It was only when the sound of a police siren disturbed me and I woke to the realisation that it was only another part of the game I was playing that I finally thought: To hell with it. Oh, why not? Go along with the charade if it makes life easier. I waited until I deposited her back at the Chateau Marmont before I admitted defeat, giving it long enough to make her think she had lost the battle.

Her attitude changed immediately. 'Darling, you won't regret it. Everything's going to be wonderful from now on.' She acted as though she had just given a leper the certainty of a cure. 'You did it for me, I know that, and I love you for it. Come up to my room and ring Mommy yourself, so that she hears it from you.'

Mrs Taylor was equally effusive in her relief, but couldn't resist a slight twist of the knife. 'Don and I just know that this way you'll start married life in a state of grace, as we did. We shall make a donation to St Jude's as a way of showing our thanks.'

Within twenty-four hours I got a call from the said Father Paul asking when it would be convenient for us to meet. The grass did not grow under the feet of the lambs of God. I agreed to see him the following night. If it had to happen, the sooner the better.

'How long does the process take?' I asked Lauren, who was all over me again. 'Is it like a driving test?'

'No, silly. All that happens is that Father Paul has to be sure that you are truly willing to accept the tenets of the Church.'

'What's the failure rate?'

'Darling, you're not going to fail, it isn't like that. Go into it with an open mind.'

I didn't know how priests talked, except those in movies, and they were always played by the Pat O'Briens, forever saving under-privileged kids or else giving the last rites to gangsters. I had never spent five minutes alone in the company of a priest, so when this Father Paul received me in his small, one-storey house situated a block from his church I expected to be greeted by somebody who looked like Pat O'Brien and spoke like Pat O'Brien. Father Paul didn't fit that mould. Maybe the Vatican runs a casting department as well as a bank; nothing would surprise me from an outfit that sends up smoke signals to announce a new model. Father Paul could have doubled for William Holden, given a good cameraman. Clean-cut, perhaps only ten years older than me – it seemed ridiculous to address him as 'Father'.

If I thought he would immediately lead me into a private chapel and ask me to kneel in prayer for divine guidance, I was again way off the mark. He showed me into a well-equipped kitchen, offered me a cup of coffee and joined me in a cigarette.

'Let's begin slowly, take our time, find our way around,' he said. 'I know a little about you, Robert, so you tell me the reason that brought you here.'

I took a deep breath. 'I'm engaged to get married. I guess you know that much. My bride-to-be is Catholic, so are her parents, and they feel the marriage will be more likely to prosper if . . . well, if I could apply for membership, join their club, as it were.'

'You and your fiancee are both in movies, I understand.'

'Yes.'

'As a matter of fact, at one time I had a hankering to go into show business.'

'You did?'

'Yes. They say there are three callings that have a lot in common – the law, acting and religion.'

'What made you choose the priesthood?'

'An unhappy love affair. It made me into an alcoholic and just before I hit the gutter somebody saved me.'

'Somebody from the Church?'

'No, strangely a woman who took in stray dogs – literally stray dogs, she had a house full of them. Extraordinary character. A widow, her husband left her pots of money. She used it to cruise the streets at night looking to find them before they were hauled off to the pound and put down. She found me on one of her nightly missions and added me to her collection. I stayed with her a year, doing odd jobs around the house, feeding the mutts, and she gradually got me sorted out.'

'Quite a story. But that doesn't explain how you ended up here?'

Like any clever interrogator he had immediately allowed me to ask the opening questions.

'No, that's something we'll go into another day. So, how do you feel about this, Robert?'

'Like I'm in a foreign country,' I answered slowly.

'Well, God resides in every country. You don't need a special visa to talk to Him. Or to me, for that matter. You came here of your own free will, and that's all He wants from you in the beginning.'

'But how do I begin? Starting with no faith at all?'

He smiled and lit a second cigarette from the glowing butt of the one in his hand. 'The fact that you said that means you acknowledge that faith exists.'

'What if I didn't come of my own free will? What if I was blackmailed into coming? Wouldn't you consider that a fraud?'

'Then put it no more than this, you made a compassionate decision to find a solution. You love this girl, presumably, and you want to please her?'

'Please her parents mostly. It was their call. And, yes, I love her, I'd hardly be here if I didn't. But I'm confused because she's told me that she's a lapsed Catholic.'

'Those who say that seldom mean it.'

He was good at it, I have to give him that, never pushing me further than I was prepared to go. Over the next few weeks we met at regular intervals and he led me step by step in and out of the maze, always patient, always understanding of my repeated doubts. It became like a chess game, whereby we both tried to anticipate the opponent's next move. If I remained privately unconvinced, I allowed him to believe he had made progress. We got stuck for a long time on the significance of the Mass, and the only occasion when he came near to losing his composure was when I described the Mass as a pagan rite.

'You officiate at a ritual that, however much you dress it up, comes down to the eating of flesh and the drinking of blood. That's pagan.'

'No, it's accepting the gift of Himself that He made to us. *Take this in remembrance of me* – the final acceptance, bonding you with the sacrifice that Christ made for our sakes,' was his rebuff.

Lauren was constantly asking me for progress reports, and she put pressure on me in another way, she refused to let me make love to her during this period, saying, 'It would seem wrong somehow, you must see that?'

'No, I don't. What's different?'

The difference was that she was applying the oldest armlock in the business. The only person I had to confide in was Woody and true to form he put the whole thing in perspective.

'Listen,' he said. 'For God's sake take the holy vows or whatever you have to do and quit giving yourself grief. The only thing that mattered to my old man was that I should be bar mitzvahed. So I went the whole schmeer like a good Jewish boy, he was happy and I've never set foot inside a synagogue since.'

In the end, more to please Father Paul than any member of the Taylor family, I allowed myself to be accepted into the one true Church, took my first confession and, with Lauren by my side, kneeled in front of the altar for the wafer to be placed on my tongue and the blood of Christ to pass my lips. The Taylors sent me a rosary by priority mail and Lauren allowed me back into her bed. Woody was right as usual – what did it matter? I didn't feel any different, my conscience was as clear as when I had put my name on Jack's script. Nobody I knew played by the rules.

37

'Madame Bovary's the answer,' Woody said. 'That's what you should write and we should do together.'

'Why?'

'Why? Because it's out of copyright, that's why. Doesn't cost us a cent. They don't come cheaper than that.'

Lauren had gone back to Denver to have final fittings for her wedding dress, and we were having dinner together in a new joint named Friar's Tuckery, which Woody had thought would be good for a laugh. The waiters wore priests' habits and the hat-check girl was done up in a scanty Maid Marian costume. The decor was Sherwood Castle, and to get to the raised bar you had to cross a drawbridge over a moat in which trout and lobsters spent their last hours. The management's philosophy was to rob the rich without catering for the poor. Gimmick restaurants like this only stayed the course for six months or so.

Woody cut into his rib-eye steak, which was certified to be prime, corn-fed and flown in from Idaho that morning. 'I've worked it all out,' he continued. 'You change the setting to small-town America, make the husband a lawyer instead of a doctor – he has a drink problem maybe, or maybe a heart condition – and she's an ex-Prom Queen he married young – he's older of course. Establish she's bored with domesticity and she's not getting sex regularly. Suddenly the town gets a new cop, they meet when he pulls her over for some traffic violation. Instant, mutual attraction, and they jump into the sack. The fly in the ointment is the husband and she convinces her lover he has to be disposed of. They arrange a murder to look like an accident, but it goes wrong, the cop is arrested and charged. The only person who could give him an alibi is the wife, but she says nothing and he goes to the chair. Oh, to get around the Code, one last twist: she relents and is on her way to get him a reprieve, but she's too late. At the very moment they pull the switch on her lover, she has a heart attack and dies with him. Could be meaty stuff, huh?'

'They made it already,' I said.

'Who made it?'

'*Double Indemnity.* It's the same story. If you do *Bovary*, it has to be a costume drama.'

'You think so? Costume dramas suck. Oh well, I'll think of something else. Have you got any ideas? Has the Duchess of El Camino earned his ten per cent and come up with anything for you?'

'He got me a couple of offers to do rewrites, but I want to follow this one with an original.'

'How about your bride?'

'They're waiting to see whether she clicks with audiences. If she does, which I'm sure she will, they've got two or three lined up.'

'So everything's coming up roses for you two. Me, I'm still waiting, but it'll come, it'll come. This steak is like Madame Bovary. Done to death.' He pushed it aside unfinished. 'What's the deal with this wedding of yours?' he said. 'I'm getting cold feet ever since you talked me into it. Do I have to make a speech?'

'Yeah, that's part of the best man's duties.'

'Jesus. You'd better write it for me, otherwise I'll panic and start telling Jewish jokes. Let's skip coffee; I've had this place. We can get dessert at Terry's – I said we might look in later. He always has plenty of goodies.'

Terry was a fifty-year-old director, a forerunner of the Russ Meyer school who dressed twenty-five and had a reputation as a swinger. Nobody quite knew how he survived and there were rumours around that he had connections with the Mob. He had a place over in Inglewood, close to the racetrack. When we arrived, there was a party in progress, half a dozen guys and the same number of girls, more or less spaced out. I know the drug scene is a big number now, but back then you didn't see much of it unless you mixed with a particular crowd and even then very few were on the really hard stuff; it was mostly just grass, occasionally cocaine. Terry's place was the first time I had ever seen it smoked openly and the first time I had ever been offered it. There was a bowl full of joints and a pile of coke, like a mound of icing sugar, on the coffee table for people to help themselves. Terry, our host, didn't know me from Adam, but I was immediately accepted as a long-time acquaintance. We sat around making inconsequential small talk for a while before he suddenly announced: 'This party's dying, let's make it movie time, gang.'

His den had a projection room concealed behind a floating panel and a screen that came down at the opposite end of the room. Nowadays when you can rent hard-core videos alongside *The Sound of Music*, and order life-size sex dolls on the Internet, pornography has become the Third Estate protected under the Constitution, but then the stuff was only available to people with the right contacts. Well-scratched prints were passed around to those who could be trusted or else had somebody from the vice squad on the payroll – police seizures were often the source of the material. This was before *Deep Throat* and other underground hits made the rounds and the early crude examples betrayed the fact that they had been shot on a shoestring.

We squatted on cushions in front of the screen, the lights dimmed and the show began. It was pretty basic: the star cast, such as they were, got down to the business in hand within the first minute. This one (untitled and with no credits) was set in a beauty salon. Black-and-white, grainy photography, cheap set, minimum lighting. Two girls wearing skimpy white tunics, one styling a weedy, middle-aged man's hair, the other giving him a manicure. Cut to an unappealing stud looking in the salon window from the street. He likes what he sees and comes inside. The hairdresser turns to give him the once-over. He leers at her and she immediately leaves the guy in the chair and disappears with the newcomer behind a screen. (Don't waste film on non-essentials.) The manicurist tells the weedy character the salon is now closed. He gets up, does his disgruntled expression and leaves. The manicurist locks the door and pulls down the blinds, then walks to the screen, peeling off her tunic as she goes. Only then did I get a good look at her face and saw that it was Tracey. Smoking the unaccustomed grass had slowed my reactions, but there was no mistaking her. She was slightly plumper and wearing a blonde wig, but it was Tracey all right. When she went behind the screen, the other two were already hard at it, the first girl stark naked and giving the stud head. Tracey slipped off her bra and panties and joined in. The trio then went through the standard routines for this art form – straight sex, anal sex, cunnilingus, straight and anal at the same time, all shot without any subtlety and ending with the obligatory spray of semen in close-up. It was about as erotic as watching the production line in a meat-packing factory, but seemed to go down with Terry's audience. 'You did it again, Terry,' somebody shouted. 'Can I borrow it for my father's birthday?' I was stunned; I couldn't get over seeing Tracey performing. You poor little tramp, I thought. Did you ever realise your ambitions! I wondered if Woody had recognised her too and when the lights went up I took him to one side.

'Did you see who that was?'

'Who are we talking about?'

'The younger girl of the two. She was the one I brought to your house on Roxbury that Sunday.'

He looked blank.

'Tracey, remember? I was shacking up with her at the time.'

'Oh, yeah, vaguely.' He was stoned by now. 'What about her?'

'Well, God, I got such a shock seeing her in that sleaze.' There was no reason why he would share my reaction, nothing really fazed Woody, but the experience made me nauseous. I went into Terry's bathroom and threw up. I stayed there, my forehead resting on the cold rim of the toilet, thinking back to the moment when I had found her in the garage, her childish excitement when she saw the ocean for the first time, how we had made love on the deck under the night sky. Pornography exists to provoke lust, but I felt only sadness.

When I got home that night I looked for the teddy bear she had left behind. I found it at the top of a cupboard. Moths had attacked its fur and I put it in the trash can.

38

Before Lauren went home we had finally settled on a new house, over-large for our immediate needs, but her choice. 'The pool's got a waterfall,' she said, as though that was the one thing in life she had been missing. The house was situated at the top of Mulholland with a fine view of the valley. Amazingly, Daddy was prepared to pop for ninety-five thousand. I had nothing to do with the finance, all the papers were sent to him in Denver. I guessed he was going to put the house in Lauren's name and there was nothing I could do about that. I was prepared to go along if that was what made him happy.

Lauren returned excited and eager to tell me how the wedding preparations were proceeding. Her dress was going to be sensational, probably on the cover of *Harper's Bazaar*, Mommy had settled on a caterer and ordered a three-tier cake from New Orleans, a calypso band had been hired to play at the reception in the golf club and, most important of all, the Cardinal had agreed to give the blessing. Daddy was also going to help with the furnishings of the new house. Woody had been right, I had become a kept man. I tried to match her enthusiasm, but more and more I felt removed from the whole process. My own plan had been to spend our honeymoon in Hawaii and I'd gone ahead and made the bookings, hoping to surprise her, but even that was taken out of my hands. Lauren brandished an envelope at me. 'Daddy's so sweet,' she said, 'in addition to everything else, he's given us these.'

'These' were two round-trip air tickets: Denver–London–Paris–Los Angeles.

'Daddy thought we should see something of the Old World before we settled down. They spent their honeymoon in Europe. Isn't it exciting? I've always longed to go to Europe, haven't you?'

'Longed to. Very generous of him.'

She must have seen something in my expression. 'You don't mind, do you?'

'Why should I mind?'

'Daddy taking over like this?'

'No,' I lied. 'Do I get to choose where we stay in both places?'

'Of course, darling. Daddy did make some suggestions, which I'm sure are worth listening to because he's so knowledgeable about these things. Talk to him before you do anything definite. Oh, and I bought you a present.' She fumbled in her luggage and it seemed to me she had brought back a whole new wardrobe. 'Here.' She produced a small box. I opened it to reveal a pair of gold cufflinks.

'I noticed you didn't have a good pair.'

'No, I don't. These are lovely. Thank you.'

'I thought you could wear them on the day. Talking of which,' ignoring the fact that she had talked of nothing else, 'have you heard back from your parents? Are they coming or not?'

'Sadly, no. Dad won't come without Mother and she just can't face meeting a whole horde of strangers.'

'Oh, thanks for calling our friends a horde.' She pouted. 'Well, I think it's selfish of her. And silly too.'

'Well, I don't know about selfish. She's old and she doesn't like change. That may be silly to you and me, but that's the way she is.' I tried a joke. 'If anybody asks you'll just have to say you're marrying an orphan.' It fell flat.

'As if I'd say that. So, it'll just be you and your best man?'

'Looks like it.'

'I ought to meet him before the wedding. Tell me his name again.'

'Woody. Woody Solotaroff.'

'What a funny name.'

'He's Jewish. So I hope they let him into the golf club.'

'Why're you in such a strange mood? Did anything happen while I was away?'

'No. All I did was go out with Woody once and make a start on a new screenplay.'

When eventually she did meet Woody it wasn't an unqualified success. He tried too hard to impress, something I was used to and thought nothing of, but I sensed that Lauren found him brash. Afterwards she said: 'It's a pity you don't have more friends out here. I thought perhaps you might have asked Howard. Daddy would have liked to have met him.'

'Howard's a two-time divorced man. That might not have gone down well with the Cardinal. At least Woody's untainted,' I said.

The trip back to Denver and the doting parents seemed to have changed her. I had never experienced the cloying relationship she enjoyed with her parents, but I made myself believe that, once the marriage was over, and we were alone together, their influence would wane. We paid several visits to our new home and I let her have her head over the decorations and furnishings. The only thing I insisted on deciding for myself was the look of my workroom.

Howard showed us the first roughs of the ad campaign. Lauren had been given 'Introducing' billing in the same size as Jason. My own name was there, too, in much smaller letters. It looked strange, seeing it on a billboard for the first time. I was more excited about the film than the wedding.

After some broad hints from Lauren, Woody and I hired morning suits for the occasion. I bought the ring and went back to Father Paul for a refresher course of what was required of me for the ceremony. I knew from Lauren that she had seen him too, so I wasn't surprised when he suggested that I should take confession before I flew to Denver. It was less of a hassle and certainly cheaper than analysis, and I used it to try and lay a few ghosts. I only gave an edited version of my past sins, leaving Tracey out of it, but I told him of my affair with Amanda and a scaled-down story of the abortion. Despite my cynicism I admit that it was a relief to tell somebody what I had bottled up for so long. He gave me absolution and later we had a social drink together and he said he had good feelings about the marriage and how pleased he was that I had accepted the faith.

Lauren flew to Denver a couple of days ahead of Woody and me. I phoned her when we got to our hotel, but I wasn't going to be allowed to see her until she walked up the aisle – Mrs Taylor had strong views on the subject. Woody and I sent our suits to be pressed and then did a trial run to the church to see how much time we should allow. To pass the last evening we took in a movie, Woody's choice, *From Here to Eternity*, which he facetiously thought would get me into the right frame of mind.

My recollections of the actual ceremony remain hazy. The church was vast, that much I remember. It was a long service with the officiating priest delivering a wandering address about the sanctity of wedlock which made my eyes water with boredom. In an odd sort of way it all seemed to be taking place without me, and it was only when I was allowed to kiss my bride that I finally believed I had actually gone the distance.

Daddy had certainly spared no expense to give his daughter an impressive send-off. The guests were ferried to the golf club in decorated school buses, which everybody seemed to think was a cute idea. A huge flower-bedecked marquee had been erected on the club lawn, complete with portable air conditioners. Woody and I were closely scrutinised as some sort of imported curiosities by the guests, but it wasn't meant to be my day, it all belonged to Lauren. A separate, smaller marquee had been put up alongside the main one to display all the wedding gifts with a Brinks security guard in attendance ('Which of the guests don't they trust?' Woody whispered). We were starting married life with a collection of silver photo frames, two complete dinner services, a canteen of cutlery, the inevitable toaster, a lot of Steuben glassware, bed linen, a Leica, several crates of wine, a set of Louis Vuitton luggage and a cigar humidor among other baubles. My parents' contribution was a highly glazed statue of a leopard and I saw several raised eyebrows.

Woody remarked, all too loudly, 'What a garage sale this is going to make one day,' but apart from that he was on his best behaviour and had delivered his speech without giving offence. Taylor made a rather pompous and over-long one which he read from typewritten cards, so when it came to my turn I kept it short. An army of waiters cleared the tables away and the calypso band took over. Lauren and I took the floor first. 'Haven't Mommy and Daddy done it all wonderfully?' she said. 'Perfection,' I said. When other couples joined us I noticed that Woody was making progress with one of the bridesmaids and later he confided that he might stay over for a couple of days.

Lauren and I changed and left the festivities in a deluge of rice and confetti to catch the redeye to New York and our connection to London the following day. The planes Pan-Am used on the transatlantic flights then were bulbous Boeing Stratocruisers cloned from the wartime Flying Fortresses, I believe, but I may have got that wrong. They had a small bar in the underbelly of the plane, reached by a circular staircase.

401

Our first aerial view of England was a patchwork of lush countryside, which gradually gave way to the sprawl of a London still visibly pitted from the bombing, very obvious as our plane started its final approach from the east and dropped lower over the devastated dock area. London airport had an unfinished drabness about it and everything on the ground seemed to have been washed in a grey monotone. Except for the arriving travellers, many of the locals had a pinched and dispirited air about them. They wore clothes that, to us, coming from Los Angeles, seemed out of fashion. After being scrutinised in Customs – the officer opening every one of our suitcases – we took a taxi to the Savoy, I having accepted Daddy's suggestion for the sake of a quiet life. We had a suite that overlooked the river. A remembered half-line from a poem studied at school – *Sweet Thames run softly* – proved misleading; the dark, sluggish water, slicked with oil and flotsam, didn't appear to be running at all.

It was our first experience of jet lag and we crashed that evening, sleeping until nearly ten the following morning, and it wasn't until after a late breakfast in the room (thick cuts of pink bacon that to our taste buds seemed uncooked, watery scrambled eggs, toast made from carpet tiles, washed down with a weak coffee) that we felt human enough to venture forth and explore the city. These were still the austerity years of post-war Britain, certain things remained rationed and London still bore many scars from the Blitz. Uncleared bombsites, where only weeds flourished, were bounded by the remains of naked houses: here a fireplace hanging crazily, interior walls bare to the sky, where fragments of patterned wallpaper fluttered – the remains of a once ordered existence. I had never seen bomb damage other than on newsreels and the reality was sobering.

For two days we wandered around taking in all the usual tourist sights. One day I got the concierge to hire a chauffeur-driven car for us and we took a ride out to Windsor Castle. The car turned out to be something called a Wolseley, which I recognised from British movies as the standard police car with a bell on the front fender instead of one of our sirens. The experience of being driven on the wrong side of the road unnerved us both for the first hour. Back in the hotel, watching the single-channel-and-no-commercials television, we found the news presenters so formal and deadpan. Our regular floor waiter told us that during the war the radio news presenters eccentrically wore black tie, but then steam radio has often had its curiosities – one of our most popular programmes was Edgar Bergen and Charlie McCarthy, and there is something inherently absurd about doing a ventriloquist act on radio. Who knows if your mouth moves?

Overall, we were left with the feeling that the effort of surviving six years of total war had drained the inhabitants of all adrenalin. Defeat is an orphan, but maybe victory is always Pyrrhic. The general downbeat atmosphere, plus the fact that it rained fairly consistently, had the effect of making us both depressed, not what we had planned for a honeymoon, and at the end of the week we cut short our stay and took the boat train to Paris.

This time I made the decision regarding the hotel, spurning the George V which Daddy had pointed us towards, and choosing a small hotel in what Hemingway described as 'more a state of mind than a geographical area' – the Latin Quarter.

'Is this a safe district?' Lauren asked when we arrived.

'Who knows? Live dangerously for once.'

I took a room at the top with spectacular views over the city, and she began to thaw. What clinched it were our first French meals, starting with *cafe complet* served in our room, a far cry from semi-raw bacon.

'So, welcome to the real *La Boheme*, Mrs Peterson,' I said.

'Say that again.'

'Welcome to the real *La Boheme.*'

'No, the last part. The Mrs Peterson bit.'

'You like that? You realise we're no longer in a state of mortal sin, Mrs Peterson? So, I'll thank you to take off your clothes and allow me to ravish you in a state of grace.'

Being in Paris had a liberating effect on me. I discovered that the much quoted 'they order it better there' was actually true. Until the bombshell hit me, I was happier than ever before. We spent the days walking, strolling, staring, lingering at bookstalls, amazed at the abundant displays of fruit and vegetables, fascinated by the flea markets, eating too well, drinking too much and at unaccustomed hours, sitting around at night listening to street musicians. Unlike the weary British we had left behind, the ordinary French seemed so alert, the women so chic, so full of the life force, the remembrance of things past not uppermost in their minds. The weather was balmy, I discovered Gauloises, Lauren discovered Hermes – the cheap and the expensive – which I suppose neatly summed up the basic difference between our backgrounds. We grew to love that room. Even now I can still conjure up every detail – the faded pattern of the wallpaper, the antique light fitting above our bed with one burned-out bulb that was never replaced, a Monet print facing us when we lay in bed, everything had a sense of permanence so that one could imagine that countless lovers before us had seen what we saw, had used the same cast-iron bath with taps like the controls of a trolley car. For the first time in ages neither of us mentioned the film we had left behind or worried about our futures; the here and now was too beguiling. Our relationship floated on calm seas free from angst. Once, at midnight, we crossed to the Ile de la Cite and attended Mass in Notre-Dame, and I have to admit that there, the whole Catholic bit got to me for the first time. I won't say it lasted, but

I definitely felt something other than a belief in myself.

One morning we split and went our separate ways until lunch: Lauren to a hairdresser's, me to wander around the bookstalls on the Left Bank. I eventually ended up on the Champs-Elysees and had a coffee and an absinthe, feeling a sophisticated man of the world while observing the passing scene. Sitting there at ease, an idea for a screenplay started to form – a romantic comedy based around two newly marrieds who come to Europe for the first time and have a series of misadventures. Not exactly earth-shattering or original, but I asked the waiter for a piece of paper and started to jot down some notes.

I think it was Jack who once told me that if you stay long enough on the Champs-Elysees you will eventually see somebody you know. Preoccupied with getting the idea down on paper, thoughts of Amanda were furthest from my mind, but as I looked up from writing, there she was, walking past in front of me, with Billy. As usual Billy was still wearing the wrong clothes for the weather and smoking the inevitable cigar. I turned to hail the waiter and pay my check, trying to keep them in sight among the crowd. Receiving my check, I slammed some money down on the table and went after them, just in time to see them getting into a taxi. It had pulled away into the traffic before I could act. I couldn't believe the coincidence – the impossible odds of us being in the same city, on the same pavement at the same time. I stood transfixed by the kerb, my heart racing, then went back to my cafe in need of another drink. So many imponderables went through my mind, then I suddenly looked at the time and realised that Lauren would be back at the hotel by now and wondering where I'd got to. When I got back to our hotel room I started to apologise for being late, but Lauren stopped me in mid-stream.

'I've got some bad news,' she said. 'I've just rung home

and just as well I did because they've been trying to track us down.'

'Bad news about your parents?' I saw her suitcases were open on top of the bed and partially packed.

'No, bad news for us. The studio has been trying to contact me for the past week, but because we'd switched hotels, nobody knew where we were. They've fired Betsy Armstrong in that film they've got shooting in the Everglades, and want me to replace her. I've got to fly there on the first plane I can get.'

'Like today?'

'Like today.'

'Jesus! D'you have to, can't you say no?'

She shook her head as she put things into a suitcase. 'No, after I spoke to Mummy, I rang my agent. I have to go or else they can put me on suspension. It's a good part, apparently, and Jerry says he can get me top billing and add some sweeteners because they're in a fix. I'm sorry, darling, but there it is.'

'Don't be sorry, not your fault.'

'But we were having such a great time, and now I've ruined it.'

'There'll be other great times.'

'If I hurry I can make the Air France flight to New York and then get a connection to Miami. But what will you do?'

'I'll come with you. Course I will.'

'No, don't do that. Don't let me ruin your holiday as well. You love it here and we've paid for this room until the end of the week.'

'Yes, but . . . don't you want me with you?'

'Of course I do, but you know what it's like at the start of a film, especially in a panic set-up like this. We wouldn't have any time together.'

'Well, O K, if that's what you want.'

'It's not what I want, I just think it makes sense.'

'How long will you be in Florida?'

'Three weeks, apparently. Chuck me that make-up bag, will you? Stay on a few more days, darling, and enjoy yourself. I'd feel much better if you did. Then when you get home you can deal with all the presents and stuff coming from Denver. What time is it now?'

'What time's the flight?'

'Four thirty. They've arranged for me to pick up the tickets at the desk.'

'You'll make it. Let me help.' We finished the rest of her packing and made a dash to the airport. She was tearful as we parted at the departure gate, but at the same time I knew part of her was excited at the prospect of starring in another movie. Ambition is a rival to love, and Lauren was ambitious.

'Call me as soon as you get there,' I said. 'Let me know where they've put you, otherwise I'll worry.'

'I will. You take care of yourself.'

'You, too. Good luck.'

We kissed, then I watched her out of sight before turning away. On the solitary journey back to the city I started to try to unscramble my feelings. The day that had begun so normally had been turned inside out within the space of a few hours. When I got back to our empty bedroom with its small reminders of Lauren – a forgotten bra on the back of a chair, a lipstick smudge on the pillow, some hair slides in the washbasin – I had feelings of guilt, telling myself I should have gone with her. Then different guilt as my thoughts turned to Amanda. I went to the window and looked out across the rooftops, wondering where in the vast city she was at that moment. A girl was sunbathing herself on a balcony below me and somehow that intensified everything. Something had been taken away from my life and something had been added. I won't say I acted on impulse because that would be too simple an explanation, it was more that I was unable to think straight. I left the hotel and walked aimlessly until I found myself in the Champs-Elysees again. I went back to the same cafe and ordered a drink. Lightning was never going to strike twice, I knew that, but as I sat there, thoughts of Amanda obliterated fidelity. I knew that no matter how stupid or futile, I had to try and see her once more. I was crazy, no doubt about that. I took out my pocket guidebook and looked up all the three-star hotels. Remembering Billy's philosophy that 'It's always cheaper to live at the Ritz' that was the first one I tried, enquiring whether a Miss Boyd was registered. I drew a blank and went on to the George V, working my way through the list but always with the same result. On the point of giving up, the last hotel I tried was the Plaza Athenee.

'A Miss Amanda Boyd?' the desk clerk said.

'That's right.'

'Yes, she's staying with us, sir.'

'Could you ring her room for me, please?'

'What name, sir?'

'Peterson.'

He dialled. I waited, trying to look unconcerned. He spoke to somebody.

'You did say Mr Peterson?'

'Yes, that's right.'

He repeated my name into the phone, then hung up.

'Miss Boyd said if you'd like to go to suite 345. Third floor. The elevators are over to your right.'

'Thank you.'

On the way up I wondered if Billy would be with her, or indeed if anybody would be with her. When I came out of the elevator Amanda was standing waiting at the open door of her suite. There was something agitated about her.

'God, I couldn't believe it when he said your name. You've no idea how pleased I am to see you. I've been in such a panic.'

'Panic? About what?' I said as we went inside.

'Billy. He's been taken to hospital.'

'But I only saw, you a few hours ago by pure chance, in the Champs-Elysees. How else did I know you were in Paris? What happened to him?'

'I think he OD'd on one of his pills. You remember he takes uppers and downers by the handful. We came back from a shopping trip and he said he wanted to take a nap before we went to a movie later. I rang his room to remind him of the time but I couldn't get a reply. So I persuaded the maid to open the door with her passkey and when I went in he was lying on the bathroom floor. I thought he was dead at first. The hotel was great, they got an ambulance and they rushed him to hospital. I've just got back.'

'And how is he?'

'Well, they stomach-pumped him and they think he's out of danger, but who knows?'

'Were you able to tell them what he might have taken?'

'Yes, I gave them all the bottles I could find.'

'Poor old Billy.'

'He hasn't been well for some time. None of his projects have taken off and he came here to meet Dino De Laurentiis. As you know he hates being alone, I wasn't working and came along for the ride.'

'And here we both are,' I said.

'Why are you here?'

I hesitated then said: 'I was on my honeymoon, believe it or not.'

'Why d'you say "was"? Aren't you still?'

'Well, like you, I've had a dramatic day. Lauren, my wife, suddenly got word from the studio she had to fly to a unit shooting in the Everglades and take over from a girl who's been fired.'

'Why didn't you go with her?'

'She didn't want me to.'

Up to this point we hadn't moved since I entered the room and were still standing awkwardly just inside the door. 'I don't know about you, but I could do with a drink,' she said. 'Come on in.' As she poured the drinks she said: 'Life is full of surprises, you might say.'

'When I'd recovered from the shock of seeing you I chased after you, but you both shot off in a taxi.'

She handed me my drink. 'How did you trace me here?'

'Persistence. I tried half a dozen hotels before I got lucky.'

'Is it lucky?'

'I don't know, you tell me.'

'Well, I'm glad to see a familiar face. I was sitting here wondering what the hell to do next. All I could think about was, what if Billy dies? They're worried he may have brain damage.'

'Do you have money to pay for the hospital and the hotel?'

'Oh, sure. Billy's good for it. It's not that.'

'What then?'

'If he dies I'm out in the cold.'

'I'm sure not.'

'Well, I haven't set the world on fire yet. You and your wife seem to be doing all right, though.'

'Touch wood when you say that.'

She looked at her watch several times during this. 'Maybe I ought to ring the hospital again and find out the latest. Excuse me.' She went into the bedroom and was gone ten minutes. 'He's amazing,' she said when she came back. 'When I got through to the ward they let me talk to him.'

'You talked to him?'

'Yes, chirpy as ever. Said that all that happened was he took the wrong pills. Desperate for me to get him discharged. Apparently all the nurses are nuns and they disturb him.'

'Will they let him out that soon?'

'You know Billy, he's a great believer that money talks. He wants me to take some money out of his room, bring it to the hospital and bribe them with a large donation. He says that always works with Catholics.'

'Are you going to do that?'

'Don't have much choice, do I?'

I went with her to Billy's suite. She found his wallet and extracted a wad of notes.

'Has Billy ever mentioned me since we fell out?'

'I can't remember. He blows hot and cold about everything and everybody.'

'This is a strange situation, isn't it? You and me alone together in Paris, my wife somewhere over the Atlantic, Billy in hospital. Who would believe the chain of events?'

'Did you ever tell your wife about us?'

'No. The only person I ever told was Father Paul.'

'Who the hell is Father Paul?'

'My confessor. Don't laugh, but you're sitting next to a Catholic convert. Lauren's parents put the pressure on me before the marriage.'

'Do you feel any different?'

'No.' There was a double meaning to my reply. 'Do you regret you and I split?'

She hesitated a fraction. 'I'd better go.'

'You haven't answered me.'

'We burned ourselves out,' she said, and walked to the door.

I put her in a taxi. 'Call me tomorrow and let me know how you got on.' I gave her the number of my hotel.

'Yes, OK, if I get a chance.'

I watched her taxi until it was out of sight. I seemed to be saying goodbye to everybody that day. It started to rain as I walked back to my own hotel, but it didn't bother me.

39

Little that is good ever comes out of a telephone call at three thirty in the morning. At best it's a wrong number or some friend abroad who has forgotten the time difference.

So when the unaccustomed sound of French phones roused me from a deep sleep I thought it had to be Lauren saying that she had arrived safely. With my guilty conscience I would have welcomed that call despite the hour. But it wasn't, it was Amanda. I shook myself awake. 'What's happened now?' I said.

'You were asleep, weren't you?'

'Yes, but it doesn't matter, I'm wide awake now.'

'Yes. Can I see you?'

'See me? Is it Billy? You want me to drive over to your hotel?'

There was silence for a moment, then she answered, 'No, I'm here, down in the lobby.'

'Here, in this hotel?'

'Yes. Can I come up?'

'Yes. Come up.'

Because of the heat under the roof I had been sleeping nude. I got up and put a gown on in time for her knock on the door. Admitting her, I said, 'What's wrong? Is Billy worse?'

'No, it isn't that. He was right, as usual. Money talks, or at least his does. Five thousand francs sprang him. He's back in our hotel, seemingly none the worse for wear.'

'So what is it?'

'I had to see you once more. We're leaving in the morning and I won't get another chance.'

'Are you going back to LA?'

'Eventually, I expect. Not tomorrow. Billy wants to go home to London.'

She looked at me, but came no closer. We both stood like statues. I had never known anybody who had the effect upon me that she did.

'I blew it, didn't I?' she said.

'We both blew it.'

'I suppose what it comes down to,' she said, 'what it always comes down to, is whether two people want the same thing at the same time, and we didn't. I often wish I could find God like you have.'

'Who says I have?'

'You told me you've become a Catholic.'

'I was blackmailed. That doesn't count.'

'I wish I believed in something other than wanting you.'

She let her head fall against my shoulder and that was the beginning of it. We kissed and it only took one kiss for all my resolve to shatter. When I undressed her, I was still not prepared for her remembered beauty. I had no conscience or guilt when we made love in the same bed that, twenty-four hours earlier, I had shared with Lauren. Even when, towards dawn, the telephone rang again and this time it was Lauren ringing from Florida, I answered her lying across Amanda's nude body, the ultimate betrayal, and the false words came all too easily. *Are you OK, what's the hotel like, were you met, are they treating you well, yes of course I've missed you, no nothing much, I sort of wandered after you left, had a meal on my own, I'll probably fly back tomorrow, Paris isn't the same without you, I love you too.*

'That was her, wasn't it?' Amanda said. 'I heard you tell

her you were going back tomorrow. Did you mean that, or was it part of the act?'

'No, I meant it. If you're not going to be here, there's nothing to stay for.'

'And beyond here, what then? When I return to LA will we see each other?'

'Yes, I want to see you again, whatever the cost.'

She eased out from under me, slid from the bed and went to the window. Nude, she was outlined against the early morning sky. 'If only everything was normal. Ordinary and normal. Nothing about my life is normal.'

'Why? Why d'you say that?'

'The things I thought would happen don't any more. I don't hang out. Well, that's a lie. I hang out with a middle-aged man who takes uppers to get up and downers to get rid of the uppers. A nice man, a kind man, a bright man, generous but lonely, who's chosen to be in a business where generosity counts for shit. It's all about power and greed. But there's one thing you should know. Despite what Oliver told you, Billy has never touched me. He's convinced he's repulsive to women. One night . . . late one night . . . I was in his room, we'd been talking about nothing in particular when out of the blue, no build-up to it, no innuendoes, he suddenly asked me if I'd take my clothes off. He said it in such a casual way, the same way as he might have asked me to pass him a new cigar. It didn't strike me as sinister and I wasn't worried it would lead to something more . . . So I did. I took everything off and stood there at the foot of his bed and he just stared at me and I saw he was crying. And that was it. It was nothing more than a model posing for an artist. All he said was, "I've missed so much being me, haven't I?" I put my clothes on again and went back to my own room. So now you know.'

She turned back to face me. 'And I'll tell you something else. I know how it'll end for Billy. One day, I'll have gone,

414

and there'll be another me, because he can't stand to be alone. There'll be another afternoon like yesterday in another hotel and chances are when it happens again he won't be found in time.' She started to pick up her discarded clothes.

'I have to see you again.'

'Is that a good idea?'

'Yes. When you get back to LA ring Julian, my agent at the Morris office. Say you're calling for Billy Fisher and ask where you can contact me. With any luck I'll still have an office at Fox, but if not, he or his assistant will know where I am. You remember Julian – he's that queen we met when we were all having dinner together at the Wilshire.'

'It's always going to be second best, isn't it?' she said, as she slipped a white bra over her breasts. When she was fully dressed I got out of bed and we kissed with sad caution as though we were both scared of prolonging the inevitable. 'Take care of yourself.'

'I always do.'

Then she was gone.

It couldn't have been more than ten minutes later when Lauren rang again.

'My God! What time is it with you?' I said. 'Must be the middle of the night.'

'Two o'clock. I'm jet lagged and too excited. You should see the suite they've put me in. I'm getting the full star treatment. Enormous king-size bed which I wish you were sharing with me.'

It wasn't the room she was talking from that I tried to visualise, but the room in the Plaza Athenee that Amanda had returned to.

'I rang Mommy to tell her I was here and she couldn't believe any of it. We've had more wedding presents, by the way. Mommy thinks we'll want to change some of them, they're a bit tacky she says. Oh, and guess what?'

'What?'

'The director came to meet me at the airport. He seems a real pussycat and very good-looking. Are you jealous?'

'I'm jealous.'

'Good. I like you to be jealous.'

'When are they putting you to work?'

'They've rearranged the schedule and they're shooting around me for the next three or four days to give me time to catch my breath. And of course I've got to have clothes fittings and meet up with make-up and hair to decide on the look. Before I forget, darling, can you do something for me? When are you going back?'

'Haven't decided yet, but after breakfast I'll go down to the airline office, see what's available and change my tickets.'

'When you get home can you send me my leather script cover, the fancy one with my name embossed on it? But before you send it can you have them add the title of our film and the date? Everybody seems to do that and it looks good. You should find it in my wardrobe trunk.'

'Will do. Anything else?'

'Keep after the decorators.'

She babbled away happily for another ten minutes. I listened, thankful that she could not see my face. The telephone is the best ally the guilty can have.

40

There was palace revolution in progress at Fox when I got back. Once again New York was challenging Zanuck's authority. A couple of years later he was to make the first of his two celebrated exits from the studio he considered his fiefdom, but for the moment he was fighting to retain his power. Battle lines had been drawn and the foot soldiers were waiting to see which faction would come out on top before making their own moves. Joe Schenck, one of the original gang who invented Hollywood, had recently resigned from the Fox board when jailed for tax evasion and perjury. He only served four months of a three-year sentence before having second thoughts and deciding to strike a plea bargain by telling all about another partner in crime. After being paroled he was taken back on the Fox lot as an 'executive producer', that nothing title handed out like jelly beans when studios couldn't think of any other way to buy off somebody. To most onlookers it proved that the old guard was still acting in character.

I kept my head down below the top of the trenches, happy if nobody noticed I was alive. There is always a period of grace before a film comes out. Have a success and you're forgiven most things. Have your name on a real turkey and the immediate future is less than rosy. Fortunately the word on our film was still good. I met with Howard and he ran the married print for me. Lauren came out of it well and the main music theme was haunting. I had private reservations about Jason's performance; he was good but too stagy for my taste. Howard had had a private showing for the front office while Lauren and I were in Europe and the reaction had been favourable although Zanuck had demanded he take a further two minutes out. It wasn't the year for long films.

I busied myself getting the new house on Mulholland into shape. Going from room to room trying to get my bearings, making myself snack meals in the state-of-the-art kitchen, sleeping alone and fitfully in the vast bedroom, I missed waking up to the scent of the sea air and the feeling of intimacy I had enjoyed in Santa Monica. Lauren had decided on most of the decor and apart from my own room I had no sense of belonging, it was like living in a hotel I couldn't afford and waiting for the bill to be presented. The wedding presents had arrived from Denver and I arranged them as I thought Lauren would approve. I spoke to her most days and she seemed happy: being the heroine who had saved the day was a role she obviously enjoyed. Sometimes I got the feeling that she regarded talking to me as an intrusion, that the film was the only thing that really occupied her. That didn't surprise me, nor did I resent it. The guilty can always afford to be generous. Her happiness salved my conscience. There were times when I fantasised a scenario in which Lauren had fallen for somebody on the film (the good-looking director maybe?), and I saw myself acting out the aggrieved husband, sorrowing but forgiving, who granted her her freedom while I rushed back to Amanda. There were times, all too frequent, when thoughts of Amanda brought about a kind of madness in me.

I took the writer's time-honoured escape route and set to work to develop the idea that had come to me at that cafe on the Champs-Elysees. As I wrote, it became a thinly disguised version of my own life. What I got down on paper moved away from being the romantic comedy I had first

418

conceived and took on a darker tone. I based the central female character on Amanda, of course, but Amanda mixed with fragments of Tracey in a way that I hoped no one would unravel. The setting became New England, and my own character a doctor. At one point I included the abortion episode, then rejected it. I knew it had no chance of getting past the Code, and instead I substituted the death of a child. As it progressed, some of the despair I had brought home with me from Paris began to fade.

Now, when Lauren rang me to ask when I was going to join her, I had the legitimate excuse that I was hard at work. To tell the truth, she didn't press the point. They, too, had run into a spell of bad weather, pushing the finishing date later, and I could tell from what she said that her nerves were getting frayed. 'It's a big responsibility for me, I'm in nearly every scene,' she said. 'The weather has cast a gloom over everything. Unlike Howard, this director loses his cool when things don't go right. It's quite an unhappy atmosphere at the moment.'

'Well, hang in. I will get there as soon as I've finished a first draft.'

I rang Julian frequently, ostensibly to let him know I was working hard, but more to discover whether Amanda had made contact. It would just be my luck if I took off for Florida at the very time she came back to LA. On one occasion, feeling particularly desperate, I called the Beverly Hills Hotel and asked for Billy, but he wasn't there and they weren't holding any reservation for him.

Julian's advice was to take two bites of the apple. 'Even if you finish it soon I don't want to go into the market with a full screenplay at this stage,' Julian said. 'Always leave them wanting more. Give me a ten- or twelve-page outline. If Fox go for it, I'll get you a development deal, but if they pass – and they might because everybody over there is running scared right now – I'll take it to Universal. I happen to know they're looking for a vehicle for Doris Day.'

'Doris Day might be a little old for the way I've written it.'

'Sweetie, Doris Day is never too old for anything.'

I needed to earn some serious money again. Funds were low and I didn't want to give Daddy the satisfaction of being able to say his daughter was keeping me. I did what Julian suggested and typed up a short outline and took it to him.

'I've been waiting for an invite to see your new house.'

'Any time.'

'How about tonight? I'll read this quickly and bring you my honest opinion as a house-warming gift.'

'Forget honest,' I said. 'Stay in character.'

When he arrived at the house he greeted me with 'How about this for service? I told Brent to hold all calls and devoted the entire afternoon to you.'

'And?'

'You want honesty, right? It's a tough piece, a long way from your last. And you're right, Doris Day it isn't.'

'But do you like it?'

'It won't be everybody's cup of tea. Did you part company with Howard on good terms?'

'As far as I know. Why?'

'My first thought is we should get a director interested, then take it as a package. Would you have any objections to that?'

'No, but tell me what you really thought.'

'Well, I like it. It's very *noir* in places, which is very me, but I'm not Ava Average, don't forget. I like my steaks to be still moving on the plate, if you know what I mean.'

'No, I don't. Put it in plain English.'

'OK, I'll cut to the bottom line, dear. It's good, but it's going to give us problems. Not unsolvable problems, and I'm sure the way to go is to get somebody like Howard on board. That could be the winning combination and if, touching wood – ' he touched the top of the wet bar.

'That's marble,' I said.

'If,' he started again, 'the Gods smile down and either you or Howard get a nomination when Oscar comes around, then we're home and dry. Which reminds me, at our weekly strategy meeting, we discussed taking ads for you at voting time.'

'I thought that was frowned on by the Academy.'

'Oh yes, dear, but nobody takes any notice.'

'D'you think there's a chance of a nomination?'

'It all depends how it does at the box office. I think your bride's in there with a chance, too.'

'Well, forget our chances at the Oscars, what if Howard passes? What then?'

'Then everybody at the agency puts on their thinking caps and comes up with somebody else. It'll happen. Shall we go eat?'

'Why don't we have something here? About time I baptised the kitchen. I haven't got a vast repertoire but I can fix us a hamburger.'

He followed me into the kitchen and watched as I went to work. 'What d'you thjnk of this place?' I asked. 'And before you answer, the decor is all Lauren's doing.'

'A little cold for my taste, but I'm sure once it's been lived in for a while it'll seem like the little house on the prairie.'

'God! You're so camp.'

I felt easier with him now, able to acknowledge where he was and what he was. Over the meal, which we ate in the kitchen, I steered the conversation to his world, a world that intrigued me. I wanted to get him to let his hair down.

'Haven't you ever had a permanent relationship with anybody?'

'Not really. A few attempts, but they never worked out. The longest lasted a year, I suppose.'

'Why not? Wouldn't it be safer?'

'Who wants safety, sweetie? That never turned on anybody.'

'But when you go cruising, aren't you worried you might pick up the wrong trick, somebody who could turn ugly, kill you maybe?'

'Yes. That's always the risk, but it's also the thrill, dear boy. I've come close a few times, been beaten up, beaten to a pulp once. But the easy tricks don't do it for me. I like converting straights, especially the married ones. I dare say I'll end up Miss Lonelyhearts, just another faded queen. Can't change things now. Too late.'

When he left I had a better understanding of the demons that drove him. That night I thought again of what Amanda had told me about Billy's sad request. My own situation seemed simpler in comparison; I was married to one woman and in love with another. It wasn't simple, of course, just another lie in the life I had made for myself.

41

More and more it was borne home to me that by stealing Jack's script I had taken possession of a poisoned chalice. It was no longer any use telling myself that it had been Jack's dying wish. The option had always been there for me to have sold it on his name and sent all the proceeds to his father instead of a token amount. The point was, I hadn't. That moment when I changed the authorship on the title page had simultaneously enhanced and sealed my fate. In my heart I knew I was never going to be as good a writer as Jack, but I was condemned to attempt further forgeries. In the first flush it had all seemed so perfect, so easy. I thought my new screenplay would automatically find a home, riding on the back of *The End of the Beginning*. But Howard's film had not yet passed the winning post and my latest effort was not the mixture as before, but totally different in style and content, something that scared an industry built on repetition.

On the strength of our recent association, Howard only took a week to read my fourteen pages, but didn't jump for it. 'I appreciate you giving me first look and I know we'll work together again one day,' he said, 'but I'm looking for a comedy. Get an idea for a comedy and come to me with that.'

Julian next submitted it to the Bernstein brothers at Universal and there it disappeared into limbo. 'Don't expect a quick answer,' he warned. 'They both have to read it and they make sure they're never in the same room at the same time when negotiating. Be patient.'

I couldn't delay joining Lauren any longer, so I booked a flight. An hour before I was due to leave for the airport, Brent rang me.

'Have we had an answer from Universal?'

'No, not yet,' he said. 'It's not that. Glad I caught you. I've just taken a long-distance call from London.'

'London?'

'Yeah, somebody called Amanda Boyd. Does that mean anything?'

'Could be. She's somebody I met way back. What was it about?'

'She wouldn't say, but could you ring her? She left a number. Said it's urgent.'

'Give it to me.'

'Grosvenor 3423. Room 524.'

I made him repeat it and wrote it down. Afterwards I shook like an ice-cold terrier. I lit a cigarette, stubbed it out, and lit a second. Since there was no direct dialling in those days, I asked for the long-distance operator and placed a call. After a delay I heard the unfamiliar sound of the British ring, so different from our own, and a very British voice answered, 'The Grosvenor Hotel, good evening.'

'I'm calling from Los Angeles,' I said. 'Can I have room 524, please?' There was an echo on the line. 'Miss Boyd.'

'I'll try for you, sir. Can I know who's calling Miss Boyd?'

'Peterson.'

'Please hold the line, Mr Peterson.'

The cigarette slipped out of my fingers into my lap. I flicked it on to the floor and put my foot on it. There was a pause and then Amanda spoke.

'Robert?'

'Yes.'

'Are you alone?'

'Yes. God, it's good to hear your voice at last. When are you coming out to LA?'

'I'm not.'

'Not ever?'

'I doubt it. That's why I rang you.'

'Why? Has something happened?'

'Yes.'

'What?'

'Billy has been taken ill again. And it's serious this time.'

'Jesus, that's too bad.' My voice echoed across the air-waves as though deliberately mocking my sincerity. There was a long pause. 'Hello? Amanda, you still there, can you hear me?'

'It's not a good connection, you sound a long way away.'

'I am a long way away.'

'Did you hear what I said about Billy?'

'Yes, I heard. I'm sorry, what else can I say? More sorry for you than Billy. Is that why you won't be coming out?'

'It's one reason.'

'What does that mean?'

'Billy's asked me to marry him before it's too late.' Again the connection played tricks and when she spoke again her words were spaced out, reaching me like stray bullets fired one after the other.

'Say again, there's such an echo on this line.' I was lying, but I didn't want to believe what she had just told me.

'I said, Billy has asked me to marry him. I wanted to tell you before you read it anywhere.'

I couldn't stop my hands shaking as I reached for a fresh cigarette. 'And are you going to?'

'Yes.'

'Why would you say yes?'

'Because I can't think of a reason to say no. He's dying.'

'Well, congratulations. If that's what you want. I'm sure

it must be nice to think of yourself becoming a rich widow.'
I wanted to hurt her now.

'I didn't say that was what I want, but I have to do it.'

'Why did you give me hope again? We were happy again
in Paris – didn't that mean anything to you?'

'Yes,' she said.

'Well, then?'

'But don't you see, we've left it too late? I can't face a
life that only gives us a few, snatched, stolen moments. That
wouldn't last.'

'It doesn't always have to be like that. Things can change.
I can make things change, if you just said the word.'

'You're saying that now, but you must see I'm right. We
had it together once, but I blew it. That place where you
are rotted us, it rots everybody,' she said in a flat voice.

'I thought you wanted a career.'

'Yes. At one time I wanted a lot of things.'

I kept talking, but nothing I said made any difference.
'When is the big day?' I asked.

'Tomorrow. It has to be soon. They've told him he
doesn't have much time left.'

'So, there it is, we'll soon both be married, but to the
wrong people.' I heard somebody else talking in the background. 'Who's that?'

'One of the nurses. It's time for him to have another
injection. He has to be cared for round the clock. I must
go in a minute; he gets upset if I'm away for long.'

'Is Oliver around?'

'No. Billy doesn't want to see anybody else.'

'Where will you get married?'

'The Rabbi is coming here to the hotel.'

'Well, it's nice to think your future's OK.'

'Don't sound so bitter, please. You'll get over it.'

'Wouldn't it be nice to think so?' I said, as the line to
London went dead.

I don't know how long I sat there, half an hour maybe, long enough to miss my plane. At the airport I managed to get on a later flight, then rang Lauren, but she was on location and I left word at the production office that I was delayed. I drank on the flight, but nothing dulled the loss. Lauren sent her driver to meet me, who first drove me to the unit hotel, then out to the location. The humidity was fierce.

'They're still behind schedule,' he told me. 'But I ain't complaining. This has been a great job for me, looking after your wife. Some special little lady. Well, I don't have to tell you that. Yes, sir, Mr Peterson, she's special, your lady.'

When we got to the location they were in the middle of a set-up and I waited by the car until it was over. I saw Lauren walk to the camera and confer with a good-looking guy I took was the director. I was walking towards them when he shouted: 'OK, let's go once more. And can we keep the eyelines clear this time?'

She went back to her start mark without spotting me. I didn't mind the delay. Watching her work, I was amazed how assured she had become since the last film. I looked at my watch. London would be asleep by now. Then, while Lauren and I slept, the marriage would have happened. The scene being acted in front of me blurred and I realised I was crying. I turned away quickly as the director shouted, 'Cut! That's a beauty. It was worth going again. Check your gate. If the gate's clear, it's a wrap.' It was then that Lauren finally saw me. She ran and threw herself into my arms.

'Darling! You finally made it.' We kissed. 'Why, I do believe you're crying.'

'Because I'm so pleased to see you.'

'Oh, darling, I never knew you were so sentimental. Come and let me introduce you to everybody.' She held my hand and took me to the crew.

'Scott, this is my long-lost husband.'

'Hi,' the director said. 'Glad you're here to help us control her. She's been impossible all day waiting for you to get here.'

I was introduced to a dozen or more people, Lauren treating them with that easy familiarity that comes when a unit has been together for weeks, while I felt very much the outsider being scrutinised (so this is the guy she's been on about?). People at work are seldom impressed by visitors. I would have had to have been Hemingway to elicit more than passing interest.

'Am I dismissed?' Lauren asked Scott.

'No, I thought we'd do some night shooting. Look at her face. Go on, yes, you're dismissed. See you around, Bob.'

Lauren dragged me away to her trailer. I saw she had our wedding photos stuck up on the mirror at her make-up table. 'I used to look at those every day and think, Did it really happen?' she said. 'Doesn't Paris seem a long time ago? Know what I found out about our hotel? Larry, our art director told me. Oscar Wilde died there. Isn't that something? I wonder if it was in the room we had? You look tired, darling. Have you been working too hard? What else have you been doing? Is the house looking good? Did you bring any pictures of it?'

'No, I should have done, I forgot. But I've been busy writing.'

'And you finished the script. Any takers?'

'Not so far.'

'Is there a good part in it for me?'

'You'll have to be the judge of that when you read it.'

'Did you bring a copy with you?'

'No, I didn't.'

'Oh, darling, you forget everything.'

'Except myself.'

'And what about our film?'

'I saw the finished print. You're terrific in it. They think you'll get a nomination. It opens the first week in December with a big campaign. This one's going well too, according to your driver.'

'It's been a tough one, though; your wife's been earning her salary. Bad weather, plus this humidity – give me California any day. Scott is such a great director. Howard was great, too, but Scott gets my vote. I was so lucky to get this break straight after our film. You didn't know you were marrying a success, did you?'

'I had a pretty good idea.'

'Does this feel strange to you?' she asked. 'Us being here, I mean? Like we just met for the first time and I've got to get to know you again.'

'Have I changed that much?'

'No, just that you seem sort of shy with me.'

'Well, I guess you're right, it is strange in a way. You know everybody here and I don't.'

She picked up her wedding ring from the make-up table, slipped it on and flourished it at me. 'I can't wear it in the film, though I forgot one day, and it was in close-up and they had to retake. I wear it at all other times, though. Darling, I'm so excited. I've arranged for us to have dinner alone in my suite and ordered exactly what we had in that little restaurant in Paris. Well, I don't suppose it'll be exactly like it was. The food's OK, but not up to Paris standards.'

'It's the thought that counts,' I said.

'I can take my make-up off later, I want to get back quickly and have you all to myself. You're in for a surprise when you see the suite.'

She was right. It was vast and vulgar as only hotels that cater for the holiday trade can be, but I made all the right noises.

'Come in here while I have a bath. Or, better still, get

in with me. We've never done it in a bath, have we?'

I undressed alongside her. 'You've lost weight,' she said.

'Pining for you.'

'Not half as much as I've been pining for you. Feel here. Feel how ready I am for you. I've been dying for this day. Darling, I want you so badly.' She pressed herself against me. Once in the bath her orgasm began the moment I entered her, and I was a long way behind. Afterwards, both of us still dripping wet, I carried her into the bedroom and went down on her warm sex, making her come again.

'But it's not fair,' she said. 'It didn't happen for you, I was too selfish.'

'Doesn't matter.'

'It does matter. Let me do something nice for you. Please, let me.'

'No, I'm probably tired from the journey. When we've had our great meal I'll be fine.'

'But it's bad for you not to come.'

'Don't worry about it. I'm here, we've got plenty of time. Which reminds me, I must reset my watch. What is it, three hours' difference?' As I changed the hands I calculated the difference in London.

Lauren chattered non-stop throughout the meal, mostly anecdotes about the film that meant little to me. Actors are never so happy as when talking about themselves. I gathered she didn't think much of her leading man ('Too conceited about his looks') though she let slip that the real reason for her dislike was the fact that he hadn't romanced her at all. 'They were amazed I could step into the part at such short notice, apparently the real reason they fired Betsy Armstrong was she never knew a line. Partied every night and came in looking like hell.'

I stayed with her in Florida for the final two weeks and before the wrap I had been accepted as part of the family. The weather improved, Scott picked up some of the lost time and when the last shot was in the can he was only three days over schedule, nothing to worry about. I usually went out to the location mid-morning, Lauren having left while I was still half-asleep. Over breakfast in the room I scanned all the papers, but I couldn't find any mention of Billy's marriage – like LA, the Florida news-sheets contained little except parochial items. It wasn't until I managed to locate a week-old copy of the London *Times*, brought in by one of the transit aircrews using the hotel, that I read his obituary. They gave him good space and said that he had been a major influence in the British film industry's resurgence, a producer who had always gone against current trends. It ended by saying he was survived by his widow whom he had married a few days prior to his death, but didn't give Amanda's name. I sent a short cable to her at the Grosvenor Hotel which just said: *Thinking of you, love, Phoenix.*

The main unit returned to the studio ten days before the Christmas holidays. All that was left for Lauren to do were a couple of back-projection shots and some looping. She was excited on the flight back to LA. 'I can't wait to see our house. Just think, it'll be our first Christmas in our own home. I'll buy the tree because I want to get one with a perfect shape. Mommy and Daddy are flying out Christmas Eve, did I tell you that?'

'No,' I said, 'but that's great.'

The Christmas decorations in Los Angeles had world-class kitsch – arched over Venice Boulevard at every intersection were a series of Disney-inspired plastic reindeers and animated Santa Clauses. I spotted a large billboard on top of one of the buildings dominated by a blow-up of Lauren. The logo read: *THE END OF THE BEGINNING introduces a Major New Star, LAUREN TAYLOR.*

'Get a look at your billing,' I said. 'You're hot. What did I tell you?' If I'd had a telescope I could have made out my own credit.

431

The moment we arrived Lauren rushed through the house examining every room. 'Yes, you've arranged all the stuff very well, darling,' she said. 'I'll fiddle with it and change a few things around when I get my breath. We'll have to go shopping. The fridge isn't exactly stocked, is it? What did you live on while I was away?'

'Love.'

'I thought you looked thinner. The other thing is we'll have to get the pool man in, the pool's full of leaves. I want everything to look perfect when Mommy and Daddy arrive.'

While she unpacked her things, I went into my study and rang Julian.

'I'm back,' I said. 'Any good news?'

'Could be, could be, sweetie. I think I'm on the verge of closing a development deal for you. I tried to ring you in Florida, but you'd already left.'

'Who with? Did Universal take it?'

'No, they passed. So I tried Fox on the off chance, but there's so much shit hitting the fan over there at the moment, you can't get any sense out of them. Last week Zanuck was out, this week he's back in the catbird seat. The only thing that worries me is this sort of fight could hurt your movie. Those pricks in New York are quite capable of junking it, just to use a failure against Darryl.'

'Christ! I hope not. Would they do that?'

'Baby, this is out-and-out war.'

'But they're taking big billboards. I saw one on the way from the airport. Why would they waste money if they were going to kill it?'

'Don't ask me.'

'Who are you dealing with then?'

'An independent with a three-picture deal over at Warners.'

'Do I know him?'

432

'I don't think so, but he's a real sweetheart of a guy I've got a lot of time for.'

'What's his name?'

'Ezra Berg. I'm looking to get him to option your script. You'll like him. He's prince people. Or maybe I should say, he's princess people, but don't worry, unlike me he never mixes business with pleasure. He's happily married to a guy who works in Bonwit's, who's nothing to do with our little world. So, don't worry, he's not going to try and hump you.'

'Well, that makes a change,' I said. 'You put it so delicately.'

'You haven't said, "Well done, Julian."'

'Well done, Julian. When do I get to meet him?'

'I'm hoping to set it up for next week. So tell me all your news. How was married life in the Everglades?'

'Fine.'

'Did you see the other bit of news while you were away?'

'What was that?'

'Your old sparring partner Billy Fisher died.'

'Really? No, I missed that.'

'And – wait for it – just before he kicked it, he married that young starlet he was always pushing. A deathbed conversion, wouldn't you say? I saved the trades for you, knowing you'd be fascinated.'

I didn't pursue it with him because at that moment Lauren came into the room. 'Well, let's hope this Berg character comes across,' I said before ringing off. 'Keep me posted.'

'What was that about?' Lauren asked.

'My agent thinks he might have a deal for my new script.'

'Oh, good. Listen, darling, I'll have to go to the studio tomorrow, but I've made a list of things for you to do. Open an account at Gelson's if you haven't already, that's the best place to go. We need most things and we're bound

433

to have extra people dropping in over the holidays, so make sure you get plenty of drink.'

'Right, will do.' I was praying that Julian's news about a possible deal materialised; I hadn't been looking forward to playing Bob Cratchit with the in-laws at Christmas.

To celebrate Lauren's return, Howard invited us both to a private screening of the film at his house. He told us that he had refused to let it go out on the Beverly Hills circuit. 'Nobody goes to those to enjoy the film, all they're interested in is outsmarting each other with wisecracks. I've been to too many over the years and they sicken me. A group of badmouthers sitting around after dinner putting the knife in. I've been to showings where you couldn't hear the dialogue on screen because of the comedians in the audience. Fuck that, I haven't spent nine months of my life just to give them that opportunity to knock us. This is just for a few friends I know I can trust.'

There were only ten people including Lauren and me at the dinner. Apart from Lauren, only the cameraman and his wife had any prior connection with the film, the rest were Howard's personal friends – his doctor, and a family of four who were nothing to do with our business. Afterwards we retired to Howard's screening room, which he had had built on to the house. Lauren clutched my hand as the lights dimmed and the first logo appeared on the screen.

Although I'd seen it before, there were things I'd missed the first time around. Now I was able to relax and view it objectively. It's a myth to say the camera can't lie, because it lies most of the time, but there was a truth to Lauren's performance and what she lacked in technique she made up for with a sincerity that can never be faked. Knowing her as I alone did, I could spot those moments, early in the film, when her approach had been tentative and how, as she became more confident, she had grown into the role so that by the time she came to the big emotional scenes she had been able to give Jason a run for his money. I even detected a sadness behind the eyes during the sequence shot in Santa Fe when she felt our relationship was on the rocks. When the lights went up, everybody showered her with compliments.

In bed that night she pressed me for my real opinion – was she really all right, had she over-played this and that scene, did I think she looked good in close-up, had I noticed the bags under her eyes she always got when she had her periods? 'You would tell me the truth, wouldn't you?'

'I've told you the truth already. You pulled it off.'

She still didn't wholly believe me.

'How about the love scenes with Jason? Did they embarrass you?'

'No, of course not. They were great.'

She interrogated me for half an hour until, finally, I took the shade off the bedside lamp and turned the lamp on its side to shine it straight into my face. 'What is this,' I said, 'an episode of *Dragnet*? I wouldn't lie to you, darling.'

'Well, let's hope the critics agree.'

When the film opened at the Fox, Wilshire, the critics did agree. She got the major share of the notices and two of them tipped her as an Academy contender, the best debut by a young actress since Jennifer Jones. Most importantly for the film, the trades were enthusiastic, *Variety* heading its review with *END HEADED FOR BOFFO BUSINESS* and went on to praise Howard, the photography and art direction. Jack's screenplay came in for its share and I was described as having a superior ear for dialogue.

This was before the days of blanket releases. The vital factor was to open as close to the end of the year as possible, not only to meet the Oscar qualification, but also to have the film at the front of Academy members' minds when the voting papers arrived. That was the strategy, and we had to wait to see if it worked. Lauren and I drove down to the

435

cinema the first Saturday to see how many people were standing in line for the last show. The line went right around the block and according to Howard, business had been building steadily and audience reaction was good.

Darryl sent us a delayed wedding present of a crate of Dom Perignon and invited us to a polo match where he was fulsome in his praise for all concerned. If he was worried about his own future, he didn't show it and maybe having a potential hit on his hands had swung the pendulum in his favour at last. He told Lauren they were going all out with a campaign to get her a Best Supporting Actress nomination. 'The competition's too strong this year for Best Actress,' he said, 'but I think we've got a shot at Best Support.' It was a heady time. We began to get invites, even a complimentary mention from Hopper, who called us 'a wholesome, happily married couple'.

Were we a happy, wholesome couple? We had money, fame was just around the corner, a house in the right location, and we played the roles of husband and wife well enough to fool most. Christmas was upon us, the tree stood in the hallway decorated with silver hearts and snow that came out of a can, there was a holly wreath hanging on the front door, the presents were wrapped, but it didn't seem like Christmas to me. I could never marry the climate to the occasion. As the actual day grew nearer, thoughts of Amanda started to haunt me again. Where was she? What was she doing? Mentally, I was always unfaithful to Lauren, but the body disguises betrayals.

Then, of course, there was the arrival of Mommy and Daddy. Mommy arrived with a mink coat ('One never knows. I'm told the evenings get very cold in the desert'). She wouldn't venture out into the garden until I had assured her that there were no snakes. Daddy came armed with his golf clubs and was immediately put out to find I wasn't a member anywhere ('I came expecting I'd get in a few rounds. Seems as though it was a waste to bring these'). He liked what his money had bought, however ('I think I made a good buy for Lauren, don't you?'). On Christmas Eve we took them out to dinner at Chasen's, which I thought might impress them because you could usually be sure of seeing some famous faces. It worked because Gregory Peck and his wife came up to our table to say how they'd enjoyed the film. Later, we all went to midnight Mass. I waited to see if I would be moved by the extra symbolism attached to that particular service, but nothing happened. I could only think of the last time Amanda and I had made love.

The day after Christmas we all went to see the film, sitting among a packed audience – the business was still building. I couldn't really tell whether they enjoyed it or not. They liked their daughter, but were, I think, shocked by the story.

'You were very good, dear, but it wasn't quite what I expected to see you in. I'm glad you didn't marry the man in the end, that wouldn't have done at all. I don't know what all our friends will think of it,' her mother said on the journey home. Her father was pointedly silent until he and I were having a drink by the pool.

'I know Lauren's doing very well,' he said. 'What's happening to you? I hope your situation is healthy.'

I told him about the option deal.

'What exactly does that mean in financial terms?'

'I get a certain amount on signature and more if the option is picked up.'

'I don't call that very satisfactory. What if they don't?'

'Then one tries to sell it elsewhere.'

'Sounds very hit and miss.' He brooded again for a while then said: 'Something else I've been wanting to talk to you about. I've read that novel of yours. Can't say I was that keen on it.'

'Oh, I'm sorry. What didn't you like about it?'

'I don't think incest is a suitable subject for a novel.'

'It happens,' I said.

'Just because it happens doesn't mean one should write about it. The film tonight was very much the same. Too much emphasis on sex.'

'It's what makes the world go round.'

'Not everybody's world. Certainly not Mrs Taylor's or mine. There's enough of all that sordid stuff in the newspapers without having to go to the cinema.'

There didn't seem any answer to that. 'Well, again I'm sorry you feel that way,' I said.

'Write a nice family story, like those Andy Hardy films, that's what people want to see.'

Having got that off his chest and doubtless because he felt he had put me in my place, he became slightly friendlier. 'I thought perhaps we could make up a foursome for bridge tonight.'

'I don't play bridge,' I said.

That encounter was the forerunner to a cheerless few days until they returned home. I felt as though a heavy weight had been lifted. That evening, when we were once again on our own, we stared at the half-eaten carcass of the goose and went out to dinner. Lauren suddenly looked so absurdly young and I leaned across the dining table and kissed her.

'What was that for?' she said.

'My guilty conscience.'

'Guilty about what?'

'Not loving you enough.'

'I haven't complained.'

It was the nearest I ever came to confessing my infidelity.

42

The New Year began well. I met with Berg and liked him a lot. He was about the same age as Woody, but without Woody's extrovert personality, though not lacking in self-confidence. 'I intend to be running a studio by the time I'm forty,' he confided at our very first meeting. 'It's the only game in town worth having. That gives me another eight years during which I want to put half a dozen movies under my belt. Good movies, that buck the trend, because believe you me, this whole scene is going to change before long. And when it happens it'll be meltdown. So when I make my move, I want to be able to double guess the double-guessers. I can only do that if I know where it's coming from.'

He had small, but smart offices in a building on the corner of Sunset that was close to Swaab's drugstore. Virtually a one-man band, his staff consisted of a secretary called Stella, who looked as though she might one day be asked to model for *Vogue*: she invariably came to work in tailored two-piece suits with not a hair out of place. 'She's all I need,' Ezra said. 'I don't believe in wasting my money on big overheads. When I start a movie, I hire the best and pay top dollar. Until then, why throw it around? Who am I trying to impress?'

Like his secretary he was perfectly coiffed, had his initials monogrammed on his shirt cuffs and didn't waste any time getting down to business. 'Know why I optioned your piece?

It's dark, but it's got heart. And last night I took a look at your movie, the one with your bride in it. I liked it – it's exactly the sort of material I want to put my name on. So we're off to a good start. You're going to enjoy working with me, because I've got taste.'

There was the usual quota of bullshit about him, one could never escape that, but he had an engaging way of putting it across and I didn't take offence. Looking back, I recognise he was one of the first of the breed that, in the years to come, took over the industry. And he did take over a studio eventually, although missing his target by a couple of years.

He gave me his annotated copy of the script containing all his suggestions.

'Your outline is better than your complete script,' he said. 'And I'll tell you why. The bones aren't covered with too much flesh. Take another look and you'll see what I mean.'

He employed combat metaphors, leaving no doubt in my mind that he considered the studio system the enemy and the average studio movie a dinosaur. 'Somehow you and Howard got lucky,' he said. 'You slipped one past them. I'm going to slip this one past them. It's got to be a guerrilla raid. Ambush them.'

I left him on a high, anxious to please, and I found his notes, although often crude, had the effect of making me take a long, hard second look at my own work. At the same time as I started working for him, things were hotting up for *The End of the Beginning*. The whole thrust of the studio campaign was directed at getting nominations. Despite the booklet the Academy religiously put out every year stating that excessive lobbying and advertising are morally and ethically wrong, unfair to those who lacked the means, nobody I knew gave a hoot. When the nomination papers went out, the trades suddenly doubled in size with the full page *For*

Your Consideration ads. Big bucks were spent by all the majors, and it was understood that everybody on their pay-rolls was expected to vote the studio ticket. Our film was doing well, but it wasn't a blockbuster, so they forgot Best Picture and concentrated on Lauren, taking page after page to boost her chances. The Morris office took out a couple of pages for me, as Julian had promised, but I was never in the running. When the papers were counted the results had few surprises. There were nominations for cine-matography and music, but Howard, Jason and myself missed out. Lauren was the only winner. The money had spoken.

From being a promising newcomer, overnight Lauren became somebody in demand. Fan magazines ran interviews and she did a dozen photo sessions. I was sometimes included, but the spotlight was on Lauren. At least half a dozen projects were on offer to her and she passed the scripts over to me for my verdict.

'What about considering mine?' I said. 'We could have Ezra over to dinner, play it cool and he might go for you in the role.'

'Do you think it's a good idea for us to become a husband and wife team?'

'Didn't hurt on your first movie. Got you a nomination.'

'Oh, I know that. It's just that I agree with Daddy that, for my next, I should take something really different.'

'Daddy's become your agent, has he?'

'Don't be silly. He's always given me good advice and I trust his taste.'

'Rather than mine?'

'No, of course not. But I do think that your new script relies heavily on the sex scenes. Maybe you'll tone it down before the next draft.'

'Maybe I will, maybe I won't. But forget Ezra, it was just a thought.'

441

'Darling, it's you more than me I'm thinking of. Be a pity if people started saying you're riding on the back of my career.'

'Perish the thought,' I said. It was the first time I became aware of how she saw the way ahead and the exchange pissed me off, especially when, the next time I took a meeting with Ezra, he brought Lauren into the conversation.

'Had a thought last night. How about your bride for the girl? If I could tie her in I think I could get the studio to give us a green light. Did you write it with her in mind? Reads like that.'

'Not really.'

'She's read it, of course?'

'I don't know whether she's read the finished script. I showed her the outline,' I stalled.

'Work on her,' he said.

'Right now, because of the nomination, she seems to be swamped with offers. But you're right. I didn't want to suggest it myself for obvious reasons.'

'Why not? Nepotism is what makes this town tick. How do you think I got a deal at Warners?'

'Tell me.'

'My cousin's Head of Business Affairs. Give it a shot when you're in bed together,' he said with a wink. 'I always find that's the best time to clinch a deal.'

If he thought sex was the 'open sesame' for Lauren, he was mistaken. After a first burst of enthusiasm when we returned from Florida, she liked to ration me by practising the Catholic safe days method – condoms turned her off. Not that I wanted to get her pregnant, far from it, and she had let me know that motherhood was not on her agenda for years. 'I want to get established as a star before I have a child.'

'How does that sit with Mummy and Daddy?'

'I've discussed it with them, and they understand.'

442

'I thought Catholics liked big families. Plenty of business for the Cardinal.'

'You can be very crude sometimes.'

'So I'm told.'

I went back to Ezra and lied, more to save my own face than to protect Lauren. 'She read it, she loved it, I worked on her, but her agent has convinced her she should accept something over at Columbia opposite Glenn Ford. Pity, but there it is.'

'Big mistake,' Ezra said.

Lauren started shooting on the new film before the Awards took place. Although the ceremony was televised it wasn't the superbowl, world event it has since become. Back in the fifties the staging was split between the RKO Pantages in Hollywood and the NBC Century Theatre in New York. Lauren had a dress specially designed by Edith Head and I wrote an acceptance speech for her should she win. With Bob Hope reading off the cue cards in Hollywood and Thelma Ritter officiating in New York, the show got under way. The Best Supporting category for an actress came at the halfway mark in the proceedings and when the nominees were named Lauren clutched my arm so tightly it cut off the circulation. Old Blue Eyes himself opened the envelope and the name he read out was Eva Marie Saint for *On the Waterfront*. Lauren's grip on my arm was suddenly no longer there. I kissed her and whispered my commiserations as she strove to maintain a plucky loser's expression, but the cameras were no longer on her. While you're still in there with a chance, you're news. Once you're out of the running, interest falls away as though you've got a terminal disease. Losers aren't worth wasting film on.

She put on a brave face, but I knew how badly she had taken it. So many people had raised her hopes – not me, I had always tried to persuade her to anticipate the worst. She couldn't stomach going to the post-Awards banquet; instead we went home to a lonely supper on our own.

43

The End of the Beginning did reasonably well at the box office. No records were broken and although it was always impossible to find out exactly what it had taken (the industry's double-bookkeeping standards were firmly in place even then, subsequently to be developed into an accounting art form), Howard told me he had been told it had yet to recover its negative cost which, translated into industry-speak, meant 'Don't ask questions because you are never going to be told the truth.' The only person to come out of it smelling like a rose was my wife. She went from strength to strength with seldom more than a few weeks between jobs, her salary climbing steadily. For long stretches she was little more than a lodger in our home. Because the hours she worked seldom coincided with mine, our relationship drifted into a platonic friendship for these periods. We were just two people occupying the same house but often not sharing the same bed – when Lauren was on early call she preferred to sleep alone. Outwardly we kept up the façade and as her circle of friends widened we ate out most of the time because she was a stranger in her own kitchen, pleading exhaustion whenever I suggested we might have people in for a meal. I found being around people who were in work and successful depressing and my own, smaller, group of friends did not fit in with Lauren's new awareness of who she was.

Despite his early brave words, Ezra failed to get a deal

with my screenplay and allowed the option to lapse. Although Julian made an effort to find an alternative buyer, nobody else showed any interest. Like everything else, scripts get shopsoiled, betraying the fact that they have gone the rounds. Few in Hollywood ever want to come in close contact with failure in case they breathe in the infection, like Legionnaire's Disease. I wasn't yet a certified failure, just one of an army hovering around the edges. When Julian's calls became less frequent, I harried him on a daily basis to get me a job, but it was a sign of the times that Brent no longer treated my calls as priority. I think it was Brent himself, taking pity on me, who eventually persuaded a producer to give me a three-week rewrite on a creaking vehicle intended for Cary Grant but which Grant very sensibly turned down. That was another thing I discovered: every second person had a script that Grant, or Peck or Bette Davis was 'interested in'. It was all part of the endless game of make-believe played out by most. Apart from the rewrite job and an even smaller 'dialogue polish' I did for Howard, there was little that came my way and I was forced to become a kept man, living on Lauren's money. I had regular calls from Daddy in Denver enquiring about my financial health and although Lauren never made a meal of it, she, too, made the odd pointed reference. 'Can't you write a new novel while you're waiting for a job?'

'I would if I had an idea.'

'Turn your screenplay into a novel then.'

'It isn't that easy.'

Gradually the batteries that had once charged our relationship lost their potency and needed jump leads to get us going again for short bursts. During a spell when Lauren was once again away on location my depression led me to pay a return visit to Madam Bee's, only to find that Pauline had left. Bee offered me the pick of her girls, but somehow the urge was no longer there. I stayed and enjoyed a drink with her on the house while we exchanged happy memories of Jack. I missed him dreadfully.

I tackled Woody, hoping he would suggest we might team up on one of his projects, but he was noncommittal and that led nowhere. In desperation, using an alias I wrote a sleazy script, a cop thriller aimed at the lowest common denominator, and to my surprise it sold immediately to a small outfit that churned out such stuff. It gave me some much-needed cash and a breathing space, but I still had to figure out how to survive long term.

Strangely, given our sparse relationship in the past, it was a chance meeting with Oliver that provided an escape route. I bumped into him standing outside the Beverly Wilshire one afternoon and was taken aback by the warmth of his greeting.

'My God,' he said. 'Robert. How good to see you. I was only thinking of you last night. How are you? You heard about Billy, of course?'

'Yes.'

'One mustn't speak ill of the dead. And actually the eccentric old bastard remembered me in his will. Left me his Bentley, which he hardly ever drove. Only six thousand miles on the clock. The rest went to his widow. You must have read that he married the delectable Amanda.'

'Yes.'

'She's now very comfortably off and enjoying her widow's weeds. What're you up to, still writing? How can you bear to live in this dreary place?'

'I'm married too and we have a house here on Mulholland.'

'Who did you marry? I'm afraid I can't keep up with all the local gossip.'

'Lauren Taylor.'

'Oh, yes. She was rather good in that film you wrote. I managed to catch it in London before it came off. Look, were you on your way somewhere or have you got time for a drink?'

I accepted his invitation because I was desperate to find out more about Amanda. We went back inside the Wilshire.

'I'm on the waggon at the moment,' Oliver said, ordering a Coke for himself, 'but don't let me stop you. While I was up at Stratford giving my Orlando I started to imbibe rather too generously. Only way I could get through it. Hated the rest of the cast, especially the stupid little bitch who was playing Rosalind. She thought she was Edith Evans. *Maurice* Evans was closer to the mark. Ghastly modern dress production, set in old Vienna. We were all made to wear Franz Josef drag. Listen,' he continued without drawing breath, 'I'm so glad I bumped into you. I've got my own film company now and I've bought the rights to a fascinating novel. I can't fathom why nobody's ever spotted it before. It was published in the twenties, considered something of a classic by lots of people. I came out here to find a writer rather than hire some dreary British scribe. Would you like to take a look at it?'

'Yes,' I said, genuinely taken aback by the offer. 'If you want me to.'

'Well, Billy always thought highly of you and though he was a difficult old sod in many ways, I did trust his taste in writers. I think somebody like you from a totally different culture could give it a completely new slant. Wait here, I've got a copy upstairs.'

He left me, returning ten minutes later with the book. 'Take it away and let me know what you think. Then, if you like it, we can meet again and talk details.'

'Well, thank you, Oliver. I'll read it immediately.'

'Just one thing. If you decide to do it, would you be prepared to come to England for a few weeks? I can't afford to stay here too long since I'm not on anybody's payroll, and I want to be closely involved in the script. I've got very definite ideas how it should go.'

'No, that's fine by me and it comes at a good time. My wife's away on location.'

'There you are then, let's hope you like it. I wait for your call.'

When I left him, I couldn't help thinking how odd it was that meeting the trio of Billy, Oliver and Amanda had twice changed my life. There and then I decided that, whatever I felt about the novel, there was no question of not accepting his offer. A paid-for trip to England held out the chance that I would be able to seek out Amanda, and that alone was reason enough to go.

That night I stayed up until I had finished the book. The author was new to me – Ford Madox Ford. The title, *The Good Soldier*, put me off at first; I thought it would be a tale about army life in England. But it was a brilliant and haunting tale of passion, written with dazzling technical skill, quite unlike anything I had read before. I went to bed excited and couldn't wait to call Oliver first thing the next morning.

'It's fantastic,' I said. 'What an extraordinary story. Takes some time to get into it, but once you do it grabs you and keeps you guessing until the last page.'

'Well, I'm glad you like it. I'd have been surprised if you hadn't.'

'Like it? I think it's superb.'

'So, are we on?'

'Definitely.'

'Who do I talk to about you?'

'Julian at William Morris.'

'Oh, that old queen. He made a pass at me once.'

'Join the club,' I said.

'I hope he won't hold me to ransom.'

'Don't worry, I'll tell him that I've already accepted.'

'I'll ring him now.'

'Give it half an hour, let me break the good news first.'

I rang Julian immediately. He was on another call, naturally, but I told Brent the score. 'Don't let him blow this,' I said, 'because I'm determined to do it, whatever the deal. Pass the word to forget his tough agent act. I want this assignment. It's a great subject, so make sure he gets the message. I'll wait in until he rings me back.'

'Understood.'

Julian rang me later that afternoon. 'Well, dear, it's your career,' he said, 'and I was Flossie Faithful and followed your instructions to the letter, but I can't pretend it's something I would recommend.'

'Never mind that, did you clinch it?'

'Of course. I do what I'm told.' I could tell by his voice that he was annoyed.

'What did he offer?'

'Not enough, and I couldn't shift him, it was take it or leave it.'

'So tell me?'

'Only twenty-five thousand for a first draft. Then, if he gets a distribution deal, which is by no means certain, as I hope you realise, another twenty-five for a second draft and fifty deferred to first day of principal photography. I tried for points but all he would promise was to give you three per cent of his, and until he gets a deal we don't know what he'll end up with.'

'Fine.'

'You think that's fine, I don't, but it's your life. Oh, and round trip air fare, of course, plus five hundred a week per diems.'

'Good. Ring him back and accept.'

'You're quite sure? I don't want you crying on my shoulder at a later date. There's no guarantee that he'll ever get it off the ground, and at best it'll only be a British picture.'

'I'm happy to risk that. And, after all, you haven't managed to get me anything else.'

'Not for want of trying.'

Just to make sure he acted quickly I got my call in to Oliver first. 'I've told the disgruntled queen the deal's O K by me,' I said. 'Not to his liking, but who cares? When do we start?'

'Well, that's great, I'm delighted. Sorry I couldn't make it more, but until I get a distribution deal I'm using my own money. How soon can you leave?'

'You say when you want me.'

'Well, now it's settled, I've got nothing to stay for. Why don't we fly over together? Let me see what the flights are like. I'll call you back.'

He made reservations for the following day and I started packing. When Lauren rang me that evening from the location, I played down my excitement.

'Darling, something came out of the blue today. I've got a writing job, but the snag is I have to go to England for a while. It's a British picture.'

'But that's wonderful. Why is it a snag?'

'Well, darling, it means I probably won't see you for ages, and I miss you. I was going to surprise you by arriving at the location this weekend.'

'I miss you too but, you know, we're both in the business of making a career.'

'Isn't it always the way? We seem to be kept apart so much these days. I'll turn it down, if you want me to,' closing my suitcase as I said it.

'Is it a good subject?'

'I think so. Brilliant, in fact.'

'Then you must go.'

'You really don't mind?'

'It's good for you to work.'

'You're so sweet, darling. I'm so lucky to be married to

451

you. Are you OK? Is everything going well on the film?'

'Yes. No problems.'

'I do miss you, darling.'

'Miss you.'

'I'll call you from London, let you know where I'm staying. Take care.' I felt nothing but an unabated excitement when I hung up.

We took the American New York flight the following morning, aiming to catch the overnight BOAC connection to London, using the time to discuss the novel in more detail. Oliver felt that because of the way it was constructed we would need a voice-over narration from the protagonist. I was happy to go along with whatever he suggested. 'It has to be sad,' he said. 'That's how Ford starts the book, after all – "This is the saddest story I ever heard" so I think we begin with that in flashback and work backwards. It has to be elegant. We must get some good locations, find out one of those wonderful old watering holes the rich frequented between the wars.'

His feeling for the material infected me and we spent most of the journey batting ideas backwards and forwards. It wasn't until we were having lunch that I casually brought Amanda's name into the conversation.

'Were you surprised that Billy got married?'

'The whole of London was surprised,' Oliver said. 'But then that was Billy's personality; he loved shocking people. What very few people knew is that he was always in pain, that's what got him hooked on morphine.'

'Morphine? Why?'

'Hard to believe, but he was a great tennis player when he was younger. Almost got to Wimbledon as a junior, but his playing career ended when he broke his leg very badly, a complicated spiral fracture and the surgeon botched it. Had to be reset twice.'

'I never knew that. I remember he took masses of pills.'

'The pills were just to jump-start him and send him to sleep. In the end the combination did for him. Billy never did anything by halves. I saw it coming.'

'I can admit it now, but when I first met him I thought he swung the other way.'

'He was neuter,' Oliver said. 'Never believed he was attractive to either sex. An enigma, really.'

'Where is Amanda now?'

'Last I heard she bought herself a set of rooms in Albany.'

'Albany, New York?' I felt a sudden panic. 'I thought you said she lived in London.'

'Yes. Albany in Piccadilly. Used to be an exclusively male refuge – Byron lived there at one time. Ex-guardsmen on the doors to keep out unwanted intruders, but they finally relaxed the rules and allowed women in. It's considered a very smart address.'

'Is she continuing with her career?'

'What career?' Oliver asked archly, reverting to the personality I remembered. He beckoned the stewardess to refill his wine glass. 'You had something going with her once, didn't you?'

'Yes, for a time.'

'Maybe you're lucky it didn't work out. I always found her too calculating. An English rose with thorns.'

I left it at that and we resumed our discussions about the novel. I managed a few hours' cramped sleep on the overnight leg to London and arrived feeling half dead. Oliver suggested that I stayed in a small family hotel in Kensington that would be within my means. I checked in and went straight to bed to try to beat the time clock. Before we parted Oliver had said, 'Give me a ring at home when you feel reasonably human and we'll start work.'

Jet lag, I find, is an unpredictable animal, sometimes savaging you, sometimes playing cat and mouse, allowing you to feel you have escaped and then pouncing a few hours later. That first night, having gone to bed mid-afternoon, I woke five hours later, had a meal, took a sleeping pill and thought I might get through the night. No such luck. I was wide awake again before long. Resigning myself to the fact, I dressed and went for a walk. I came across a British bobby on the beat and asked him to direct me to Albany in Piccadilly. 'It's right opposite Fortnum and Mason's,' he told me, as though this was a map reference I couldn't possibly miss. Seeing my blank expression, he gave further instructions. 'That's a large store on the right-hand side if you're heading towards the Circus.' Then, as I obviously still didn't have a clue, he volunteered to walk part of the way with me. As we approached Knightsbridge he spoke to a young hooker lingering in an alleyway. She had a poodle on a lead.

'Don't press your luck, Ida,' the bobby said with amicable familiarity. 'You've had three appearances in court this month. Go home and look after your little boy.'

'Got to make a living, dearie, haven't I?' Ida rejoined.

'How are tricks then?'

'Business is slow.'

'I'll give you another half an hour, but if you're still here when I come back I'll have to book you.'

'Is that the way you operate?' I asked.

'Yes, well, live and let live is my motto. I know most of the regulars by name and, personally, I turn a blind eye most of the time.'

'Funny she had a dog with her.'

'No, that's part of the act. Meant to give them an alibi. They're not soliciting, see? They're out walking the dog. Now then, keep straight on to Piccadilly. Look out for Fortnum's. Albany is opposite on the left-hand side.'

I thanked him and walked on. I found Albany and went into the courtyard where two or three vintage cars were parked. The doors to the main entrance were closed, but I saw a uniformed man observing me from a side window. Doubtless I looked suspicious. Retreating, I found a Lyons Corner House open and had some breakfast, then rang Oliver from a public call box. Like me, he hadn't slept and was keen to get started. He lived in Chelsea and I took a cab there.

It was somewhat obviously an actor's apartment; framed posters of his stage appearances decorated the stairwell and he had a signed photograph of the Oliviers placed prominently on his desk. It was furnished in a mixture of styles – some good antique pieces side by side with a few modern additions – functional chairs that typified the starkness of post-war design. The television set, I noticed, was small with a bulbous screen and had an aerial perched on top of it.

After making a pot of coffee he said, 'I thought if we went over my notes you'd get an idea of how I see it. I'm not a writer myself, but I see the shape it ought to go very clearly.'

We spent the morning mapping out a rough outline. I was quite happy to let him make the decisions and many of his ideas were good. He knew the novel backwards and had underlined key passages in his copy. At lunchtime we took a break at a local pub where they served a rough-and-ready lunch and warm beer. Then we resumed work until he confessed that he was bushed. 'Why don't you go back and mull over what we've discussed?'

'What I need is a typewriter. Can I hire one?'

'I'll get on to that for you. Anything else you need? Apart from a good night's sleep, that is?'

For the next week we met on a daily basis and I began to get the script down on to pages and make some progress, the plan being that once he felt I was on the right lines I should return to Los Angeles and finish a first draft. When I left him every day I made a point of going back to my hotel via Piccadilly, lingering outside Albany in the hope that I might see Amanda. That never happened, but on the last week I was there Oliver gave me a farewell meal in a fashionable theatrical restaurant, Le Caprice. There he was greeted effusively by the owner, Mario, and we were seated on one of the plush banquettes.

During the course of the meal I looked across the restaurant and saw Amanda being shown to a table. She was with an olive-complexioned young man who I took to be an Italian. As she sat down she suddenly became aware of me. I saw her colour before looking away.

Oliver noticed my change of expression. He turned around. 'Good God,' he said, 'what a coincidence. Do you want to go across and say hello?'

'Not at the moment.' I was in turmoil but tried not to show it. 'I will before we go.' The rest of the meal passed in a haze. Whenever I stole a glance Amanda's companion seemed to be engaging in an intimate conversation with her. I half listened to Oliver's comments about the script, all the time trying to decide what my next move should be. We finished our meal and got up to leave. It was then that I walked to Amanda's table. I excused the interruption to her companion, who viewed me with barely concealed hostility.

'What a surprise to see you,' I said.

'I was thinking the same thing. Are you here on holiday with your wife?'

'No, I'm just here for a short while working with Oliver on a new script.'

'Yes, I saw you were with Oliver.'

'I'm sorry about Billy.'

'Yes, but it wasn't unexpected.'

Her replies were formal.

'I'd love to see you before I leave,' I said. 'Any chance?'

Her companion tapped on the table with a knife.

'Well, I'm busy at the moment.'

I nodded. 'Should you get a free moment, I'm at the Holland Hotel in Kensington. Give me a ring if you can.'

'The Holland?'

'Yes. Do please, if you have the time. I'd love to have a talk.'

I nodded to her sullen companion, whom she studiously had not introduced, and rejoined Oliver at the exit.

'How was the widow?' Oliver asked. 'I didn't say hello myself because I thought it best to leave you two together. Who is she with?'

'I've no idea.'

'Looked like a gigolo to me. I expect there are quite a few after her money.'

The first thing I did when I got back to my hotel was to change my flight home, allowing myself a further three days in London in the hope that Amanda would contact me. I never left the hotel in case I missed her call. It wasn't until the late afternoon on the second day that she rang. For so long I had thought of her as Amanda Boyd, that I had a momentary blackout when the name 'Mrs Fisher' did not register.

'Darling,' I blurted, 'I couldn't believe it. First Paris, now London. The gods must want us to meet.'

'Though not always with Oliver, I hope.'

'Don't be too hard on Oliver, he's employing me.'

'Employing you?'

'Yes. He has ambitions to be a producer. I'm writing a script for him.'

'Well, bully for Oliver, but Billy must be turning in his grave. How long are you in town?'

'If I hadn't seen you at that restaurant I'd have been back in LA by now, but I delayed hoping you'd ring me and we could meet.' She made no immediate response. 'Are you free this evening?'

'This evening? No, I already have a dinner engagement.' There was a formality about her reply.

'Can you get out of it?'

'Not really.'

'Tomorrow then, how about tomorrow? I'll change my flight again.'

'No, tomorrow's not possible. I'm leaving tomorrow.'

'Leaving? Where are you going?'

'We're off to Nice.'

I felt a creeping numbness. 'Who's "we"? That number I saw you with?'

'You can't resist those awful American expressions, can you?'

'You know me, consistent. Saying the same old things in the same old way. Like, I love you.' I waited. 'You know that, don't you?' I waited again.

'Oh, Robert, it's too late for both of us,' she said finally. 'Perhaps we could have made it work once, but the chance has gone.'

'It worked again in Paris.'

'Paris isn't now.'

'I'll leave Lauren, never go back, if you'll say the word.'

'You mustn't say that.'

'Why not? It's true. There's never been anybody else for me. Don't you believe me?'

She met my words with a long silence. 'Yes, I believe you,' she said finally, 'but we spent all the love we had in Phoenix.' Her voice was so empty, as though to check me pleading further, putting herself beyond my reach.

In desperation I said: 'Darling, we've passed that. You came to me in Paris and it was the same as ever, you know it was. Why throw that away?'

'I already did,' she said. 'I married Billy.'

'But Billy's dead. I don't mind any of that, all I know is that I still love you. I didn't marry Lauren for love, I married

458

her because that way I thought I could block you out of my life for ever ... but I couldn't, I can't, and I'll make any sort of bargain to keep you.'

'It's too late,' she replied. 'You'll see that one day. Not now, when you're hurt, but I know I'm right. I was never the person you thought I was. Just somebody out for the main chance. We're too alike, you and me, birds of a feather. Admit it. That's why it could never last.'

'No, you're wrong. We both made mistakes, but they're behind us. Darling, are you there? Answer me. We can't say goodbye for ever over the phone.'

I said something else, one last, desperate cry that now I can't remember, but suddenly her answering voice was no longer in my ear. Afterwards I sat in the silent, darkening hotel room for a long time. All I could think of was, we would never make love again and that, like Wharton's hero I once modelled myself on, I faced living on without her in the ruins of time.

44

LOS ANGELES 1980

The secret of survival in the film business (or perhaps in any business for that matter) is to make sure you choose your enemies more carefully than you choose your friends. Friends seldom employ you, while people you despise are often in a position to do so. I learned that by degrees during the years when my marriage to Lauren died a slow, quiet death. There was nothing newsworthy about our separation; it was just that the currents of our separate careers flowed in opposite directions, taking her boat towards success while more often than not mine was becalmed. When the moment could be delayed no longer, her mother's muscle with the Cardinal prevailed and that which God had joined together, God's Holy Roman servants pulled asunder. The house and contents went to her – Daddy saw to that – and I settled for cash, no point in playing the gentleman. The end of my marriage also saw the end of my religious conversion. Lauren subsequently married again, to her dentist as I recall, and, when the movie roles dried up, became the queen of television mini-series. I caught one of her appearances by mistake the other night while surfing the channels to try and find a news bulletin. Her teeth looked good, I will give her that.

Although I continued to make a living, nothing happened to send me spinning upwards; my status as a screenwriter still hovered just above the level of a janitor, since for most of us it is a profession that specialises in rejection. I completed Oliver's commission, turning in what I thought was a passable version of Ford's novel, but Oliver never succeeded in getting it to the starting post. Years later I happened to catch the BBC's successful attempt, but of course they didn't use my script. Thwarted in his ambition to be a producer, Oliver went back to the theatre he once professed to despise. He was made Sir Oliver in due course, though I've never understood those fancy British titles, especially when dames become Dames.

That visit to London was the last occasion I ever saw Amanda. I did write to her, but she never replied. Perhaps she lost my address. From time to time old wounds bleed again if her name crops up in the fashion pages of *Vogue* and *Harper's Bazaar*, those indefatigable chroniclers of the idle rich. From all accounts, she seems to travel a lot and I read that she has settled in St Tropez where a lot of the dropouts water and bronze themselves. For all I know, she's there still. When in my cups, I sometimes wonder what our child would have looked like, but that is a country I try not to explore too often. I loved differently in the past. No more. I still date, but take care not to become involved; perhaps, finally, my early fantasy has come true – love unrequited now comforts me like a favourite childhood blanket.

If love for Amanda corrupted the heart of my life, the quest for fame completed the process. All too late I realised that another *End of the Beginning* was never going to come my way again; I had accepted the Danegeld and by so doing sealed my fate. Not so long ago I re-read my first and only novel, hoping to discover something there to recharge my creative batteries. I found that, instead of striking full chords, my youthful imagination had only achieved a few, thin notes without the authentic music of life, yet it served to remind me of a time when the barometer of hope was always rising, a time of first love and happiness.

Putting the novel back on the shelves, I was forced to admit that I didn't have the talent that separates the men from the boys, now I was just another writer in the Hollywood pack who had sold out, that Hollywood itself had sold out: everything immoral is now OK if it sucks up to the amoral majority and pays off at the box office; virtue is politically incorrect. To justify the fact that some of us earned more than the average novelist, whopping by the standards of ordinary living, we provided the blueprints for a sterile popular culture, never writing for ourselves as real writers do but instead writing to order. We had surrendered our identities no matter how we pretended otherwise. I took any assignment that Julian managed to get me; writing, but more often than not rewriting, a raft of forgettable scripts all over the place – Seattle, Chicago, Vancouver, Arkansas and once, God help me, Phoenix, for, as the industry changed, more and more films were made away from Hollywood to escape the monstrous studio overheads. There were no longer any true tycoons running the show, only the ersatz variety; Harry Cohn was dead, Jack Warner and Mayer had gone, Zanuck likewise. Monsters they may have been and yet much of the product they were responsible for now seems to have an enduring core of morality. When they were deposed it became the age of the package deal as a new breed moved into the vacuum only to create their own vacuum. The executive playing fields were populated with a motley army – agents, accountants, ex-hairdressers, oil men, Las Vegas hotel owners, you name it – who knew little of cinema, cared little about cinema, and set about brainwashing the rest of the world into accepting that theirs was the power and the glory.

Where was I during all this? I took what came my way and turned in the pages wherever the job took me, in the process becoming over-familiar with most Hilton bedrooms across America. I smoked my quota of grass when under pressure, occasionally did some cocaine if that was the social norm, moved out to San Diego when the smog in LA became intolerable, often ill at ease but adapting, chameleon-like, to whatever colour the dense undergrowth demanded. Eventually, the effort of grafting away just to sustain a lifestyle courtesy of American Express made me see the light. Since I was never going to lick the system, why not join it? It was a game plan others had followed with success. I used whatever influential contacts I had, for I had learned the smart, breakfast meeting, easy-speak of the copper-bottomed phonies. My persistence finally paid off. When the next round of musical chairs commenced, I eased myself into a vacant seat. Now my name is on the door as *Vice President, Creative Affairs* at this studio – a title as meaningless as they come. I sit in a stylish office with a rubber mat under my desk to save wear and tear on the carpet, two telephones, and a secretary who can't take longhand let alone shorthand but who mixes a mean whisky sour at the happy hour. I have a constantly renewed stack of legal pads with my title printed on them, a parking space on the lot, and I pull down a steady hundred and seventy five a year plus a generous health plan and pension on a contract that has three years to run. Producers, who not so long ago wouldn't return my calls, now solicit half an hour of my valuable time. I enjoy that – it's much more rewarding to sit in judgement of others than to sit in judgement of oneself. Often I find myself interviewing writers who bring back sacred and profane memories of my earlier self; young hopefuls lured, as ever, by the promise that Hollywood dangles in front of them. I don't have any real authority, of course, nor would I exercise it if I did. Much too dangerous. I listen attentively when a pitch is made to me, but never actually commit. I don't have any ambitions to be a hero. Recently there have been rumours that those wonderful people who gave us Pearl Harbor have their sights fixed on this company. If and when they move in I should walk away with a nice golden handshake to keep me ticking over in my old age.

There were casualties along the way of course – friendships that, for one reason or another, had to be phased out. That's the price demanded for crossing the line and joining the enemy. Poor Julian didn't live long enough to become Miss Lonelyhearts, he died a while back – an early, undetected victim of Aids, I suspect, for he cruised to the end. Arnold is still teetering on the fringe, though his bride expired on one of those extended holidays they took. Perhaps the Galapagos tortoises got her; nature usually has the last laugh. Of course now I don't need an agent.

The other day my secretary fixed an appointment for a Mr Solotaroff without first checking with me. To my shame the name didn't register immediately with me and it wasn't until Woody walked through the door that a forgotten penny dropped.

'Why, Woody,' I said. 'What a long time it's been. How good to see you.'

'No, good of you to see me. I know you're busy.'

'Never too busy for you. How are things?'

He hadn't worn well. The life hadn't yet been squeezed out of him, but he was less bushy-tailed, dowdier, his suit needed pressing, but some of the old chutzpah remained. 'Great,' he said. 'I've got a real humdinger of a project I'm developing and I wanted you to have first look at it. I said to myself, "Take it to a real filmmaker, Woody, go to the best."'

'I appreciate that, Woody.'

'Know what I always think? If only, way back, you'd brought me that script of yours – what was it called?'

'*The End of the Beginning*, you mean?'

'Yeah, that one. I could have parlayed that into something really big.'

'I'm sure you're right,' I said.

'That was the best thing you ever wrote.'

'Yes. Too bad lightning didn't strike twice.'

'Still, you landed on your feet here.'

'Tell me about this new project of yours.'

He launched into a well-rehearsed spiel, attempting to sell me a real dog of a script, a remake of *Bringing Up Baby*, this time with a kangaroo. 'Neat twist, huh?' he asked. I heard him out, but behind his manufactured enthusiasm I detected that familiar note of desperation.

'Can't wait to read it,' I said. 'Leave it with me. I'll give it my blessing and see that it gets to the right people.' From the few pages I bothered to read later, it was about as funny as Nixon's tapes.

'You know something,' he said as I walked him to the door, 'you never changed. A lot of the jerks in this town do, but you've stayed the same talented, straight guy I first met. That's so rare and beautiful.'

'I've tried,' I said. 'It hasn't always been easy, but I've tried.'